Wild Ride

HEATHER VAN FLEET

HER
Wild Ride

bookouture

Published by Bookouture in 2019

An imprint of StoryFire Ltd.

Carmelite House
50 Victoria Embankment
London EC4Y 0DZ
www.bookouture.com

ISBN: 978-1-78681-834-8
eBook ISBN: 978-1-78681-833-1

To Bella. You took that picture on the sly from the van, then boom, this story was born. Thank you for being the most awesome nine-year-old a mommy could ever have.

CHAPTER ONE

Niyol

Club life didn't leave me many options when it came to the choices I made. And since I'd been born into the world of the Red Dragons, I never really had the desire to find a way out. So in some fucked-up way, the day I was sent to prison two years ago was probably a karmic punishment I deserved for being an outlaw. Technically, I hadn't done nothing wrong to get put behind bars, but at the same time I'd broken enough other laws for the club in the past that maybe I did deserve the sentence I'd served.

One thing I didn't warrant was my stepmom and stepsister's wrath about my attitude toward women. More specifically, the woman we were sitting in some random diner, at nine at night, waiting for.

"All we're saying is that you tend to be a little overbearing when it comes to the ladies. Play nice, and there's no doubt that things will go great." My stepmother, Lisa, patted the back of my hand, then pulled a cup of coffee to her lips.

"I could've found another way to get there if you're *that* afraid I'll rough her up." I glared between the two of them.

"Like how, hitchhiking?" Emily snorted.

I gave her the middle finger. "Very fucking funny, smartass."

"You two…" Lisa sighed and shook her head.

"I said it before and I'll say it again," my stepsister continued. "Flying him to San Diego is the quickest and safest option."

"Which costs money that he does not have, remember?" Lisa argued, sticking salt into an open wound. "Whatever money he's got tucked away needs to go toward building a new life *away* from here."

I rubbed a hand over my forehead, wishing this was a hell of a lot simpler. Taking my bike would've been the perfect way to travel, but my old Harley barely ran no more, and I couldn't afford the parts to get it fixed. Lisa had offered to help me out financially as much as she could, but she'd done enough already by letting me crash in her basement. The last thing I wanted was for a trail of money to lead from her to me when it might put her in danger.

It was hell to be broke. One week out of a two-year stint in prison, and I barely had a dime to my name. That was just one of the reasons I'd decided to haul ass and move to San Diego. A second chance, a new location, and freedom from the club that had been fucking with my life for twenty-plus years.

The other reason I was running? The Red Dragons as a whole.

My old man—the Red Dragon Club Pres and Lisa's ex-husband—had all but ruined my life pre-prison. Now, thanks to my mouth, he was locked away in the same Illinois State Pen I'd been in, for the very crime he'd tried pinning on me.

To get early parole, I'd narked him out, tired of living like the liar he'd made me out to be. Siding with the DEA, turning the name of my father's biggest dealer over to them, wasn't one of my prouder moments. But I wouldn't take it back. It got that fucker off the streets.

Three days before my release, though, I'd gotten a letter with the RD logo on top. There were few words, but enough to make a point. If I ever showed my face back at the club then I'd be wishing for death compared to what the remaining RDs, the ones who were loyal to my old man still, promised to do to me.

I didn't take time to figure out who wrote the thing. I knew they meant business, and I wasn't stupid enough to think that sticking around town long was a good idea. Already my stepmom, just by giving me a place to lay low for the week, would be on their shit list if they ever found out she was helping me.

Which is why I needed to leave, tomorrow. A week, post-prison, was already too long to stick around Rockford. Hell, I would've been out of here the day after I was released if I could've. But finding a ride cross-country wasn't as easy as I'd thought.

I pinched the bridge of my nose. "Your mom's right, Em. This is the only way."

Emily sighed, slowly shaking her head as she leaned back in the booth. My guess was, she was worried I'd corrupt her best friend who'd, last minute, agreed to drive me so my stepsister could go on some cruise with the guy she was supposed to marry.

"Good. I'm glad that's settled then." Lisa smiled wide.

"And I promise to be nice to your friend." I took a drink of my own coffee, cringing from the lukewarm, bitter taste. I set it on the table and pushed it away as I finished. "Just as long as she's not a huge talker."

Emily's lips twisted.

Lisa looked out the window.

I picked up my fork and pointed the end between them, before stabbing at my half-eaten waffle. "You two aren't being real encouraging there."

"Here's the thing…" Emily bit her lip, ripping up her napkin. "Summer is kind of the most talkative person you'll ever meet."

I tipped my head back and groaned. "Jesus. There is no 'kind of' about it. She either talks a lot or she doesn't."

"See? There you go with the douchiness again."

"Sorry." I held up my hands. "Momentary lapse in judgment."

"That will *not* happen with Summer, correct?" Emily asked.

I nodded, the good little boy in the big asshole body.

The old me wouldn't have agreed so easily. But I was reformed now—or trying to be—and ready to prove I wasn't the asshole she, Lisa, or any other woman out there remembered me to be during my RD years.

"Good. Glad we've cleared that up too," Lisa huffed.

I'd only seen this Summer once before, and that was when Emily was in college. It had been six months before I was sent away to the pen, before everything in my life had gone to shit.

One night, I'd slipped away from the club, a little lost in my head after getting into it with my old man. Pops had been drunk off his ass, like always, telling me I was going soft. After one of our club brothers was busted during a run, I'd asked if we could maybe lay low for a while, back off the drug running to get off the authorities' radar. I also made the mistake of telling him we needed to find other ways to make money. Expand our autobody shops, maybe even open another outside of the compound. Course he'd gotten pissed at that, called me unworthy of the tat on my back, then told me to get the fuck out of his face. And because I was sick of his shit, I was all too happy to oblige.

I hadn't thought twice about where I wanted to go when I'd hopped onto my bike and taken off that night. Lisa had been my sounding board since the day she and Pops first met. An instinctual connection was what the two of us had—I couldn't really describe it as anything but. Her house was the only place that felt like home to me, aside from the compound.

When I went to leave Lisa's, Emily pulled into the drive the same time I was pulling out—home for the weekend from college. The only thing I'd seen that night was my stepsister's wave and the shadow of her friend in the passenger's seat. Otherwise, I had no idea what my *chauffeur* was like—except for the fact that she taught at the same middle school Emily did.

Emily and Lisa started arguing again, talking like I wasn't even there. I wasn't good at paying attention, and soon found myself tuning them out.

The perfect distraction came into focus seconds later, a sexy little waitress working her magic with a coffee pot behind the counter. She was all smiles as she walked from table to table, sporting a pair of sparkly eyes. I couldn't make out the color, but I could see the happiness on her face; at the corners of those eyes when they crinkled from grinning most of all. There was a natural ease to how she moved, how she spoke to people as well. Fluid like a dancer—a ballerina, maybe. A people person and the exact opposite of who I was.

On instinct, I scanned her, head to toe. Not just because she was good-looking, but because I tended to compartmentalize every person I met. Label them. Safe, or not safe. Good, or bad. A habit I'd picked up from my years as an RD.

She wore a pair of white tights, a short little blue-and-white checkered dress with an apron, and white laced-up Converse tied in two, perfectly symmetrical knots. She wasn't my type at all, too hoity-toity. But there was something about her that drew me in.

Her long blonde hair was pulled back at the nape of her neck, nearly hitting the top of her ass. The real kicker of it all was the fact that she wore this big white bow around it. She reminded me of a cheerleader.

Like she could sense I was looking, the waitress' stare slipped my way. At the sight of her full on, my heart kicked into overdrive. Fuck, she was stunning. Beyond just simple and sweet.

Emily kept talking, Lisa might've said my name, but nothing could break my concentration. Not a damn thing. It'd been a long time since I'd taken up with a woman—felt her soft skin, kissed her neck, tasted her... Had I decided to stick around, not pursue the new life I was aiming for, Hottie Waitress could've been my first in a long, long time.

Curiosity lit the waitress' gaze the longer I stared at her. Head tipped to the side, she waved at me, slow, tentative, unsure...

"—and conversation isn't a bad thing to have, Ny."

I blinked, refocusing on Lisa. "Huh?"

She glanced over her shoulder to where I was looking, but the waitress was gone, like a figment of my imagination. I rubbed at the back of my head, trying to brush the image out of my mind.

"Are you listening to *anything* we're discussing?" Emily huffed. "Oh, wait, who am I kidding? You never flipping listen."

"I'm listening." I squinted at her, then Lisa. "What'd you guys say again?"

Lisa laughed under her breath, while Emily groaned, probably to try and keep her shit together. I knew I was pissing her off, but I also didn't care much either. I loved her, but she drove me nuts.

"What I said was, you have conversations with me and my mom all the time. What's so hard about making idle conversation with anyone else?"

I shrugged, then, because I couldn't help it, looked for the waitress again. She came back out from the kitchen, hips swaying as she moved around the counter to serve some trucker in a corner booth. *Not a figment. Definitely real.*

Waitress dropped her head back, laughing at something Trucker Man said. Even over the low Elvis music playing on the speakers, I could hear the sound. It was cute as hell, warming my chest like fire. I put a hand over my heart, trying to scrub the sensation away.

She captivated me. And I didn't have a damn clue why.

"—and Maya. You used to talk to *her* all the time."

At Maya's name, I refocused on Emily and scowled. "Not the same."

Maya Davenport was the reason I'd chosen San Diego as my place to escape.

She'd been my best friend when I was nineteen. The first girl I'd ever slept with, too. Maya was also one of the only women I'd ever been able to count on in my life—the reason I'd decided not to write off all women in general.

Once a month during my stint in prison, she'd always manage to call me—talk me through my shit. Maya had given me a reason to want to get out of prison, when most days I'd felt like death. She'd been my everything once; my savior from the past, and the main reason I was finally able to nut up and do what I had to do to get out of jail in the end.

Now I was hoping she'd accept me back into her life, minus my cut. As a guy alone, no brothers, no future, and not a dime to my name. If she was smart, she'd tell me to stay away. But I didn't know what the hell I was going to do if she did. Which was why I hadn't bothered to call her and tell her I was coming yet.

"We love you, Ny." Emily moved out of the booth and stood. "But it's time to re-evaluate your stance on communication."

I grunted in response.

"I'm going to the bathroom. Try to be nice if she—"

"Yeah, yeah. I'll be nice to the chauffeur when she gets here."

I searched the rest of the diner once Emily left the table, wondering why this *Summer* hadn't bothered to show yet. Besides two waitresses, the trucker, a chef, and us three, the restaurant stood empty. It worked out well, seeing how I wasn't looking to be discovered. But still, places like this gave me a horror-movie vibe.

"We know this is hard for you," Lisa said, her voice softer than her daughter's had been. "But it's for the best that you go with Summer. I promise, she's a really nice young lady."

"But nice doesn't necessarily mean much in my world."

Nice was the prison guard who snuck me in smokes, then turned me in the following day for having the things illegally.

Nice was my old cellmate—the guy who claimed he had a woman back at home he was getting out for, only for me to find out he was mental and talking to his dead wife in his sleep.

The one he'd killed.

And nice was my father. Charles-Motherfucking-Lattimore. The one who put me behind bars in the first place for the sole fact that he didn't think I was the proverbial son after all.

Sighing to herself, likely pissed that I couldn't find a reason to be positive, Lisa picked up her purse, claiming she needed to make a phone call outside. I nodded, barely giving her the time of day. It was her idea I ride with Summer, while Emily had been against it. Between the two of them, Em was the one who didn't trust me, while Lisa was the one who couldn't seem to get rid of me fast enough. Either way, I'd be out of their hair for good come tomorrow.

"You look like you could use a piece of pie," a soft voice piped up from my left.

Two long legs, covered in those white tights, leaned against the side of the table. Nostrils flaring, I inhaled the scent of something flowery, just as I jerked around to find the culprit.

Waitress.

One blink, then two. My mouth opened and shut.

This woman, Jesus… She wasn't just beautiful. She was *epic*.

And her eyes? They were even prettier up close. Thick with emotion, shiny like the sea… one-hundred-percent baby blue. She was young, too, twenty-three, maybe twenty-four, no older than Emily. Innocent. Untainted. Ready to be dirtied.

Just not by you.

"Pie, huh?" I grinned, ignoring my inner voice.

She set a plate in front of me. One side of her lips curved. "Well, in the words of Ms. Jane Austen, *Good apple pies are a considerable part of our domestic happiness.*"

"That so?" *Jane, who?*

"Of course. Though with pie, you also have to have a good cup of coffee." She pointed to my cup, nose scrunching. "And it looks to me like your waitress screwed you in that department."

I picked up the cup and looked inside. "It is pretty fucking bad."

"I'll fix that for you." She cracked her neck from side to side, like she was readying for a battle, and damn if my cock didn't instantly react. Hard, shifting against my zipper, imagining what exactly it'd be like to sink inside—

"Do you want cream or sugar?"

I shook my head, watching as the top button of her dress popped open. Not realizing she was showing me her goods, she leaned over the table to pour me a fresh cup. I stifled a moan in the back of my throat and looked away, vowing to keep myself from going there.

Gorgeous or not though, I needed to keep my priorities straight. Which meant getting out of this town and starting over as someone other than the son of a really bad fucking man.

After she finished pouring, Waitress untied her apron and sat across from me in the booth. I froze, eyes narrowed, watching her, my mind racing.

Wordless, and still smiling, Waitress reached for the cup Emily wasn't using and poured herself some.

"Now *this* is the good stuff." She sighed and lifted it in the air like it was liquor. "Cheers?"

Transfixed by her every move and word, I lifted my old cup. Forward and fearless... a woman after my own heart.

"What are we cheers-ing to?" I quirked a brow.

She hesitated for a second before she touched her cup to mine. "To road trips."

I scowled, watching her over the rim of her cup, through the steam that lifted and misted across her nose and eyes, unable to take a drink myself because I could've sworn she'd just said, *To road trips.*

Before I could question her, Emily was back. "Oh, good. Your shift ended."

I watched my stepsister sit next to Waitress in the seat, only for the two of them to hug.

"Summer." Emily motioned a hand my way. "Meet my step-brother, Niyol."

Holy shit.

Waitress was my ride to Cali?

"Hi." Summer blushed a sweet pink, giving me a little wave like she'd done earlier.

My response? "Fuck. Me."

CHAPTER TWO

Summer

Maybe I'd grown a second head. Or my mind had been invaded by little green aliens. Because if there was ever a time I should have considered myself crazy, it was the moment I agreed to a road trip with Niyol Lattimore, my best friend's *incredibly* sexy stepbrother.

"I can still change my plans, you know. Drive him myself. Sam said our travel dates are interchangeable, so it's not a big deal if I need to postpone." Emily stared down at the gravel drive, her feet dangling over the front bumper of my Range Rover.

"Not happening." I swung my feet like her, bumping our shoulders together.

"But what about your job at the diner? I *hate* that you have to quit."

"Not me." A summer without perverted truckers would not be disappointing. Plus, I didn't necessarily need the money. Sure, the tips I earned from waitressing were nice for an occasional manicure or massage, but those things weren't necessities. Besides that, I only worked there as a favor to my cousin—the manager of the place. I'd spent every summer since I was sixteen working at that diner. Now, at twenty-four, I was more than ready to call it quits and actually have a summer vacation like teachers were supposed to.

Emily was six weeks away from starting back at work too—she was a science teacher at the middle school where I taught English.

The two of us had been friends since college, floormates, instantly clicking over a late-night study session in the library.

"We've already been over this, Em. You deserve time with Sam, just like I deserve a few weeks of R and R on the road." Even if the R and R was with a semi-stranger who'd gifted me with a lifetime's worth of material to paddle my pink canoe.

"But what if—"

"No buts, what-ifs, or anything remotely close to an excuse. You just got engaged. Go *celebrate*." I smiled at her. "Have loads of crazy sex and forget that you even have a crazy stepbrother while you're at it."

My best friend didn't have a single bone in her body made for arguing, at least with me, therefore I knew she'd let it go. She wasn't a pushover, so to speak, more a woman who preferred the calm to a storm. It was what made us such a crazy-awesome pair. We were not two peas in a pod by ordinary standards, but we were each other's lifelines. So, the second she'd told me about her dilemma—having to choose between driving Niyol to San Diego or going on a surprise cruise with Sam—I'd known what I needed to do.

Emily twirled her engagement ring around her finger. It was huge and sparkly, everything I'd wanted four weeks ago. Everything I'd *had*, I should say.

The dress had been altered, the reception hall booked, the table decorations designed, now stored in the rafters of my father's garage. And the honeymoon to Bermuda...? Well, Landon, that bastard ex-fiancé of mine, was currently there with his new girlfriend.

I swallowed hard, tears instantly blurring my vision at the thought. No. I wouldn't cry. I'd gone an entire *week* without doing so. Why was I letting this get to me now?

"You know you don't owe me anything, right?" Emily interrupted my thoughts, touching my forearm.

Nonchalantly, I wiped at my cheeks beneath my sunglasses with one hand, keeping my face turned the other way as I answered. "I do. But this is what best friends are for."

"I'm just…"

"Just what?"

"Worried."

"About me?" I put my hand on my chest, facing her again. "*Please*. I'm fine."

"You're vulnerable, and Niyol can be a real asshole. He's incredibly conniving when he wants something. If your intentions are to go on this trip and get over Landon, then this may not be the way to go about doing so."

"I can handle it," I said after a long pause. "Seriously, Em. I'm not some damsel in distress, in need of a hero to remind me what it's like to be a woman."

If anything, after Landon, I wanted nothing else to do with the male species. Not when it came to love. Not when it came to a happily ever after. And certainly not for booty calls.

For my entire life, I'd counted on a man to protect me, love me, *honor me.* But I was done. Done with a capital D.

"And even if you were, Ny's not some sexual Superman. He's an ex-con and—"

"A former member of the Red Dragons, blah, blah, blah. I get it."

She glared at me.

I winked, thankful for the emotional reprieve.

As a teacher who dealt with hormonal middle-school kids ten months out of the year, I knew a thing or two about dealing with enigmas. And that's exactly what Niyol was. Instead of being the twelve or thirteen-year-old type, though, he was the twenty-six-year-old kind.

The moment I sat across from him in that booth last night, I had him pegged. Tormented and broody, secrets running amok in his head, angry at the world, but willing to give it a shot, regardless.

In a way, Niyol and I were kind of alike. I, too, wanted a new shot at life. A shot where I could just be me, forgoing my past and my pains for a chance at reinventing myself. Who I was as a woman, most of all. No longer would I be someone's second in life. Not to my father, who always chose my brothers or his job over me, and certainly not to guys like Landon, who found other women to satisfy their sexual needs.

Emily stared at the front door of her mom's house, the wheels in her head spinning. I touched her shoulder and smiled in reassurance when she faced me again.

"Please don't worry about this. Or me. If I didn't think I could handle the trip, then I wouldn't have suggested taking him."

"You'll at least call me, right? If it gets too bad?" Emily frowned.

"Of course." I patted her hand just as the screen door banged shut, drawing our attention to the front porch.

Unwittingly, my breath caught at the sight of Niyol, just like it had done the night before across the length of the diner. In all his six-foot-plus glory, he sauntered down the front porch steps, a duffle bag slung over his shoulder. The color of his bag matched his midnight hair. Thick, heavy layers hanging over his forehead, just barely touching the tops of his tan cheeks. The patch of scruff he sported around his lips covered the lower half of his face, while his dark brown eyes took control of the world and everything in it. He was one-quarter Native American like Emily. Niyol Lattimore may have run the gamut of trouble, but he was one hell of a gorgeous sight.

"So, quick question," I whispered conspicuously into Emily's ear. "Does he always look so grumpy?" I continued to watch him, licking my lips, his sexy swagger tripping my heart up a beat regardless of my new man-ban. The soles of his black boots could easily crush a hand or foot. Probably had crushed their fair share of hearts too.

With his hands tucked into his back pockets, and his chin to his chest, he looked like a warrior on the verge of destruction; his coat of armor consisting of black jeans and a black tee. His movements were slow, deliberate, and his thighs, the massive muscles encasing them, bulged with every step he took. Niyol was *massive*. Even standing at five-foot-nine myself, he towered over me by at least four inches.

"Maya doesn't even know he's coming," Emily whispered back, ignoring my question. "It has to be hitting him what he's about to do, you know? Surprising her like this."

"Stop talking about me like I'm not here." His throaty words crackled through the air, as though he smoked a pack a day. Maybe he did.

"I'm just worried about you, Ny." Emily's shoulders dropped, worry for the guy engrained between the dip of her brows.

"You need to *stop* worrying about me." He tossed his duffle bag into the backseat with a grunt and slammed the door, never looking in my direction as he moved to stand in front of his stepsister. That was a change from the night before. Definitely not the best ego-booster either.

"I'll always worry about you." My best friend grazed his shoulder as she jumped off the hood.

"I'm fine." He took a step back and knifed a hand through his hair, as though her touch were poison. I could totally relate to dealing with Emily's constant pessimism, but did he have to be such a dick about it?

Trying my best to ease the tension, I pounded on the hood of my Range Rover, just once. "All right, it's time to jet."

Emily held her finger up to me, eyes widening. "Hold up a second, I forgot something inside."

Nodding, I brushed off my hands on the back of my jeans and walked toward the driver's side. From over the roof, I started to tell Niyol our plans for the first leg of our five-day trip.

"I want to make it to Des Moines before the sun sets. My grandparents are expecting us for the night. I need to warn you first, Grams loves to talk. My grandpa, on the other hand—"

"I'll sleep in the car."

I narrowed my eyes at him from over the roof. "Excuse me?"

"I *said* I'm gonna sleep. In. The. Car." He tipped his head to the side, studying me. *Challenging* me.

"You'll sleep in the car," I huffed, annoyed.

"*That's* what I said." He leaned over the roof and set his elbows on top, dark brows rising mid-forehead.

"You can't sleep in the car. Not when there will be two perfectly good beds for us to sleep in at my *grandparents'* home."

His lip tilted up on one side in a smirk, highlighting a scar beneath his nose. "Gonna set one thing straight before we do this, Princess. First off—"

"Did you just call me 'Princess'?" My eyes widened.

"Anyone driving a car that costs more than a house is a princess." He glared at me.

"Well…" I swirled my index finger in a circle, attempting to spit the words out, whatever they might be. "You, I… This…"

Nice diction there, Summer. Two minutes in this man's presence and I was suddenly losing all semblance of normalcy.

Before I could tell him off, Emily bounced back out the front door. When I glanced at her, Niyol snuck into the backseat, mumbling something under his breath that I'm pretty sure I didn't want to hear.

Breathless, like she'd been running, Emily shoved her hand out in front of me. She opened her mouth to say something, but lifted her brows in suspicion as she stared between me and the back window.

I jumped in front of her, blocking the view. "What's up, Buttercup?"

"Take this."

I stared at the silver container on her palm, nose scrunched. "Pepper spray?"

"There are a lot of scary people out there in the world, you know."

I wondered if she was secretly referring to Niyol.

To appease her, I grabbed it and stuffed it into the pocket of my shorts. "You do know I have super ninja skills, right?"

"Uh, no. You don't." She moved back when I opened my door.

"Thanks for the vote of confidence." I kissed her forehead before sitting in the driver's seat. "I'll miss your face."

"Take care of yourself," she called through the open window, giving me a little wave.

I glanced into the backseat, finding Moody Booty with his eyes narrowed as he scrolled through his phone.

Smiling the brightest smile ever, I turned back toward Emily and said, "Don't worry. Everything will be fabulous. Promise."

Famous. Last. Words.

CHAPTER THREE

Niyol

I couldn't stand her music. Over and over, she played this twangy shit, singing along with every song from a playlist I'd come to learn—not by choice—was called *Road Trip Beats.* Had I known I'd be riding alongside the Karaoke Queen, then I would've brought some ear plugs.

"Can you turn it down?" I groaned.

She clicked her tongue against the roof of her mouth. "I would, but I'm really freaking tired and having the music loud helps me stay awake." She paused for a second. "What kind of music do you like listening to? I can change the station at least. Compromising is the best and cheapest lawyer."

Whatever the fuck that meant.

"No. I got a headache. Need silence." I rolled over to my side and grabbed my cell phone from the floor, squinting at the time. 5:45 p.m.

"But—"

"How 'bout you let me drive instead." I pushed up to a sitting position between the front seats. I wouldn't mind getting behind the wheel of a pretty car like this. Mostly so I could fuck up the engine by going too fast.

She scowled at me in the rearview mirror, then refocused on the road. "You just said you had a headache."

"Fine. Then pull over at the next exit." I ran a hand over my face and sat up completely. I probably should've curbed the dick routine, but she wasn't the only one who was exhausted, not to mention on edge.

I'd been up all night, worrying over the fact that I'd be stuck in a car for three days with *her.* She'd cast a spell on me at that damn diner, and I wasn't about to be sidetracked from my main goal.

When I wasn't tossing and turning in bed, thinking about Summer's sparkling eyes, I was feeling like an asshole because I'd been bitched at by my cousin, Slade, and best friend, Archer, who'd showed up at Lisa's unannounced round midnight.

Since getting out of the pen, I hadn't made the effort to see or talk to either of them—or anyone else from the club for that matter. I had known it'd be hard to avoid the two of them. They were always loyal to me, always knew where I was, unlike the rest of the RDs who I'd somehow managed to avoid, having my back on runs, calming me down when Pops laid out the law and fucked me over in the process—that's who Slade and Archer were. Which was why I did owe them some kind of explanation as to why I was leaving cold turkey instead of trying to talk it out at the club.

I didn't want to admit that I'd been threatened in prison. So I told them the semi-version of the truth. How I wanted to start over, and I wanted to do it in San Diego.

They'd begged me not to go, even went as far as threatening to chop my nuts off if I did. I knew they'd be pissed, which was why I'd been trying to leave town under the radar. Me running from the club was one thing. Running from those two was a whole other fucked-up notion.

Thing was, they didn't know what it was like to live with the guilt of being a rat. They were solid with the club, good brothers who could do no wrong, unlike me. Maybe someday I'd be back, accept whatever fate awaited me with the RDs. But I wasn't ready yet.

Hell, I might never be.

"We'll be there in less than an hour. Can you wait just a little longer?" Summer asked.

"No. There's an exit up ahead, and you can grab some coffee or an energy drink. I want a smoke." My lower back cracked, proof that I should've sat up front with her. But I'd needed to try and get some rest, stretch my legs in the process. Otherwise, I'd be dragging ass if she asked me to drive.

Thankfully, Summer stopped arguing, taking that exit like the devil was messing with her foot. I'd likely pissed her off. Something I swore to Emily that I wouldn't do. Tomorrow, I'd do better. Tonight, though? I was too tired to care.

The white sign to the right said *Winterset: Covered Bridge Capital of the World.* The sign next to it said: *Birthplace of John Wayne.*

"This place is quaint." Her voice was happy as we drove further into town. Perky, really—everything Emily was not. "I'm kind of glad we stopped, actually." She took a left, then a right, until we wound up on some random street.

I stared out the window and watched the streetlights pop on. I hadn't been in a town like this before. *Quaint* wasn't what I'd call it. Old and run-down, like something out of a thirties western, was more like it.

She parked in front of a coffee shop and only then did she turn her music down. It was the quietest she'd been all day. I met her gaze in the rearview mirror. My gut got tight at the view, and I quickly looked back down at my lap. She might've said something, but I couldn't hear it. Not when a buzz was filling my ears. Not when the intensity of her blue eyes was damn near swallowing me whole.

Focus, Ny.

Keys jingled in her hands. "I'm gonna head inside and grab some coffee. Meet back here in ten?"

I jumped out of her fancy-ass car and mumbled, "Fine."

I missed my bike. The open air, the smells, the noises… Had my Harley been in better shape, I would've set out on this trip alone. Would've been a hell of a lot better off, that's for damn sure.

The bell over the door jingled when I stepped inside the convenience store. The stench of sweat smacked me in the face. I made my way to the front counter, meeting up with an old man.

"Marlboro Reds." I pointed to the shelf behind the register, digging in my wallet for a ten.

He turned to grab them, just as the door's bells chimed again. I glanced over my shoulder, finding a couple of preppy boys who looked like college kids. They shoved each other, laughing. My guess was they went to school up at Iowa State. One had a frat shirt on, the other a Polo.

"You need some help?" I asked the old guy. He was up on a stepladder now, knees shaking.

"No, I've got this, son. Don't you worry." Sure enough, he made his way to the top of his ladder, holding onto the edge of the highest shelf. This guy was gonna have a heart attack if he wasn't careful.

The preppy guys stood directly in line behind me. "She wanted me," guy one said.

"No, you idiot. She blew you off. I told you all blondes were bitches," the other guy said.

"It's what I like. Can't help myself. Plus, her rack was fucking fantastic. Did you see that pink tank she had on? Damn." He whistled. "Nipples for days."

I shifted my weight back and forth between my feet. Sweat pooled along my neck the closer they got. Still, I kept my mouth shut, not wanting to start anything. The old Niyol would have been all up in their faces, telling them to back off. But new leaves had to be turned.

"We don't have all day," one of them called out.

I pulled my phone out of my jeans' pocket to check the time. It'd taken the guy five minutes to get my pack down. There's no telling how long it'd take him to ring me up.

After what felt like forever, the old man climbed off his ladder and made his way to the register. "That'll be nine forty-nine, young man," he said.

I handed him the ten.

The idiots laughed under their breath, only for one to say, "Can you hurry the fuck up?"

My body went rigid, blood boiling hotter as one of them practically dry humped my back.

"Step. The hell. Back," I growled.

One of them snorted out, "Pussy."

Rage flashed red behind my eyes when I closed them. I tried to breathe—*in through the nose, out through the mouth*. But the louder they got, the more the temperature inside of me heated.

In the end, I managed to keep myself in check, head down as I moved to the door. I tucked my smokes into the front pocket of my t-shirt, just as one of them whispered under their breath, "Go on now, cry to Mama."

I flattened my hands on the door and squeezed my eyes shut. "Screw it."

I spun around. Two steps forward and I was chest-to-chest with the Polo-wearing fucker.

"You got something you wanna say, then say it to my face." Not giving him a chance to speak, I punched him in the jaw. His body flew back and knocked a display shelf to the floor.

Racks of Hostess shit flooded the tile, but I didn't care. I was driven by the fight, hate at the wheel. His frat boy buddy came up behind me, wrapping a forearm around my neck. The struggle was nothing as I shoved my foot back against his dick. He groaned, falling to his knees.

Blood trickled down the corner of the Polo's mouth when he stood back up. He faced me, eyes on fire. "You hit me."

"And I'll do it again." I squeezed my hand into a ball, my knuckles barely sore.

The store door flew open then, capturing my attention. A shadow stood there, eyes wide, a hand on her mouth. Summer.

"Niyol? Are you okay?" She raced over, and my eyes widened when I got a better look at what she had on. Tight pink tank, spaghetti straps, and no bra. She hadn't been dressed in that before.

Jesus fuck. Those pricks had been talking about her.

Distraction short-lived, Polo guy came at my side, slugging me square in the kidneys.

I doubled over as Summer screamed, "Stop it!"

When I managed to stand, I froze at the sight of her jumping onto Polo's back, her arms in a headlock around his neck, legs locked around his gut.

"Holy shit." I blinked, watching as she scratched his temples and forehead, then nearly laughed my guts out when he started screaming like a little girl.

A double click drew my attention back to the old guy behind the counter. "Ah, hell." On the guy's shoulder sat a shotgun, one with the barrel pointed at me.

Instinct pulled my hands into the air. "It's all good, man," I said. "We were just leaving."

Slowly, I took another step back, wrenching Summer off the guy along the way. She squeaked, but landed on her feet in front of me, my arm wrapped around her waist. Her chest heaved as she took in air, and her body shook with unchecked rage.

"Get outta here. I don't want to use this on ya. I know those boys are to blame."

Nodding at the old man, I reached for Summer's hand, pulling her through the front door. A cop rounded the corner of a building a few seconds later, lights flashing. The two of us took off across the street, feet slapping against the brick sidewalk. We hopped into her Rover just as he parked in front of the convenience store.

"What… was that?" Summer started the engine, but waited a second to leave, panting as she glared at me from her seat. She tapped the gas once the cop was inside the store, pulling back out onto the road.

High on adrenaline, I couldn't help but grin as I leaned back against the headrest. Man, it felt good to use my hands again.

"Seriously. What was that? You're not in prison anymore, Niyol. You can't just start random fights with random groups of men!" she yelled.

I pulled my smokes out and started packing them on my palm. "Those guys were idiots. Called me a dumbass."

"Well, they called me a bitch in the café when I wouldn't give them my number, but was that a reason to start a fight? *No.* Absolutely not. They were words, Niyol. That's it."

I tugged a cigarette from the box and placed it between my lips, swallowing hard at her admission. I should've done far more to the guys for saying what they did to her.

"Didn't see you walking away," I pointed out.

She huffed, foot growing heavier against the accelerator as we hopped back on the interstate. "I was *saving* you."

"Whoa, there. You didn't *save* me from nothing. I had it handled." I lit my smoke and rolled down the window.

She laughed, the sound so evil I glanced at her to see if she'd sprouted horns. "There is no way you are smoking in here." She grabbed the cigarette from my mouth and tossed it out her window.

"Hey. Those were expensive."

"I don't care if that was the last cigarette on earth *or* if you had to pay a million dollars to get it. You will not. Be smoking. In my car. Ever."

"Man, you take all my fun stuff away. Won't let me fight. Won't let me smoke…"

"Look at it this way." She lifted her chin, all high and mighty like. "Not fighting means no concussions or worse. *And* not smoking means no cancer."

"You're a regular little Superwoman, huh?" My smile grew wider.

Her cheeks grew pink, rage likely the cause. I could tell she was the type to not lose control very often. "No. Just a woman who likes to stay positive." She glanced at me out of the corner of her eye before refocusing on the road. "But I'm not opposed to *that* pet name if you feel the need to call me something other than Summer."

"Nah." I shook my head and kicked my feet out onto the dash. "Princess fits."

"By whose standards?" she scoffed.

"Mine." I shut my eyes, tired now that my adrenaline was crashing.

I needed to feign sleep. End the conversation. This woman was fire, ready for anything to burn in her wake, and *nothing* like I figured she would be. Arguing with her was just as dangerous to me as looking at her was.

Things grew quiet after that, other than the sound of the Rover's engine. For the first time since we'd left, I finally felt myself relax a little.

Until she started in again.

Jesus. She really did like to talk.

"Tell me something about yourself. To make this work, I think we need to get to know each other. Be friends, or at *least* cordial."

Funny, seeing as how Emily had said the same thing.

"I mean, Em adores you, so you must have some good qualities underneath all that black you wear."

Ignoring her comments about my clothes, I hit her where it counted. "We're not gonna be friends, Princess. No point. You're my chauffeur, that's it." When she didn't speak, I reopened my eyes and caught sight of her white-knuckling the wheel.

Shit. There I was, being a dick again.

"Just enlighten me, would you please?"

I sighed, and grabbed another smoke out, threading it through my fingers. "You don't wanna be friends with me. I'm not a nice guy."

"I'd like to be the judge of that one, if you don't mind." Her voice grew softer, an odd soothing melody to my racing, fucked-up heart.

"I already know you," I said. "And I'm betting you know me, too. So, let's cut the polite bull."

She was the goody-two-shoes who likely got everything she wanted in life. Perfect grades in high school and college, daughter of two perfect parents, raised right and rich and girly. I could already tell she was a poster child by the looks of her clothes and car. What else did I need to know?

"You don't know me," she whispered, looking away, bottom lip pulled between her teeth.

There were a lot of things I wanted to say just then. *I can't know you. I can't start liking you. I can't let anything hold me back from getting out of Illinois.* But I didn't. Instead, I thumped that idiot away in my mind, and let the old Niyol "Hawk" Lattimore lead the way.

"Maybe there's a reason people like you and I shouldn't know each other. Ever think of it like that?" I sighed, leaning my head back against the seat.

This woman… every goody-two-shoes, sweet, innocent inch of her, did not want to know who I was. And it was my job to make sure she felt the same way.

CHAPTER FOUR

Summer

By the time we arrived at my grandparents' house, I was nearly dead on my feet. I didn't bother to wake Niyol before leaving my Rover, but I did leave it running, with the AC on low. The air was stifling, and heat lightning popped in the distance proving so. Out here on the sparseness of my grandparents' farm, away from the city, it was beyond uncomfortable for nine at night in mid-July. The last thing I wanted was for him to sweat to death if he really did decide to sleep in there. He may have been a bit of a jerk, but that didn't mean I couldn't be the bigger person.

I walked toward the front door of the old white farmhouse, excitement brewing deep in my belly. The welcoming sight of Grams and Grandpa's two-story home was everything I remembered. Knowing they were waiting for me was like a warm blanket ready for me to crawl under.

"Hello?" I called out as I opened the front door, struggling to keep myself balanced as the weight of my suitcase nearly toppled me over. I might have overpacked, but a girl never knew when she'd need heels or boots, shirts or shorts, especially on a cross-country road trip.

"Summer!" My grandfather, who could have very well been Santa Claus' clone, came barreling through the kitchen to greet me with a hug. "I can't believe you're here." He pulled back and held me at arm's length by my shoulders.

My mother's father was the most charming man I knew. And even though I'd never known his daughter, my mother, I felt as though he and Grams were everything that my mom might have been.

"I've missed you guys so much." I squeezed him again, just as tightly as I could.

"We've missed you, too." The scent of chocolate cake hit my nose as we walked toward the kitchen. Like it had a mind of its own, my stomach growled, proof I hadn't eaten all day.

"Hungry?" Grandpa smiled, eyes zeroed in on my belly.

"Starved." I laid my head on his shoulder. "Where's Grams?"

"Backyard. That crazy cat of hers is being a pest. Killed a nest of baby rabbits this morning. About broke her heart." He shook his head as he motioned me toward the table. "I'll get you something. Have a seat."

I plopped my bag onto the floor next to the wall and sank into a chair. The old wood squeaked beneath me, and I couldn't help but grin at the sound. God, it was good to be there.

My gaze traveled the length of the room, over the yellow walls and sunflower border, only to land on the picture I'd painted for them when I was ten. It hung on the fridge, a magnet farm of animals keeping it in place. I smiled. This place hadn't changed at all. Same furniture. Same set-up. Same hominess I'd never tire of.

During the summers, up until my senior year of high school, when Dad worked, took my brothers camping, or drove them to their football, baseball, hockey, or soccer camps in between, I preferred staying with my grandparents for a few weeks. This was my mother's house growing up, so it always made me feel like I was at one with her, as strange as it sounded. I knew her only from pictures and stories told, but one look into my eyes and she'd supposedly been in love with me. Until she died, three hours after I was born, from a pulmonary embolism.

I hadn't been there in two years. Mainly because I'd been so over-the-top in love with...

No. I'd promised myself to stop with the Landon regrets. Bigger and better—that was the direction I intended to take now.

The porch light flickered off, and the back door swung open seconds after. I shot a glance toward the frazzled-looking woman with gray hair down to her elbows, my eyes welling with tears at the sight. My grams. Dressed in a flowing green skirt and gauzy white top, she looked just as gorgeous as ever, even at sixty-six.

"Oh, my sweet heavens," she cried, eyes meeting mine.

"Hi, Grams." I smiled and prepared to stand.

"Don't get up. You look exhausted." She took the final steps to get to me and regardless of what she said, I pushed out of my chair to meet her in a hug that rivaled the ferocity of my grandfather's.

"My goodness, you are so beautiful, just like your mother." She rocked us side to side. I caught my grandfather's smile from over her shoulder, followed by his wink, then quickly wiped an escaping tear before Grams could see. "Sit. Let's feed you. It's obvious you don't eat."

"I eat plenty, Grams. Promise."

She scoffed and waved her hand at me. "You're too skinny."

Grandpa placed a plate on the table. I sat down in front of it, smiling, watching as they positioned their chairs across from me. I pulled my hair out of my ponytail and into a side braid instead, trying my best to ignore the ginormous elephant in the room.

They knew I was coming. I'd called them last week when this whole road trip thing had transpired, asking if I could swing by and stay for a night's visit. I never bothered to explain where I was going, who I was with, or why I was doing it in the first place. Heck, Dad barely knew the details himself, thinking I was going away with Emily—not her ex-fugitive of a stepbrother. No doubt if he had known the truth, there would have been some major drama. Still, I was twenty-four, rented my own loft, and had a decent-paying job. I loved my father, but he didn't need to know *all* my secrets.

"Meatloaf and mashed potatoes. I see you still know my favorites." I picked up a fork, moaning as my taste buds nearly exploded in satisfaction.

"I'd never forget." Grams set her chin onto her palm and an elbow on the table.

"So. Who's the gentleman?" Three bites in, and the question I'd been dreading was dropped by none other than my grandpa.

I wiped my mouth with a napkin and grinned with innocence. "What gentleman?"

Grandpa folded his arms over his chest. "The one sleepin' in the front seat of your vehicle, that's who. Scary-lookin' fella who is not Landon."

I choked, coughing. Bits of food spilled from my mouth as I reached for a glass of water.

Grams laughed, standing to pat me on the back. "I'm sure we'll find out soon enough who the fella is. Leave the girl alone, honey."

My face grew hot. Yet I wasn't sure if it was because of my choking or my grandfather's abruptness. Out of the two of them, he had always been the quiet one. Maybe his age had made him more vocal.

After clearing my plate, I leaned back and folded my arms over my stomach. "That was delicious. I've missed your cooking." I smiled at Grams, hoping they'd moved on to other topics.

"Spill it, Summer Marie."

"Paul," Grams scolded. "I said let her be."

I squirmed under the full force of my grandfather's gaze before looking to Grams. "It's fine. Landon and I..." I looked to my plate, inhaling through my nose, exhaling through my mouth. "We broke up."

"Oh, good. I never did like that boy." Grams spoke up first.

My eyes popped wide at her confession. "You didn't like Landon?"

Grandpa spoke next. "Neither of us did. He wasn't good enough for you."

I blinked, taken aback by their confession. They'd never given me any indication before.

"Why didn't you tell me? We were two months from getting married."

"Because, honey. You seemed to love him." Grams shrugged. "And all we wanted was to see you happy."

I nodded slowly, trying to piece things together. The two of them hadn't been overly excited about him and I getting engaged, I remembered that much. But I'd figured it was because they thought we were too young to get married. But now, to know that they'd never liked him? Well, it eased something in my chest, like a loosening bolt.

"So, spill about the gentleman in your car," Grams said, a sly grin on her face.

Nervous for some reason, I licked my lips, glancing between them before I answered. "He's just my friend's stepbrother. I'm driving him to California." I shrugged. "A summer vacation kind of thing."

"Are you dating him now?" Grams leaned back in her chair, folding her arms.

"Oh, no, no, no." *God, no.* "He's just an acquaintance." *If that.*

"Are you going to bring him inside, so we can meet?" She lifted her brows.

"Yes." Carefully, I looked up to regard my grandpa.

His eyes were narrowed like mine, except he was glancing through the kitchen entryway toward the front door.

"It's getting late. I suggest we get the intros out of the way while we're still awake."

"Oh, wonderful. I'll get my cake ready." Grams stood and took my plate to the sink. "New guests always require the good china." She clapped her hands, completely giddy, flying toward her curio cabinet sitting in the corner of the kitchen.

"Um, no. Don't do that, Grams. It's late, and my guess is he's gonna want to just go to bed when he gets inside anyway." If I could even *get* him inside.

Grams turned back around, four small white plates in her grasp. "Everyone loves my wacky cake, Summer. And it's still warm. That's when it tastes the best."

I stood and moved next to her. "I know. It's just that there's no need—" The front door slammed shut, cutting me off. I turned to find the seat at the kitchen table where Grandpa had been sitting empty. "Shit."

"Dear, don't cuss." I faced my grams again, her frown suddenly replaced by a conniving smile. The corners of her eyes twitched as she pressed a free hand to my cheek. "It's unbecoming of a young lady looking for a new suitor."

Dear God. What had I gotten myself into?

CHAPTER FIVE

Niyol

The pounding wouldn't stop.

Boom, boom, boom.

Slowly, I opened my eyes, reaching for the Glock in my pocket that wasn't there. All these years later and my instincts never failed.

Boom. Boom. Boom.

"What the…?" I sat up slowly, eyes narrowed out the window. Standing on the other side of the glass was… "Santa?" I jammed both palms into my eyelids. Obviously, I was hallucinating.

"Get up. There's cake in the house for you," the old man yelled.

I reached over to turn off the car, then opened the door a crack. "Who're you?"

"The owner of this house." He lifted his chin, eyes narrowed. "And Summer's grandpa."

Two shadows behind him caught my eye from the porch of a huge white house. It was Summer standing next to some old lady.

"Fuck," I whispered under my breath and pushed the door open the rest of the way, nodding a greeting at the old man.

"You don't talk, boy?"

I shrugged, following him up a winding sidewalk.

"It ain't polite not to answer your elders."

"I talk fine." I swallowed.

"Good. Because when you meet my wife, I expect you to hold a better conversation with her than you do me."

Damn. This man gave me running for asshole of the year. I liked him already.

Summer stumbled over a step on the porch, eyes flitting between me and her grandpa. The lady, who I assumed was her grandma, stayed inside the doorway, stance cautious as she grinned from behind a screen door.

"I'm sorry," Summer whispered as I walked past.

I kept my voice low as Summer's grandpa stepped inside the house first. "I told you I'd sleep in the car."

"I had every intention of letting that happen." She tucked some of her hair behind her ear and glanced back over her shoulder before looking at me again. "But they saw you out here and wouldn't let it go." She bit down on her bottom lip—a move she'd been doing a lot. I followed the plump curve of her mouth, the way those teeth sunk into the flesh, completely and utterly distracted by thoughts of doing it myself.

Not a good idea, motherfucker.

I looked away and cleared my throat before uttering, "It's fine." Being inside a house like this made my skin crawl. Too homey. Too nice. Too unfamiliar.

Before I could head in, Summer touched my shoulder. "Please be nice. It's been a really long time since I've seen them and…" She blinked those aqua blues, trailing off into a world I couldn't help but want to know.

My shoulders fell at the thought of her having demons like me. New Niyol made a rare appearance as I dug my fingers through my hair. "Hey."

Something in my stomach leapt when she looked at me—expectant, fearful, curious.

"Yeah?"

I blew out a slow breath. "I'll be nice. Promise."

Slowly, Summer smiled—a smile I didn't deserve. She was too sweet for the likes of me, and damn if I didn't want to corrupt her, new life goals be damned.

With a shaky sigh, she mouthed, *Thank you*, and skipped ahead. I dipped my head back, eyes to the sky as I slammed the door on my thoughts again.

"Welcome to our home, you strapping young man. My name's Peaches." The grandma—*Peaches?*—slapped her palm against my back as she shut the door behind me. "I think you'll do just fine for my girl."

"Uh…" I scratched the back of my neck as she led me through their living room. "I'm actually going to stay in Summer's Range Rover tonight." I jabbed my thumb back toward the door, stopped, then stuffed my hands into my pockets. "Just feel more comfortable out there is all."

Summer, now standing in the entryway of the kitchen, stiffened at my words.

Her grandma, on the other hand… "No, you will not. There is a perfectly made-up bed for both you and Summer to share upstairs. I'm not that old-fashioned, you know."

Summer spun around and grabbed her grandma's hand. "Grams, no. I told you. Niyol and I are not—"

"You know what?" I stepped between Summer and her grandma, the RD who loved corruption coming to the forefront of my mind. "I do think I'll stay inside now." I winked at Summer, finding her pink cheeks now even pinker. Then, because I couldn't help myself, I backed up and wrapped an arm around her waist, fingers grazing the warm flesh of her hip just under her shirt.

Consider it payback for all the talking she'd done so far.

Her grandma's eyes nearly bugged out of her head as she pressed her hands together beneath her chin. "This is just *wonderful*."

That was a first. An old lady, thinking I was *wonderful?* Fuck. I wondered what she'd think if she knew that, inside my black duffle,

I carried a knife the size of my forearm for protection. And that was only because I couldn't get my hands on a gun before I left town.

"Cake's all served up and ready," the grandpa called from the kitchen.

Grinning from ear-to-ear, Peaches headed toward her husband, patting Summer's cheek along the way. When they were both out of earshot, Summer pushed me away.

"Are you insane? Grams is going to have us married and cursing us with pregnancy juju by the time we're out of here tomorrow." She glared up at me, those blues shimmering with barely checked rage. Her reaction only made me smile wider—made my cock twitch a little too.

"You wound me, Princess." I lowered a hand to my heart and grinned, deciding to play a game. If her grandparents thought I was her soon-to-be Prince Charming, I'd play the part, no problem.

She stabbed the back of my wrist with her finger. "I'll do more than *wound* you if you don't watch it." And then she was off, her tiny shorts catching my gaze, and damn if I couldn't look away.

CHAPTER SIX

Summer

Last night was the worst. At least the part *after* Niyol came inside. Grams was being ridiculous, asking us how long we'd been together. Niyol didn't even try to correct her; too seduced by her wacky cake to even acknowledge anyone's existence.

He was a traitor. A total man. You put a little good food in his stomach and he succumbed to anything and everything a woman wanted, especially the sixty-six-year-old kind.

After we finished eating, I headed upstairs to take a shower, ignoring Niyol's rumbly voice and boisterous laugh. He had my grandparents eating out of the palm of his hands in a matter of minutes, and it was the strangest, most unnerving thing I'd ever encountered.

Exhausted from the drive, I had plans to head straight to bed when I was done with my shower. Yet when I got to the room Grandpa had put my stuff in, I noticed the extra bag on the floor... and the big body already asleep in what was supposed to be *my* bed. Grams hadn't been kidding when she thought Niyol and I should sleep in the same room together.

I thought I'd fallen asleep on the floor, but when I opened my eyes this morning, I found myself buried under a blanket on the bed instead.

Nervous energy kick-started my heart when I rolled over. I blinked, letting go of a breath when I found the spot behind me cold and empty. Had I been sleepwalking? Because there was no way Niyol would have put me in bed with him willingly.

I slipped out from beneath the sheets, the pull and promise of coffee drawing me toward the kitchen. But when I went to open the door, a voice from the hall gave me pause. With careful ease, I pressed my ear to the wood and listened.

"*I don't know if you'll get this message. But we need to talk, Maya.*" He paused. "*I'm out of prison and I'm coming to California. I'm hopin' you'll let me stay with you.*" He sighed, sounding incredibly defeated for a man with so much grit. My throat grew tight with empathy, all my bitterness from last night slipping away. I'd *known* he held a softer side than what I'd encountered so far. It was what made me want to keep trying to get to know him.

He was Emily's stepbrother, a guy who was a little broken, but needed some tape to fix him right up. *A sad man was truly no man at all*—that's what my father used to say. Not because they were any less a person, but because they needed someone to help them feel un-sad. I could be that person for Niyol temporarily. If he'd let me.

The door whipped open before I could step back. I fell to the floor with a groan, hands braced out at my sides. A lightning-sharp pain shot up my tailbone and tears instantly welled in my eyes. Pain tolerance was the one thing I lacked.

"Jesus, Summer, what are you…" Niyol froze, dark eyes narrowing as he held my gaze. Quickly, I wiped my damp eyes before he reached forward to help me stand. He dropped my hand away, rubbing a palm against his jeans.

"I…" Ass on fire, I brushed off the back of my sleep shorts and blinked up at him, my equilibrium still out of whack.

His brows furrowed. "Were you spying on me?"

Swallowing hard, I took a step back, stopped short by a wall. "I wasn't *spying*, per se. At least not on purpose. I just needed to go to the bathroom and accidentally overheard you talking."

That dark scar by his lip was more pronounced up close. My fingers twitched against my thighs with the strangest urge to touch it—an urge that needed to stand right down. His nostrils flared, as though he was smelling something, surely *not* me. A natural reaction had me inhaling too, and the scent of soap and menthol filled my senses. Clean, masculine, and one-hundred-percent Niyol.

My gaze dropped to the ends of his hair as droplets of water fell onto his massive shoulders. Massive shoulders which were encased in yet another black tee.

"The bathroom is that way." He pointed toward the en-suite door to his left, eyes still narrowed.

"Who were you talking to?" I asked, because, apparently, I was a glutton for punishment.

"Nobody you know." His rough voice crackled through the air, angry and vicious, yet filled with a tinge of regret and sadness too.

I shivered. "Are you in trouble?"

His eyes darkened at my question.

I held up one hand. "Sorry. Just… ignore me." I shook my head and moved to my left. He followed, a hand landing next to my head on the wall. He didn't trap me in, but clearly, our conversation wasn't over.

"You don't need to spy on me," he said. "If you've got questions, ask them." His words were the most civil things he'd said to me since we'd left Lisa's house. Yet at the same time, I could feel the tension between us, his dark anger most of all. I wasn't sure if he was mad at me or the world more.

"For the last time, I was not *spying*," I scoffed, folding my arms between us, needing the barrier. "I was just wondering why you were talking in the hallway when you could talk in here. Or outside."

He licked his lips, eyes darting quickly to my cleavage, then my face. My throat grew warm, as did my cheeks. It was the first time he'd looked at me like I was something other than a pain in the ass. And I liked it *way* too much.

No more men, Summer. Remember that.

"I didn't want to wake you. That's why I didn't talk in the room." He paused, rubbing a hand over his mouth before leaning forward and caging me in, his hands pressed against the wall along the sides of my head.

I blinked as the scent of his aftershave caressed my nose. Holy hell, he smelled good.

"And I didn't want your grandparents thinking I was running off or hiding shit."

That was actually quite... *respectful.* "Oh."

He cocked a brow. "Why does it matter where I talk anyway?"

I dropped my arms and our chests brushed together. The heat coming off him was nearly asphyxiating as my shoulders grazed the wall. Raw man-power emanated from his body, and I shivered once more, hating how the single brush of his dark shirt against my tank top made my insides tingle.

This was how it always started for me, my body overtaking my mind. Blinded by a pair of gorgeous eyes and pretty man-lips, I was in serious trouble when it came to hot dudes.

Two years of my life I'd wasted on Landon. The only reason I'd found out he'd been cheating was because I'd caught him in the act—literally on the desk in his office one afternoon. Week after week, he'd been coming home, smelling like cheap perfume, and I'd been too much of a freaking idiot to recognize the signs. Too blinded by thoughts of a happily-ever-after most of all.

Had I not discovered the truth, then I would've been walking down the aisle soon, in the five-thousand-dollar dress I'd burnt to a crisp in my fireplace just last week.

Therapy had never been so expensive.

I shook my head to rid the memory. "It doesn't matter. And again, I'm sorry for listening in like I did. It won't happen again. I respect others' privacy. Trust me."

He nodded once, but didn't respond, nor did he look convinced. Thankfully, the anger in his eyes simmered a little, though the replacement wasn't much better. Smoldering, dark, and everything I wasn't expecting. My breath caught a little, nipples tightening against my tank.

Good Lord, I needed to get laid. *Self-imposed-ban-on-men, say what?* Maybe I had this ban all wrong. Maybe I needed to screw my ex from my system. I could almost bet that Niyol would be amazing at taking the itch away. He had a certain dominance to him, edged with a bad-boy sex appeal, and would no doubt give me the ride of my life if I asked him to.

On the other hand, fantasizing about the giver of any of my future orgasms being a man I was going to be trapped inside a car with for the next week or so was probably not a good idea. Plus, he was a law-breaker, and from the sounds of it, hung up on someone else... though a man in love with one woman shouldn't have been looking at me the way Niyol currently was. Like he wanted to taste me, touch me, bend me over the very bed I'd woken up in...

His tongue snuck out of his mouth and something shiny caught my eye as it clicked against his teeth. Distracted, not thinking of anything but the sudden ache between my thighs, I whispered, "You have a tongue ring."

He nodded. "I do."

The longer he stared back at me, the darker his eyes seemed to grow. They were black holes of unnerving nothingness and everything at the same time. My heart raced uncontrollably in my chest and dampness coated the back of my neck from sweat. *Since when did it get so hot in here?* I shifted from one foot to the other, but all that did was cause his leg to graze the sensitized space I was dying to get relief from. He tipped his head to the side, studying me like a puzzle. One he was fighting against figuring out. Before I could make the decision for him—before I could jump in his arms and wrap my thighs around his waist—he dropped his hands away from beside my face, pressing them to my hips instead.

"When did you get it pierced?" My voice was a whisper, the breath grazing my lips like tiny fingers.

"Twenty-first birthday present to myself."

I cleared my throat. "Did it hurt?"

"No."

Unconsciously, I arched my hips against his, one, slow push and pull. At my movement, Niyol's breath seemed to catch, and the sight of his already dark skin flushed even more.

Power washed over me at the sight, a sudden urge to bring this hardened man to his knees suddenly my biggest need in life. So, again, I arched my hips, loving how his eyes shut, how his lips parted too. Loving the low growl in his throat. Wild. Uncaged. A beast ready to explode.

In the process, my thong grazed my clit, sending delicious shockwaves through me. I gasped at the sensation and he reopened his eyes. A new look surfaced there in his gaze, one which sent goosebumps dancing over my arms.

Desire. Need. Lust.

It spurred my next question. "Are you pierced anywhere else?"

A full-wattage grin lit up his face, dark with promises of pain—the good kind. Pair that grin with the heat in his eyes, and I was ready to eradicate my sudden celibacy for one simple shot at this man. One orgasm would be more than worth any consequences. I was sure of it.

"You interested in finding out, Princess?" He arched one brow, teasing. Niyol knew exactly what he was doing, and I could tell he was enjoying it. But instead of taking advantage of what I silently offered, he took a step back, his hands dropping away and ending the heat.

I let go of a breath, realizing just how wrong this was.

I *had* to be rebounding. That's all. Because there's no way on earth I'd ever find myself being drawn to a man like Niyol Lattimore as something more than eye candy. He was a bad man who'd done bad things, with his very bad... tongue? No, no. Not his tongue. His tongue was far from bad. In fact, that tongue was killer sexy and—

God, I wanted him against me again. I wanted to be kissed by those full lips. Touched by those large hands. On my breasts, between my thighs... Who was I kidding? I wanted to experience the bad side of life in the form of a man who'd likely been to the deepest, darkest depths of it.

Most of all, I wanted that tongue in my mouth.

"Are you willing to show me, or is that an earned privilege?" I asked. It was a dangerous question, one I had no idea I was capable of asking. But with this man, I suddenly felt like I could take on the world in his presence.

His jaw clenched, those midnight eyes lowering to half-mast. Still, he didn't reply. He didn't need to. Niyol's gaze spoke the words his mouth couldn't—lowering to my breasts, studying their fullness, then moving back up to my lips. In turn, I pulled the bottom one between my teeth, a surge of heat washing over me at my unspoken invitation for him to kiss me.

But seconds passed, followed by what felt like a minute, then two. My skin grew itchy, unnerved. And the more Niyol continued to study me from a distance, making no other move to touch me, the more I realized I'd been reading this situation entirely wrong.

Never did he urge me closer with his words or his hands. Instead, his expression faded from enraptured to... blank. Emotionless. Hard.

Then, as if some internal decision had been made in his head, he grabbed his duffle bag off the floor, tucked it over his shoulder and said, "I'll meet you in the car."

My hands stayed frozen at my waist, oxygen trapped in my throat as I blinked back tears of embarrassment.

Oh, God, what had I been thinking?

♥

"Sorry, kiddo. Car's dead. Not turning over at all." My grandpa slammed the hood of my Range Rover shut, his hands greasy, and his arms coated in the same mess.

I glanced at Niyol out of the corner of my eye, painfully aware of his presence, now more than ever. Smudges of dark oil covered his strong nose and cheekbones; a bit on his temple too. Adorable. Sexy. And scary as hell. A man I'd nearly thrown myself at… only to be blown off in the end. Something I was sadly used to in the past, even with the men who supposedly loved me. Men like my father. My brothers, my own fiancé…

At least I had my grandfather to count on.

"Did you turn the ignition off after you got out last night?" I asked Niyol, attempting to keep my voice even.

"Yes," he answered, his voice emotionless.

I fidgeted with my hands, peeking up at him finally. His eyes were drawn together, focused on the hood.

"So, it's not the battery then?"

Grandpa answered me first, wiping his hands on the towel flung over his overalls as he did. "Ny checked that out. Said it was good and charged."

I bristled at the nickname, rubbing my upper arms at the same time. *Ny?* Since when had they jumped into nickname territory with one another?

"We're on a *schedule*," I huffed, frustration pulling at my chest like a game of tug-of-war. I wanted to get to Denver before nightfall. Do some shopping too. I had plans, and a broken car didn't exactly coincide with them.

When my schedule was compromised, I struggled to compromise. I was the type of woman who needed order and control to stay functioning. A creature of routine? That was me. This feeling of helplessness was not a good one to have.

"Since when?" Niyol folded his arms, narrowed eyes refocusing on me.

I shivered at the intensity. "Since when what?"

"Since *when* did we have a *schedule*?"

"Since before we started driving." I just hadn't had a chance to tell him was all. "I have an itinerary in the glove compartment, if you want to see. It's one of the reasons I agreed to drive you. I want to see the states. Do a few touristy things." Enjoy life and the freedom of travel. Find myself when I felt so incredibly lost, most of all.

Niyol frowned at me, forehead creased. Another second passed, then two. I rolled my lower lip between my teeth, nervous for his response.

Thankfully, my grandpa chimed in before I said something I didn't mean. "Ny thinks it might be the radiator. He and I are gonna run into town, grab some fluids and change the oil."

"I just had the oil changed, that's the thing."

"Don't worry, Princess." Niyol glared at me. "This is what I do. Fix cars. I'll figure it out and get you on the road in no time. Would *hate* for you to go off schedule."

I mouthed out, *Asshole.*

Niyol's reply was a snarky wink.

A few minutes later, I pushed through the front door of the house, livid. What I needed was some comfort food to cleanse my internal irritability.

"Sweetie, I heard the news…" Grams stood at the kitchen sink, her lips turned down in sympathy.

"It sucks. I have reservations at hotels, plans, things I wanted to do along the way too." I plopped down at the table in the kitchen, greeted with a plate of pancakes and bacon. Orange juice sat to my left and I picked it up, guzzling the cool liquid before I continued. "I just had the thing in for service. Everything was fine. I don't understand what happened. The oil was freshly checked, and the battery was good. The muffler's in top-notch shape too. I'm just so… so *mad.*"

Mad at myself for letting Niyol get to me upstairs.

Mad at myself for not being able to adjust to things when they went awry most of all.

"Eat. One more night here won't hurt. You and Niyol can even have the place to yourself for a while this evening, rest a little before you start back up on your trip. Grandpa and I go to bingo Saturday nights, and then play bridge with a few other couples afterward."

I stabbed at my eggs with a fork. "Grams. For the last time. Niyol and I are not…"

The back door squeaked open, and in came Grandpa, laughing at something Niyol was saying. "You'd make a fine fishing buddy, my boy."

Grinning from ear-to-ear, Niyol sat across from me like everything was just fine and dandy—maybe to him it was. My fingers tightened around my fork even more at the thought, and suddenly the pancakes on my plate were his eyes as I stabbed each piece.

"Fishing would be fun, sir."

I snorted, then coughed to cover it up. *Sir?* Did Niyol really just throw down the manners when he'd rarely shown me a single bit of courtesy since we'd started?

"I haven't done that since I was a kid," he finished.

Niyol put his hand around the back of Grams' chair. She leaned close to him, patting his cheek. "Maybe Paul can take you to the farm pond about a mile up the road this afternoon. You two can get some afternoon fishing in. Catch some crappie for dinner."

Niyol's smile grew even wider, more genuine, sending a shot of anger and sadness into my belly. Again. Growing up, visiting my grandfather, that's what the two of *us* always did. Fish together at the pond. Talk until the sunset about my mother, what she'd been like as a kid. Now *Niyol* was the one getting to do the thing I craved? Not fishing, exactly, but spending time with one of the only males in my life who I didn't feel abandoned by.

"I'd like that." He nodded at Grandpa, who was grinning like he'd won the lotto.

I bet Niyol didn't have a single clue how to fish. He was just playing like he did to piss me off; grow close to *my* grandparents, pretend that he was a first-rate asshole instead of a lowly asshole.

"Oh, good. Summer and I'll run to the store for some sides. Cornbread and whatnot. We'll make a huge meal of it tonight before we head to bingo."

Niyol nodded enthusiastically, nothing about him in that moment reminding me of the guy who'd basically written me off as a waste of space. A ride. What was it he'd called me? His *chauffeur?* At the thought, I gritted my teeth, losing my temper and all sense of who I was—losing my patience most of all.

"Gee, *Ny.* I didn't know that fishing was a big pastime for guys like *you.*"

He stiffened at my words, eyes narrowing at his plate, not me. His reaction had me smiling wider, batting my lashes; innocence guarding my irritation. I'd gotten to him.

"I fished growing up," he managed, twirling his fork through the butter on his pancake. "Might take it up again when I get to California. Who knows?" He leaned back in his chair with a shrug. The picture of impassive yet again.

Ugh. What would it take to crack this man?

I shoveled food into my mouth, mumbling around it. "Sure. Keep telling yourself that, *Hawk.*"

I heard his quick intake of air, saw his fingers tightening around his fork like my own. I knew little to nothing about Niyol's life in the *club*, other than what Emily had told me. One of those things she'd mentioned was the fact that all the club members received names after patching in. And Niyol's name? It'd been given to him by his father. A man who was no good and had nearly ruined his life. According to Emily, he refused to go by the nickname anymore, especially when it came to civilians. The fact that I'd just rubbed it in and used it? Well, it wasn't very nice, to say the least.

Surprisingly, Niyol didn't lose it on me. In fact, after that little outburst, things grew fairly quiet, albeit tense, except for the occasional conversation between Grandpa and Grams—who seemed oblivious to the emotional beatdown I'd basically just given to Niyol in the form of a simple *name*.

The longer we all sat there, the more guilt wrangled my chest into submission. God, I was stupid. Jealous, too. After that, Niyol refused to look at me, talk to me, even acknowledge me. Instead, he stared at the uneaten food on his plate as though it were his worst enemy, only occasionally nodding at something my grandparents said.

Halfway through our meal, I'd grown too upset to eat. I wasn't a mean-spirited person. If anything, I was a pushover. I hated how I'd let Niyol get to me upstairs, that was all this was. Why I'd snapped like I did. It wasn't a worthy excuse by any means. And I was certainly not proud of calling him what I did either. The fact of the matter was, though, I couldn't take it back. But I *could* try to make things right.

Somewhere along the way, the two of us had gotten off-track. Now, it was my job to rectify things. Bring us full circle and start over once and for all.

Decision made, I sat up straight and cleared my throat. "Would it be okay if I went fishing with you guys—"

Abruptly, Niyol stood and shoved his chair away from the table, interrupting me. He nodded at my grams and said, *Thank you for breakfast*, completely ignoring me again as he headed outside. I jumped in my chair when he slammed the door shut in his wake.

Crap. I'd *really* messed things up.

CHAPTER SEVEN

Niyol

I'd gone fishing once, damn it. On my tenth birthday with Flick, the second in command for the RDs. Granted, it had been in a shallow creek just outside the compound, and *only* because Pops had been too busy getting drunk and fucking groupies to even remember what day it was.

But still, it was fishing.

"Niyol?" Summer's voice cut through the air from the front porch. I stiffened at the sound, wishing she'd just leave me the hell alone. Ignoring her would be even more critical now, especially since I'd let her get to me.

Hawk. She'd called me fucking Hawk.

How had she known?

One day with her and she'd sunk her claws in deep. The second she'd sat across from me in that booth, I'd known she was trouble. Old habits die hard when it came to bad men wanting to corrupt good women. Which was exactly why I was determined to get away from her as fast as I could. Get to Maya and San Diego most of all.

As Flick's niece, Maya wasn't good in the traditional sense that Summer was. If anything, she was just like me. A former member of the club, in her own right, raised in the MC world and taught wrong more than right. Besides Slade and Arch, she'd be the only one who'd understand what I went through—what I was *going* through, more like it.

"I'm so sorry." Summer's feet shuffled through the gravel as she approached, tiny whimpers slipping through her lips at the same time. "I didn't mean to be such a bitch. I'm just stressed. About the car and the delay and… other personal stuff. I didn't mean to upset you."

"How did you know?" I gritted my teeth. "About my club name."

A pause. "Emily told me."

Of course she did. My stepsister had a big mouth on her. I spun around to look at Summer, but wound up scowling at her feet. Fuck. Me. She'd come out here, walking on gravel, barefooted, just to apologize?

"Where the fuck are your shoes?" I asked, looking back under the hood.

"Oh," she laughed a little. Nervous. I could tell. "I wasn't thinking. Just took off outside."

"You'll cut your damn feet." And why did I care?

"I'll walk in the grass on the way back inside." Her voice was softer then. Maybe she thought I was being nice. Maybe I was.

The thing was, I wasn't pissed at Summer. I was pissed because everything she'd said inside was true. The life I'd lived, my lack of a father… the whole fishing thing. The lack of real-life experience when all I'd ever known growing up was law-breaking and getting drunk, club life, and all that came along with it.

There I was, running from a place that I was ninety percent sure was where I was meant to be all along. But going back now? I'd be deemed a traitor even more than when I'd ratted out my father. Which was why I had to keep going. I'd made my decision, and now I needed to live with it.

"Niyol?" she whispered my name like she was afraid I was a bomb, seconds from detonating. "Scream at me or do whatever it is you feel like doing. Just please, don't shut me out. We've got days left to go on this trip, and the silent treatment will only make this thing between us worse."

I grunted, still not looking at her. There wasn't a *thing* between us. Never would be either. Which was why ignoring her was so futile.

In a way, I deserved her attitude as much as she did mine. It was a reminder that people like Summer and I weren't meant to be friends—weren't meant to feel what I'd felt with her upstairs in that bedroom. That fire sparking between us, ready to engulf us if doused with gasoline.

Bottom line? I was driving cross-country for a chance at a new life. And Summer was a distraction I couldn't afford.

She leaned back against the bumper and flexed her hands together. "Are you listening to me?"

I glanced down at her pale legs, swallowing hard at the view. The things were endless; muscled and elongated by ass-hugging cutoffs. Fucking sexy. Upstairs I'd wanted them wrapped around me. I'd wanted to *bury* myself between them. I'd wanted to strip her naked and fuck her until she was limp in my arms. I still did. But again, we weren't right for each other. If anything, I belonged with someone like Maya, someone who understood where I came from, who I was. Even if I didn't feel that way about her anymore.

I wiped my hands down the front of my shirt and slammed the hood shut. "Yeah. I'm listening."

"Okay, good. Because I'd really like it if we could start over. Get to know each other the right way."

Slowly, I leaned my hip against the front bumper, arms folded. "Fine. Whatever you need." Though there wouldn't ever be a right way for anyone to know me, especially not this woman.

She fidgeted with the bracelet she wore around her wrist, crossed and uncrossed those legs, too. "You're not still mad at me then?"

I reached out and tugged the end of her braid, not even thinking, just reacting. "No. I just think you're a pain in my ass, is all."

Doe eyes blinked up at me like she'd been caught in my net, and a sweet smile grazed her lips.

"I am kind of a pain, sometimes. I know. I've always said what's on my mind, not necessarily thinking things through beforehand. It's probably my worst quality in life, to be honest. But, I'll try harder to tame it down, okay? Maybe not be so blunt."

If this was her version of being *blunt* then I'm pretty damn sure she didn't know what that word meant in my world. Regardless, my damn chest grew all warm at her confession, the way she looked at me too. Slowly, I dropped my hand away, gaze going to her lips, her pink cheeks too. Fuck, she was pretty. Too pretty for the likes of me.

"It's fine. I don't care one way or another. You're my ride, remember? That's all."

"Yes. Okay. Your ride." Her throat worked over as she swallowed, the movement drawing my gaze to her throat. She had two freckles that sat in the center of her neck, and they danced together as her skin moved up and down. "I'll remember that from here on out." But her voice caught at the end, proof that she didn't believe what she was saying.

"Good." Because someone had to.

She fidgeted some more. "I'm thinking of calling an old friend, seeing as how we'll be here another night. Her name is Ashley. She's super funny and charming. Doesn't talk quite as much as I do, so you're safe there." She waited a beat. "Would you mind if I go out with her tonight?"

"Not your keeper."

Summer nodded, as a heavy, humid breeze blew across our faces. Pieces of her long hair flew upward from under that braid, smacking her across the nose. She sneezed in turn and, Jesus Christ, even that was cute.

I spun around to study the rows of corn beside the house, refusing to look at her any more than I had to.

"We'll talk later then?" She touched my shoulder. "At dinner? You have to go be all manly and find us food." She lowered her voice, acting like a caveman.

I stuffed my hands into my jean pockets, fighting a smile. "Yeah. Okay."

The sound of her *ouch* had me turning to watch as she walked back to the house, through the gravel, and on her tiptoes. Fingers balled into fists, I fought the urge to scoop her up, carry her inside. But I wasn't a hero. I was a bad dude who'd done bad things. And the sooner she understood that, the better off we'd be.

♥

Summer's grandpa drove me to an autobody shop so I could grab the new cooling belt for the Range Rover. With the old man at my side, I spent the afternoon working on it, teaching him all I knew about car repair. He was a good dude, a fast learner too. Rough in his own right. Served in the military for ten years and came from nothing, kind of like me. I liked the guy. A lot more than I thought I would.

Around three that afternoon, we'd gone to the farm pond, fished like he'd promised. He told me war stories, and, to my surprise, I told him about the club and what had happened to me, preparing for him to either kick my ass, or tell me to leave.

What he told me, instead, was a hell of a lot different.

"We don't get to pick the life we're born into, ya know," he paused. "Summer sure didn't."

He squeezed my shoulders as we headed back to his old pickup. The weeds were tall, up to our knees, and the sun was low in the sky. Who knew the country farms of Iowa could be so damn soothing.

"Summer doesn't know the kind of life I've lived." Never would either.

He paused behind the truck bed, bushy white brows lifted mid-forehead. "You don't know much about my granddaughter at all, do ya?"

His words were accusing. Protective too. I shouldn't have said what I did, but at the same time, I wasn't gonna hide who I was. Nor would I hide thoughts just to please others. That wasn't me.

"Not really, other than she's got a good job and is best friends with my stepsister."

"Hmm."

I frowned, rubbing a hand over the back of my sweaty neck. "Listen. Summer and I… we barely know each other. Come from two different worlds. I'm not sure what she's told you about our relationship, but we're not together like that."

"I know, son." He nodded, grabbing the tackle box from my free hand, then shoving it into the truck bed beside our poles. Once he shut the tailgate, he brushed his hands together and continued. "But you should know that her life wasn't always easy either. She's been through her fair share of problems, still goin' through them, actually. Just don't jump to conclusions is all I'm saying."

I looked to the high grass and swallowed, hating how I was curious to know what Summer's version of *hard* was compared to mine.

"Now. Let's get these fish on home. They ain't gonna fry themselves."

Thoughts heavy, I jumped into the passenger seat, thankful for today, for the chance to get to know this man who reminded me of my own grandpa. The man who'd abandoned my father and I all those years ago when Pops wouldn't let me leave the club. When *I* didn't feel safe enough to do so myself.

He lived near Vegas. Part of me wondered if we'd have time to visit him. The other part of me knew we'd likely not be welcomed.

Slade had mentioned me swinging by on my way. But the thought of him running me off was enough of a deterrent to keep me away.

At a little past five, when the two of us were walking back into the house, Peaches scared me shitless, jumping out from the living room like a ninja.

"Summer's left already for the evening. Has some dinner plans with her friend." She buttoned her sweater-thing, then looked at me with accusing eyes. "There won't be a fish fry after all this evening, I'm afraid."

I scratched at my chin, the stubble rough beneath my fingers. Even growing up the way I did, nobody made me as nervous as this lady.

"You know when she'll be back?" I asked.

"Late, I suppose." She set her hands on her hips, red painted lips pursed. "She's out with an old friend of hers, like I said. Not sure if it's a gentleman or lady." She pulled her purse off a hook by the front door and shouldered it, looking to her husband. Summer's grandpa silently settled an arm around her shoulders, giving me pity eyes.

"Thanks." I waited a sec. "For letting me know." I smothered my grin with my hand when I figured out the woman's angle. She was trying to make me jealous about Summer going out with a friend—a friend I already knew was a chick.

For some reason, Peaches wouldn't let the idea of me and her granddaughter being together go. Unlike her husband, though, she didn't have a clue who I was, or what I'd done in the past. She sure as hell would be changing her mind about me if that were the case.

"Now, we're going to bingo for the night, remember?" Peaches huffed. "You're more than welcome to join us if you'd like."

"No, thanks."

They left twenty minutes later, leaving me alone in their huge, old house. Apparently, they trusted me enough to do so—most people wouldn't have. It was… different. Kind of nice.

The rest of my night was spent watching TV or trying to call Maya. Her phone kept going straight to voicemail, though. At least I knew I had the right number.

Sometime later I fell asleep on the couch, waking to the sound of shuffling feet, followed by a thump, and Summer saying, "Oh, shit."

Curiosity kicked my ass, and I got to my knees and peered over the back of the couch. She was bent over, picking up some wooden frame off the floor, her perfect ass right there on display. Instead of making myself known, I waited to see if she'd notice me first.

She hiccupped, then mumbled something else under her breath as she set the picture back on a shelf. Then she hiccupped again, leaning back against the wall by the door before sliding to the floor, her eyes shutting along the way. With a heavy sigh, she tugged both knees to her chest. Long bits of her blonde hair stuck to her face and neck as she dropped her forehead to her knees.

Minutes passed without a movement. I thought that maybe she'd fallen asleep… until I heard it, even over the loud rumble of thunder outside. Sniffles. Followed by a sob.

"Fuck," I whispered under my breath. Something was wrong. And no matter how much I wanted to, I couldn't ignore it. If there were problems, I dealt with them whether they were my business or not. It's who I was. What I did. The Red Dragon in me that'd never let up.

"You good?" I crouched down in front of her a minute later, running a hand through my hair.

Slowly, she lifted her head and met my stare. "Niyol?"

Her cheeks were wet, black shit running down both sides. Her bottom lip… It trembled so hard that it made my gut tighten. Made me feel something I wasn't expecting.

Fear.

"What's wrong?" I touched her hand, out of my comfort zone.

She shut her eyes again, breathing heavy. "Everything."

"Did someone hurt you?" I sat beside her against the door, wondering if her grandparents could hear us. They'd gotten home about an hour ago, and I'd played like I was asleep, not wanting to talk.

"I'm so tired, Niyol." She laid her head against my shoulder, shocking me. Wetness dripped onto my bare skin, and I swallowed hard, not used to the intimacy—regretting immediately that I hadn't put on a shirt.

I'd never been a touchy-feely guy before. Sex and foreplay were as emotional as I got. Until this woman came along apparently.

Why was that?

"Let's go to sleep. I'll stay on the couch tonight."

"No. Not tired like that." She sniffled, snuggling closer, her head dropping to my bare chest. Lips grazed my nipples as she spoke, and I sucked in a breath. "I'm tired of hurting. I want to feel good again."

"You'll feel better in the morning when you sleep this all off."

She mumbled something over the rain beating against the door that I couldn't hear. Then finished with, "He told me that I was the only thing he'd ever need. That he loved me. How can I sleep that away?"

I frowned, keeping my arms at my side. If I didn't, I'd wrap her up in them. "Who?"

"Landon."

Before I could ask who Landon was, she started in again. "He told me he loved me, and he gave me that ring, and I bought a dress…"

Shit. So she'd been engaged then?

More sobs, more tears. And because I couldn't stand the sound, I dropped an arm around her waist and squeezed her a little closer, setting my chin on top of her head. I didn't make a move or speak after that, but I felt her breathing even out against me. Heard the small tiny snores exhaling from between her lips not long after too.

She'd fallen asleep on me. Another first in my book.

Weirdly transfixed by her confession, her body laying so trustingly against mine, I rubbed a hand over the back of her blonde hair, pretending for a second that this was normal. That I had every right to comfort her. Guess I couldn't help myself. Pressed close to me like she was, Summer fit.

Tossing my head back against the door, I looked to the dark ceiling, telling myself I didn't need this right now. But as I tried to push the feeling away, I kind of liked the sensation of being wanted like this, even if all I was, was a drunken shoulder to cry on. Growing up in a club full of guys and the groupies who were there for only two things—protection and sex—I didn't have much of a need to feel the emotional shit when it came to women. Not even Maya, who'd been an important part of my life, had ever made me feel like this woman did.

This softness in Summer, her vulnerability, it brought out a side of me that I never thought I'd want to explore. A need to protect something when it wasn't club related. A need to feel something that stemmed beyond just fucking too.

Question was, would I?

CHAPTER EIGHT

Summer

We'd driven two and a half hours in near silence. My nerves were shot, and my head thundered loudly against my temples. I couldn't take another minute of hangover driving, nor could I deal with the tension ricocheting between Niyol and me. What I needed was fresh air, ibuprofen, greasy food, and a bathroom to either pee... or possibly puke in.

After yesterday, I was truly regretting everything I'd done since agreeing to do this for Emily. Nothing had gone right, and the tension between Niyol and me had only thickened, twofold. I'm not sure what happened after I fell asleep against him, honestly, but I can tell you what I did know.

Niyol had put me to bed—*in* bed.

Then he'd tucked me in, under the covers.

And then this morning? He pretended like I didn't even exist. Again.

Had my confession freaked him out? The one I'd apparently felt the drunken need to divulge in? Probably. Did I want to apologize? Absolutely. Had I? Of course not. I felt awful, and if I spoke about last night, how I'd spent the first half of my night giggling with an old friend, only to spend the latter half of it sobbing when I'd confessed my broken relationship, then I would likely start crying even more.

"I'm stopping," I finally said somewhere outside of Omaha, Nebraska.

His answer was a grunt. No surprise there.

I pulled into the parking lot of a gas station, but Niyol forwent my invitation inside—like I figured he would—and fell back asleep.

What I needed to do was check in with Emily before she boarded her cruise ship. Give her an exaggerated version of how well this was going. My fingers hovered over the call button as I stepped out of the Rover, hesitating even still as I peed. As I strolled the aisles of the convenience store, cherry Slushie in one hand, Doritos tucked under that same armpit, I found myself shaking at the prospect of chatting with my best friend.

At the last second, in line at the checkout, I chickened out and decided texting was the best option. If I didn't, I'd probably spill my guts—which would only cause more problems.

She got back to me within seconds, no surprise there. My guess was, she'd been waiting by the phone.

Thanks for checking in. Miss you, and love you, too. ☺

My shoulders slumped as I read her words. Little did she know that I wasn't happy. More so I was *miserable* and ready to turn this car around and say screw it. This was feeling like way more work than pleasure.

When I got back into my Rover, I made an executive decision, even if it wasn't on my itinerary—the thing was already shot to hell anyway. "We're gonna stay in Omaha for the rest of the day, and the night."

Niyol barely stirred against the door. At least he wasn't sleeping in the backseat anymore. It was a small win I'd take.

"We've only been driving for two hours," he managed.

"I'm sorry, but I can't deal right now. My head hurts." Not to mention I was an emotional mess. Perhaps after a shower and a nap, he and I could do an early dinner in town and talk a little more. I'd apologize for my behavior from the night before. Then fix the issues once and for all between us.

"Whatever you need, Princess."

I rolled my eyes—secretly thankful he didn't argue with me.

With a renewed sense of purpose, I punched in the GPS for the nearest, and classiest, hotel I could find. I'd splurge if I had to. Get a suite with a whirlpool tub to soak my woes away in.

"I'll pay."

"Huh?" I blinked, thrown off by his words.

"For the hotel tonight."

His announcement had me frowning. And utterly confused. "It was my idea, so I'm fine with paying for the rooms. Emily said you were short on cash, so—"

"I *said* I'll pay." He paused and took a deep breath. "Just let me, would ya?" He glared out his window, fists tight on his lap.

I narrowed my eyes, unsure of how to respond. Every second longer I spent with this man, he did, said, or acted in a way that eradicated all my preconceived notions of him—even if he had a rough way of going about it.

"Thank you," I finally replied. "I, um… appreciate your offer."

Another grunt. That's all he seemed to be capable of doing today. Caveman Niyol—a name I'm sure Emily would back me on. I grinned at the thought, for the first time in hours, imagining him in some sort of leopard-print sarong, swinging from one tree to another.

Niyol nudged me with his elbow from over the console a minute later. "And I'm sorry for being an ass today. Just got shit on my mind."

I shrugged. The asshole part bothered me, yeah, but it wasn't like I wasn't used to it. *Sad, sad, Summer, always so accepting.*

"It's fine. I'm kind of used to assholes."

"You shouldn't have to be."

"How do you mean?"

He cleared his throat. "Be used to assholes, I mean. It shouldn't ever be okay."

Not knowing how to respond, I could only shrug his comment away.

As I reversed out of the lot, he got quiet again. The silence was easier than it had been before, though I still wasn't a fan of it. Thankfully it didn't last long.

"Where would you be right now? If, you know…" He motioned his hand between us.

"If I weren't driving you?" I got back onto the highway, swerving through traffic.

"Yeah."

"Hmm." I thought for a second about my answer. "I'd likely be at home, practicing cheers. I'm not only an ELA teacher, but also the head cheerleading coach for the seventh-grade girls at my school. Tryouts are coming up, and I need to create some new routines for the upcoming year." I shrugged.

"Damn." He chuckled, the sound surprisingly nice. "It's no wonder you got all this energy." He lifted his hands from his lap and did a set of spirit fingers.

I hit his thigh with the back of my hand, fighting a grin. "Don't make fun of me. Cheerleaders are the only athletes who can fly, you know."

He rolled his eyes and kept at his teasing. "Give me a N, give me an I, give me a Y, O, L."

I glared at him, opening my mouth, only to wind up giggling at how ridiculous he looked. This big, bad, darkness-inducing man actually had a sense of humor? Who would've thought? That also sucked in its own right because a funny Niyol was a *charming* Niyol.

"You are the strangest man I know."

A hint of a smile crept over his full lips as he pointed toward a row of large complexes and buildings to our left. We twisted through the interstate, the downtown already coming into view.

"See that over there?" He jabbed a finger toward a tall hotel that could only be described as a Mandarin meets a Hilton—definitely *not* the semi-classy one on my GPS, but a full-fledged luxury joint. "We're staying there."

"Uh, no. It's going to cost a fortune."

"You're not paying for it." Another grunt.

I wasn't sure where he got *that* kind of money, but at the same time I was too exhausted to argue. The last twenty-four hours had drained every bit of emotional energy I could spare—the highs and lows of it all too much. So, I'd let him pay the four hundred bucks if it meant a nice, snuggly bed to cozy up in. "Whatever you say."

A valet came toward his door as we pulled into the turnaround about ten minutes later. He was dressed in a suit with a green bowtie and had this handlebar mustache like something out of the 1920s.

"Welcome to your palace." Niyol smirked from over the roof when we got out. "Every princess needs to stay in one at least once in her life, right?"

I didn't respond to his smartass remark, just shook my head and grabbed my bags from the trunk. This man would be my undoing in some way or another. The question was, could I find a way to keep myself safe in the end?

CHAPTER NINE

Niyol

On the fourth ring, after the tenth time in two days, Maya finally answered her phone.

Now, there I was, sitting on the edge of a hotel bed, attempting to say something that made sense. Nearly seven weeks had passed since I'd last heard her voice, so nothing about this was easy or simple like it once was.

"You're really coming to San Diego?" Maya asked.

"Sitting in a Nebraska hotel as we speak."

"And everything is fine?" She paused. "Things are safe? Because my uncle said shit back at the club is—"

"Yeah. Everything's great." I rubbed a hand over my forehead, the need to call my brothers damn near painful.

If something was going on back at home, I'd feel even more like a dick for running. I didn't want to get into club business over the phone, no matter. Was damn shocked Flick had even mentioned anything about it to Maya at all, especially since she hadn't bothered to show her face in Rockford for the last eight years. Plus, anyone who wasn't a brother, didn't follow the code or wear the patch, had no rights to anything said behind the compound doors in the past. Maybe with Flick in charge, though, it was different.

"God, Hawk. I just…" She cleared her throat. "I can't believe you're coming."

I winced at the sound of my club name. Unlike Summer, she hadn't used it out of spite. She'd used it because she didn't know me as Niyol. Nobody but Emily, Lisa, and now Summer, did.

"You good with that?" I held my breath, worried she wouldn't be. I had no plan-fucking-B. Hadn't even thought of one.

"Yeah, yeah. How soon will you get here?" Maya asked. "I've got a couch with your name on it. "

I fell back onto the mattress and blew out a relieved breath. "Four days? Maybe less? Depends on things." Summer things, mostly. Her and her *itinerary*, for starters.

At the thought, I sat back up and glared toward the bathroom. The shower was still running. She'd been in there for at least a half hour. *Naked. So very fucking naked it's not even funny.*

I cleared my throat, my heart racing at the thought. Christ, what was my problem?

"Are you there?" Maya asked.

"Sorry. I'm here." I gave my head a quick jerk, trying to relax. "It's been a rough couple of days, is all."

"You wanna talk about it?"

The shower turned off finally, and I jerked my head toward the door. Through it, I could hear Summer humming, the song sweet and light and everything she embodied.

"Hawk?" Maya's voice brought me back to reality again.

I scrubbed a hand over my face this time, struggling to get my head on right. "Nah, I don't want to get into it. We'll talk when I get there."

"Okay."

We hung up not long after, never discussing our plans; not even figuring out where to meet when I got to San Diego. She told me to just call her, and that she'd come to me, wherever I was.

For the first time in forty-eight hours, getting to San Diego, to Maya too, wasn't my number one priority. No way would I stop to think about what that meant.

"Um, the shower's free."

At the sound of Summer's voice, I lifted my head, body stiffening at the view.

Jesus, she looked incredible. Everything about her tiny outfit and the body that lay beneath it had my blood simmering, my hands sweating too. Her skin was flushed red, that skimpy tank she wore barely covering her curves. The material of her skirt kissed the tops of her thighs and was practically see-through white. The woman had the body of an athlete, one who trained hard and got good results. And because of that body, my dick hardened for the hundredth time since we'd met, the need for release stronger than ever.

"Are you okay?" she asked, eyes narrowing slightly as I perused her body.

"Not really." Not with her looking so phenomenal. Not with me wanting to strip off every damn inch of her tiny outfit. I shot up off the bed, teeth gritted, unwilling to elaborate, of course.

Without looking at her again, somehow, I grabbed some clothes out of my bag and headed to the bathroom, slamming the door shut behind me.

"Jeez, cranky much," she mumbled through the wood, no fear of who I was, what I could do to her... where I'd come from most of all. She didn't know me and my world. She just knew what Emily had told her, and what I'd come to show her over the past three days too. Our time together had been mild compared to what it could have been. In all senses.

I knifed a hand through my hair, pulling it, wondering why the fuck the idea of having her sass me, not judge me, *fight me* made me so damn confused.

"Just... It took you a long-ass time in here," I yelled back.

That wasn't *too* much of dickheaded thing to say, I didn't think.

"What are you, the shower police?" She laughed, the sound only adding to my frustration.

Needing to de-stress, rid myself of the nerves buzzing through me, I yanked down my zipper and gripped my cock. Pulling once, twice… hard enough for pain, but soft enough for pleasure. It was torture either way I looked at it.

The bed squeaked from behind the door. I squeezed my eyes shut, thumping my head back against the wood. Inhaling to steady my breath, I was met with the scent of flowers. Flowers like body wash, or shampoo…

Christ. The entire *bathroom* smelled like it. Like *her*.

Steam fogged up the mirror still, other than a small space where she'd rubbed it clean, with her hand—I could see a print. Heavy breaths, panting, I squeezed my dick even harder, stroking faster with an open-mouthed, silent groan. Not wanting to come all over the bathroom tile, I stepped into the shower and flicked on the hot water, barely getting the rest of my clothes off in time.

I shuddered, pumping faster, imagining things that I shouldn't.

Summer on the bed, laid out naked.

My face between her thighs, then my cock filling her tight, wet pussy.

I slammed a palm against the shower wall, head slumped forward against my chest as I came all over the drain.

I was a dirty son of a bitch.

CHAPTER TEN

Niyol

Half an hour later, Summer and I were walking side-by-side toward the hotel lobby. Sad part was, I was more on edge than before I'd jerked off.

Whenever Summer moved, her arm would graze mine, sending little shocks over my skin—electric charges, it felt like. Whenever she spoke, my head would spin, making me dizzy. Then whenever she looked at me? My fucking heart would jump into my throat, choke me, really. I'm not sure what was happening to me, just knew I didn't like it.

When we finally got to the lobby, and her ample tits had just barely grazed my upper arm, I lost it.

"Jesus, I need some space, all right?"

Pain shot through her gaze, those blue eyes questioning my bad mood. I pointed to the concierge desk, lowering my voice. Again, it wasn't her fault.

"Can you find us a place to eat, please?" I reeled in the last of my anger. "I'm gonna go out and smoke."

The first thing I did when I stepped outside was breathe in the night air, then light a cigarette. Several drags later, I thought I had myself under control… until she appeared again, messing with my mind in ways she couldn't help. Ways I hated myself for.

She pushed through the front door of the hotel, avoiding my eyes to look at a brochure in her hands. "Apparently there's a good bar and grill down the street, close enough that we can walk to it. See some sights along the way, maybe a few stores we could pop into on the walk back." She shrugged. "It's still early."

"Fine." I took the last drag of my smoke, then stubbed it out with the toe of my boot. There would be no tourist shopping on my end, but she could do whatever she wanted.

The strap of her tank top slipped down her arm as she brushed against me. That drew my gaze back to her body, more so to her breasts as they peeked through her thin shirt. Her nipples were hard, poked against the material, and I licked my lips at the sight, my tongue ring clinking against my teeth.

Summer stopped whatever she was saying and zeroed in on my mouth. Both cheeks went pink when she discovered what I was doing. Lip pulled between her teeth, she tugged the little sweater thing that was wrapped around her waist over her shoulders, tying it at the neck.

I was such a bastard.

Pulling the brim of my baseball hat down over my eyes, I took off ahead, not knowing if I was going in the right direction. Must've been, because a minute later she was at my side once more, her sparkly flip-flops slapping the cement along the way.

"Is there a fire I'm unaware of?" she asked.

"No." At least not one she could see.

Though I'd been nothing but an ass to her since we left the room, she started talking to me anyway. Part of me wondered if the real reason she never stopped was because it made her feel in control when she was nervous. Funny how, after three days, I already knew her quirks.

She went on and on about the city and the streets, about how she'd never been west before. Maybe if I listened to her, *tried* to be friends like she wanted, then I could picture her as another Emily.

It was worth a shot.

"… and my dad was always with my brothers or at work, so he never took me places growing up. I've always wanted to travel though."

"Brothers?" I asked.

"Two of them." Summer smiled fondly. "Twins, actually." Her little nose scrunched up. "They're athletic junkies and both play sports semi-professionally now."

"Which sports?" I didn't do sports. Ever. No time, desire, or opportunity.

"One plays football for a traveling indoor league. The other plays hockey somewhere in Canada."

I could hear the pride in her voice. It's obvious she looked up to the guys. Loved them a shit ton, too. I could relate to that. Emily made me proud with all her smarts. Even her choice in men was decent. A pretty-boy fiancé, a stable life, a stable job… good things she deserved.

Growing up, I didn't have anyone but my club brothers, and we were all the same person. But once Pops married Lisa when I was seventeen, I welcomed Emily as my little sis, even if she didn't want anything to do with me or the club at the time.

We landed in front of a brick building with a white door about a half mile away from the hotel. Thankfully, the open air had given me a chance to regroup. Going back to the hotel room would be a whole other issue later, but this was a minute-by-minute situation now.

"This is it, I think." Summer peeked up at me from under her long bangs. She was nervous, likely thinking my shit mood was still there.

Squinting, I took note of the sign hanging above the door and smirked. "Jarkey's, huh?" *Home of the best burgers in Nebraska*, the logo read on the window.

"Don't knock the name." She reached for the knob, but I blocked her, opening it myself. I urged her in first, a hand along her lower back. Gentlemanly and shit. She gave me a tentative smile, thanking me with a nod.

I cleared my throat. "Not knocking the name. Just hungry and don't wanna be let down if they don't actually serve the best burgers in Nebraska."

"Like all good things in life, you have to give the unknown a chance." She winked, then moved toward the hostess. Secretly, I wondered if that was what she'd done when it came to this trip; driving me.

Inside the bar, I lifted my gaze to the ceiling, then surveyed the rest of the room. Anything to keep my eyes off her ass. The place was small. Clean wood, smelling like fried foods, with the dull roar of sports games on the TV that echoed through the speakers. I could handle this, even if it wasn't my typical joint.

The hostess led us to a table in the dining section where Summer and I sat at a high-top table. "What can I get you two to drink?"

"We'll take whatever beer you have on tap, please," Summer said as she studied the menu.

I frowned, not used to having anyone order for me.

When the waitress was gone, I looked at my menu and asked, "You still hungover?"

She set her menu on the table and rubbed her palms flat over the surface. "A little." She pulled the blonde braid she always wore over her shoulders and played with the ends. Another nervous habit. "I'm sorry about last night."

"What're you sorry about?" I narrowed my eyes.

"Getting drunk-weepy. I tend to do that when I have vodka and the place we went was definitely a vodka kind of joint."

"You remember everything you said?"

She licked her lips. "Yes. I do. And I was incredibly stupid. Just… had one of those nights, ya know?"

I didn't know. Mainly because I didn't cry. Ever. Hadn't experienced an emotion to make me in life, not since I was a kid and my old man broke my arm. I didn't say that though.

"Sure." I leaned back in my chair, stretching my legs out under the table.

She played with her fork and napkin, not looking at me as she finished. "I don't want to talk about it though."

"Which part?"

"All of it, really. I promised myself I was done talking about…" She cringed, cutting herself off.

"Your ex?"

She blew out a heavy breath and nodded.

"Then we won't." I shrugged, not caring one way or the other. I knew what it was like, not wanting to share your shit. And we didn't know each other well enough to do so.

"I'm over him, by the way."

I blinked, deciding to stir the pot a little. "Didn't seem like that last night."

"I was drunk. That's why. When I drink, I get emotional, I told you. I know it's a lame excuse, but—"

"And I told *you* we didn't have to talk about it." I took a drink of my draft. The cold liquid nearly burned my throat, proof that it'd been a long time since I, too, had gotten wasted.

"Don't you, ya know, want to though?"

I opened my mouth to tell her I didn't give two shits, but I saw her cringe, realizing that maybe she wanted me to say yes after all. Wanted to spill her guts to someone, even if she said otherwise.

Therapy in the form of me. Funny shit, that was.

"Listen, Princess. If you've got shit to say, I'm not gonna stop you from saying it."

"For the last time, stop calling me Princess. Please."

"It's just a nickname." I held my sweaty glass between my hands, scowling. I was trying to make her laugh, get under her skin even, not make her feel all sad and shit.

She set her elbows back on the table, waiting a sec before she asked, "Don't you ever regret being so rough?"

Ah, so she was turning this around on me then. "I have a lot of regrets in life. But that's not one of them."

"I'm sorry. I shouldn't have asked that."

"Nothing to be sorry for." I finished my beer, then pushed it to the middle of the table. "Shit happened in my life that I can't take back, and now I'm trying to make up for it."

"While you were in your motorcycle gang?"

"Club."

"Huh?"

"It's called a motorcycle *club*." Though *gang* was a phrase that most folks around Rockford and the Chicago area used for us.

"Oh, well, what was the bad *shit* you did?" she asked.

"You really wanna know?"

She nodded slowly, not looking too convinced. Maybe if I told her what I'd been through, what I was like, she'd stop trying to be friends with me.

"We did bad shit, Summer. Sold drugs, killed men, broke a hell of a lot more laws than I'm sure you even know exist." Her eyes widened a little. Fear filled them, which was exactly what I wanted to see. "We never got caught, but we were always hunted."

"Hunted?" She bit her bottom lip.

"Yeah. Sometimes by rival clubs, but mostly the DEA."

"As in the Drug Enforcement Administration?"

I nodded. "My old man dealt with a lot of illegal shit, mostly drug trafficking. Occasional prostitution too, but that stopped when a couple of the groupies round the club got pregnant. I didn't like the way things were run, but I never got a say as to how things went down either." I shrugged, wishing it hadn't been that way.

"If you were the leader—"

"The Pres, you mean."

She rolled her eyes. "If you were the *Pres*, what would you have done differently?"

Nobody had ever asked me that before. Probably because they didn't want it to get back to Pops that someone was questioning his role. But I'd thought about it. A lot. Especially when I was in prison. And for some reason, I wanted Summer to know what my plans had been, even if I'd never get to follow through with them.

I leaned back in my chair and tucked my hands behind my neck. "Before I got put behind bars, I'd always dreamed of taking over the club one day, reforming it."

"How so?" she asked.

"I wanted to turn it into a more family-oriented place. Most of the older brothers had jobs outside of the compound, a few had families too. The ones who didn't, like me, worked in the onsite body shop and just needed the club as a place to kick back. Lots had fucked-up families like mine. Some were former soldiers who didn't wanna go back into the real world after getting out of the military." I shrugged. "I wanted a place where we could all come together. Be that family. Enjoy the occasional party, but also have each other's backs."

"So you wanted to be a mechanic and turn the whole compound into a roughed-up version of a country club then."

"Guess so." Her analogy was spot on, but it still made me laugh. "I wanted to expand on the business aspect too. Possibly open up another repair shop outside the compound. Look for other ways to make money instead of doing it illegally."

The Red Dragons could've been so much more than what they were. Hell, maybe they were already changing, and I didn't know it. Arch and Slade hadn't said much about what was going down back at the compound, club rules restricted non-members from knowing their business. They'd mentioned Flick had taken over, which was a good thing. But he didn't always know right from wrong either. Still, any of my ideas were pipe dreams now, long fucking gone the second I decided my own freedom was more important than the club's reputation.

"And now you're running away from it all." She tapped a finger against her lips.

"No." I grunted, hating the lie on my tongue.

"Then what do you call it? Escaping?" She tipped her head to the side.

I rubbed a hand over my mouth, still not answering. I didn't want her to know that there was a small chance I was currently being hunted right now by anyone who was pissed about what I'd done. She'd freak out, kick me to the curb. And seeing as how I was a dumbass, offering to pay for her expensive hotel tonight, I'd basically just shit away most of my money. Whether I wanted to admit it or not, I needed Summer.

"I'm just trying to figure you out, is all." She reached across the table and set her hand over my wrist. I froze, looking at her skin compared to mine. Pale, untouched, smooth, while mine was rough, knuckles lined with scratches and bruises. Scars from past fights and being whipped across the hands by anything my father could use for a weapon when I was a kid.

"You're an enigma to me, Niyol."

I frowned, watching the edge of her thumb run once more over my knuckles. Did she realize what she was doing?

"We may not know each other well, but I can be a good listener if you ever want to talk." She cringed, finishing with, "I don't *always* lead the conversation."

I pulled my hand out from under hers, using my other hand to rub at the skin she'd stroked under the table. It prickled, a ghost of her touch still there. That scared me off far more than anything. If I started to crave physical contact from her, then I wouldn't be able to stop.

"We should get back to the hotel." I motioned for the waitress, avoiding Summer's eyes.

"I wasn't trying to make you uncomfortable, Niyol."

Ignoring her, I reached into my wallet and pulled out some cash. Once I slapped a few ones on the table, I stood.

"I'm gonna take off. Walk a little." Before I grabbed her and hauled her onto my lap. Before I ruined her like I ruined everything else in my life.

"Wait." She pushed in her chair and stood in front of me, her hands flat on my chest. "Don't go."

I looked in her pleading eyes, jaw locked as I willed her to leave it be.

The more time I spent with her, the more she reminded me of my stepmom in the sense that she had this undying need to make others feel better. Comfortable. A need to get people to open up, when that was the last thing they wanted.

"Sit." She puffed out her bottom lip, pouting—a last-ditch effort, no doubt. "Please, Niyol."

I breathed a heavy sigh, shoulders falling a little. Because telling this woman no wasn't in my vocabulary it seemed, I did as she asked.

She moved her chair next to mine this time, the legs screeching across the dirty bar floor. Eyes bright and eager, she waited for me to continue speaking, though I'm not sure what the hell else she wanted me to say. When I didn't open my mouth, she leaned back, leading the conversation. Again.

"Talk to me some more. About anything. I just… I want to know you for some stupid reason."

She was stupid all right. Stupid for being so sweet to me. Stupid for wanting to know me. Stupid for looking at me like I held the universe in my hands with my fucked-up life. A life she was obviously curious about but wouldn't dirty herself up enough to ever get too close to.

Maybe that was why I felt my chest squeeze. Why I felt like flipping this table, scooping her up, hauling her over my shoulder, and making her mine. I wasn't good enough for a woman like this. She was too pure for my world. But I wanted to. More than anything right then. And because of that, I turned on my inner asshole and let her have it again.

"You've got life all mapped out, don't you?"

Her gaze flickered with unease. "I, um, have *plans*, if that's what you mean. Goals and a job in the field of work that I love."

I glared down at my boots, the same pair I'd been wearing the day I stepped into prison. They were filthy; broken laces and scuffed. Summer's shoes though, were tiny and sparkly. They looked brand new, like something straight out of a magazine. It was almost like they'd never seen the world. Virgin-shoes was what I'd call them. Shoes that hadn't seen the bad shit like mine did. She was the princess, whether she liked to be called it or not. While I was the type of guy who'd been beaten by his father, left for dead in an alley, only for him to come back an hour later and say: *Get up, start acting like a man.* All because I refused to kill a guy for not having Pops' money.

Shit like that happened to me all the time growing up. And I dealt with it because that's what a Red Dragon did. Now, though, was my chance to start over. Forget those memories and just be someone else altogether, even if I wasn't sure how. And no matter what happened, she didn't want to be with me in any way shape or form when it all went down.

"Must be nice." I scowled down at the floor. "Knowing what's to come in life. Being prepared for a future."

"I worked hard to get where I am, if that's what you mean." She toyed with the end of her bracelet once more. I looked closer, finding a small shell set in the middle of it. "I got good grades all throughout school, stayed out of trouble, and even went to the same college as Emily."

"Don't bring Emily into this." I scrubbed both hands over my face. "This is about *you* and *me*."

"There is no *you and me*. As far as you are concerned, we're not even friends, remember?"

"No. We're not." But I'd never tell her that a huge part inside of me was dying to *kiss* her, taste her shiny lips, lay her on a bed and show her what it was like to be with a man who had no soul.

I pulled a smoke out of my pocket and twirled it in between my fingers instead.

"I want to understand you, Niyol. Is that too much to ask?" Her voice went soft.

"Why?"

"Because…" She took a shuddering breath. "Behind all your hard tendencies, I can almost bet there's an incredibly decent guy just waiting to be known."

An incredibly decent guy… That was laughable. Nobody *complimented me* for the hell of it. Nobody ever called me decent, either.

"Fine then, Princess. You wanna know me, then listen up." I folded my hands on the table top and she scooted closer to me. It was like she was readying for a bedtime story.

"My mom ran when I was a little kid. Two, I think." Not that I could really remember. I wasn't allowed to ask about her. The one time I did, Pops slapped me across the face and shoved me against a wall. "I stayed with my Pops, lived in a house with him about a mile from the Red Dragons' compound. Then at sixteen, I prospected, and a year later, I was patched in." Not wanting to see her reaction, I stared at the TV behind the bar.

"Life was decent enough. I had my cousin, Slade, who didn't have a mom either. She ran off like mine just days after he was born. His dad died later on, and when they couldn't find the lady, he moved in with Flick."

Slade was a quiet motherfucker, fiercely protective of me and Arch, even being two years younger. For a long time, we never saw him with a woman. Never saw him look at one even, up until he was close to eighteen. His head was always buried in a book, learning about everything he could that wasn't club related. People used to think he was slow. Stupid 'cause he didn't talk. But me and Archer knew the truth. Slade was a damn genius who only hid from the world because he didn't know what he wanted out of it.

Be an RD, or run away.

Eventually he made his choice and, as far as I knew, he didn't regret it.

"And the other guy? Archer?"

I refocused on Summer. "He's a buddy of mine. His dad was the Road Captain. Planned all the runs and took over when the VP or Pres weren't there." I paused, letting that sink into her mind. "Archer grew up in the club like I did, but overseas. Then came here when his father got transferred. He patched in around the same time as me. " I shrugged. "His old man died after a run gone wrong, and Arch's been a bit of a drunk since."

Not only that, but Archer was the goof-off, the guy with no goals, other than fucking and drinking. Blond hair with an Irish accent that the ladies fell to their knees for.

No matter what, he and Slade always had my back, like I had theirs.

Until I'd abandoned them.

"So, what, you didn't go to school? Get an education?" She frowned, her pretty lips dipping in pity.

"Couple of the old ladies round the club did what they could for me when Pops let them." Which wasn't very often. "I didn't need an education to deal drugs and work on cars though." Or fuck or get drunk either. None of those things needed a teacher.

"Where does Emily come into play in all of this?" Summer twisted her napkin, then flattened it back out on the table top. "I mean, I know she's your stepsister, but she's never told me much else."

Probably because she didn't know a lot.

"The night I got patched in, after celebrating at the club, Pops made me go with him on a run, while the rest of my brothers stayed behind at the compound."

"A run?"

"Like, we'd go out, run drugs, weapons, shit like that. Club stuff."

But it wasn't that kind of run. At least, not the night I was patched. Pops took me into town instead to find me some ass; a fucking virgin hooker to celebrate with, instead of one of the groupies who hung around the compound. One of the few things my old man said to me that night was, *No son of mine needs tainted ass on his first night as a brother.*

If he'd known I hadn't touched the girl he'd paid for, and instead given her an extra hundred bucks, then told her to escape out the window, he probably would've killed me on the spot.

As messed up as it was, at least at the time, I thought that was Pops' way of showing me he loved me; like him taking me to that girl was his version of trying to be a real father.

"On our way home, he saw Lisa and Emily stranded on the side of the road. They'd been out of town, shopping or some shit for Em's birthday. Their car had broken down. Pops pulled over to help. Didn't think he had it in him to care like that, to be honest."

I shook my head at the memory of Lisa's eyes. All big and green as she looked up at my pops through the rolled-down window. Then she looked at me, and I swear to this day she started crying. I must've scared her even worse than Pops had.

Emily, on the other hand, was in the passenger seat, scowling. I'd been half drunk on whiskey, yeah, but I'd never forget the look she gave me. One that promised a knee to the nuts if I even so much as looked at her.

"So, what, it was love at first sight then for the two of them?" Summer asked.

"Something like that." I shrugged, not really knowing the whole story. "Pops just had this way with women, I guess."

"He was charming, then." She frowned.

"No. The man's a master manipulator. Always in control, no matter who knows him or who doesn't. That goes for both women and men."

She reached over the table and squeezed my hand again. "I'm sorry you had to go through all that."

This time I pulled my hand back right away. "Nothing to be sorry for. Pops gets what he wants in the end."

At least he used to.

If I'd been smart at the time, then I would've warned Lisa away. Had I done so, though, I might have missed out on a lot myself. Selfish bastard that I was, if it meant not having Emily and Lisa in my life, I wouldn't have changed a thing. Outside of Slade and Archer, they were the only two people I could count on.

"Did Emily and her mom live with you guys?" she asked.

"Nah. Pops bought them the house Lisa lives in now. He went and stayed there maybe once a week." Most of the time, though, he was too busy doing runs, or fucking groupies to even remember he had a wife. "But her and my old man fought a lot. They only stayed married for six months, I think." If that.

"But you stayed in touch with Emily and Lisa still."

I nodded, drumming my fingers along the table top. "Nine years later, and they're still more my family than Pops ever was." Holidays, get-togethers, nights of just doing nothing… Pops never knew I used to visit them as much as I did. But Lisa became the mom I never had and Emily the sister I didn't think I wanted.

"I'm glad you have someone."

I looked up, finding a wide smile on Summer's face. I didn't get a lot of real in my life, but for some reason, she was fast becoming an exception to that.

"Me, too."

A few seconds passed before she began again. Summer really did love to fucking talk. And the scary part was, I wasn't minding it as much.

"So, what happened? How did you wind up in prison?"

I leaned back on my stool, tapping only my thumb along the edge of the table. "I got in a fight with Pops one night after I saw him hit one of the groupies. I'd just turned twenty-four and felt like more of a man than I'd ever been." The kind of man who apparently thought it was okay to test the RDs' club president, father or not. "I'll never tolerate men hurting women."

"And what are, um, groupies exactly?" She bit her bottom lip.

"Women who like to fuck. In turn, they get shelter, food, and protection from shit most are hiding from outside of the club."

"Like protected prostitutes."

"Sure." I didn't bother correcting her. Unless you grew up in that lifestyle, you wouldn't understand it.

"What happened after you got into it with your father?" Those sweet eyes of hers continued to study me, curiosity making them even lighter it seemed.

I shifted and looked down at the table. "I wound up moving out of Pops' place. Lying low for a while. Hiding out in abandoned buildings, shit like that. Slade and Archer brought me stuff I needed. Food and clothes. Money."

"Slade and Archer sound important to you," she said with a sad smile.

"They're my brothers." I glared at the table, avoiding her eyes. Every day I missed those two. But unlike me, they wouldn't walk away from the club. Their devotion to the RDs was forever, no matter who led it or what rules applied.

"So, what happened then?" Summer asked, scooting her stool even closer. So close, our thighs pressed together.

"Pops found me. Came alone." She nodded me on, her eyes wide, fearful. "He said we needed to talk. That he'd had a *change of heart* and wanted to see shit my way for once."

The little kid inside of me who longed for love from his father had needed to believe him. That was why I'd agreed to go.

Had I known what would happen, I'd have never gone.

"I should've known something was up. Slade was blowing my phone up the entire ride back, but I didn't answer because I was on my bike, following my father. By the time I read his texts, it was too late." I folded my arms behind my head and looked at the ceiling.

This was where shit got bad.

"What do you mean, too late?"

I scrubbed a hand over my forehead while memories buzzed in the back of my head.

"Niyol?" Summer asked on a whisper.

Instead of looking at her, I grabbed a smoke and tucked it behind my ear, then lowered my hands to hold my empty glass.

"I got back and found the DEA swarming our house just outside the gates." I sniffed, the picture still fresh in my mind, even two years later.

Lights flashing, bikes stacked alongside the fence, guys I'd once considered uncles and brothers—*family*—all staring at me, pity in some of their eyes, disgust in others.

No matter, everyone's hands were tied anyway. My father always got the last word.

"I remembered how smug Pops looked when he got off his bike and walked over to one of the suits." He shook the fucker's hand, sealing my fate. "Apparently, he'd asked for club immunity from the law to forgo all their debts, if he'd turn in his number one dealer. That dealer, supposedly, being me."

Summer shook her head, disgust in her eyes. "Your own father set you up?"

I nodded. "While I'd been staying away, Pops made it look like the place was all mine, not his. He'd stashed part of the club's drug supply inside. Even had the fucking balls to put a makeshift meth lab in there." I scrubbed a hand over my face, trying to push the memories from out of my head, failing every second longer I kept talking. "He was so pissed that I'd taken off, that framing me was the only retaliation he had."

"God, that's awful," Summer said with a hiss.

I shrugged. "As the president's son, the jail time was easier punishment than what the club could've handed out."

Summer leaned back. When I looked up at her again, I noticed her narrowed blue eyes focused on the table in thought. I swallowed at the view, wondering what was going through her mind.

"Why didn't you stand up for yourself? Tell them the truth?" she finally asked.

"I wasn't a rat," I grumbled. "Least not then. Plus, they didn't believe me and everyone was too fucking scared to stand up to my old man."

"Even your supposed friends? This Flick guy, too?" Summer's upper lip curled in disgust.

"You don't get what it was like. Pops had so much damn control over everything in everyone's life that one wrong move and you, or even the people you loved, would be dead. Nobody was willing to risk it. Least not then. I accepted that fact." Even though it didn't make it any easier.

"But eventually you told the truth to the police, right? And they believed you?"

I shrugged. "People got sick of the way things were going down. Especially Flick. He's the one who wound up gathering evidence to help clear my name and put my father behind bars instead."

He'd gathered a bunch of my brothers for support, the first two to show were Archer and Slade, of course. It took them a long while to get everything together, to get their stories straight too, but I understood why. My father wasn't the type to let shit go, and if he'd found out what was happening before he was taken away, then it wouldn't have ended well for any of them.

"And you were in prison for two years?" Summer asked.

"Yeah."

She frowned. "That's a lot of time to hold onto secrets."

"Better than the original five years I'd been sentenced with."

The waitress interrupted, setting our plates down on the table. I glared at my food, not even hungry now. I'd already said too much. Opened my mouth and told her shit I'd never told no one. Not even Maya. Which meant now, more than ever, I needed to get out of there. Away from her. Get drunk. Pass out. Sleep. Something. *Anything.*

"I need to go." Ignoring her wide, confused eyes, I dropped a fifty on the table, and said, "Don't wait up." Then without a glance back, I walked out the door—away from her and away from my memories most of all.

CHAPTER ELEVEN

Summer

My eyes shot open, finding the ceiling of a dark hotel room. Sweat dripped down the back of my neck, dipping into my shirt and soaking the collar. The sheets tangled around my restless legs, pinning me in place. Even if I could have moved, my mind was too paralyzed to let me because of the dream I'd just had.

Landon was there in my sleep once more, this time at the foot of my bed, watching me, telling me he was sorry, just as he shoved a faceless woman against the mattress and took her from behind.

I shuddered, toying with my bracelet at the same time. Loneliness encompassed me, something I didn't enjoy. I craved companionship, someone to talk with constantly. Without that, I felt more alone than ever before.

What happened with Niyol and I at dinner had continued to weigh heavily on my mind for the rest of the evening. I wasn't the only one who'd needed a shoulder to cry on, apparently—though there were no tears shed on Niyol's end, unlike the night I'd gone out in Des Moines.

I'd been thinking about that more and more, the reason as to why I'd opened up to him that night at my grandparents'. Was it because we had so much in common, even if our lives were on entirely different spectrums? Insisting that he opened up to me tonight was maybe my way of saying, *You owe me.* I'd told him my darkest secret, now I wanted to know his.

Either that, or I was growing more comfortable with the guy. The guy who had broken my heart with a tragic story and an enormous amount of pain in his eyes. A guy that was also getting under my skin like Landon had, but in a different, deeper, sort of way.

Whether Niyol knew it or not, I was very aware of what it felt like to lose things, even though my losses were nowhere near as terrible as his.

I also knew what it was like to want to start over. It's why I was taking this trip in the first place. Driving across country, hitting the San Diego beaches… Not only did I want the chance to rid Landon from my mind, but I'd also hoped that seeing the Pacific Ocean for the first time would somehow help me feel closer to my mother.

At twenty-one, she and my father had gone to California together. It was their first trip, post-college, as a real couple. While they were there Dad had given her the bracelet I always wore. Having it around my wrist constantly made me feel close to the woman I never knew.

In a way, Niyol's and my mindsets were very similar, both of us never knowing our moms. Unlike him, though, I had a father and brothers who loved me. Although he did have his club brothers, and Lisa and Emily.

A low groan sounded from the side of the bed. My heart skipped at the sound. I swung my feet over the edge of the mattress to the floor, finding Niyol asleep on the carpet, shirtless and thrashing.

Without a second thought, I dropped to my knees beside him. His yells grew louder, more desperate. Not knowing what to do for him, I pressed my hand against his slick, sweaty back to try and wake him.

"*No!*" he shouted and swung his arm, nailing me in the chest.

I winced but kept trying. "Niyol, hey, stop." I rubbed his back harder, faster, feeling like a mother. "Shh, it's okay."

"Fuck." He darted upward, seeking me out with his arms. Our chests crashed together as he grabbed my waist. Breathing ragged, he whispered against my neck, "*I'm sorry, I'm so fucking sorry.*"

"It's okay," I repeated, attempting to soothe him. Regardless of my feigned calm, my hand shook as I rubbed it over the back of his head. His hair was damp as he brushed against my cheeks, likely from sweat. Because I couldn't help myself, I snuggled my nose into his scalp, inhaling. Fresh, flowery, with hints of musk and cigarettes. He'd used my shampoo.

"Do you want me to turn the light on?" I finally asked.

He shook his head and the stubble along his chin and cheeks brushed against my neck. It was a delicious burn, one that had my nipples pebbling against my shirt.

Not the time, Summer. So not the time.

Despite how he made me feel, I accepted his need to hug me; it was something a *friend* would do. Any minute now, he'd realize what was going on, though. Then he'd accuse me of trying to take advantage of him, jokingly pushing me away I'm sure.

Niyol was the hardest person for me to read, cursed with a personality that straddled the fine line between a boy who'd lost so much, and a hardened man who'd been through hell.

"Do you want to talk about it?" I asked.

Seconds passed before he finally said, "No."

Swallowing the lump ensnared at the base of my throat, I decided to do something I might regret, but felt confident—and exhausted enough—to suggest anyway.

"The bed is big enough for the both of us. You don't have to sleep on the floor if you don't want to."

The thought of him continuing to sleep down here, even after he ran out on me during dinner, was something I couldn't stomach, as dangerous as it might be to share a bed. I knew I wasn't in the right frame of mind to be so close to a deliciously sexy man. Especially one who harbored so much pain and vulnerability. But at the same time, I craved his nearness more than I craved any kind of distance between us.

Surprisingly he nodded, pulling back enough to look me in the eyes. His dark eyes were lost, broken like a puppy in need of a home. My heart ached for him even more then, wondering what was going through his mind. But before I could ask, he stood, his hand in mine as he pulled me up. Soft, yet firm. Protective, yet easy.

He was such a big man. Tall, constructed of muscles that could easily crush me. Yet his tender fingers proved that he could let his darkness fall away whenever he wanted it gone—which wasn't often, it seemed. Niyol was very much in control of himself. That fascinated me as someone who struggled to relinquish control over anything. My schedules, my plans, my perfectly mapped-out life that was now in shambles... How different would it be if I'd been cursed with a life like Niyol? I shivered at the thought.

Together in the dark silence of the room, we moved back to the bed, shoulders touching while we laid on our backs. The air conditioner came on with a rough grumble, and he pulled the sheets over our bodies. It hummed throughout the room, and the chill of it pulled me deeper under the covers, but also made me more aware of the warmth now laying so close to me.

"Are you sure you're okay?" I wanted to face him, comfort him some more, but the chicken inside of me laughed in my face and told me to get a grip. Niyol was a man who did not like any sort of pity, even if it were well-intended.

"Not really."

I shut my eyes and nodded. "I'm here if you want to talk or whatever."

The bed creaked as he rolled over onto his side. Feeling suddenly brave, I did the same, facing him. He searched my gaze like before, only this time, he seemed more at ease and even more vulnerable in the soft light reflecting off his back from the street outside. At the same time, he also appeared far more dangerous than anyone I'd ever encountered.

My cheeks grew hot as he continued to look his fill, my stomach knotting in an even more unnerving mess. When he didn't speak, I fidgeted, opening my mouth, then snapping it shut. Was he pissed at me for something again? Was he regretting accepting my invitation after all?

When I couldn't take another moment of his quiet, I asked, "Can you at least tell me what you were dreaming about?"

"It doesn't matter." Short answers, a hard tongue—those were the responses I'd come to know from him. The normal ones. Not like the long conversation we'd had at dinner. That was a rarity. One I couldn't get used to no matter how much I found myself liking it.

"It *does* matter." Hands trembling, I lifted one, tentatively laying it against his cheek.

He shut his eyes, his face seeming to be tortured by my touch. I should have stopped, moved it away, should have rolled over and ignored him, respecting his need for quiet. But being so close to him, feeling his breath on my face, inhaling his skin, forced me to become someone else. Someone needing more than a friend. Someone needing to ease the ache creeping up in her lower belly. Someone selfish who wanted to forget boundaries and ultimate goals.

I traced the scar by his lips with my forefinger. "How did you get this?"

"My father," he whispered back, eyes opening once more.

I swallowed hard, pained for the broken boy, then braved a moment for the sake of his pain. Slowly, I leaned closer and kissed the mark, leaving my forehead pressed to his. It was a quiet *I'm sorry* this time—my version of a healing touch.

His breath shuddered on an exhale over my lips. I'm not sure if he was affected by me, or his memory more. Either way, I knew, from that moment on, there would be no escaping this man.

When I moved back, he began to search my face again. In turn, I trailed my fingers down his chin, then his neck, unable to resist touching him now that I had begun. I couldn't see his tattoos, but I could feel them in a way; the outlines, several scars in between. The power they held, the reasoning behind them all.

"Summer…" he breathed my name, pain residing over features, the downturn of his lips most of all. Still, he didn't pull away, didn't tell me stop, didn't plead with a no. His fingers, though, they dropped onto my hips, then dipped beneath my shirt, lifting up to the base of my ribs. I sucked in a sharp breath at the initial contact, never feeling so richly devoted to in my life.

This was so incredibly wrong. Neither of us were in a place for whatever was stirring between us. But the lines of muscles and tattoos scattered over his arms and shoulders and chest? They were a new sort of drug I couldn't resist. A temptation I couldn't shake. Niyol Lattimore was my addiction in the making.

His body trembled, as did mine. Licking his lips, he made no move to kiss me, but he looked so starved. I wasn't sure what was happening, what he was thinking, but I knew I didn't want to stop it.

We both moved even closer, me first, then him. Then a growl reverberated through the room, and before I could take a breath, I was beneath him, his hands pressed on either side of my face against the mattress, while his long hair hung over his cheeks, just barely grazing my own. My eyes widened, chest rising and falling as he straddled my waist.

God help me. I was his prisoner. And I liked it.

"This is wrong…" His words mirrored my earlier thoughts, but he didn't move away. Instead, he squeezed his eyes shut tighter than before, finishing the last of his words on a painful breath.

"But, Jesus… You make me wanna do *really* bad things to you. So I'm gonna need you to tell me no, Summer." Then he said on a whisper, "Please, tell me no."

"I…" No thoughts. No regrets. "I can't."

At my words, he winced, just as one of his hands ran down my hip, then my thigh, hitting just below my knee. He latched a hand onto the skin and wrapped my leg around his back.

"Christ, I'm gonna need to—" He groaned deep as he pushed his erection between my thighs, cutting off his own words.

"Tell me." I was breathless, back arched, shaking, desperate for him to make the pain go away. The pain between my thighs… The pain in my heart most of all. I was done playing it safe in life. It was time to throw myself under the bus. Or in this case, under Niyol.

Fingertips still digging into my skin, he ground his hips against mine once more as he said, "There's no fucking way I can stop this anymore."

"I don't want you to." I tugged his head closer, fingers threading through his long hair. "Please. I need this."

His eyes met mine, a battle raging through them. Then just like that, he nodded, losing himself in me with a kiss.

Soft, tentative, exploring. The initial touch was everything I'd been missing, and then some. His tongue wasted not a second to slip inside, the barbell colder than I expected. I gasped, sucking it in deeper, wondering how magical that would feel between my thighs. I groaned at the thought, fully lost in the taste of him, then grazed my fingers down his arm, the firm muscles trembling even more at my touch. Slowly, carefully, I lowered my hands and guided them around his jean-clad ass, whimpering when he drove himself harder against me.

"Summer." My name on his lips was a warning, a desperate plea. In turn, he hissed, moving faster against me. He lowered one hand from my face and pressed it to the curve of my waist, trailing his fingers up higher and higher, until his knuckles grazed the undersides of my breasts.

"Touch me more," I whispered. "Don't stop." I licked a line up his neck, tasting the salt of his skin.

Another growl sounded from his throat, but he didn't touch my breasts. Instead, he pushed his hand lower, grazing the dip of my belly until the tips of his fingers were deliciously snug beneath the waistband of my shorts.

"There. Yes, there," I hissed. "Lower, please."

Breath heavy, he trailed kisses from one side of my chin to the other, down my neck, to the curve of my breasts peeking just over the top of my camisole. The teasing was too much, so I buried my hands into the back of his hair and forced his mouth back to mine.

But he didn't kiss me, not this time. Instead, he held his mouth just inches from mine and stared into my eyes, letting his breath wash over my lips. "This can't be more."

Was he telling me, or himself? Regardless, a look of *Do I stay, or do I go* filled his stare. He was tortured with going through with whatever we did, but I was too lost to tell him to stop—too selfish.

Guilt and desire are two of life's most powerful emotions. Niyol was currently battling with them both.

It didn't take me long to realize what needed to be done though. My desire to erase the pain in his eyes, giving me the control my body craved. I wanted to piece him back together. Make him whole, if only for one solitary moment in time.

Holding my breath, I traced my fingers along his cheeks some more, enjoying the rough stubble beneath my touch. I wanted Niyol to touch me, in all the ways a man could touch a woman. But if I guilted him into doing so, even wordlessly, he might never forgive himself. Or me. Which was why I needed to be the one to touch him first.

Before I could talk myself out of it, I urged him onto his back by his shoulders, never faltering from his stare. He didn't speak, just watched with hooded eyes while I kissed my way down his chest, his belly, too. Hard muscle greeted my lips with every inch, and my body hummed with the need to be pressed naked against him. It wasn't the time, probably never would be, but I'd be crazy not to think about it.

I landed at the top of his jeans and popped the button, stopping at the zipper.

"Summer." He held my wrist with his hand. "You do this, it changes everything."

I blinked up at him, unsure of what he meant, but also not caring either. "It's okay. I want to."

One barely-there nod later, and I was pulling down his zipper, then freeing his erection from his boxers. My eyes widened as something glistened from under the head of his cock. A piercing that nearly matched the one in his tongue. Part of me wanted to giggle with glee, but that likely wouldn't go over well. So, instead, I went to work pulling his jeans and boxers down, thankful for his relinquishing of control.

As he arched his back, I yanked his pants to his knees, then pulled them off his feet, tossing the black denim to the floor. I crawled back between his thighs, spreading his legs at the ankles. He hissed as I wrapped my hand around the base of his cock, then whispered, "Jesus," as I licked a circle around the tip.

Pushing any last doubts away, I crawled over him and sucked him in deep, using my other hand to stroke what I couldn't take inside my mouth.

"Feels so good." His legs shuddered around my head, but he played it cool, his fingers trailing over my forehead, down my cheeks; tender fingers from such a rough man.

I looked up at him again, finding his eyes shut. The moonlight crept in through the curtains a little more, exposing a larger expanse of his face. Seduced like this, Niyol was stunning.

Groans sounded deep in his throat, and he pushed his chin to his chest, muscles pulling tight across his stomach at the same time. My mouth was stretched and aching, way out of practice a few minutes in, but seeing him let loose, relax, knowing it was because of me, made it worthwhile.

Over and over, I stroked him, kissed him, sucked him, until he came hard, growling out my name. His warm release reached the back of my throat, the salty residue filling my mouth before I swallowed it down. Slowly, I pulled back, my gaze never leaving his face.

But then he opened his eyes, and that's when I saw it.

A flicker of regret. The problem? I'm not sure what it meant.

On my knees, I stayed there watching him momentarily, ignoring the burn in my throat at the same time. It's amazing how quickly I could become a slave to this man, when all along I'd been determined to keep myself *away* from the opposite sex in general.

I wiped some of the remaining stickiness from his release off my hands and onto the sheets, then slowly stood from the bed. Unsure of what to do or say next, I headed toward the bathroom, determined to get it together. Once inside, I locked the door, flicking on the light as I tried to catch my breath. Hands clenching the edge of the sink, I leaned forward, elbows outstretched, head down.

This was Emily's stepbrother, a man with demons, not someone who I could ever bring home to my father and brothers. Not a potential forever after.

"Stupid, stupid, girl." I narrowed my eyes in the mirror, knowing exactly what I needed to do.

I would forget that the entire thing ever happened, even though, deep inside, I knew just how hard that would be.

CHAPTER TWELVE

Niyol

I fucked up. Big time.

And now there I was, being an ass again because of it.

Talking wasn't my thing, that was the problem. Especially not when all I wanted was to take the wheel of this SUV, yank it back in the direction of the hotel, scrap my plans to get to San Diego, and camp out in a hotel for the rest of my life with a woman who I'm pretty sure would always be too good for me.

Pre-prison, I would've run with that idea.

Post-prison life, I was trying to be better, though that shit failed the second I let Summer suck me off.

Now, instead, I was battling all sorts of thoughts and what-ifs.

What if escaping the RD life was a mistake?

What if the person I wanna be isn't who I'm meant to be?

What if there's more out there than I ever thought?

Case in point, the sexy blonde blasting her country music once-a-fucking-gain.

The last thing I wanted was to set her off, ask her to change the channel for the sake of my sanity. It seemed this shit-kicking stuff soothed her, and who was I to judge? This was her ride after all.

Ever since we'd loaded our bags and took off from the hotel, Summer had grown weird on me. Distant. Cold. Less… cheerleader. When she'd stepped out of the bathroom, she played it off like nothing had happened. Just packed up her stuff, and left the hotel, me trailing after her like a lost puppy.

I needed to apologize. Again. But I didn't know how to go about doing so without bringing up the unmentionable. The unmentionable that I hadn't been able to get out of my head all day.

Her mouth, my cock…

I shut my eyes, swallowing hard, a total asshole for reliving it in my mind for the thousandth time today.

We were just outside Colorado Springs when an idea hit me. Like she could sense my thoughts, Summer, shockingly, piped up first.

"So. Where exactly are we headed now?" The wipers and the steady rain on the windshield, along with her music, made for the worst background noise ever. "The hotels I booked are no good because of our extra day in Des Moines. Furthermore, we're at least a day behind schedule."

"Keep driving." Open air, plenty of space to get away from one another… My idea was perfect. Hopefully she'd agree.

"Please tell me an actual answer, would you?" she whispered, then sniffed, then sighed.

I jerked my head to look at her, needing to make sure she wasn't crying. Which she wasn't, thank fuck. But I could tell she was barely holding it together.

"I'll tell you where to turn. Just stay on this road." Per the sign we'd just driven by, we didn't have much further to go.

"Have you ever been camping before?" I finally asked, needing to fill the silence with something other than my crazy thoughts. Thoughts that included pulling over and reciprocating what she'd done for me this morning.

She glanced at me out of the corner of her eye. "A little, when I was a kid."

"Ah, I forgot." I bounced my knee in place, impatient, on edge.

"Forgot what?" She frowned.

"That you're high maintenance."

"I'm not high maintenance." She rolled her eyes. "It's just that when I discovered hotels, I preferred those over tents." I thought maybe she'd stop talking, but then she surprised me and kept going. "Whenever my dad would take my brothers camping and fishing, I learned that staying behind with friends, or going to my grandparents' house, was a much better option."

"In other words, princesses don't like to get dirty. I get it."

Other than a little twitch of her lips, she didn't react. But her knuckles whitened as she tightened her fingers around the steering wheel, proof she was losing her shit. I wanted her to snap at me, react in some way other than this comatose shit. It was driving me insane, especially since it was my fault.

I leaned back in the seat and I kicked my feet on the dash. "Take the next exit."

"What'd you say?" She jerked her head my way.

"I said, take the next—"

Something thumped beneath the car, and Summer squealed, losing control of the wheel. The Rover swerved to the right, and I gripped the oh-shit bar, putting my feet flat on the floor.

I fell to the side, then looked at the side mirror, eyes narrowing at the view. Dust and rock kicked up behind us as we slowed to a stop along the side of the road.

"Fuck," I muttered under my breath.

The engine hissed. The radio was still playing the same twang I hated—louder now that we weren't moving. I reached forward to shut it off, but Summer beat me to it.

"Leave it," she snarled.

I put my hands up.

With a loud huff, she pressed her forehead against the steering wheel, knocking it twice.

"You good?" I cringed.

Her narrowed eyes shot my way. "Get. Out. Of my. Car."

"Uh…" I scratched at my throat.

"I said, get. Out."

"I'm not getting out, it's still raining." As if mocking me, the sun flickered through the clouds.

"Yes. You are."

"You can't make me, you know." I tapped my finger along the door, messing with her. A riled-up Summer was so much easier to deal with than a quiet one.

"What, are you *five*?" She grabbed her door and shoved it open. "Get. Out!"

I watched her through the windshield as she maneuvered her way to my side, stumbling once against the front bumper. Trying like hell to curb my smirk, I opened the door, intending to help her stay upright. But she managed herself, eventually making her way to me.

She ripped my door open the rest of the way and yelled, "Now, Niyol." She gripped my sleeve and yanked.

"Hey, watch it." I laughed—because I couldn't help it.

Relentless, Summer kept pulling until I finally gave in. When I stood, she jumped back, squeaking as she lost her balance and fell flat on her ass, right into a mud puddle.

"Jesus, you okay?" I reached down to help her stand.

She shoved my hand away. "You stupid son of a—"

"No need for the language." I wrapped my arms around her waist and helped her up anyway, but only for her to jump back, hands at her side like I'd burnt her. I couldn't help but grin as I scanned the length of her body. She looked like she belonged in a ring with a bikini.

"You're dead." The wetness hit my face so fast, I didn't have time to jump and cover.

She'd nailed me with a ball of mud?

"So, you wanna get a little dirty after all, Princess?" I curled my lip.

Her face was like a fireball—ready-to-explode red. Then before I could stop her, another ball of mud flung from her other hand, this time landing on my thigh.

I arched my eyebrows. "Another one? That wasn't very nice."

"What? You don't like to get *dirty*?" Her lips pursed.

"Oh, I like it dirty." I tipped my head to the side, stalking her as I moved close.

"Oh, I bet you do." She crouched to grab two more handfuls of mud, then stood, her lips pulled up on one side. My dick twitched behind my zipper at the view, his mind on one thing, and one thing alone.

Summer wound her arm back.

"Don't do it."

She batted her lashes once, then twice, before flinging another handful at my cheek this time. It stuck to my chin—cold and wet. I reached up to wipe it off with my fingers, half smiling, pissed, and ready to strip her out of those white shorts to show her how *dirty* my cock wanted to get.

"You are in a lot of trouble." Like I was a soldier headed to battle, I ran to her and swooped her up and over my shoulder. She screeched, beating my backside with her fists.

"Stop it. Put me down."

I laughed again and held my palm on her thigh beneath her ass.

"I wouldn't do that if I were you," I growled.

She froze while I slipped my hand just beneath the edges of her shorts. "Did anyone ever tell you what a nice ass you have?" I taunted.

"Wh-what are you…" She all but melted, her voice like a kitten's purr.

I traced the skin just beneath the fringe of her cut-offs, distracted and trying not to linger. If I kept exploring, I wouldn't be able to stop.

And God help me, I didn't want to.

"It's so round," I kept going. "Just the right size to spank."

"You wouldn't," she hissed.

I took two small steps forward and shrugged my free shoulder. "Yeah, you're—"

Without a warning, I slipped, falling to my knees, only for Summer to slide from my hold, landing face first, somehow, back in the mud.

"Shit. I'm so fucking sorry." Covered from hip to boot in my own bath of mud, I watched as she laid there, frozen.

"You *jerk*." A second later, she was up again, facing me. "Look what you did!"

"Total accident. I swear." I held up my hands, trying not to laugh as she attempted—more so failed—to brush the mud from her face, her clothes…

Cringing, I took the free moment, ignoring the wild noises and words I'd inspired from her mouth, and inspected the damage on her truck. The tire was in crap shape, flattened down to the rim.

I rubbed both hands over my muddy face and sighed. Of course, this was my fault—everything else on this trip had been so far. And I had no doubt she'd let me know it too.

Fuck. My. Life.

CHAPTER THIRTEEN

Summer

"But we don't even have a tent. Haven't you ever heard of wild animals?"

Niyol quirked a brow at me, unnervingly calm. "You got nothing to be afraid of."

"Well, excuse me if I'm a little worried about staying at a place *named* Swift Wolf where, in fact, there might very well be *wolves* lurking around us while we *sleep*."

He rolled his eyes. "If we keep the fire going, we'll be fine."

I pushed ahead of him, ramming my shoulder against his as I walked over to the nearby picnic table and plopped my bag down. As I straddled the seat, I attempted to enjoy the scenery, the way the trees whispered in the warm wind. How the sounds of birds could be heard from miles away, but not a single camper tarried about. Maybe *that* fact should have alarmed me, but the promise of a few more hours of sleep was distracting me enough not to care.

Niyol moved about the campsite, his steps sure and confident, the same black boots he always wore crunching through the brush. In front of the firepit, he stacked some wood and shoved bits of newspaper just beneath, then peppered it with lighter fluid that he'd purchased at the ranger station. A second later, he took a step back and frowned, studying it like an unsolvable puzzle.

Standing there like that, with his dark hair covering one eye, lips pressed into a thin line, Niyol looked like a powerful warrior wanting nothing more than to overpower the world. Or at least this fire.

I, on the other hand, looked like a yeti—covered in mud from our roadside-war earlier. The looks we'd earned when we reserved this spot were almost enough of an incentive for me to head toward the dirty shower stalls a little way up the road. But in the end, exhaustion held me back. Soon, though.

"Grab the rest of the dry wood from the trunk, would you?"

"Ever heard of the magic word?" I huffed.

He rolled his eyes. "Pretty please gimme the wood, Princess?"

Now he was just being a smartass. Still, I went and got his *wood*. Why? Simple. Because I was an idiot.

After I handed it to him, I stepped back and brushed off my hands on my shorts. They were caked in mud, just like my body, and no amount of bleach could make them white again.

A yawn escaped me right then. The need for a nap had me peering around the campsite for a spot to crash. By the back bumper of my Rover, there sat a sleeping bag spread out on the ground, with another on top, which would serve perfectly as a pillow. I'm not sure where they'd come from, the ranger station again maybe. Either way, it looked a lot more appealing than the ground or the backseat of my Rover.

Regardless, if I'd never run off the road and got a flat tire, we'd at least be in Denver by now. Possibly at a nice hotel with clean linens and *real* pillows.

"I'm such an idiot," I snorted under my breath, wiping sweat off my brow beneath my long bangs.

Niyol moved in next to me, his arm brushing mine. "You talking to yourself?" he asked.

"I was thinking out loud, actually."

"Hmm." He struck a match and dropped it into the pit; seconds later our fire was born.

"What do you mean, *hmm*?" I narrowed my eyes, watching every move he made.

"You do that a lot?" He crouched down to adjust some wood with a long, skinny stick.

"Think out loud, you mean?"

He nodded.

"Yeah. It's therapeutic." It was part of my personality, to talk things out, figure out problems, solve them with my words. There wasn't a crime against it, yet Niyol's comment made me feel like a fool.

Lips twitching, he glanced up from under a dark patch of his hair, studying me again. He did that a lot, and it made me uncomfortable. Made my skin itchy. Like, I constantly had to touch my face to make sure there wasn't something on it.

"Why are you looking at me like that?" I finally asked, shifting from one foot to another.

"You're just…" He blew out a slow breath, losing his smile, before looking into the fire.

"I'm what?" Impatient, I tapped the toe of my foot.

He scowled at it. "Nothing."

"It's not *nothing*. Did I do something to make you mad again?" Because I wouldn't be surprised if I did. My new name should've have been: Niyol Lattimore's Antagonist Extraordinaire.

"Christ, Princess. Don't get all moody-sensitive on me. I was just thinking you were funny, is all."

He stood, putting his back to me—all man and woods and… God, he had nice back muscles. I could see them beneath his shirt, shifting and pulling at the material, like it was ten times too small.

"No one's ever called me funny before." I cursed my stupid thoughts, his compliment most of all, and looked to the sky to pray for strength to get through this night.

Of course he ignored me. What was new?

Two could totally play that game.

Niyol was messing with me again. Running, then staying, fighting, then pretending that everything was some big joke. It was both exhausting *and* infuriating and… fascinating. So fascinating, because I wanted to know what made him that way. What went on in his head most of all. Wanted to know for reasons I didn't have any right to know for too. I was starting to care about him. Starting to be concerned about whether or not he was okay—whether he needed me to help him, hit him, or run from him altogether.

All of those were viable options that I should have been looking further into.

Unfortunately, I needed a nap first.

"Hey," he hollered at my back as I walked toward the sleeping bag.

My feet just barely hit the edge before I decided to answer. "*What*, Niyol?"

He paused, exhaling heavily before he said, "Get some rest."

My shoulders dropped. I frowned, fighting the urge to analyze the tone of his voice again. Instead of doing so, I fell to my knees and landed face first onto the sleeping bag that served as a pillow, drifting to sleep within seconds, dirty body, broody biker boy, be damned.

Take that, black silky sleeping bag.

CHAPTER FOURTEEN

Summer

I think I was having an out-of-body experience. One of those moments where you're there, but you are not at the same time. At least, that's what it felt like as I opened my eyes and found myself blanketed in darkness, other than the flicker of a campfire.

Then I heard an owl hooting in the distance, followed by something else that sounded close to a wolf. Or was it a mountain lion? A rustling in leaves had me gasping for breath, and I shot up, ready to fight, hands extended. *Where the hell's my pepper spray?*

Panic thickened in my chest, like murky watery mud. My back throbbed from the way I'd been lying, and my skin was on fire from what was likely a thousand and one mosquito bites. I spun around to look for Niyol, finding him by the fire, relaxed as ever.

"You okay?" He was sitting on the ground, leaned back against a tree stump.

I took a shuddering breath, beyond thankful I wasn't amid some serial-killer spree.

"Yeah." I stood and stretched my arms above my head. Bright sparks shot into the air from the fire at the same time. I had to admit, it was a pretty sight. "How long have I been out?" I asked.

"About four hours."

"*What?* Why didn't you wake me?" My shoes were off, and I fumbled around until I found them lined up at the foot of the sleeping bags. Had Niyol done that for me?

"You needed rest." He shrugged.

Despite my arguing with it, my heart took a little sputter into Swoonville: population one. How could this man be so sweet and grumpy at the same time?

"Oh. Well, thank you for, you know…" I pointed at my feet.

"No problem," he said, gaze never straying from the fire.

I scanned the campsite. Everything around us was neat and organized. It shocked me, seeing as how most men I'd been around—my dad, brothers, Landon—could barely do laundry or dishes, let alone tidy up an entire area.

On the picnic table, there were several items of food, and my stomach growled on instinct. I hadn't eaten all day.

"Hungry? I cooked us some hot dogs not long ago." He stood like me, his frame tall and intimidating in the shadows as he stepped toward the table. He'd changed out of his muddy tee, but his jeans were still caked like mine.

I frowned, pointing at the paper plate holding the food. "Where'd you get them?"

"Ranger station. Got them when we were checking in. You were too busy staring at the animals on the walls to notice." He chuckled under his breath.

I shuddered at the memory of those wolves and pumas. They decorated every bit of the area in the ranger station. Taxidermy was an art form I could never get down with.

"I'm starved." I folded my arms and attempted to rub my hands up and down my bare shoulders to fight away a chill, only to encounter another three, itchy bumps.

"Cold?"

I nodded. "A bit. Mostly just itchy and grossed out by all the mud."

He swatted a bug, then reached for the hem of his hooded sweatshirt. "Here. Take this then."

I watched him, mesmerized as the base lifted enough to reveal a tattooed, dark belly. Beneath the hoodie, he wore yet another black tee that framed his massive chest. Unabashed, I took him in, my mouth practically watering at the memory of the ridges I'd just barely explored that morning. In a way, he really did remind me of Tarzan, but with darker complexion, eyes, hair… his entire persona, more so. And instead of swinging from trees, he strode around on massive calves, the movement far more animal than human.

His fingers grazed mine as he handed it over, and my heart beat a little faster. He looked around for a second, as if hearing the noise, but then turned away and walked back to the picnic table.

I sighed, watching him go, wondering if things were ever going to be somewhat *normal* between us.

His sweatshirt was warm on my skin when I slipped it on over my head. The scent of his body lingered on the material. In secret, I turned my head away, burying my nose into the cotton neckline. It's scary how obsessed I was becoming with this man. And I wasn't sure if I was all that bothered by the prospect. It wasn't like I wanted Niyol as a boyfriend. But there was no denying I wanted to explore his body a little more. I'd only ever had sex with Landon. And though it got better, I'd never really felt passion with the man like I was pretty sure I was supposed to. Perhaps his cheating had been a blessing in a sexual disguise.

Regardless, it wasn't a wise decision to think about Niyol the way I was, mostly because we were two very different people, heading in two very different directions—both physically and metaphorically. Niyol was running from something, while I was simply taking a break.

Under my breath, I laughed, then walked to the picnic table, quickly readying my food before I sat beside him. Our thighs brushed together. And regardless of what I knew was right, I couldn't find it in me to move. Niyol didn't either, other than to eat some food himself. In fact, the longer we sat that way, eating in silence, the more relaxed I became—as did he, it seemed.

One and a half hot dogs in and hallelujah bells chimed in my stomach. Unable to hold back, I moaned when the last greasy bite slid down my throat. Niyol cleared his throat, drawing my gaze back to him.

His eyes narrowed as he spoke. "Be careful there." He nodded to my now bare plate. "You might just bite into your arm."

Grinning, I licked the dribble of ketchup off the corner of my mouth. His eyes zeroed in on the movement, and I immediately lost my smile. Everything this man did was sexual, and I was beginning to think he'd been planted in my life just to test my resistance. What I needed to do was move past Landon, be my own person, not lust after some bad dude. Even though one night with said bad dude would most definitely be worth it on the libido front. Niyol wasn't all sweet innocence himself. And those super, not-so-secret, sexy stares he gave me were like tiny orgasmic explosions just waiting to happen.

"Why don't you get some rest? I'll be okay on my own." I stood from my seat and brushed the mud off my jeans the best that I could.

He scowled down at the fire but didn't respond. I knew he had to be tired, especially since he'd been the one to do all the major work today. In fact, the more I thought about things, the worse I felt. Shoving the duties onto him this afternoon and going to sleep like I had wasn't one of my finer moments. Plus, our little argument, and what had happened between us, still weighed heavily on me.

Niyol never did answer, so I looked up at the dark sky, savoring the warmth as the fire filled the air.

The night was sticky and humid, yeah, but there was something soothing about the heat of a campfire, in hot or cold temperatures. The stars and moon were at their brightest tonight. And though my aversion to nature and the outdoors had always kept me in hotels and resorts in the past, I couldn't help but wonder if I'd been missing something all those years by never going with my brothers and Dad. This was incredibly peaceful, fear of wild animals or not.

My thoughts jumped to Landon for some reason again. He always took me to fancy hotels and the finest of restaurants, never one for outdoorsy stuff either. If anything, Landon was more of a *princess* than I was. That thought made me smirk. It was easier to think of him as a wuss than it was to think of him as any sort of royalty.

Two days before I found him with that woman last spring, we'd just had blueprints drawn up for a house—the one he was having built so we could move in together after the wedding. Over and over, I'd told him I didn't need to have fancy things, that his apartment was fine, but Landon was loaded—a trust-fund baby. There wasn't anything that he couldn't buy, except for me, of course.

I liked simplicity. I liked things uncomplicated. From life events, to the type of house I thought he and I were going to be raising our children in.

Sitting there now, eating hot dogs in the middle of the night next to an ex-con, of all people, I'd never felt more at ease. More simplistic, though I knew things were anything but. And the best part of it all? There was no more terrible longing in my gut. Not a single burn of unease in my throat when I swallowed. I wasn't sure if I was losing my mind, or if it was just the processed foods messing with my head. Either way, I liked feeling completely content. And I liked it even more that I could do it without having Landon with me.

Smiling to myself, I leaned back and patted my stomach, then wiggled my back against the edge of the table to scratch another itch. A shower would be on the agenda soon, but the night sky was so beautiful that I wasn't quite ready to stop looking at it. The Colorado stars truly burned brighter than any others I'd seen.

"What time should we leave in the morning?" I asked.

When Niyol didn't answer me again, I turned to him.

His jaw flexed as he stared at the fire. Did the flames mesmerize him like they did me? I touched his arm to get his attention and he jumped a little, only to move and grab a bag of marshmallows at his left.

"Early."

Face unreadable, he drew up two sticks from the ground and handed me one.

"Thank you," I whispered as I grabbed it. Following his lead, I rummaged through the bag of marshmallows with my other hand. Both of us put three on the ends of our sticks. "I've never done this before." I grinned, weirdly giddy at the prospect.

"What, roast marshmallows? How could you not have?" His eyebrows rose. "Even *I've* done it."

We stood and leaned over the fire.

"Guess it's just another thing to knock off the ole bucket list." I nudged him with my elbow.

A bigger frown covered his lips at my words, while secrets found homes behind his eyes once more. I wanted to ask him what was upsetting him this time, even though I kind of already knew. It was me and him, together. What happened between us, most of all.

When the silence got to be too much, once the marshmallows were consumed, I found myself making a terrible decision. One that would forever haunt me.

I just didn't know it at the time.

"Let's play a game." I sat on a log that served as a seat next to the fire. Once the marshmallow gunk was wiped off my fingertips, I inched as close to the flames as I could without getting scorched. Even though it was mid-July, the weather warm, I couldn't get close enough to it.

"What kind of game are we talking?" To my surprise, he took a seat on the ground next to me.

"How about Never Have I Ever?"

"Isn't that a drinking game?"

"Yup. But we'll improvise." I shimmied in place. Mostly to try and ease the itches on my back.

"And how will we do that?" he asked.

I considered my answer, thinking of all the different ways we could do this, until an idea popped into my head.

"Okay, so, see this?" I held up my marshmallow stick. With the end, I traced a line in the dirt in front of us. One side labeled *N*, the other *S*.

Niyol leaned over, eyeing my work. "Yep."

"You know how the game works, right? One of us asks a question and if you've done it, you have to take a shot, or whatever." He nodded, eyes drawn together in concentration as I continued. "Since we don't have either a shot glass or alcohol, then I'll mark a tally in the dirt under the correct initial instead when you haven't done it. In the end, whoever has the least tally marks will win."

"And what'll the winner get?" he asked, dark brows bunched together.

"Hmm…" I tapped my chin with my finger. "How about we get to ask one major favor of the loser?"

"Anything?"

My stomach dipped when our stares collided. The firelight reflected in his eyes, made him look beyond tempting. Maybe I should have disregarded the stakes altogether. Or figured out some other game that might not cause me to possibly wind up as his sex slave—not that he *wanted* me to be his sex slave. But I'd have done anything to know the person behind those dark-brown eyes of his, and this was the quickest way of doing so. Which was exactly why I said what I did.

"Yes. Anything."

More silence followed, other than the echo of insects. His elbow grazed my thigh, and I looked the other way again, not wanting him to see how one simple touch of his skin against mine turned me into a puddle of mush.

I swallowed, then looked back at him once more—he was just that magnetic. His hair covered his forehead like always, his eyes barely visible through the strands. The stubble he'd been sporting yesterday was already thickening. I broke my gaze away once more and refocused on the dirt. My hand shook as I brought the stick to my lap and he cleared his throat, likely sensing the tension.

"Okay," he began as I twisted my hands around the wood. "Never have I ever flown in an airplane."

I stayed still, while Niyol marked a line. "You've never ridden in an airplane?" I asked.

"Nope. My turn. Never have I ever kissed a dude before."

"Duh," I huffed out. "Okay. Never have I ever read a book for pleasure." I stayed still, because reading had always been a pastime of mine, but he didn't move either, surprising me. So, I added in a clause. "A book that wasn't required reading for school."

Still, he didn't mark a tally.

I frowned. "What have you read, exactly?"

"Does it matter?" he grumbled, instantly defensive.

My eyes narrowed, the word *yes* was on the tip of my tongue. But the challenging glare he gave me back wasn't worth the fight.

"I spent three months in solitary. Books were all I had." He dropped his chin to his chest causing his hair to drape over his cheeks and eyes even more.

"Why were you in solitary confinement?" I asked.

"People run their mouth behind bars, and I've got a temper. Beat the shit out of another guy who called me some names."

"Do Emily and Lisa know?"

He shook his head. "No point in upsetting them if it's already in the past."

The silence between us grew stagnant after that, the air pressing tightly inside my lungs. I struggled to breathe. Niyol was so young when he was put in jail—just barely a man. Yet he'd been through so much. With his own father, what the man did to him, most of all.

Without thought, I reached for his hand. No matter how many times I told myself to leave him be, I couldn't help but touch him in some way or another.

"Hey. You don't have to talk about it anymore. It was stupid of me to even ask. I'm not even sure why I did. Sometimes I just talk and don't know what I'm saying and before I figure it out, the questions are already out, and regrets are made and I… I'm rambling." I bit down on my thumbnail, looking between his stick and the fire.

"You're good." Two seconds passed, then five, then fifteen… something flipped at twenty, and the soft mood he'd shown me briefly was eradicated. He pulled his hand away and said, "But I'm done with these sissy questions."

He stood; tall, proud, angry.

I blinked quickly, trying to shrug it off. "We can stop playing. It's just some stupid game." I swallowed hard, looking away.

"You scared, Princess?" Energy radiated off him like barbed wire with an electric charge. He reached into his back pocket, grabbed his ratty blue hat, and shoved it on backward over his mop of hair. That's when he turned to me and said, "Because I'd really like to make this game a little more interesting if you don't mind…"

Crap. *Now* I was scared.

CHAPTER FIFTEEN

Niyol

"Never have I ever jerked a dude off."

Not that I was surprised, but she didn't reach over to put a fucking tally under her stupid box like me.

Her eyes no longer lingered on mine the way they had when she'd first woken up though—like all she could ever see was me. Thank fuck for that, because one of us had to get our shit together and it sure as hell wasn't looking to be me.

Summer was getting to me, pushing me off track with her sweet blue eyes, pretty lips, and soft personality. And I wasn't as strong as I thought I was.

When she was asleep earlier, I'd sat on the picnic table for a long time, trying to figure out how to tell her that I was sorry for being a dick this morning, but at the same time, I needed her to know that what happened between us was still a mistake. More so on my end than hers. I should've told her no, stopped her, it wasn't right of me to want it, when she and I weren't meant to be nothing more than two people who shared a car and a week together. But the man in me couldn't say no. Fucker that I was, Summer's mouth around my cock was the most beautiful thing I'd ever witnessed in my life.

Still, no matter how many ways I spun the excuse around, about her and I keeping our distance, I couldn't let myself agree. Not when all I wanted was to figure out a way to make it happen again.

"It's my turn now so—"

"I get five in a row. That's how I wanna play."

She scoffed. "That's not how this works."

"And I'm not one to follow the rules, don't you know that by now?" I looked at her and winked.

"You're being... *mean*."

I laughed.

Mean? I don't remember the last time someone called me mean, if ever. Arrogant, fucker, dipshit, douchebag, those were more the norms.

Ignoring her, I kept at it with the game. "Never have I ever given a blowjob." I leaned forward, marking another tally, knowing damn well what her answer was. If being an ass, or as she put it *mean*, meant keeping her at a distance, then so be it.

Chicken-shit move for a chicken-shit guy. Apparently, I was more like Pops than I'd hoped.

"I'm not answering that when you damn well know the answer." She stood and shook her head. "I don't understand this. I'm trying so *hard* to get along with you. But it's like, the harder I try, the more of a jerk you become." She tossed her stick into the fire, stomping on our initials.

Apparently, the game was over. But if she were forfeiting, I won by default.

Why the hell, though, did winning make me feel like shit?

"I'm going to the bathroom to shower, and *you*... Just go to bed. Maybe a little sleep will help you become less of a *jerk*." She grabbed the flashlight off the table and took off toward the Rover.

I stood to follow, forgetting the stakes of the game. Asshole or not, I would never let her go shower alone in the middle of the night when any random dipshit could be out there waiting to pounce.

"You're not going anywhere without me." I snaked an arm out in front of her.

"Yes. I am." She put a hand on her hip, challenging me with a smirk.

When all I did was stare at her, she huffed and went to get her bag from the Rover.

I pulled the hat off my head and dragged my fingers through my hair, trying to get it together. Calm the fuck down.

"If you're gonna shower, I'm coming, too."

"Fine. Whatever," she fired back, her voice now muffled inside the trunk.

Wordlessly, I dug through my duffle on the picnic table, first needing to find my knife, then my smokes. After a few minutes, I came up empty in the cigarette department. I took a step back, looked under the tables, around the campfire, but found nothing. Now that I thought about it, I hadn't had one since I got up this morning.

"Summer," I said as I spun around. "Have you seen my cigar…" I blinked. Summer was gone. "Damn it, woman." She'd gone on ahead without me.

It wasn't even two minutes later that a loud scream sounded from the other side of the road. I could see the lights from the bathrooms, the open door, too. I took off across the road, jumping through some low-slung bushes to get there faster. I drew my knife from my boot, ready to defend, to kill whoever or *whatever* the fuck was out there. An unseen threat, a pissed-off RD who wanted revenge for my dad, or even an animal looking for his latest meal. The thoughts spurred me through the woods even faster, my hands shaking as I gripped the handle of my knife against my thigh even tighter.

God, if something happened to her…

Heart in my throat, I raced through the first layer of brush and trees even faster, then I bolted through the bathroom doors, only to stop short at what I saw. Summer was curled in a ball on the floor, wearing nothing but my sweatshirt. Her wide blue eyes were filled with tears and the second she saw me, she began to sob harder.

"Are you hurt?" I dropped to the floor beside her and pulled her to my chest. When all she could do was gasp, I said, "Talk to me, Summer. Please."

"Th-there was something in here. An animal. He was big, h-had four legs…" She sucked in a shuddering breath. "I scared him away when I screamed, but I don't know if he's gone."

"Hey, shhh, he's gone. I promise. You're okay." I took a deep breath and let it go, thankful that was all it was.

I tucked my knife into my boot before I grabbed her hand and helped her stand. She was shaking so bad she didn't notice I had it. Not sure what she'd say or do if she knew I carried the weapon, but now wasn't the time to think about it. I reached around her body to yank her dirty jeans off the floor.

Her whole body trembled now as I helped wrap a towel around her waist. Against my chest she laid her head and squeezed the back of my shirt. "I'm sorry."

"For what?" I swallowed, stroking a hand over the back of her head.

"For freaking out just now." She sighed, dropping her voice to a whisper. "And for this morning. What happened between—"

"Stop." I touched her lips with my finger, failing to ignore the spark. "I didn't tell you no. If anyone needs to say sorry, it's me."

"But it was wrong. I know you love Maya. I mean, you're driving cross-country for her."

"She and I aren't together like that." Hadn't been like that but for one night, really. If anything, Maya was my escape, a friend. A woman who'd been there for me through a lot of my shit. That was all.

"Oh. I didn't know."

"Didn't expect you to." I squeezed my eyes shut, exhaling. "I'm not in a place for a relationship anyway."

"Yeah." She laughed a little. "Same. We're both kinda messed-up right now, so I guess this trip feels a little like fate. Two lost people, coming together to find a little light at the end of our dark tunnels."

"My whole life's been dark. No light for me." But I'd like to think I could find myself a flashlight along the way.

As much as I didn't want to, I couldn't help but agree about the fate part of her analogy. This kind of did feel like we were meant to take this trip together, even though fate had always fucked me over in the past. What made it any different now?

I wasn't supposed to be happy, not with a good girl like Summer. If anything, I was supposed to be a miserable shit, who lived a miserable world, with miserable people, who never found anything good. It was hell to think such shitty thoughts, but when you grew up the way I did, optimism wasn't reality. It was a dream.

"Hey, Niyol?" Her eyes were rimmed red when I lowered my chin to look at her again. More tears had slipped out of the corners, and I brushed them away with my thumbs. I hated seeing women cry.

"Can we be friends now?" Her bottom lip quivered.

Christ, this woman… Was she trying to rip out my heart?

I pulled her into another hug, inhaling her hair as I stroked the long strands. "Yeah, Summer. We can be friends." But anything other wasn't possible.

After soaking my shirt with her tears, I leaned over and kissed her temple—a natural reaction. A *friend's* reaction.

"Let's get you back to the campsite. We'll both shower in the morning."

She nodded and laid her head on my shoulder.

As we stepped outside, though, an uneasy feeling washed over me. I stiffened, my arm tightening around her back. My knife damn near burned a hole in my pocket but reaching for it would likely freak out Summer.

It felt like we were being watched. It was a feeling I'd had every moment of my life.

I looked left, then right, eyes narrowing.

Summer must've caught on.

"Everything okay?" she asked as I flashed my phone screen around the woods.

Other than something scurrying up a tree, I couldn't see a thing.

"Yep." I clicked it off, hurrying her through the wooded trail, hoping my paranoia was caused by my lack of sleep.

Within minutes, we were back at the site, the fire still blazing hot. Summer seemed to have relaxed a little, but I was a livewire, unable to shake away the feeling that someone was out there. Someone was watching. Someone was hunting us.

"You thirsty? I got us a couple bottles of water." I cleared my throat and grabbed one from my bag, hoping she didn't see my shaking hands when I handed it over.

"Thank you." I watched as she sat on the bumper of her car, bottom lip pulled between her teeth as she opened the lid. Seconds later, she guzzled it half down.

If I hadn't been such an ass to her during that fucking game, none of this would've happened. I shook my head, vowing—a-fucking-gain—to knock off the attitude.

"God, I'm so itchy." She squirmed, reaching behind her back, under her shirt.

"You want me to look?" I stood in front of her, frowning. "Could be poison ivy or something."

She nodded, then gulped the rest of her water back, wetness dribbling over her chin.

More movement rustled the trees to my right, and a huge gust of wind pushed through the site. Instinct had me reaching into my pockets, though my knife was in my boot. Yet nothing popped out, other than something small and furry. Black and white. A damn raccoon.

I gritted my teeth and wondered why I was so fucking worried. Was it because of Summer? This new need to protect her? Nobody knew where we were, as far as I knew—other than Lisa and Emily.

There again, you should never underestimate the RDs. Especially ones who might be looking for vengeance.

Most of the time, my instincts were right, which was why the decision I made was the right one.

"Thinking we should sleep in the backseat of your truck tonight." Lock the doors too. Every noise, every gust of wind, every snap of the fire would be fucking with my head if we slept outside. If anything, I should've packed us up and left, found a hotel nearby, but freaking her out any more than she already was could end badly. And being on the road at night? We'd be like sitting ducks if there was a rogue out there.

"Because of the animals?" she asked.

"Yeah," I lied. "And it feels like rain too."

Summer didn't argue. Instead, we worked side-by-side to push the seats down in the back of her Rover. It'd be hell to sleep so close to her, but it'd be worth it at the same time. Even though she said she'd stay up and keep watch, too, I knew she wouldn't make it. And I didn't want her to have to, either.

Once the doors were locked, and my knife was tucked behind me out of sight, Summer lay face down next to me.

"Let me see that back now." There wasn't much I could do for her if she'd gotten into something. If she had, we'd grab meds tomorrow at the ranger station on our way out.

She yanked her arms out of my sweatshirt and tugged it up and over her shoulders. The material bunched around her neck. I almost told her to take it all off, so I could see better, but I knew that wouldn't be a good idea.

I only had so much control.

Bare skin, covered in tiny bumps, met my stare in the dome light. "It looks like you've been bit by something."

She groaned, squirming. "I'm so damn itchy." My heart started racing as she reached around to unclasp her bra. "I don't want anything to touch it."

Holding my breath, I glanced up to study her profile, exhaling heavily through my nose. Her eyes were shut, face pinched. She looked uncomfortable as shit.

"I'm sorry," I said, feeling guilty. Something I wasn't used to. Letting her lay on the ground earlier, even over the sleeping bag, probably hadn't been a good idea.

"It's not your fault."

"I can put some water on it. See if that helps."

"Okay."

I reached for another bottle of water, wishing I'd have thought of bug spray, even ice. Using a spare shirt of mine, I poured the warm water over it, soaking the bottom. Holding my breath once more, I worked the wetness over her back. In the spots where she wasn't bitten, her skin was smooth and warm. Intoxicating to touch. Next to my darkness, her pale skin shone bright in the light. I was tainted compared to her. Dirty, even.

Pleasure and fear combined inside me as I continued to clean her. Bits of mud washed away, which probably hadn't helped with her itching. My gaze flickered to her face again. Her lips were parted, breathing unsteady—whether from me or the itching, I didn't know. If I hadn't been freaked out about what might happen afterward, I'd have bent over and kissed each mark until I had her moaning beneath me in pleasure. No matter how hard I'd fought this connection we'd developed, Summer had wedged herself under my skin. And I was ninety-nine-percent sure I liked her there.

"Are you done?" she whispered when I paused, my hand frozen in the air above her back.

My fingers shook when I set my hand on my knee, and I nodded, even though I knew she couldn't see me.

Blonde hair hung over the top of my hoodie, covering part of her face now. Unable to help myself, I reached down and tucked it over the other side, my fingers trembling even more. She shivered at my touch, and tiny goosebumps erupted over her skin.

Touching her like that reminded me of the time when I was thirteen and first had my hands on a woman's naked body. Even though I never actually fucked her, it still terrified me.

No matter, I continued to run my hands through the length of her hair, that same flowery smell I was already hooked on hitting my nose deep—making my gut go tight.

"Hmm," she moaned, her body soft, compliant. The sound causing me to shut my eyes.

How the fuck could I feel this way for a woman I'd only really known for three days?

God, I was nothing but a bastard who thought with his dick. That had to be it. Summer was the first woman I'd been alone with in two years. The first woman I'd touched, kissed…

Her skin was a softness my hands hadn't known in a long, long time.

Reopening my eyes, I greedily moved the tips of my fingers down her back, around her bites, letting myself savor the maze between.

She shivered. "That feels nice."

Her words were my last straw. The reason I lowered my forehead to her cheek and whispered, "I'm so damn sorry."

She froze. "For what?"

"Everything." I squeezed my eyes shut and pulled back before I dropped a kiss to her shoulder.

Slowly, she slipped her arms back into my sweatshirt, pulled her bra off underneath, then rolled over onto her side, facing me. "You have no reason to be sorry."

I settled down next to her, mirroring her position. The edge of the folded-down seats dug into my ribs, but I didn't care.

"I've been a dick." Temptation had me settling my hand along the curve of her waist, while desire and the need to be closer had me pressing my forehead to hers.

"It's okay." She shivered. "I haven't exactly been a sweetheart either."

"Hmm." Little did she know that everything she'd done and said within the past three days was a sucker-punch to my heart—the best and worst kind.

"You need to sleep." She reached over, touched my hand.

No matter how tired I was, sleeping wasn't an option. Not only was I freaked out about whoever could be outside, but being this close to her, her hot breath grazing my lips, made me feel like the universe was at my fingertips and she was the bright sun circling me. The little bit of goodness I'd been searching for. The goodness that Maya had given me once, only it was two times more powerful with Summer.

"I don't want to do it anymore." I stroked her cheek, holding her gaze.

"Do what?"

"Fight with you."

"Then we won't." She leaned back a bit, saying the words so fast, I had to wonder if she even knew what she was agreeing to.

I *knew*, though. I also knew that if I didn't argue, things would get worse between us in other ways. Being away from the RDs and going to stay with Maya was what I needed. The right thing to do. But Summer? She was proving to be the thing I suddenly wanted more than anything else.

"And about this morning…" She sucked her bottom lip in, eyes skimming over my face. "I just wanted to make you feel better. You had that dream, and I had a dream, and we were both broken and—"

"You had a dream too?"

It couldn't have been any worse than mine. Pops finding me, tying me up, knifing the dragon tat off my back… It was the way of the RDs. You leave, turn your back on the club for good, you lose everything, including the permanent ink on your skin. I'd seen it done before. Too many times. I'd gotten out of it because of my prison sentence, my quick escape out of town. And if Flick really was the leader now, he wasn't as set in Pops' ways.

But it could still happen.

"Yeah, but it was nothing." She shrugged it off, messing with her bracelet again. Her eyes were distant as she stared over my shoulder. I reached out and touched her hand.

"You okay?"

She blinked, refocusing on my face with a small smile. "I'm tired."

"Liar." I frowned, touching her chin. "Tell me about your dream."

"It really was nothing. Just stuff to do with my ex."

My jaw clenched. I had no right to be jealous, but something in me was. Something very stupid and new.

"He hurt you?" I asked.

"Not physically, no."

I shut my eyes, breathing her in as comfort. If any man so much as laid a finger on her, I'd kill them.

"Back to the point of this whole conversation." She leaned back, touching my shoulder with her own. I reopened my eyes, already missing her warmth. "Me doing what I did to you this morning? It was unacceptable."

I couldn't stop myself from grinning back at her. The rat bastard in me thought what she'd done was *perfectly* acceptable. Phenomenal, really.

"Don't look at me like that." She rolled her eyes, dropping her head to the side. "Besides, I don't really *want* anything like that in my life right now."

"Why're you bringing it up then?" I was just as much to blame, seeing how I didn't try to stop her.

"Because I want you to know that it won't happen again, it was a mistake."

It was a mistake in her world, but I didn't want it to be. I wanted her to want me, fight for me, as much as I suddenly did her. Even if all we had together was this trip.

"And you can trust me to drive you without having to worry about me... *seducing* you, by the way."

"Seducing me?" I laughed. She was fucking cute if she thought what she'd done was just seduction. Her mouth on my cock was a top-fucking-notch *memory*, one I'd take with me everywhere now.

It didn't matter what she said, or how many times she tried to play it off as nothing, because there was no way in hell I could *stop* thinking about it. And the longer I lay there with her, her flowery scent invading me, the more I realized that my guilt over wanting to be with her was lessening. And without that guilt, resisting anything else she offered me would become impossible.

CHAPTER SIXTEEN

Summer

"Tell me about Maya."

I knew things were getting dangerous between us, the sensation in the air stifling, like pins prickling my skin. Regardless of how much I wanted to curl into Niyol's side, tell him to ignore any last doubt he might have had and be with me, even if only for the night, I couldn't. He'd hate himself if he did.

I wasn't dumb. I knew he was likely going to San Diego not only to get away from his old life, but to see if he could rehash something with this Maya woman. He might claim not to want her like that, but he wouldn't know until he saw her. And the last thing I needed was to become someone's second choice, someone's *fling*.

Surprisingly, he leaned back like I did—relaxed, staring at the roof when he answered. "I met Maya when I was nineteen. Her uncle's Flick, actually." There was no emotion on his face as he spoke, but I could hear the genuine adoration in his words at the same time. Awe, really.

"And who's Flick again?" I asked, ignoring the lump in my throat.

"The club VP, now president. Apparently he took over after Pops went to prison."

I nodded as he continued, having no idea what the role of a VP or president was. Motorcycle clubs were something of a conundrum to me, like Niyol was. All I knew was what was portrayed of them in movies and TV shows: they often broke the law, but rarely got caught.

"One summer, Maya and her mom moved into Flick's place. They'd been running from Maya's crazy-ass dad, who was the VP of some club out in Arizona." His dark brows furrowed in thought. "Anyways, I rode over with Flick on my bike to help them move in. The rest is history, I guess."

All too easily I could imagine Niyol on a motorcycle. The thought had my tummy fluttering with excitement. Dressed in one of those black leather vests, long hair blowing around his face… It was a hazardous thought to have, mainly because I could effortlessly envision being the girl on the back of his bike, hands tightly wrapped around his muscular torso.

"Come on, there's more to it than that." Though I meant to sound playful, I was barely holding it together. I was a fool to think I would ever be someone he could fall for, but my stupid heart just wasn't getting the memo like my brain. Besides that, if Niyol was looking for romance at all, he probably wouldn't choose it with me.

He grinned at me, adding a wink. "Well, she did remind me of an anime character when I saw her. All big, hazel eyes, porcelain-like skin. Cute as hell and dressed like a badass in leather pants and shit."

"Oh. Is she, um, Native American like you are?"

"Nah, half Chinese, half white."

My lumpy throat burned even more with unwelcomed jealousy. "I bet she's stunning."

I felt him shrug against my shoulder. "The two of us would sneak away together when I came by on the weekends after that. We'd talk and shit. Archer would always get mad, telling me bros before hos, but Slade wasn't even a brother yet, just seventeen. He was too busy putting his nose in a book to notice where I was half the time back then." He paused. "Maya was actually the first girl I'd ever really been friends with. She was fun. Listened to my shit. Made me laugh, too."

"Bet you lost your virginity before you even knew what virginity meant." I nudged his thigh with my knee.

He groaned. "You make me sound like a fucking slut."

"Were you?" I asked, genuinely curious.

"No. Maya was my first."

For some reason, that hurt me a little more, though I didn't have any right to feel that way. God, why was I asking?

He blew out a slow breath. "Most of that summer was spent surrounded by crazy-ass bikers. If anything, she was like a sister to me, least at first. Then the night before she was set to leave, we got a little too drunk on moonshine and started messing around. She wanted to do it and I thought she was cool."

I slowly rolled to my back and looked to the roof. The last thing I wanted was to see his face light up for another woman.

The stars weren't as bright now through the sunroof, the moon hiding behind a layer of clouds. We might have been locked inside a car, but I could still smell the campfire flames from outside. It was distracting, and I needed that.

"Tell me about this." He tugged at my shell bracelet, breaking me out of my thoughts. I pulled my arm up and toyed with the ends. "You're always playing with it," he added.

"It was my mother's."

"Was?" he asked.

I nodded. "She died giving birth to me. When I turned sixteen, my dad gave it to me."

"Shit. I didn't know." He rolled over to face me, his warm breath barely smelling of cigarettes. I hadn't seen him smoke all day, and secretly I knew why. He'd be angry if he knew, but I was saving his life when I threw those things out the window this morning when he'd fallen asleep on the road.

"I'm fine. It's hard to miss someone you never met."

"That's how I am about my own mom," he said, surprising me with his truth.

"Yeah?"

He nodded. "You ever wonder what she was like?"

"Mmm, yes. All the time, actually. That's part of the reason why I jumped at the chance to drive you." I smiled, feeling my throat close off a little. "Mom loved the beach. Especially the ones in San Diego, according to my father. By going there, I feel like I'll be closer to her somehow."

"Did she name you?" he asked, his voice going a little softer. Shyer, maybe. I could see the blush on his cheeks.

"Nope. That'd be my dad. I was born in the Summer. July. My father thought it'd be a nice dedication to her, I guess." But really, I hated my name. The memories I never got to experience with a woman who had died because of me.

"Enough about me." I shook my head, feeling my smile wobble a little. I didn't talk about this for a reason. It was too hard. "What happened to Maya?" I asked, changing the subject—hating how I had to use his first lover as my scapegoat. "How did you guys end things?"

"She moved to California at the end of that summer. Said she couldn't do the biker life anymore."

I rolled back over to my side, too curious not to see his face. Loss accompanied his dark memories this time, I could see it in his eyes. I longed to comfort him but didn't know how.

"That had to be hard."

"It was. But not because I wanted her as my old lady. She was my best girl-friend. One of the only people who understood what it was like, besides my brothers."

"That's so sad."

He shrugged again, his go-to movement when he obviously didn't want to expand on a subject.

"After she left, did you two keep in touch?" I asked.

A nod. "Yeah. We tried. Besides my stepmom and Emily, she was the only one who called me when I was locked up."

"And now?" I held my breath, waiting.

"And now what?"

"Are you *interested* in her... like that?"

"You mean, do I want to fuck her and make her my girl?"

I rolled my eyes and shoved his shoulders. "You are such a crass, dirty man."

He laughed, then reached up and held my hand over his heart. "I don't know what I want..." He waited a beat, then shut his eyes. "Other than to get out of Illinois. Away from the club. It'll be good to see Maya, sure, but I'm worried if she sees me she'll change her mind. Tell me to go. I'll be fucked."

My stomach tightened at his words. Niyol had been pushed aside by his family for his entire life. Abandoned and disowned, abused... He didn't know his mom, and his own father was a monster. Sure he had Emily and Lisa, but they weren't blood.

"She'd be an idiot to turn you away, Niyol." He blinked, narrowing his eyes at me. I rolled mine at his shocked expression. "I'm serious." I tightened my hold on his shirt, squeezing. "Like I've said before, you act all hard and tough, even mean sometimes. But there's this underlying softness inside of you that any woman would be a fool not to notice and love."

I winced at the L-word, knowing I'd said too much. Letting down my guard, exposing my vulnerable, aching heart, was a bad habit of mine. What I needed to do was shut my mouth and go back to sleep instead of telling him the truth that I couldn't hide.

Niyol *was* a good person. He'd just never been told so before.

"You trying to make me cocky, Princess?"

For once, I was thankful for his nickname and sarcasm. "It's amazing you can eat, seeing as how you are so *full* of yourself."

He made a goofy face, squinted his eyes. The view was so silly and... so not the Niyol I'd come to know.

"Will you ever go back?" I asked, too nosy for my own good.

He frowned. "Go back to the club?"

"Yeah. There." This was really none of my business. But for someone who talked so highly about his friends, Slade and Archer and even Flick, I couldn't help but wonder why he was so adamant about getting away.

"I'm not welcome there anymore."

"How do you know? Did they tell you that?"

He seemed to think about his words, eyes narrowed, lips pursed. Then finally, he sighed and rubbed a hand over his mouth, like it pained him to speak. To say what was on his mind.

"It's complicated."

"Because of what you did to your father."

He nodded.

"But did they actually *tell* you that you weren't allowed?" I asked again.

"No. But I got a letter before I left prison."

"What did it say?"

He groaned. "God, you sure do ask a lot of questions."

"I'm pretty sure I was an investigative reporter in my previous life." I smirked. "I kind of have a knack for being nosy."

Reaching over, Niyol tapped said nose, only to trail his knuckles down the back of my cheek. "You got a cute nose, by the way."

"Nuh, uh. No subject changes." I grabbed his hand, pulling it down, but that was a mistake because, soon, he interlaced our fingers together, holding me still.

I swallowed hard, blinking in surprise, but I made no move to pull away.

Against my palm, I savored the touch of his rough callouses, wondering, again, how they might feel against my naked flesh. If he was trying to truly distract me, it was working, because suddenly, looking him in the eyes, feeling his simple, yet intimate hold, I lost every single word inside my very frazzled brain.

"What are you thinking about?" Niyol searched my face, his voice cracking a little.

"I-I don't know."

"Summer…" He leaned on his elbow to look down at me, eyes filled with warm curiosity, and a softness he was starting to share more than not. Strong cheekbones met wide brown eyes, two lips I imagined kissing all night, though I knew that ship had sailed. Still, I took in all of his features, greedy for every inch I could devour with my gaze—in lust with the scruff on his chin and the small tattoo that ran down the side of his neck. "Tell me."

I swallowed the painful lump in my throat and averted my gaze. "I'm tired."

"Look at me," he ordered less than five seconds later. His voice cracked again, desperation clinging to those three simple words.

Pulling my lower lip between my teeth, I did as he asked, clinging to the top of the sleeping bag, begging for a shield that could hide whatever emotion I might have been exposing.

His eyebrows furrowed. "Tell me what you're thinking about."

"I don't know, I told you."

"I don't believe you."

A finger touched my cheek, holding me in place, the sensation sending tiny bolts through my body. I shivered as he moved his hand down my neck only to stop when it settled over my heart. He continued to search my face, like he wasn't sure what he was looking for. A sign from God to back away? To move closer?

"What are *you* thinking about?" I turned the question back on him, needing to know the secrets behind his eyes first. The dark coiled emotion hidden in those muddy pools called to me.

A crackle of lightning sparked through the air outside of my Rover. I jumped, automatically leaning closer to him. Droplets of rain hit the glass just seconds later, peppering across the metal roof. The loud boom of thunder that followed had me letting go of his hand and wrapping my arm around his waist. He mirrored my position, squeezing me close and murmuring soft words I couldn't make out.

In the end, though, it was the look on his face that had my breath catching. What it meant most of all.

Desire.

Need.

Something more.

"Please," I swallowed. "Tell me what you're thinking." My composure was slipping, my heart racing in my chest. The thunderous beat was surely louder than the ones outside.

The air grew thicker, stifling. The unspoken words clung to us like millions of electric molecules.

"How 'bout I show you instead?"

That's when he did the last thing I expected him to do.

He kissed me.

CHAPTER SEVENTEEN

Niyol

My mind and body weren't my own. Summer looked so damn sad and beautiful. I couldn't handle it, hated even thinking that I might be the reason for that pain in her eyes.

But then she moaned against my lips, parting her own, accepting me. *Taking me.*

The taste of marshmallow invaded my tongue, and I knew right then, this was where I wanted to be—where I was meant to be.

Needing her closer, I laid down on my side, both hands cupping her neck as I sampled every inch of her mouth. The windows fogged up, humidity blanketing the space. Sweat crept down the back of my neck, but I still shuddered, craving her skin against mine.

Summer's legs wrapped around me, drawing me closer as I moved to lay on top of her. I groaned, unable to stop the sound when she rolled her hips upward. It was just like this morning, but deeper, closer, needier. Desperate. I was so fucking desperate. For her.

Something different flickered between us now, and as I pulled my mouth back, dropping kisses to her neck, tasting her sweet and salty skin, I realized how much I didn't want this to end.

Her and me, this thing we had, this connection? It was everything.

My hands roamed over her thighs, rubbing up and down, until they landed at the edge of her shorts. I lifted the sweatshirt up to her neck, urging it off. No hesitation, she lifted it over her head, blonde hair pooling around her like wings.

I groaned at the sight of her, naked, exposed, and moved lower, kissing the undersides of her creamy breasts, then sucking slowly on one, pink nipple. Right then and there, I looked into her blue eyes and finally lost the rest of my control.

I lost me.

"Sit up," I grumbled, pulling back just enough so I could watch her.

Eyes wide, she did as I asked, biting down on her lip. "Are you sure?"

"Yes."

So trusting, so fucking sweet… I'd never had a woman look at me the way Summer did. And I fucking loved it.

At the thought, I lost even more of my control. "Take off your shorts. I want to see every inch of you."

She paused, something in her holding her back. I touched her face with both of my hands to keep her with me, to tell her that this wasn't a mistake. If she craved me even half as much as I did her, then I wouldn't stop. I couldn't. I'd be the one dealing with the backlash later, not her.

"I'll make you feel good, Summer. Will you let me?"

She finally nodded, trembling at the same time. My fingers tightened on my lap as I sat up on my knees, mirroring her position. The rain fell harder, blocking us from the world outside. Possessiveness struck me with a slap to the heart, and I touched one hand to the curve of her waist to curb the sensation.

"What is this?" The question was whispered, her eyes alight, confused, but needy.

I reached up and touched the window to my left, tracing through the steam with messy letters. *B. E. A. U. T. I. F. U. L.* I spelled out. That's what this was between us.

Dressed in nothing but her panties, Summer grinned shyly as she lifted her own fingers to write something herself. *S. E. X. Y.*

I chuckled, lightness breaking through the terse emotions flaring through me. Then when she slowly turned her head to look back at me, with a smile so sweet on her lips, I couldn't help but say the words this time.

"Closer." I pressed my nose into her hair and inhaled.

"Anything." She did just that, bringing her naked chest against my shirt.

I could barely catch my breath as I wrapped my hands around her lower back, the chill of her skin the perfect counter to my hot hands. She shivered even more as I rubbed my palms over her bumpy shoulders, a circular motion of lust and comfort.

"Tell me to stop. That you don't want me like this." I breathed out the words in between kisses to her cheek, her chin, her neck.

She pulled her head back, blinking up at me. "I can't tell you to stop. Not when I need you."

The man in me who craved this woman cheered, and I pressed her hand to my chest as she rose on her knees even higher.

Slowly, she urged me onto my back. Then she straddled me like she'd done this morning. Hands frantic, she pulled my shirt up and over my head this time. I tossed it somewhere in the front seat, growling when she lowered her lips to my chest, then my nipples. She sucked on one, drawing circles around my stomach with her fingertips. But then she went lower—moving beneath the waistline of my pants. Her hot breath against my skin had me grinding my hips. I groaned, tossing my head back. She wrapped her tiny hand around my cock and stroked it up and down, pre-come already spilling from the head.

"Fuck." That felt good. This woman knew exactly what she was doing.

I rolled her back over and grabbed her hands, raising them above her head. Our breathing matched, chests rising and falling in sync.

"You're good at that, Princess."

She whimpered as I bit down on her shoulder blade, hard enough to leave a tiny mark, but not hard enough to hurt. God, I wanted to claim this woman—every inch of her—even though she never would be mine to claim.

"Don't move. Let me make you feel good." I sucked her bottom lip between my teeth, causing a low hum to sound in her chest.

When she whimpered out a soft, *Yes, please,* I continued to kiss and touch, moving down her gorgeous body, landing at the top of her panties. They were black, cotton, simple. Perfect. I nibbled on her hip, using my other hand to start the process of pulling them down—and down they went with the wiggle of her thighs and the fling of her foot.

"I've wanted to taste you since the second we first met." I nuzzled my nose against the soft patch of hair covering her pussy.

"Niyol," she whispered my name like a prayer, arching against my mouth.

I shut my eyes, losing myself as I parted the lips of her pussy, and licked her warm clit with one long stroke.

She shuddered. "Yes, that…" Then arched her back even higher—giving me just enough room to get my hands beneath her bare ass. My face was sweating, beads of it dripped down my temples, but I didn't care. Nothing else mattered.

Positioning myself deeper between her thighs, I sent out a silent prayer, asking for a little help, because foreplay was about as foreign to me as sex was these days. I'd only ever went down on one woman, and I'd been nineteen, though blowjobs were an almost day-to-day occurrence for me during my time at the club. Now the thought of anyone else's mouth around my cock besides Summer's made my chest throb.

Fuck was I in trouble.

As I covered her clit with my lips, she hissed, moving her hands from over her head. I let it happen this time, watching her under the dome light, using the sensation of her fingers digging into my scalp to calm me. Settle me. I sucked and pulled and licked like my fucking life depended on it.

"Niyol, yes. Like that. Don't stop."

My cock ached with the need to fill her. But I would not—*could not*—let that happen yet. So, I dug the pads of my fingertips into her skin instead, pulling one hand away to plunge a finger inside of her. She cried out even more, the sound wild and feral like the animals that probably surrounded us. But it wasn't enough. I wanted her screaming.

She arched even more, her knees squeezing my head. And soon she was coming hard against my lips, calling out my name on a long, shivering moan.

That was the exact moment I lost a piece of myself to her. One I should have done anything and everything to try and get back but didn't.

Probably never would.

CHAPTER EIGHTEEN

Summer

Thunder clapped in the distance, the sound sinister as it echoed off the mountains from outside the car. Niyol was still asleep, hair strewn over his face in a sexy, tousled way I was beginning to adore. With an arm thrown over his eyes, he looked younger, softer, and nothing like the broken man I'd come to know.

Shirtless, he was a sight to behold—all layered muscles that set my pulse racing when I stared too long. I studied the tattoos that lined his stomach and chest even more this time. Most were of the script variety, except for the tail of a red animal that drew my attention to the top of his left shoulder. Without even looking at his back, I already knew it was a dragon.

Unable to help myself, I reached out and lightly traced what I could see, wondering if it would forever be a reminder of a past he no longer wanted to embody. Could he have it removed? Did he *want* to have it removed? I knew so little about him. His wants and needs, other than starting over. Making a new life. A life I was suddenly hoping to be a part of somehow.

I wasn't stupid enough to think that a bout of amazing foreplay and an all-night cuddle-fest meant more than it did. But the romance-loving, girlie part inside of me was hardcore, attempting to take the reins and steer me in that direction.

Not wanting to go there this morning, I squeezed my eyes shut, forcing myself to remember the truth. That come this time next week, I'd be back at home, and Niyol would be in California, starting over.

A few lonely raindrops were still falling outside, landing on the roof of the Rover. From the looks of the sky through the sunroof, there was another storm brewing, but it seemed we had a while until it hit.

I slipped out of his hold, unlocking the trunk door. Niyol didn't even stir as I maneuvered my way onto the campsite. According to my cell, it was one in the afternoon, yet the thought of being behind schedule no longer mattered to me.

Regardless, I picked up our camp, needing something to do to bide my time until he woke. Most items outside were sopping wet from the night's storm. His duffle was the only thing that seemed unscathed, tucked beneath the picnic table where he'd left it.

The fire had long gone out, leaving just a dusting of smoke, along with a pile of gray-and-black ashes. The shift in weather from the day before was dramatic. Even hotter and stickier, like we'd been thrown in a pile of Colorado soup. Sweat dripped down my neck, into my hair, and by the time I finished, I knew I would need that shower I didn't get last night sooner than later.

An hour or so later, I woke Niyol and asked him to accompany me to the bathroom. No way was I going to take that trek by myself anymore.

"Are you okay?" I asked as we walked toward the outhouse, soap and shampoo tucked under my arms, our changes of clothes in his.

He nodded, staring down at the brush below our feet. "I'm good. Just ready to get on the road." His gaze darted from the path, then down to his right, an edge to him I couldn't ignore.

Was he already regretting what we'd done? My shoulders drooped at the thought. I'd wanted to hold on to our night for a little while longer. But it was looking as though that would not be the case.

Our hands brushed together as we approached the shower block. If he were any other man, I would have grabbed his fingers, interlaced them with my own. But this was Niyol, and I was Summer. Two very different people with two very different life goals.

With my stomach in my toes, I said over my shoulder as I walked inside the women's room, "I won't be long."

Head down, he nodded and walked toward the men's side. "I'll be quick too, and right next door if you need me."

Ten minutes later I slipped my slimy feet back inside my flip-flops, my body as clean as my back would let me get it. The bumps were still itchy as hell, but thankfully seemed to be scabbing over.

The wind had picked up outside, banging against the small building's shutters. Ignoring the sound, I put on a pair of cut-off sweats and my favorite Cubs' jersey. It had been a gift from my father on my twenty-first birthday. Though it was ten times too large, and clearly made for a man, I adored it because he'd picked it out for me on his own. Something he rarely did.

I loved my dad to pieces, but he was a workaholic, always at the hospital or his clinic. Usually, he had his receptionists or one of the nurses do the shopping for him, buying me perfume and makeup, expensive purses I never used. But this shirt, this *gift* had been from the heart for once.

There was a small circle mirror that hung over the one sink, and I wiped the steam away with a paper towel to study my face. I brushed my knotted waves back and pulled my hair into a side braid that hung over my shoulder. The spots on my neck brought forth by Niyol's mouth sent a blush to my cheeks and a smile to my lips. The memory of his face between my legs had my heart skipping beats at the same time.

I shouldn't have felt so giddy about any of this. But there I was, wondering if it was going to happen again. Wondering, too, if next time we could take it a step further.

A weather siren sounded in the distance. I blinked at my reflection, then pocketed my old underwear. As I gathered the rest of my stuff, something hard whacked against the side of the building.

"Holy crap." I jumped in place and dropped my shampoo bottle onto my toe. The one glass window on the building rattled as rain slapped the pane. A crash of lightning lit the room and the lights flickered—on, off, on, off.

Panicking, I unlocked the door and yanked it open, only to have it pushed back against my nose and forehead from the wind. Dizziness washed over me, and I gasped in pain, pressing a palm to my forehead as I fell back against the wall. Blood seeped out from over my eyebrow, and I quickly grabbed a paper towel to wipe it away.

A voice yelled from outside the door. I whipped my head to the left, just barely able to make out what he was saying over the whirling wind.

"Niyol?" I mumbled, somehow finding the strength to stumble toward the door again.

Just a foot away, I watched through the sudden downpour and wind as Niyol raced toward me from the men's room. My head thumped an angry rhythm against my skull, and I stumbled back to the wall, dizziness taking me over again.

The wind whipped through the trees while the weather siren wailed louder in the distance.

"Get in," he shouted over the ruckus. He wrapped an arm around my waist and hauled me back into the shower. "Hold onto me. Don't let go."

A noise, sounding a lot like a train, whistled. I knew the sound. Heard it many times before as a child who'd frequented Oklahoma a ton growing up.

"Oh, my God," I whispered. "Tornado."

As quick as his shaking hands could go, Niyol undid his belt from around his waist and tugged me to the ground. We landed with an oomph, and immediately I felt like Helen Hunt in *Twister*, as Niyol attempted to connect our bodies with it. It didn't work, of course, and he cussed, his eyes flickering up to meet mine in fear, even as he said, "It's okay. We'll be okay."

With my head still throbbing, I gripped his hand and lowered my cheek to his chest. We were at Mother Nature and God's mercy now. Nothing but a miracle could save us if a tornado struck this building.

CHAPTER NINETEEN

Niyol

"We'll get through this," I whispered into Summer's ear once more, her body trembling against mine.

Even as I clung to her, I couldn't help but wonder if this was it for me. For us both. Death in a Colorado campground. *Fucking hell.*

Something smashed against the side of the building, just as the glass from the window shattered to the floor. It sprayed over the stalls, barely missing my back. Summer's hands tightened even more around me as I gripped the back of her jersey. The lights went back on for a sec, only to go out completely. The roof creaked, rattling like it was seconds from ripping off. The building was made of cement, though, so if the roof held up, we'd be fine.

God, I hoped we'd be fine.

Pipes under the sink banged around, like it was more of an earthquake than a storm. I glanced back behind me to make sure things weren't breaking off, only to notice the door rattling open.

"Damn. I gotta go close that."

"No." She gripped my arms tightly as I began to pull away, her eyes glazed over. I frowned, watching her face. That's when I noticed a bloody bump along her hairline.

"You're hurt." I went to touch it, but she pushed my hand away, doing the unthinkable.

She yanked her body from mine with a grunt. I fell back, my shoulders slamming against the wall. Before I could blink, she stood and ran to the door, then used her shoulder to shove it closed.

"Get down!" I yelled as a branch flew through the broken window toward her head.

She yelped, falling to her knees. I crawled toward her, my throat tightening, the edge of her jersey torn.

"What the hell were you thinking?" I yanked her back toward the stall, never letting her go.

"I'm okay," she insisted as I pulled her to my chest.

Then with our backs plastered against the wall, hands interlocked, we waited it out until the end.

CHAPTER TWENTY

Summer

"The landlines are dead, I get that. But you mean to tell me all cell-phone towers are down as well?" I leaned forward onto a desk in the ranger station, avoiding the yellow glares of all the taxidermy on the wall.

This place was creeping me out, and the man running it today wasn't helping matters.

A monstrous pipe filled with tobacco in one hand and his yellow-and-green bird in the other, Mr. Park Ranger/Mountain Man Sam leaned back in his seat, eyeing me like a pirate. He'd not been the guy we checked in with the night before. If he had, I wouldn't have agreed to stay here. His gray brows matched his beard, but his head was bald with a tattoo that said *Mama's Boy*. God. We were officially in the Twilight Zone of Colorado.

"Yuuuup. Storm took out pretty much anything in its path." He tapped one hand across the wooden counter, gaze a little hazy. "Y'all got lucky it didn't get ya."

I shivered, watching him. Was that tobacco he was smoking in his pipe, or something else? I wouldn't be surprised—this *was* Colorado.

"You've *got* to be kidding me." I stepped back and folded my arms.

I wasn't mad at him, more so I was mad at our luck in general. My Rover was trashed. A huge tree had implanted itself into the roof. And my car held all of our stuff, including the phone chargers. Not that they'd work right now anyway.

Thankfully, I had insurance on my vehicle. But I kind of needed to talk to someone on the actual *phone* to get the rental car process started.

The door jingled as Niyol came barreling in. He moved to my side, hair pulled back and reminding me of a sexy samurai, minus the sword. I glanced down at his hands, noticing his duffle. It dripped along the tiled floor, building a puddle by his feet. Somehow, it had gotten blown under the car, managing to stay on our campsite. At least one of us had our stuff.

"Don't worry," Sam winked at me. "I'll get you two to town." Pirate Sam dumped his pipe gunk into a cup and tucked his parrot back into its cage. He motioned for us to follow, and after a shared look, Niyol and I did just that.

♥

With the advice of the nice car-rental man in the nearest town, we were able to find a quaint little bed and breakfast just a few blocks from a shopping center. Unfortunately, we couldn't get a replacement vehicle until that night. Something about hail damage from the storm, and a shortage of vehicles. My insurance company had also been slow to get back to me due to the phone lines being down. Then when we finally did connect, it took forever to get the proper paperwork in order. It was a huge mess, but I was dealing with it the best I could.

Inside the bed and breakfast, a lady with long brown hair and a sweet smile greeted us at a wooden desk to the left of the front door. Niyol hung back to my right, leaning over a couch. He'd looked at his dead phone at least twenty times in the past hour. I wondered who he was expecting a call from.

I glanced around the small lobby as we waited for our keys. The B and B was beautiful; homey-looking, in an antiquated sort of way. Buttercream-painted walls, paisley furniture, and hardwood floors that looked freshly refinished. There was also a fireplace, and a small love seat that sat kitty corner to a couch in front of it.

I was scared the owner would be disgusted by the sight of us, both dirty and disheveled—which was more my MO lately, it seemed. Thankfully, there was one room left, and she didn't blink an eye when she handed over the key.

She offered us cookies but apologized for not having anything for dinner. Told us about a restaurant down the road that we could get takeout at, and then let us be. I was wholeheartedly okay with her hospitality.

"You can shower first." I pointed to the bathroom when we stepped into our room.

Niyol set his duffle on a dresser, then sat on the edge of the bed with a low groan. He was just as worn down as I was.

"There's a Target close by. I'm gonna go grab some new things to get me through, then maybe pick up a couple of burgers for dinner."

In the middle of taking off his shoes, he froze, eyeing me from under his hair. "You're not going anywhere without me."

I rolled my eyes and sat next to him, nudging his shoulder with my own. "What, you think the big bad wolf will eat me alive along the quaint streets of this small Colorado town?" I snorted.

He didn't laugh. "I'm serious, Summer. Don't go anywhere without me."

"What's the big deal? I'll walk and be back in an hour, if that."

"Jesus, Summer, when I ask you to wait, just fucking wait, all right?"

I stiffened, my good mood faltering. So much for not fighting with me anymore. Instead of telling him off like I wanted, I decided to play the agreement-card. Secretly though, I'd just leave when he was in the shower.

"Fine. Go shower then." I scrunched up my nose. "You smell almost worse than I do."

He glared at me, distrusting, but did as I asked.

To ease that look in his eyes, I leaned back against the pillow on the bed, feigning relaxation as I flicked on the TV.

Once the shower began to run, I did what I said I wouldn't and snuck out fast, careful to let the door shut with a quiet click behind me.

At Target, I picked up a spare bra and some underwear, along with a few pairs of shorts and some t-shirts. Then I headed to grab the burgers I'd mentioned, even scooped up a bottle of wine for later at the gas station next door. Wine cured all ailments—made me numb, too. And after the past few days, numb would be a welcome feeling.

An hour later, just like I'd said, I was back in the lobby, half expecting Niyol to be waiting for me by the door, his demon eyes flaring. He wasn't though, and I couldn't help but grin in success as I rounded the hallway corner to head to our room.

Touting my fantastic skills, I giggled under my breath and said to myself, "See? I am perfectly capable of taking care of my—"

"Hey, there." I stalled at the deep voice, my elbow smacking the corner. At the view, my heart lurched into my throat.

An attractive, yet rugged-looking, blond guy stood outside our room, hair just barely grazing his shoulder, green eyes sparkling. Next to him was another hot guy, chin pressed against his chest, black hair, and eyes as menacing as Niyol's, glaring at me like I'd killed his puppy.

Scanning them quickly, I immediately spotted names on the fronts of their black leather vests, swallowing hard at what they said.

Slade and Archer.

Oh, God. These were Niyol's club friends. Question was… where was Niyol?

I looked to our door, before flashing them both a fake grin. "Can I help you gentlemen with something?"

The blond guy grinned wider, crossing his legs at the ankles. He reminded me of a young Fabio, but with so much more potential. Yet under all that hotness, I sensed danger. Something deadly with intent and mistrust, all directed at me. He was the one who spoke first. The one whose name patch said *Archer.*

"Nice night, yeah?" He tipped his head to the side, an even bigger smile lighting up his face. Two huge dimples encased his cheeks and, for a second, I nearly lost my grip on the bags. Scary or not, this man was incredibly good-looking.

"Um, yeah." I nodded fast, taking a slow step toward the door.

"Goin' somewhere, sweetness?" His accent said Irish. Thick and laced with an unspoken edge.

Words, dummy. Form them. Form. Them. Now.

"My bags are heavy." I pointed toward the door. "Just gonna set them in my room."

Slade stepped away from the wall, finally showing his full face. I gasped, dropping one of my bags this time. He looked nearly identical to Niyol, just a little shorter. Muscle mass, thick arms, a square jaw and full lips.

"Where is he?" he growled at me, lip curled. "We know he's here. And we know you're fucking with h—"

"Hold tight, brother," Archer said, his hand smacking across his friend's chest.

I stared back at Slade, swallowing. "I don't know who you're talking about. I'm here with my fiancé."

Archer's charming grin was probably meant to be calming, but all it did was make me wonder if I needed to grab my wine and use it as a weapon.

"You stayin' in there?" he asked, looking at my bags, the door, then my face.

"Y-yes." My knees shook, threatening to buckle. I cleared my throat. "Now if you'll excuse me, I just need to get inside."

Archer nodded, the movement slow, grin fading as he said, "Heard there was a guy on this floor. His name's Hawk. Real tall, dark-lookin' fella."

I gulped. "N-no. I don't know anyone named Hawk." I lost the grip on my other bags completely then. One fell sideways onto the floor, my new panties slipping out onto the carpet.

Slade walked over, picked up a pair, and twirled them around his finger. "Pretty." He smirked, but it wasn't a playful view in the least. Not like the other guy.

Face hot, I snatched them out of his hand and tucked them back into a bag. "I think you should go," I said, voice still shaking.

Archer took a giant step back and stuck his hands into the front pocket of his jeans. "Nah. We're just gonna wait right here for our friend." Both of his brows waggled at me playfully.

"Oh, well, suit yourself then." I'm not sure why I was lying. Niyol had seemed fond of these men when he spoke about them. But he was also running away from the club for a reason, which was why I didn't spill.

As if on cue, Niyol flew down into the hall just seconds later, flushed, eyes wild, hair in disarray, and a long knife in hand. I gasped, eyes flashing between the blade and his face.

The second his gaze met mine his shoulders dropped, likely in relief. That was until he saw who stood at my sides.

"Jesus, Christ. You guys really fucking followed me?" His eyes said murder, teeth flashing like a wolf's. At the same time, he slowly tucked his giant knife back into the waist of his jeans. I shuddered at the view, wondering if he'd had that all along.

Letting go of my breath, I eyed the three men, unsure of what would go down.

"Course we did." Archer's smile grew cocky, only for him to charge at Niyol, paying no mind to the weapon he'd stored away.

Like long-lost brothers, the two of them hugged, slapping one another on the back.

I'd never been more confused in my life.

"Why, motherfuckers?" Niyol stepped away first, moving to my side. His hand went around my waist like it was the most natural reaction.

Swallowing hard, I glanced up, catching Slade's narrowed eyes on Niyol's hand.

"You're a hard man to find, Hawk." His face went neutral when he caught me looking. I immediately noted a scar that ran the length of his cheek, leading down his neck. I couldn't help but stare, my heart thudding at the thought of how he got it.

"Good to see you too, cousin." Niyol nodded at Slade, then narrowed his eyes when he looked back at me. "Get in the room, Summer."

"No." I held my chin up.

Archer laughed. "Summer, huh? Damn pretty name." Then he looked me up and down. "Matches that pretty face."

I rolled my eyes and folded my arms. "Fuck off."

He laughed at that, looking to Niyol who'd stepped in front of me. "Leave her alone," he growled.

Archer's brows lifted in curiosity, then understanding a second later when he nodded.

I sure as hell didn't understand anything about this *or* these men.

"The name's Archer." He jutted his hand out to shake one of mine, respect suddenly covering his face. "Sorry if we scared ya." He motioned to Slade, then himself. "I'm a good friend of your *fiancé* here." He winked and immediately my face heated.

Regardless of my embarrassment, I lifted my chin even higher and stepped back around Niyol. "Well, *Archer*, I'd like to say it's been a pleasure—" I glared at him then Slade, who wouldn't even look at me now "—but it hasn't been."

Because I didn't want to deal with the devil eyes being drilled into the side of my head by Niyol, I spun on my heels and headed back into the room, making sure to leave the door open a crack.

Archer roared with laughter from the other side. "She's feisty, that one."

"She's also off-limits," Niyol hissed.

The other guy, Slade, barked back, "You got claim on all women now or what?"

"No, idiot. That's Emily's best friend. My ride. She's—"

"Hot as hell." Archer laughed again.

"And too damn good for any of us."

Butterflies danced in my stomach. Niyol's words growing sweeter with every second that passed, it seemed. Was that really what he thought? It broke my heart a little. Whatever it was he thought of me, I knew there was no way I was better than him. Just… different.

I dropped my bags on the foot of the bed, then reached into my pocket to grab my phone. I wasn't going to call anyone, it was still dead, but I needed a diversion in case I was caught listening… which was exactly my intention as I tiptoed back to the door.

"Came here to warn ya. There're some rogues on your tail," Archer said, his voice growing serious. "Don't stop any more than you have to. We got eyes on ya at all times, though. My buddy and his Vegas crew."

Rogues? Vegas crew?

I frowned, and a queasy feeling replaced the butterflies in my stomach.

"*Fuck*," Niyol hissed. "How many?"

"Not sure," Slade answered. "A half dozen or so left the club when Pops was taken in. Lifers, mostly. Rage, Dom, to name a few. Don't know if they got outsiders joining in or not."

Niyol pinched the bridge of his nose, looking so pained that I wanted nothing more than to go back out into the hall and hug him. My guess was, though, that he was in no mood to accept my coddling at the moment.

"Flick sent us to let you know," Archer jumped in.

"Why the fuck does Flick even care?" Niyol barked.

"Because he knows who you are, Hawk. What you've been through," Archer yelled back, losing some of that cool-guy persona.

"I'm a fucking nark. No way am I going back when that label will always be on my head."

"Oh for Christ's sake," Slade yelled, bumping his chest against Niyol's. I stiffened, ready for fists to fly. "Quit being a fucking pussy and get over your one-man pity party. Not everything's about you."

Archer held out a hand between Niyol and his cousin, his narrowed gaze flashing between the two men. When Slade finally took a step back, and kicked one foot back against the wall, I knew right away who held the power between the men.

More unheard whispers were said, but their voices inevitably rose once more.

"Explains the camp then." Niyol sighed. "I knew something was off. Felt it."

The camp? He'd sensed something there? Why had he not told me? I was a big freaking girl, could easily manage anything. Why did he think he needed to handle me with kid gloves and keep secrets like that?

What else had he been keeping from me?

The trio grew quiet again, likely realizing how much of their business they had been sharing with the world out loud. That stunk for me, seeing as how I couldn't hear them, but at the same time my little old heart could only take so much more.

Niyol had a lot of explaining to do.

"You guys got a spy in the midst," Niyol told them, the tension in his voice thick.

"S'cuse me?" Slade asked. "A spy?"

Where was Niyol going with this? I held my breath, waiting.

"Three days before I left the pen, I got a letter. Someone inside the compound. Figured it was Flick, warning me off."

"Obviously not," Slade grumbled. "Flick is pissed you didn't come back. It's why we're here now, damn it."

"No. Obviously not, smartass." I could imagine Niyol's face, pursed lips and narrowed eyes directed at his cousin. It was horrible to say, but I was kind of glad his angry attitude was directed at someone other than me for once.

"You got this letter with you?" Archer asked.

"No. Left it in a drawer at Lisa's."

"All right then," Slade said. "We'll get it. Figure it out and then get you back home."

"I'm not ready. Not yet," Niyol said, sighing. "I need more time."

Even I couldn't understand his hesitation. Was this because of Maya? He'd insisted they were only friends, but maybe he was hiding something from me about that, too.

"It was always supposed to be you leadin' the club someday. Flick's only temporary. We need you back."

My eyes widened at Slade's admission, and pressed a hand over my mouth to hide my gasp. I tried to rationalize what I'd just heard, even repeated it in my head. *Niyol* was supposed to be the leader of the Red Dragon Motorcycle Club?

Holy. Crap.

On one end, I suppose that made sense, because his father had been their leader once. But it was still hard to wrap my head around the fact that the man I'd spent this week with was intended to be some big, bad leader of some big, bad motorcycle club.

"I'm not a leader," Niyol replied. "Never *wanted* to be a leader."

"You were born into like we were," Slade said, sounding almost bored now. Talk about someone with serious mood swings. Maybe it ran in the Lattimore family.

All this talk of Niyol being a leader and coming back to Illinois not only confused me but left me wondering exactly *why* he seemed so adamantly against it. Especially if there was a chance he could help revamp the club like he'd mentioned to me in Nebraska.

One thing I did know for sure: escaping wasn't the solution to someone's problems. Take me, for example. I was on a soul-searching mission of sorts myself. But I'd still go home. Still deal with my issues too. There was no running away forever. Just running for now.

Archer's voice grew a little louder, grabbing my attention once again. "Listen, brother. Once you get whatever shit you're dealing with out of your system, then you get your ass back home and make this right."

I heard a slap, like someone was pounding on someone's back. Curious, I leaned forward on my tiptoes, not wanting to get caught, but dying to see what was going on too. The first person I noticed when I peeked around the door was Niyol, face in his hands.

"Not going home," he mumbled. "Told you."

Archer barked back with, "Why the hell not? Give me a good reason."

"Because I don't want that life anymore."

"Bullshit! We're family, Hawk," Slade yelled, then started to laugh, almost manically. It sent a chill up my spine. "This about Maya?" He folded his arms and quirked a brow.

There was a pause. Then Niyol lifted his head and growled out a simple, "No."

There was a longer pause, until finally, Archer tipped his head to the side, smirked, and said words that were definitely not meant for my ears.

"Holy shit. It's about the blonde, isn't it?" Archer motioned his chin my way, eyes narrowing when he caught me spying through the crack. Quickly, I backed away, my chest heaving as I struggled to breathe.

"*She's* the reason you ain't comin' back?" Slade jumped in. "Christ, it's like Maya all over again."

That wasn't true. Not in the least. Niyol and I barely knew each other. Most days we didn't even get along, and when we weren't fighting, we were just… doing… *other* stuff.

He and I were *not* like that. Nope, not at all.

I mean, I didn't *think* we were. After a while, I heard a heavy sigh… but not a single answer from Niyol. Crap.

"So, that's it then? We can't talk you out of it?" Archer asked. "Flick's gonna lose it, you know."

I frowned. Out of what? Going to San Diego? To Maya?

Silence met my ears. Either Niyol was whispering, or he didn't have a good enough answer to share.

"And what's gonna happen if the rogues find you first?" Slade asked this time. "Archer will keep his buddy on you as long as he can, but they've got their own shit to take care of right now, and we gotta get our asses back home."

I frowned, trying to ignore the tension in my belly at the mention of those rogues again.

"I can handle it," Niyol said, his voice steady. "Won't be long now."

More whispered conversation passed between the three guys. I held my breath, unmoving, a hand over my lips still. Then seconds later, soft goodbyes were said, followed by footsteps in the hall.

And just like that, they were gone.

As quietly as I could, I snuck back toward the bed and sat on the edge of it. Eyes trained on the floor, I waited for the bomb that was Niyol to drop, knowing it would be one hell of an explosion.

The hinges squeaked as the door opened slowly, and my throat went dry when I attempted to swallow. Slow, methodic footsteps echoed in the room until he stood in front of me.

"What in the hell were you thinking? I told you not to leave, damn it. I've been out there scouring the fucking streets looking for you, Summer."

I glared up at him, unapologetic—also avoiding his question. "What was that all about?"

With a long sigh, and completely ignoring my question too, Niyol walked over to the window and pulled back the curtain just in time for the rumble of bikes to come to life outside.

Like a lost puppy, I followed him, and stood by his side. One half of me wanted to apologize for leaving, because I knew I'd worried him. But at the same time, I didn't want to be some fragile damsel in distress who needed him at my side every waking minute. I *could* handle things my own, and other than my mini-breakdown last night over some random, wild animal, I was perfectly fine.

I looked out at the lot, finding Archer and Slade's bikes as they pulled onto the main street. The backs of their vests held the Red Dragon emblem; a dangerous and fantasy world combined.

"You don't know how fucking dangerous my world is." Fingers closed around my wrist, and Niyol tenderly pulled me closer, until his arm was around my waist.

I blinked up into his eyes and scoffed, "Apparently I do now."

"I warned you." Unmoving, he studied me through bloodshot eyes, chest rising and falling in time with mine. "And you didn't listen." One step, two steps, then three, until my back was pressed against the wall. "I'm a really bad guy, Summer. But believe it or not, there are worse assholes out there who'd make me look like Jesus in comparison."

"I swear to God, Niyol, if you don't tell me what's going on, I will call the police. Or your sister—"

Before I could finish, I was on my back in the bed, hands above my head and trapped beneath his grip. Both of my legs were pinned beneath his straddled thighs and his hard erection pressed against my center through his jeans and mine.

Oh, God. I moaned on contact, suddenly able to think of only two things in that moment.

One: how big he was.

And two: that ring buried beneath the head of his cock—how it would feel inside of me.

"Do you like danger, Princess?" Hot breath washed over my lips as he pulled back to kiss my cheek, my chin, my neck… I shut my eyes, the sensation of having him so close to me again overwhelming. He was trying to scare me. And I liked it. "Because in my world, that's all there'll ever be."

Was that a warning? Why? He was going to be in California, while I'd be back in Illinois, this time next week. Niyol wanted nothing from me but… this. Whatever *this* was.

Fingers moved down my arm, over my neck, the side of my breast. I shivered, skin breaking out in tiny goosebumps. Internally I answered his question. *No. I hate danger.* Hated everything that came along with it. Give me simple. Safe. Yet the only words able to slip out were the wrong ones.

"I like *you.*"

He froze, body so tense, I was sure he was seconds away from shattering.

Nose buried against my cheek, he whispered, "That was the wrong answer."

Reality smacked me in the face with its wicked ways. My breathing grew difficult, painful. And then I couldn't think or feel or do much of anything but—

His lips closed over mine before I could finish my thoughts, rough and wild, he kissed me like death was knocking at our door—which, at this point, it very well could have been.

Somewhere along the way, I lost myself in his kisses, like my body was made to be calmed by this beautiful, dangerous man. I was already far too addicted to his touches as it was, and each day we spent together, it was growing harder to think of what would happen in the end.

I kissed him even harder at the revelation. Harder than I'd ever kissed any man before. Then I wrapped my hands around his shoulders, forgetting who I was, let alone what was happening.

Over and over, Niyol devoured my mouth, his hand creeping under my shirt, his warm lips tasting me like he was starving.

"Fuck, Summer." He pulled away, kissing my chin, my neck, pulling on the skin with his teeth. "I want you so much."

"Have me," I moaned. "Please."

But then he froze, his forehead pressed to mine, breathing heavy. Labored.

Pained.

"We can't do this." He squeezed his eyes shut, propping himself up, one hand on either side of my face.

I blinked, opening and closing my mouth, one-hundred-percent confused.

Had I misjudged this all over again? Because I was beginning to think I was no longer a good judge of *anything*, whether it was character, situations, or life in general.

Biting my lip, so as not to rage out my frustrations, I rolled out from under him. Instead of going to the bathroom this time, I sat along the edge, praying my voice didn't shake as I said one simple word. "Oh."

Fingers gripped my elbow, light touches like feathers. "Sum…"

Why the nickname? Why did it have to sound so good coming out of his mouth too? Nicknames like that one were heartbreaking because they made me think there could have been something real between us, but he was just too damn stubborn to let it happen.

"I'm so sorry," he whispered.

Because I was getting tired of his head games, I couldn't give him my forgiveness. Not now. Maybe not ever again.

"We should probably leave, right?" I spat, fingers tightening into fists. "Especially if there's a chance we could be in *danger*. What, with those *rogues* after you and all."

He dropped his hand away. "You're pissed."

"Nah." I waved him away. "You know I don't mind the hot-and-cold stuff. Or the lies either. Nope, not at all. Keep them coming, Niyol, because you've been spouting them off since the day we met."

This time I stood and grabbed my Target bag, shoving dirty and clean stuff back inside from off the dresser and floor. My eyes started to blur unwillingly, and I was so angry at myself for them, because I knew exactly what they meant.

I'd started falling for this man.

And there was nothing I could do to stop myself.

CHAPTER TWENTY-ONE

Niyol

It was midnight when we finally pulled out of the parking lot. We didn't talk, not that I was surprised, just jumped into the tiny rental that Summer had managed to secure. I could've stretched out in the back, slept a little, but that probably wasn't a good plan. It was late, and dark highways meant more places for rogues to jump out from. Now, more than ever, I needed to be on the lookout for anything suspicious. Especially after what Slade and Archer told me.

Everything inside of me now said my running away was wrong. Hell, even Flick wanted me back. I could be on my way home, doing the shit I'd wanted to do for so long. Best part of it all? There'd be no Pops around to beat my ass.

Yet there I was, heading in the opposite direction. My reasoning? She was sitting in the driver's seat.

Slade and Arch had been right. I felt shit for Summer. Stuff I didn't understand. First though, before I told her the truth, there was something I had to do.

Something important.

Something I'd be fucked over for.

Something nobody would understand. Maybe not even Summer.

I scrubbed a hand down my face and leaned my head back against the seat, wishing for some sort of manual on life and how to deal with the shit in it, mainly when it came to women and brotherhood.

"Are you sure you don't want me to drive? You can sleep in the backseat."

Summer shook her head and yawned, already finished with her gas-station coffee. "I'm fine."

A two-word answer was better than the nos or nods she'd been giving me since we left. I got that she was pissed at me. And I couldn't blame her; I'd fucked up, kept things from her. But somewhere in my dumbass head, I'd thought by not telling her about the possibility that we were being followed, I was protecting her. We'd already been through so much. The part that was feeling things for this woman wanted nothing more than to make her smile. Keep her happy. I guess I just had a really jacked-up way of going about it.

"All right then." I cleared my throat. "But we're gonna need to make a detour around dawn. Head north. See about getting another vehicle to drive."

"Why?"

"Because it's necessary."

"I need an actual reason, Niyol," she groaned. "And I also need answers. I'm tired of just doing as I'm told. This is my gas we're riding on. My car that got messed up because of some *stupid* tornado at a *stupid* camp where *you* decided to stay at."

I pinched the bridge of my nose, elbow on the window seal.

I had to tell her, get it out once and for all.

So, I did. I told her everything Slade and Archer had told me. About the rogues. Who they were. What they wanted. And how they likely wouldn't stop until they made it happen.

"You're telling me we're likely being followed right now?" Surprisingly, she was calm, but I saw her arms tense in the dark, her hands clutch tighter around the wheel.

"Yeah. Probably."

"Like, there are seriously a bunch of big, bad bikers out there hunting you down at this moment in time, looking for revenge on you because of your stupid, guilty *father*?"

I reached over and touched her thigh, giving it a reassuring squeeze. "This is about me, not you."

She laughed sarcastically. Manically.

"Yeah, because crazy-ass bikers will take one look at me and assume I'm nothing to fear, obviously."

I scratched at my throat, then shrugged. "I'm not that worried about them. You shouldn't be either."

Least not yet. Archer said his Vegas buddy's club were tracking them down—or trying to. In turn, Flick had, for some fucked-up reason, asked for them to stay on us. Keep us safe until I got us to San Diego. Those guys knew the area better than anyone else. I told Summer this too. She still wasn't impressed.

"Had I known that there was a freaking chance that we'd be stalked by crazy-ass people, then I would've never agreed to this," Summer whispered this time.

The words on my tongue were stuck. The ones that said, *Then we would've never been together.* But there I was, being selfish again. So, I told her what I knew she wanted to hear.

"You're right. I should've told you."

"Good." She lifted her chin. "Glad you can at least admit *that*."

I winced, covering my mouth.

She got quiet on me then. Too quiet. I had to look at her a couple of times to make sure she was awake. But her eyes were always wide. Her hands at ten and two. She was nervous.

Just before I begged her to pull over and let me drive, she gave me a one-two sucker punch.

"Why are you *really* running away, Niyol?" I almost didn't hear her. The words were that quiet.

I rubbed a hand over my forehead, not really having an answer myself. I'd left it open with Slade and Arch, telling them

I wasn't sure when, or even if, I'd come back. I needed another couple of days to think on it. Figure shit out. They said they'd give me one—mighty fucking good of them. But I also knew their reasons why.

Flick was generous. But not *that* generous.

By not going home last night, I knew I was setting up Summer and myself for trouble. Not just with the rogues either. My lack of commitment to the club wouldn't go unnoticed by Flick and the other brothers. They'd likely get pissed, then I'd be out for good, retaliation and consequences be damned.

But to tell Summer the real reason I wanted to go to San Diego now was too risky for me to share yet. I was fucking scared. Big time. Why? I had no idea of the outcome.

Uncertainty really fucking sucked for someone who had a control issue like myself.

"I'll tell you. Just... not yet, okay? Soon."

Her shoulders fell. I could tell she was done with me. But if she'd just give me a little more time, then everything would make sense.

"We're also gonna get a bike to drive the rest of the way. It'll help us get where we need to go."

"If you ask me that's a stupid idea. We'll be more out in the open like that."

I shook my head. "Not with the kind of bike I'm planning on getting."

Surprisingly, she didn't argue again. I wasn't sure if that was a good sign, or not.

"Just... tell me where to go."

I punched in the address on the GPS, then leaned back in my seat, fear and regret eating at my gut. Every so often, I'd steal a glance at Summer to help me get through, memories of our time in the back of her Rover together flashing through my head like a temporary bandage.

We stayed quiet like that for a while, the open road widening, and the thick tension slowing dwindling the further down the road we went. Eventually the sun slid up into the sky and I got to watch my first sunset in two years.

Couldn't enjoy it though. Not when I was keeping secrets again.

"Where are we going exactly?" she asked after I told her to get off the highway not long after six.

"My gramps' place. He owns some bikes. Runs a Harley repair shop too."

Pops' dad was a big, tough-as-shit guy who I hadn't talked to since I was sixteen. Needless to say, I wasn't sure how he'd react to seeing his long-lost grandkid—the son of the guy he swore off a long time ago. Hell. I'm not even sure if he still owned the place—Slade said he was pretty sure he did, but at this point, I was willing to put my money on any bet just to get us out of this car.

"Is he a psycho like your father?"

I shrugged. "In his own right."

"Great. Just what I need. Another crazy Lattimore in my life."

I laughed a little at that, mostly 'cause she was right. Us Lattimores were a bunch of fucked-up fools.

"Can he turn this car back into the rental place for me at least?"

"Yeah. He can."

"Okay." She breathed, smiling softly at me. "I guess I don't have any other reason not to trust you, Niyol."

My chest got tight at her admission. That trust was a gift to me, whether she knew it or not.

We drove for another three hours until we finally crossed the Nevada border and made it to the small town. Sure as shit, the building was still there: *Lattimore's, owned and operated by Sani P.*

My hands started sweating at the thought of seeing him. Would he know who I was? Tell me to fuck off? Or welcome me with open arms? Slade talked to him more than I did, had even suggested I come here for a bike, but Slade's dad wasn't *my* dad.

Bikes of all shapes and sizes sat in front of a small, dilapidated building. Next to it was an even smaller house, which was more of a trailer. Gramps' place. The closest business was a good three blocks away due to the sheer size of the land which he owned and ran his business on.

I'd been here once when I was a little kid, barely seven, I think, but it wasn't the land I remembered most. It was the look on Pops' face when Gramps told him not to come back. It was the first time I'd ever feared my father.

"We're really going to do the Harley thing then." Summer's lips twitched as she put the rental car in park.

I grinned, using my smoothest voice. "You wouldn't mind, would ya?"

"I'm beginning to realize that with you, I don't necessarily get a choice." Smile dropping at the corners, Summer's blue eyes went a little sad.

Those words she said could go a lot of ways, but I wouldn't call her out on them, not when I was thinking the same thing myself. Every second of every moment that Summer was near me, I started liking her a little more—*wanting* her even more. And yeah, anything she wanted, I'd do it, no hesitation. Especially if it made her eyes light up.

"Come on." I squeezed her shoulder. "Let's go inside and meet the old man."

The bell dinged as we stepped inside the building, the smell of incense and pipe tobacco filling the air. Some kid sat behind the small desk just inside the door to our left. He looked no older than fifteen.

"'Sup," he said as he stabbed the butt of his cigarette into an ashtray. I'd not smoked in twenty-four hours, and I was feeling it.

"Looking for Sani," I said.

The kid stood, grabbed his leather coat from the back of the chair. He eyed me from head to toe, then moved his gaze to Summer, eyes nearly popping out of his head.

"And you are...?" He licked his lips and stepped around the desk to stand in front of her. The kid was short, his head hitting the tops of her tits. Tits he couldn't stop ogling.

I stepped in front of her. "Tell him Niyol Lattimore's here for him."

"Chill, man." He held his hands out in front of him, his gaze giving Summer a last once- over before he left the room.

"Is this what bike shops normally look like? I've never been inside one before." She rubbed her arms and took a step back. Summer's pretty looks countered the grease and grime of the shop. It was a damn nice view.

I smiled and looked away. "Yup."

Summer walked around the small office, fingering the different Navajo heirlooms along the way. Instead of watching her like I would've liked, I sat down in the chair by the desk and put my face in my hands, rubbing it.

God, I was a fucked-up mess. The rogues, the guilt over not heading back with Slade and Archer, the feelings stirring in my chest for Summer most of all... It was wrecking me. Four days with a new pair of legs and I was second-guessing what I'd been dying to do for two years. Sad part was, this was only just the beginning.

CHAPTER TWENTY-TWO

Summer

"Well lookie here."

A smoky voice sounded from behind me. I twisted around, finding a man just a little taller than Niyol, with gray hair that hung down to the middle of his arms. He wore a red bandanna on top of his long hair, and was dressed like Ny: black jeans, black shirt, black boots.

He hovered in the doorway between the office and what I'm assuming was a shop, while the creepy kid remained at his right, arms folded over his chest, winking at me.

"Gramps." Niyol stood from his chair and pushed his hand out to shake the man's. "It's good to see you again."

The old man didn't budge and Niyol's hand was left hanging in the air. My teeth clenched together at the view. I couldn't take disrespect when respect was given. It was my biggest pet peeve.

"It's rude not to say hello when someone greets you," I snarled, glaring up at the man.

The boy laughed under his breath, hiding it with a fist. Everyone ignored him but me. I flipped him off this time, which only made him laugh harder.

"And who're you exactly?" Niyol's grandpa focused on me, his dark eyes penetrating.

I shuddered at the look, instinct pulling me closer to Niyol's side as I answered. "I'm Summer Parks."

The man glared at me for another few seconds before sitting on his chair and leaning over the top of his desk, hands folded.

I looked to Niyol, watching as he spoke again. "We need your help, Gramps."

"No." The old man didn't hesitate with his answer. "Don't do nothing to help with that group your father's got you involved in. You know that."

"I'm not—"

"What part of *no* don't you understand?" Hatred poured off the man like a thick, foggy morning. It was the only analogy I could think of as I peered into his dark, hazy eyes. Staring back at us, he reaped nothing but abhorrence.

"Please, sir," I added, ignoring the goosebumps along my arms. "Niyol is a really good person. Nothing like his father. He just wants peace and happiness and he *really* wants to get away from those... those *men*." I sucked in a breath, then said, "If you don't help him, he might never be able to leave that club. Find a new start. I can't stand the thought of that happening, and as his grandfather, you shouldn't want that for him either."

When I was sixteen, I was the queen of the debate team. Not the drama club. But I was hoping to combine the two ideas together. So, I sported a few crocodile tears—waterworks always sealed the deal with men. Add in the fact that I was blonde and, well... crap. *Something* had to work out in our favor, right?

The old man sat back in his chair, eyeing us both. He folded his hands over his chest, and said, "Why should I help you, boy? You chose this path."

"Because I didn't have a choice," Niyol spat.

"You had a choice." He pointed a finger at Niyol. "You could've called me."

"And you really think Pops would've let me go? I was a kid, for Christ's sake. Had nothing but the patch on my back and the bike beneath my legs."

And a girl he was traveling across country for—though I kept that one silent. For some reason, I couldn't admit it out loud anymore.

"I could've sent for you." His grandfather frowned.

"He would've *killed* you."

"Guess you'll never know, will ya?"

Niyol shook with undisclosed rage. It had me pulling straws from mid-air in turn. If his pleading didn't work, then maybe my lies would.

"I'm pregnant," I shouted over their bickering.

Niyol stiffened, as did his grandpa, but I kept going, no time to waste.

"Niyol's the father. If we don't get a bike to drive, those men will come after us and... and..." I lowered my hand to my stomach and worked up as many tears as I could this time. "They'll kill our baby."

Niyol's eyes shot to my face, burning me with a glare. But I couldn't stop with the lie now that I'd spilled it.

"Please, sir," I whispered. "For the baby? Your great..." I sniffed. "Grandchild?"

The old man stared back at me, dark eyebrows furrowed, pink lips pursed. Then he looked at my stomach and a change passed over his features, a softness I could only hope was him relenting.

"Pregnant, huh?" He tapped his lips with a finger.

I nodded slowly, leaning against Niyol even more—praying to God that we looked like a real, legit couple in love, pregnant with our first child, and on the run from the bad guys.

"Yes," I whispered, bringing Niyol's free hand to my stomach before pressing my palm over the top of his knuckles. He stiffened but didn't make a move to stop me.

Ny's grandfather stood from his desk and lifted something out of a box on the shelf where he kept what looked to be hundreds of dream catchers. Under my wet lashes, I watched him, his movements slow and sure. Something jingled in the air, the sound of keys, I guessed. I held my breath thinking we'd gotten what we came for. But when he turned back to face us, he curled his lip in disgust and shook his head, that softness eliminating.

"Lying ain't okay, girl." He tossed the keys in the air and Niyol caught them mid-swipe. "But because you've got some balls, you two can take this bike, keep it till you get your issues worked out."

My face grew hot, and I looked at the floor, wondering if hell's gates were going to open right up for me. I wasn't a religious woman by any means, but if I were, I'd have a year's worth of repentance to serve for these last five days alone.

"Thank you, Gramps." Niyol urged me closer to the desk, keeping his hand along the small of my back. "I'll get this bike back to you soon as I get Summer where she needs to be."

My back stiffened at his words. Where *I* needed to be? I quickly shook my head and tried not to read into his words.

CHAPTER TWENTY-THREE

Niyol

I really shouldn't have been enjoying the hell out of the fact that Summer was on the back of this purring Harley, body flush with mine. There was something right about riding with her arms wrapped around my waist like she was. It was like everything I'd been missing had finally clicked into place.

It could've been the fact that my Gramps and I were on speaking terms again too. That the last thing he said to me after he fed us a bucket of chicken and told us a few stories about the history of his tribe was, *I'm sorry, Niyol. I should've tried harder.*

He hadn't known about what'd happened to me within the last couple of years. Had no idea I'd been behind bars either. And he sure as hell didn't know that his own flesh-and-blood son had been the one to put me there. Wasn't his fault in the least, but he still blamed himself.

Thing was, he couldn't have stopped my dad from making me into an RD if he'd tried. And he couldn't have taken me away from the club either. That was my life back then. And I loved it.

Until shit got out of control.

The only thing I'd allowed Gramps to be sorry for was not trying harder to keep in touch, even if he did hate my pops as much as I hated the man myself.

"Tired?" I asked through the helmets, our ear coms in sync if we needed to communicate. Normally I didn't wear one when I used to ride—too restrictive—but it helped keep us undercover this way. No RD would recognize me with the oversized helmet on my head, or the sidecar attached to our right that held our bags. We looked like a couple of old hippies taking a cross-country journey, nothing more.

Instead of speaking, Summer wrapped her arms tighter around my lower stomach, sending a shot of heat through my body.

"We're gonna stop for the night soon."

She nodded against me.

We wound up driving another hour until we were just south of Vegas. Found a cheap motel that sat along a busy street. It reminded me of something out of a B-grade horror movie. Summer didn't seem to mind, though. But she did follow me around like a lost puppy, her head hanging, and doing as I asked, no questions. It bothered me seeing her so submissive; tight-lipped and sad. Maybe she was scared. Because, God help me, if she was regretting this trip, what'd happened between us, I'd never forgive myself.

"Let's grab something to eat." I pointed toward the restaurant next door to the motel as she unlocked our room. She nodded but asked to shower first. I didn't argue, knowing what girls were like when it came to hygiene. Emily had been crazy about showering twice a day.

I changed my clothes when she got in, then headed into the main lobby to grab some ice. After I got back to the room, she was sitting on the edge of the bed, dressed in a black, flowy skirt and a bright blue tank that hugged her chest. My dick immediately hardened, loving the view, but I couldn't touch her. Not now.

Side-by-side, we walked next door to the restaurant. It was a mom-and-pop type barbeque joint. The kind with a pig on the front sign wearing a bib. He was smiling with a fork in one hand and a knife in the other, sitting on top of a pot that was on a stove. It was fucking ridiculous and ironic but made me laugh all the same.

"What's so funny?" Summer asked, looking at the sign.

"Poor pig has got no idea what he's getting into."

She didn't laugh like I thought she would. Instead, she whispered, "I can relate." Then tugged open the doors, leaving me behind.

CHAPTER TWENTY-FOUR

Summer

This was all becoming entirely too comfortable and familiar. Diners, hotels, late nights wrapped in each other's arms… For nearly five days now I'd become this disoriented, crazy loon with lust and desire complicating the fear and the facts of what was really going on. And I hated it.

We scanned the menu in silence, ate in silence, and then when we walked away from the restaurant, the only thing I wanted to do was *silently* go to sleep. Niyol tried making small talk, but I could tell he was only doing it to get through dinner. I always answered him, but my words were short and curt. After a while, I could feel his mood changing, the tension of the night eating away at his nerves. For a guy who liked silence, he sure didn't act like it anymore.

By the time we made it to the front door of our motel, I realized just how badly the two of us needed some time apart, even if it was only for the night.

"Maybe it's best if I get my own room tonight," I said, secretly wishing he'd beg me to stay. I wasn't an idiot. I knew what had happened between us the last few days wasn't something we could continue to keep doing. But one more night, that was all I wanted. A conclusion to this madness we'd been living through.

Or maybe, just maybe, he'd tell me he didn't want to go to California after all, as crazy as that thought was. That what the two of us had shared during this trip was something worth exploring. I shouldn't have been silently pleading for this, crying on the inside for a chance. But there I was, doing just that.

Niyol stood behind me at the door, a dark force that warmed my back, even if he was being cold.

"Not happening. Not with the rogues out there." He touched my hip, the sensation burning through my tank top as he finished. "I'll sleep on the floor if you have a problem sharing a bed."

I dropped my hand away from the knob and let it hang by my side as I turned to face him. "No, it's not that. I just... I need to be alone for a while."

He held my stare, his emotions shifting from one spectrum to the other. Hurt, fear, sadness, only to end in resolve.

"Fine. Whatever you need. Just... don't answer the door to nobody but me." He pulled that knife out of his pants. The one I'd finally gotten used to, now that he was open with it. After he set it on the dresser, he put his boots back on. "Gonna go to the bar about a block away. There are eyes in the lot, watching our door."

"Who?" I stiffened.

"A couple of guys from Archer's brother's club showed up earlier. Gonna trail us the rest of the way to San Diego."

"Are they bikers too?" I asked.

He nodded. "Yeah. A brother club."

"Okay." I turned back around, eyes blurring with unshed tears as I struggled with the zipper of my bag.

After tomorrow, Niyol and I would be going our separate ways, and the reality was hitting me way too hard. So hard, I wanted nothing more than to keep as much distance between us as I could. Both physically and mentally.

Out of the blue, he came up behind me, his hand on my waist again, his lips pressed to my ear in a whisper. I shut my eyes, holding my breath.

"Summer… Make me stay. Tell me you need me."

Tears fell. Wet, warm, painful. But the words wouldn't come. Not when I knew the regrets would ultimately follow—for the both of us. Not just me.

"I-I can't."

Slowly, he dropped his hands away, his boots echoing on the floor after that, noisy with his exit. A warm wind brushed against my neck, and my hair flapped around my face like wildflowers in a breeze when the door opened. I waited for it to shut, holding my breath once more. Instead of a slam, though, all I heard was the sound of his voice instead.

"You've got every right to hate me, Summer."

I blinked, not expecting those words. Surprise had me turning to look at him.

"I don't hate you." I never could. Not anymore. "It's just that you pull me close, then you push me away. One second I think we're barely acquaintances, then the next, it feels like so much more." *Too much.* "I'm really confused. And tired…" I smoothed a hand over my scratchy throat. "I'm *so* tired."

"Tired of me?" He looked to the floor, rubbing at the back of his neck.

"No." I shook my head, my voice uneven, desperate. "I'm tired of not being someone's everything."

He lifted his head, searching my face, lips parted, eyes wide.

It was selfish of me to say, but it was also the truth. I'd been my father's second in life, the first being his job. I'd been Landon's second as well, but to another woman. And in a way, I'd also been Emily's second to her fiancé. I didn't want attention on me all the time, I didn't even want pure devotion. I just wanted someone who would treat me like I was worthy of being a priority every once in a while.

His answer was like a punch to the gut. One I needed desperately to hear, no matter how much it hurt.

"I can't explain what's going on, but I do get it. Just know this…" He paused, taking a heavy breath. "I'll never, *ever* regret a second we've spent together."

I nodded, not bothering to wipe my tears away. More than anything, I wanted to tell him to stay. I did. But knowing tonight would be our last night together would hurt me too much to do so. Which was why I stayed silent and let him go. It was easier that way. For the both of us. Letting Niyol go was the right thing to do, even if it was the hardest.

CHAPTER TWENTY-FIVE

Niyol

I revved the engine at a stoplight, heart thundering in my ears. Next to me was another bike, smaller than the one I was on, but faster. I recognized the RD patch out of the corner of my eye when I'd stormed out of the motel room. Locust, his club name, was patched across the top of his cut on the front, just below the one-percenter patch. On the back was a giant red dragon in the middle, with the words *Las Vegas* written above. It was all the proof I needed that Archer's Vegas buddy had come through after all.

I didn't deserve him. Nor did I deserve Slade. But damn did I want to. Just like I wanted to deserve the woman I'd just left behind.

A horn honked from my left, loud in my ears. I growled through the madness in my head, feeling the heat of the car's bumper as I swerved around it. I pushed the visor up and over my face, soaking in the night air, then dropped my chin and squeezed the handle tighter, needing the rush. The speed. Anything to clear my mind.

I lost the guy following me after a few turns, the town we'd landed in for the night bigger than I'd thought. He didn't need to follow me anyhow. I was fine. And even if I wasn't, maybe karma would come for me after all.

I gunned it harder, taking a sharp right, heading down an empty street, then veering into an alley. Could've gone faster, if it weren't for that stupid fucking cart attached. But I'd take what speed I could get.

Around a dumpster, through a tight hole, I took off faster, eyes narrowed ahead.

Fuck me. Not only did I not deserve Summer, but I didn't deserve the club. The place where I was meant to be all along. I didn't deserve their forgiveness, even though they were offering it up, but I was damn glad I'd been offered.

I slammed a fist against the handles, swerving a little at my realization.

What the hell would I have done in Cali anyway? Maya had a job, a life there without me. Staying with her would fuck up her world, no doubt. Unlike me, she'd been able to live without the club, thanks to her mom and Flick. Sure, she'd always be a part of it, would understand what I'd be missing if I stayed in Cali, but she had a chance to be her own person, whereas I didn't.

Nor did I want to anymore.

I belonged with Slade and Archer.

I belonged on a bike.

And most of all, I belonged back in Rockford... with my brothers, with the cut on my back too, even if that was the only thing I'd ever do again. I'd figure out who sent that fucking letter. Take care of shit and get the RDs in order. I could do it.

I *wanted* to do it.

Sighing to myself, I slowed my bike until eventually I stopped at a stop sign. It was quiet, other than my engine, and I took in the dark streets as I dropped one booted foot to the cement.

Summer, though.

Sweet, sweet Summer.

I hadn't expected her. But now she was all I could think about. Was it because she was forbidden? My stepsister's best friend? Was it because she wasn't part of my world? I needed to go back and face her, no matter what my reasoning was. Tell her the truth once and for all. Why I wanted to finish this trip—with her.

I revved the engine and went to pull away, intending to head back to the hotel. Face the music once and for all. But a pair of headlights flickered on ahead of me. A car sat along the side of the road, parked about twenty yards on the right side. Slowly, it pulled away from the curb, inching closer, a snail's pace. My eyes narrowed as I watched it. Uneasiness drifted through my veins, urging me to go, to run back to the motel, find the Vegas guy I'd outrun. I reached for my phone, intending to call Summer, until the car's engine grew louder, more threatening.

Fuck. This wasn't good. I needed to get out of there. Sure as hell didn't have time to call anyone either, which left me with one option.

The car's lights flickered on, blinding me. I lifted an arm, held it over my eyes, trying to see inside the old Buick. But the windshield was tinted. My head had been too fucked up to care whether I lived or died, that's why I'd been so unaware of my surroundings. Idiot fucking mistakes I knew better than to make.

Trying not to look like I gave a shit, I pulled away, keeping at the speed limit. I felt them behind me a minute later, following so close the hum of their bumper vibrated against my bike tires.

"Motherfuckers." I revved the gas, coming up on a busier street, faster, pushing forward, I raced around a car, then another, but they kept pace.

And then I heard it.

Felt it.

A sharp shot in my back, blood, poison… death.

Blackness.

CHAPTER TWENTY-SIX

Summer

I lifted my head off the pillow, eyes swollen as I turned to look at the clock on the bedside table. Three-twenty in the morning and, from the looks of things, Niyol hadn't been back yet.

Earlier, by the time eleven o'clock rolled around, I had attempted to call his phone at least a dozen times, even got the guts to talk to the two guys out front on bikes. When I saw their patches on the back, then saw the *Las Vegas* written above the dragon, I knew they were safe. There for us, most of all. Guy one, who'd followed Niyol, said he lost him around nine, figured he needed to be alone. Unfortunately, he hadn't come back after all.

I thought maybe Niyol was giving me the space I asked for, so I'd settled into bed and told myself not to worry. It didn't work. I had been ridiculously childish about the entire situation, feelings or not. We were adults. The two of us could have easily shared a hotel room and not let our impulsions get in the way of our goals. Some good that did me now.

Somewhere between eleven-thirty and twelve, I must have fallen asleep, too tired with the idea of figuring out what I should do to fix the mess we'd gotten ourselves in. I didn't have the slightest idea where to look for him now though. Maybe he'd slept outside the door, or even in the lobby?

After I grabbed my shorts off the floor, I slipped out of bed, and got dressed. For my best friend's sake, I'd scour the town to find him if I had to.

Nervous energy radiated through me as I walked outside and headed to the lobby. Weirdly enough, both of the Las Vegas bikers were gone. I tried not to let it bother me, but when I reached the parking lot where Niyol's spot sat empty, fear snaked through me in the shape of a shudder.

I folded my arms like they were a shield, gaze darting left and right from nerves. The outside of the hotel was apocalyptic-quiet at this time of night, with the m-light flickering off the distant *motel* sign, making it read more like *otel*. Anyone of those rogues could be out there, ready to strike if they wanted to. I was an open target, even if Niyol said they wouldn't likely touch me.

Regardless, the idea still kept me on edge as I made my way toward the front lobby. Pure adrenaline alone was the only fuel getting me there.

The second I stepped into the front lobby, I knew something was off. And it had everything to do with the two police officers standing near the front desk. I froze, eyeing the area, looking for Ny, only for the receptionist to look over their shoulders and point a finger at me.

"God, Niyol. What'd you do?" I sighed to myself, picking up speed to meet the officers halfway.

"Do you know a Niyol Lattimore?" the taller officer asked me.

"I do. He's my friend. Is everything okay, officer?"

"He's been in an accident."

"An accident?" My chest grew cold, my knees wobbly.

"Mr. Lattimore was shot this evening while riding on his motorcycle. He's in the hospital, unconscious at the moment, but stable. We found a key card for this hotel in his wallet." the second officer said, voice grave. "We've been trying to get in touch with someone who might know him, just in case."

I pressed my hand over my mouth, stifling a sob. "Can you take me to him? Please? I-I don't know where the hospital is, and he's my ride…"

I reached into my pocket for my cell, cringing when I wrapped a hand around it. Emily would be in the middle of the Atlantic somewhere, and his stepmom was likely in bed. I'd call them in the morning, let them know what was going on. There was no need to alarm them until I knew the full extent of his injuries.

"Sure, we can take you, Ma'am." Officer number one smiled politely.

Twenty minutes later we were in the parking lot of a hospital, the red emergency sign brightening the dark, morning sky. The scent of cleaning supplies had my stomach churning in knots as I stepped through the entrance.

There was no doubt in my mind that those rogue members of the Red Dragons had slipped past Niyol's friends. They wanted Niyol dead and wouldn't stop until it happened.

Where are his supposed brothers now? I snarled at the thought and shook my head in disgust.

One of the police officers stayed in his car, while the other stuck with me. He was young, probably mid-thirties.

"Are you all right, Miss?" he asked, eventually leading me toward the elevator.

No. I wasn't okay. My hands wouldn't stop shaking and my head was killing me. Basically, I was in my own version of hell.

After reassuring the officer that I was fine, I walked toward Niyol's room, telling the nurses I was his fiancée. Thankfully, they didn't question my sincerity, just led me toward his room. They explained that he was heavily medicated for pain—he'd been shot in the back of his left shoulder. They also told me that he'd lost consciousness but didn't have any bleeding in the brain or a concussion for that matter. They weren't sure why he hadn't woken up, which didn't help with my unease in the least. His one saving grace? The fact that he'd been wearing that helmet he hated so much.

When they shut the door behind me, I covered my mouth at the view to hide my gasp.

The drip of an IV echoed off the whitewashed walls, along with the heart monitor. I inhaled through my sudden tears, taking in the scent of man and hospital—a smell that had me breaking out in a cold sweat.

Niyol's helmet and clothes were in a bag at the foot of his bed, and once I composed myself enough, I grabbed them and began searching through his pants for his cell phone.

Twenty-seven missed calls. Twelve from me, the rest from Slade and Archer.

Swallowing hard, I tucked it into a pocket, before I finally chanced a look at his face through watery eyes. I sucked in a breath at what I saw. Though the lights were off, I could still make out the shadow of his profile—asleep and so peaceful, you wouldn't think he'd been through what he had. Yet my chest tightened the closer I got to the head of his bed. He looked like death. It was terrible, unnerving, and it made it that much easier for me to make my decision once and for all.

"I'll be back," I whispered, before placing a kiss on his forehead.

Out in the hall, I searched through his contacts, finding *her* name. It rang three times, and when she picked up, I asked on a shaky breath, "Is this Maya?"

CHAPTER TWENTY-SEVEN

Niyol

If I was in hell, then somebody needed to turn on the fucking light.

But then I heard a beep. And another. Followed by the dripping of something, then whispered voices. I blinked open my eyes, *déjà vu* hitting me as a nurse hovered over my bed. It was just like the time I'd OD'd after partying too hard when I was sixteen, only now it wasn't self-induced misery.

"Jesus." I winced as I tried to move, the back of my left arm ripping—at least it felt like it—from the place where the bullet had gone through. Every other inch of my body hurt too, probably from the fall. But I was alive. No idea how I got so lucky. Maybe the Big Guy had a special place in his heart for dickheads like me after all.

"You're awake," the nurse said as she removed a blood-pressure cuff from my good arm.

I cleared my throat, reaching for some water. "Is there a woman waiting for me?"

The nurse held the straw to my lips. "There is. She's right outside the room. Are you up for visitors?"

"Yeah." I blew out a breath, relieved Summer was okay. Just the thought of her getting hurt had my blood pressure rising, no doubt. "How long have I been out?"

"About eight hours." She smiled at me and set the cup on a table.

Damn. That was a while.

I needed Summer with me until we got to San Diego even more now, by my side at all costs. Not only so I could protect her, even in my jacked-up state, but so I could tell her how sorry I was.

Leaving her like I did was one of the stupidest fucking things I'd ever done. Any one of those rogues could've shown and messed her up. Even with the Vegas brothers around, nothing would stop someone looking for vengeance.

The nurse finished up and said she'd let her in. Squinting to ease my aching head, I looked toward the door, waiting, holding my breath. But when it finally opened, it wasn't Summer standing there.

"Maya?"

With one arm folded over her stomach and her free hand at her side, she looked like she was walking toward death row—me being her executioner. It was a shit thing to do, but I found myself looking behind her, expecting Summer to be right there.

How was Maya here and Summer wasn't?

"God, Hawk." She dropped her hands and threw them around my neck like no time had passed at all.

I winced as the pain in my arm intensified but still smiled a little despite it. "Hey, My."

She pressed her forehead to mine. "You're a flipping mess."

"Least I'm not dead, yeah?"

Maya groaned. "Not funny, idiot."

Eventually, she leaned away, holding my face between her hands. Her hazel eyes were rimmed red like she'd been crying. But the Maya I knew didn't cry over stupid shit like me getting shot.

She'd changed too, at least looks wise. A shit ton, actually. Taller, thinner, but rounder in all the places a woman was. I studied her, head to toe, compartmentalizing yet again. But instead of feeling that old spark we'd once shared at nineteen, all I felt was satisfaction that she seemed to be doing okay without me.

I'd imagined this scenario before. More times than I could count. It was the one thing that got me through prison. Made me believe that I had a chance on the outside; that someone besides Emily and Lisa were waiting for me. Only now that it was happening, it didn't feel right. Not the way I thought it would. The way I'd hoped.

"I've missed you," she finally said.

"Nothing about me to miss," I laughed, but then started to cough.

She reached behind me, fluffing up my pillows. "You still smoking?"

I winced through the pain but managed a nod.

"You're an idiot."

"And you're still good about busting my balls, I see."

"Eh, I'm not as bad as I used to be." She winked, smiling for a second before sitting beside me on the bed. "Care to tell me why you're getting shot up?"

I shut my eyes, trying to breathe without it hurting. If this was pain on meds, I'd fucking hate to see what pain was like off them. "Rogues."

"Huh?"

"Lifers on Pops' side." Her eyes narrowed a little, confusion there. Apparently, Flick hadn't told her much. "Brothers who left the club and decided to take vengeance on my ass 'cause of my old man," I clarified.

"That stupid club." She gave my legs a shove, then curled up next to me on the bed. Lucky she was so tiny, I barely had to move to make room. "I'm so glad you're done with them."

I cringed and looked away.

"Haaaawk?"

"Hmm." Still couldn't face her.

"Don't you dare tell me you're going back. Especially after this and what your dad did to you."

She made sense. Going back *was* stupid. But to me, club life was *my* life and ignoring it wasn't possible, no matter how far away I ran. There was no point in starting over somewhere else when I could've been starting over with the RD world first.

"Flick's taken over." I shrugged, trying for casual.

"So?" she huffed, ignoring my reasoning—still the hardass even all these years later. "My uncle is an old man. He may be good to me and my mom, but he's not gonna be able to lead a motorcycle club much longer. You know that as well as I do."

Another reason why I knew I had to go back. I didn't want to be Pres. But maybe, someday, I wouldn't have a choice.

"Don't be pissed at me about this," I argued. "I had every fucking intention to leave, but what the hell would I do if I made it to Cali anyway? You would've grown tired of my ass mooching off you. Admit it."

"You could've gotten a job. Or gone to school and gotten your GED. *Something.* Anything else."

I touched her hand, squeezed her fingers too. "Maya. Be serious. I fucking hated school and learning new shit."

"I *am* being serious. You have loads of potential, but never had the chance to explore how much. Now you do."

There may have been potential in me for something, but it sure as hell wasn't the things she'd mentioned. Plus, I didn't have any motivation, let alone fucking patience, to follow through with anything but the only life I'd known. If only I could've realized that before I left Illinois.

There again, I'd have missed out on Summer.

Summer, who was still not there...

I shook my head, refocused on Maya. "I have to do this. For Slade and Arch. They need me. And I want to do good by the club."

"And where was the *club* when you were getting shot up in the streets, huh?" She jumped off the bed. "I can't believe this.

All these years later, and you're still the same idiot who lives and breathes the illegal life."

A tear slipped out of her eye, but she wiped it away quick with the back of her hand and started pacing the floor.

So this new version of Maya had grown soft. Why was that? I wanted to ask, hell, I probably should've, but she didn't let me, her next question catching me off guard.

"Tell me something," she whispered, stopping long enough to face me. "Does this have anything to do with the woman who called me?"

"What woman?"

"The pretty blonde who's sitting in the waiting room, looking half dead."

"Summer?" *Summer called Maya? Summer was here? At the hospital?*

I looked at the door again, waiting for her to pop inside.

"Yeah. Her," Maya continued. I could see the curiosity in her gaze, a little bit of confusion too. If she was jealous, though, she didn't show it.

I loved this woman in front of me like I loved Emily and Lisa. That's it. There was nothing there otherwise. Not a flutter in my gut. No racing heart. None of the stuff I was supposed to feel. The stuff I felt with Summer.

"It's complicated." To the point where I needed to finish our ride back to San Diego before I could tell her the truth I'd been holding onto. Explain that our trip had been necessary after all, just not for the reason we both thought. If I told her that now, though, here in this hospital, she'd leave me in a heartbeat.

Which was why I'd have to lie to her. Again.

"Real complicated, I'm sure." Maya rolled her eyes and sat beside me on the bed again. "As in, you got it bad for her, but she's too goody-goody for someone like you?"

I cringed, then rubbed a hand over my face.

Maya pulled it away, her eyes a little sad. "If you want something like that in your life, Hawk, all you've got to do is treat her right. Not like you would if she was any other woman at the club."

"I treated you good." I smirked.

"You fucked me on the dirt road outside the compound when we were half buzzed on moonshine. That, Hawk, is not how a girl like your blonde deserves to be treated."

I shook my head, hating the memory. Not because I didn't want it, but because it was wrong. Growing up, that's how women around me were treated. I'd only followed through with what I was taught, even if I tried to be a little better. Now though, I knew it was wrong—refused to ever let a woman be treated as anything below perfect for the rest of my fucking life.

"I'm sorry." I sighed, wishing I had the right words. "You deserved better than that."

"We both did." Her eyes went hazy as she stared ahead. I almost asked her what she was thinking about, but I knew her well enough to know that she held secrets tighter than I ever did.

"Yeah." Maybe we did. But I wouldn't regret it.

Maya stared at her hands, folding them on her lap. "Your girl asked me to finish driving you to San Diego, by the way."

"She did?" My brows shot up. Summer was gonna bail on me? No fucking way could I let that happen. Not now.

"Yeah. Sorry, though. I've just got a lotta things going on right now."

"It's fine. I'll figure it out."

She patted my cheek. "You always do."

The room grew quiet, other than our breathing and the machines hooked up to me. I could feel her tension against my side, though. It was all I needed to know that she was still pissed at me about going back to the club.

"Don't hate me, all right?" I finally pulled Maya to my chest, needing to say goodbye. It'd be hell to do so, but better for the both of us.

"Not hate, Hawk. Always love."

And just like that, I knew we'd be okay, even if it wasn't in the way I'd originally planned.

CHAPTER TWENTY-EIGHT

Summer

My father told me when I was thirteen that I'd forever be his baby girl no matter what age I was. He swore to protect me and love me, be with me through every good and bad experience. But now, eleven years later, I realized how little like a fairy tale my life had become. And without my dad there to hold my hand while I sat alone in a hospital waiting room, saddled with a breaking heart and a nervous brain, I felt lost.

The door to the lobby creaked open. A nurse poked her head inside, smiling brightly with a handful of papers. "He's ready."

I didn't hesitate to follow this time, knowing what was coming.

Goodbyes may have hurt, but the thought of not saying goodbye was unbearable.

I'd spoken to the biker men who'd been outside my and Niyol's hotel room the night of his accident. They'd swung by the hospital, not to check on him, but to ask if I'd seen anything suspicious. When I said I hadn't, they then told me I needed to stay quiet about the entire situation, explaining how they'd taken care of things on their own… whatever *that* meant. For some reason, the Vegas motorcycle people had been adamant about keeping the police out of this whole ordeal—I hadn't seen a single officer pour in or out of Niyol's hospital room since he'd been admitted. Nor had any officer of the law come to me. But, I wasn't about to question it.

In a warped way, I was kind of starting to trust those two men anyway. And, believe it or not, I was also starting to understand just how different their world was compared to mine.

That was ultimately why I'd kept my lips sealed shut.

During the three days Niyol had been here, I never went into his hospital room to check in. Thankfully, though, his nurses were always sweet enough to update me. But because I'd avoided Niyol, he'd blown up my phone with his millions of messages and texts. Around the million and one mark, I'd finally decided to reply with a simple text saying: *I'm safe, still around, and won't leave town until you're discharged.*

After that, I'd turned off my phone, only turning it on to occasionally communicate with his stepmom and stepsister. I hadn't told either Lisa or Emily what had happened. There was no point in worrying them if Niyol was going to be okay. But I did say we had gotten lost along the way, which was why we'd taken a little longer than planned.

It seemed to satisfy Lisa, but Emily didn't sound as convinced.

My growing feelings for Niyol were tearing me up. At the same time, being alone the last couple of days left me with way too many what-ifs to make sense of anything else. Like, what if I would've gone with him the night he'd been shot? What if I'd ignored my sudden bout of emotions and become the strong woman I knew I could be instead? He might not have left the motel at all, if that was the case. Worse yet, I might have gone with him and been hurt too.

I could be home right now, making lesson plans for cheers, creating new routines for the upcoming tryouts. Yet had I gone the safe route, stayed behind in Illinois and not agreed to this entire trip, then I never would have met Niyol... which could have been a good thing.

Or not.

But then Emily would have had to miss out on her cruise with Sam. And Lisa couldn't miss any work, or she would've lost her job. What kind of friend would I have been if I had let those things happen? Though I had every intention of thinking selfishly, I knew it wasn't me.

I lived for my friends and family. Making them happy was what made me happy. Being someone's second wasn't all that bad, not that it mattered anymore. I'd chosen my fate, made up my mind. What-ifs did me little good in the grand scheme of things.

I stepped out of the waiting area and walked toward Niyol's room, mentally preparing myself for what I was about to see. Him and Maya, cozied up and ready to live out their version of a happily ever after.

Outside his door I sucked in a breath and tapped my fingers against the wall behind me. That's when the sound of a wheelchair and a woman's laugh echoed into the hall. I looked over, expecting the dark-haired beauty I'd met a few days prior, but only seeing Niyol and his nurse.

"Hey." I bit my lip and gave him a tentative wave.

He smiled at the sight of me, eyeing me from head to toe. For the first time since we'd met, it wasn't a sexual look, but a look of pure relief instead.

"Thanks for not cutting out on me, Princess."

I swallowed the lump in my throat at his nickname, then shrugged. "Figured you needed your stuff." I hitched his bag up on my shoulder a little higher, peering into his room at the same time. It sat empty, no Maya in sight. "Where's Maya? I was hoping to say goodbye to her too."

He frowned, dark circles appearing deeper beneath his eyes. In the span of three days, Niyol looked as though he'd aged ten years. Still, his handsome, rugged face never failed to make my palms sweat. I wiped them against my shorts.

"Gone." He frowned at his lap.

"Oh, um, I thought she was driving you the rest of the way to San Diego."

He glanced up at his nurse. "Can you give us a few minutes?"

"Five minutes." She tapped her imaginary watch. "I'll use the bathroom, then I've got to get you pushed to the front and head back to work."

Nodding once, he looked from her to me, a brightness in his gaze that wasn't there two seconds ago. "I have a favor to ask you."

My heart skipped like a traitorous villain. "And I *may* or may not have an answer."

He chuckled. "If you don't have plans to rush home, I still need that ride to San Diego after all."

The breath in my chest stalled out. Or maybe I'd lost the ability to breathe at all; my lungs declaring me gone, even though my heart still beat. "What about—"

"Maya had to get back to work." He looked at my neck, avoiding my eyes.

What was he not telling me?

"Oh." Damn it, this man. I swore to myself I could handle this—his inevitable rejection was always there in the back of my head. It was what I'd been preparing for. Yet now he'd thrown a wrench into my best-laid plans, short-circuiting my already misfiring brain.

"Why did you call her?" he asked on a whisper.

I didn't have to think about my answer. "Because you love her."

He opened his mouth to say something in return, but I interrupted. "Maybe you should just fly the rest of the way. Or take a Greyhound. I'll pay for the ticket if you need." I took a step back, but he grabbed my wrist, stopping me. "It's only a few hours," I continued, desperate to run—to keep distance between us before I fell even harder than I already had.

"I *can't* fly."

"It's not so bad to fly, I promise. My guess is, you'll literally be in the plane for, like—"

"I'm not gonna fly, Summer. And I'm sure as hell not riding in a Greyhound. *You* are gonna finish driving me."

"But what if I don't want to?"

He lifted his hand and squeezed my elbow, lowering his voice as he said, "You have to. I need to do something there, and only *you* can take me."

"That makes zero sense," I huffed.

"It will. I promise you."

"So, what, you expect me just to be at your beck and call? Your servant *and* your chauffeur now? Hell, you don't *need* me anymore, Niyol. Yet you keep pulling me back and I… I can't do it. I can't."

God, that hurt to say. All of it. Not because of the driving or the trip, but because my heart wanted him so badly to need me as his, like I desperately wanted to call him mine.

"Please. Just trust me."

"Trust." I snorted. "Funny how you can throw that word around so easily."

I felt him stiffen, saw the dark regret fill his eyes too. But it didn't last long. And soon determination took hold of his face, so fierce I couldn't look away.

"Damn it, Summer. I can't tell you why until we get there, but I can promise there's something in it for you."

"There's nothing I need from you." My bottom lip wobbled, my eyes blurred.

"You *do* need this," he nearly cooed at me. "Finishing this trip is as much for you as it is for me."

I looked away, my heart thundering loudly in my ears. "We don't even have a car, remember?" I was grabbing at straws, desperate. "Our experience with them hasn't been the best."

"Gramps is pissed as hell about his bike, but he's also got a soft spot for blondes, so he sent us a limo." I heard the grin in his voice, likely thinking he had me right where he needed me.

"A limo?" I scowled.

"Top of the line." He waggled his eyebrows up and down.

"Don't you have to have a special kind of license to drive one of those?"

"Probably."

I dropped my chin to my chest. "Ugh. Why can't you drive alone?"

He caressed the back of my elbow, causing goosebumps to form on my skin. "I need a nursemaid."

I away pulled my arm, not liking his soft caresses, let alone his excuses, then turned to look at the bathroom door. Where was that nurse?

"What if I told you I've already booked a plane ticket home?"

"Cancel it."

"That costs *money.*"

One side of his mouth kicked up. "I'll reimburse you."

"How? By robbing a bank?" I huffed.

"Don't tempt me." That's when he grabbed my hand again and pulled me to his lap.

I squealed, nearly falling over. "What are you doing?"

With his arm wrapped tightly around my waist, he leaned close to my ear and whispered, "Please, Summer. Finish this adventure with me."

Irritation itched my nerves at his choice of words. Adventure? This was no adventure. This trip had been a test of my wills, my sanity even. No longer did I want to be near him, be close to him, or let him touch me even. No longer did I want to think of the 'what-ifs' when we'd only wind up a 'never-could-be.'

But his eyes darn near twinkled. Add that to all his sweet, sudden charm, and I could only be so strong. Someday I would learn. But apparently that day wasn't going to be today.

"Why, Niyol? Why does it matter so much that I do this with you?" I asked.

It wasn't his fault I felt the way I did. He'd told me from the first moment we'd touched that anything between us couldn't happen the way I would likely want it to. Yet there I was, wholeheartedly feeling things for the one guy I couldn't have but wanted so much it hurt to even breathe in his presence.

Fingers slid just under the back of my shirt, sending tingles across my shoulders. I swallowed my hiss and ignored his flaring eyes, the hot breath of his mouth against my neck and chin. But his whispered words? They were impossible to deny.

"Because I need you more than I need anything, or anyone, right now."

"Well, you can't have me anymore, damn it." Frustration had my hands balling in my lap.

Before he could respond, the nurse popped out of the bathroom and headed our way. I took the moment and rose from his lap, my back turned to him as I slowly whispered the words I'd probably live to regret. "I'll drive you to San Diego. I'll finish this *trip*. But after that?" I shook my head, refusing to look at him for fear I wouldn't get the words out. "I can't see you again."

And then I left him there, locking myself inside the bathroom. Separating myself from the pain while facing the reality alone in the confines of a small stall. My mistaken feelings for Niyol were bittersweet and honest, but something I could never live out.

CHAPTER TWENTY-NINE

Niyol

Twenty-four hours had passed since I'd been discharged from the hospital. Yet there we were, back on the road like nothing had changed. At least for me it hadn't.

Summer was a whole other story.

"You're quiet today." I leaned against the window, wincing. Even on pain meds, my body was sore as shit. Some broken ribs from the fall off the bike, adding to the GSW in the back of my shoulder. Guess I shouldn't complain. It could've been worse.

"I don't have anything to say."

I nudged her thigh with my foot over the console. "You *always* have something to say."

"Not today, I don't."

She stared out the windshield of the limo—or should I say, the hearse—with a blank expression. Not real sure where Gramps had gotten this beast. Hell, I'm not even sure how Summer was driving it. I'm betting he'd sent it on purpose as some sort of sick joke for fucking up his bike—not that it was my fault. The only good thing was, it'd get us to San Diego in one piece.

Just before we started back on the road, I'd gotten a phone call from Slade. He and Archer had covered for me after all, telling Flick and the brothers that I *was* coming back, but had to go see

Maya first, my Gramps too. Either the two of them were in my brain and could read the future, or they were lucky-ass guessers, because I'd never said yes to returning.

But I'd never said no either.

Still, I was thankful as fuck to still have them at my back, especially since the club was my next stop after today.

I blew out a slow breath and studied Summer in the driver's seat. Summer, with her extra-large coffee tucked in between her thighs like always. Summer who hadn't bothered to look me in the eyes all day. Summer who'd apparently given my phone a workout with all her calling.

Not only had she called Maya, but she'd also called Archer, which was how he'd found out about the accident. In turn, he'd called Flick and the brothers back at home, then bought return plane tickets—two of them.

The thought of Summer calling the people who mattered the most to me set her a notch above everyone else in my life. I just hoped she wasn't too pissed when she found out *why* I wanted to finish this trip with her.

"Let's play another game," I suggested, all too aware of what had happened during our last one. She must have felt the same way, because her cheeks turned pink. Another thing I fucking loved. The woman was all sorts of bashful but had a whip-fire tongue when she needed it the most.

Instead of ignoring me like I expected, she smirked and said, "My choice?"

I nodded. "What'll it be? The license-plate game? I spy?"

She shook her head. "No. I'm not into kids' games."

I chuckled. "Don't I know."

Her eyes narrowed. "I want to play ask me/ask you."

I stretched my legs out and scowled at the dash. "Not sure if I like the sound of that."

"What?" she huffed. "Are you scared?"

"Yeah. I kind of am." Honest-to-God terrified of where this could lead. Yet I found myself curious about the prospect of getting inside her head, even though I didn't want her in mine just yet. "I'm tired of the quiet, so shoot. Ask me anything. About my past, my present, or my future."

"Fine. Where's Maya?"

Not the question I was expecting.

I shifted in my seat. "Told you she had to go home."

"You're telling me, the supposed love of your life couldn't stay—"

"Hold on now, Princess. I told you before, it's not like that with us now."

She pursed her lips but didn't reply. I'm pretty sure I'd stumped her for once. The idea made me grin.

"My turn now." I cleared my throat. "Who fucked you over before you came on this trip with me? The guy you were crying about that night at your grandparents' house?"

"I…" She chewed on her bottom lip before finishing. "How do you know I was fucked over?"

"Doesn't take a genius to figure it out." Emily didn't give me a lot of detail in the diner about her best friend's past, but from the way Summer had acted that night in Des Moines, the things she'd said? It wasn't too hard to figure out.

"He wasn't just an ex."

I raised a brow at her, waiting as she tapped her fingers on the wheel. She cleared her throat and finished with, "Landon was my fiancé."

I knew that, but it still bugged the shit out of me hearing it anyway. Maybe that's why I was a dick when I replied, "You're too damn young to be engaged."

"Seriously?" she huffed. "My parents married straight out of high school and had three kids by the time *they* were twenty-four." A shrug. "Age is nothing but a number. Now it's my turn."

I held up my hands in defense. "Go for it."

"Why am I still driving you when we both know you could've found another way to San Diego?"

Of all the questions she could've asked, it had to be the one I couldn't answer yet. Not because I didn't know, but because it would ruin everything I'd planned.

"Come on, Sum. I already told you I can't tell ya that."

"I have every right to ask. It's part of the *game*. No holds barred and everything, remember? So if you're refusing to answer the question, then I win, end of story. And what I want for my prize is to be done with this trip and you too."

I pinched the bridge of my nose. "Jesus, tell me how you really feel, why don't ya?"

"Screw you, and the ship you sailed in on, Niyol Lattimore. You're *just* as bad as my ex was when it comes to being a dick and I am *so* over it."

Fuck, fuck, fuck. I didn't want to argue with her.

"Summer, I—"

"I'm done with your games. Just stop talking."

I turned to her, finding her lower lip quivering. My fingers itched to reach over, tug her hand into mine, kiss her pain away. But her wall was up. And the confession that was on the edge of my tongue wouldn't budge. So, I shut my eyes and let it go.

She'd know what was going on soon enough.

CHAPTER THIRTY

Summer

"What's the address?" I asked, my hand lingering over my cell phone's GPS.

We'd made it. Seven-thirty at night and we were sitting in a parking lot, six blocks from the ocean.

I should have been relieved that the last leg of our trip had been incident-free, but the heavy weight on my chest from our earlier fight wouldn't eradicate itself no matter how much I willed it away.

Niyol's dark brows furrowed as he held a small piece of paper in his hands. Over and over he flipped it, the small words written across the lines seeming like a puzzle to him. It was obviously private, so I didn't attempt to read it. Instead, I studied his profile; the way the setting sun hit his face through the window. It was the first time I'd given myself permission to look at him all day. And just like I figured, it hurt.

It hurt so bad I couldn't breathe.

He wore his hat today, such a strange but wonderful combination to his persona. The brim was now folded almost in half. His hair hung in waves over his ears, and the light hit him at an angle where he appeared adorably boyish—scruff and all. In that moment, he didn't look like a big, bad, gruff biker. Instead, he looked exactly like the Niyol I had come to know. A guy who was sweet when he wanted to be, harboring a touch of danger always hidden just below the surface.

"Just turn left. Head to the beach."

I cringed, unable to tear my gaze from his face at the same time. How ironically bittersweet it would be seeing the Pacific where my mom had once been, with him and Maya reuniting again right there in front of it. Even if they weren't together, it still hurt knowing she'd get what I couldn't: the boy *and* the man.

I stared down at my lap, inhaling through my nose. "Yeah. Sure. Whatever you need."

I knew he was studying *me* this time, but what for? What was he thinking?

"Okay. Let's go then." He cleared his throat as he motioned me ahead with his finger.

I swallowed hard and nodded, before pulling us back out onto the road.

My jaw locked as I drove two blocks, then four, and five, until we came to the road that ran alongside the beach.

"Turn here." He pointed to a smaller road, as if he knew the location well.

Terrified to speak for fear I'd beg him to stay with me, or worse yet, sob, I did as he asked. My strength was weakening every second longer we sat in this car. My hope was that the open air would clear my head. I made a mental note of where I wanted to come back to after I dropped him off. There was an old-looking wooden bridge to our right, long and crafted beside the edge of the water. It was beautiful, the perfect place to just let myself be—think about my mom. The perfect place to walk and think and… cry, too, something I'd been trying hard not to do all day.

"There. Stop there." He pointed toward another parking lot.

"The beachfront lot?"

"Yeah. It's perfect."

"Is this where you told Maya that—"

"Come with me, okay?"

Lost in his gaze, I broke down and agreed. It was selfish of me to act this way when he was just moments from finding the beginning of the new life he'd been searching for since we left Illinois.

Wordless, he slipped out of the car once I parked. Regardless of my inner turmoil, I unbuckled and said a silent prayer to God as I followed Niyol out, praying for strength to get me through this.

The early evening air was warm and humid, sticking to me like a second skin. I brushed wisps of my hair away from my face as I stood next to the front bumper of the hearse. It seemed appropriate to drive one, seeing as how close to death I suddenly felt. Dramatics were not my normal flair, but I blamed it on exhaustion.

I could do this. No problem. I needed to function on my own, and I sure didn't need the trouble that came with a man like Niyol. Or any man for that matter. I hadn't been single since college, boyfriends off and on, constantly by my side. I'd go home, start back at work, and be free to be me.

Except there was a huge problem: the thought of never seeing Niyol again hit me harder than the thought of leaving him behind.

Maybe the two of us could keep in touch as friends. *Distant* friends—not like how we'd become, obviously, but acquaintances. I wouldn't call us besties by any means. But at the same time, I knew I was starting to feel for Niyol something far deeper than I had for any guy before. That should have been a warning in itself, but I refused to let myself believe that six full days in the presence of a man who was virtually a stranger to me could be the thing I'd been searching for when I wasn't even looking.

I sighed, taking stock of the place where we would say our goodbyes. The beach was deserted except for his dark towering frame near the edge of the water. Niyol looked like a dark angel wrapped in black, in the midst of heaven and hell combined.

Soft waves crashed over the sand, and I moved closer, resolved in my need to at least dip my toes into the water. I hadn't seen the Pacific before. Not even as a kid.

Just like my mom.

The tide rose and fell over Niyol's bare feet, the sound of it crushing like the ache in my stomach. With careful ease, I kicked off my flip-flops and finally stepped into the water.

"Brrr, that's chilly." I shuddered but continued to revel in the sensation.

Niyol's arm brushed mine and my breath caught, trapping the salty air inside my nose. "You okay?" he asked.

I could feel him looking at me, but I couldn't take my eyes off the ocean. I felt as though I was at the end of the earth, with nothing left before me but perfection in the form of water.

Was this how my mom had felt?

"Yeah." I shivered. "It's really beautiful here." A white flag flew from a lone boat, and the image of a family aboard developed in my mind. I twirled my bracelet, feeling a lump form in my throat at the same time.

"This is your first time seeing this, right?" he asked.

I nodded and turned away, refusing to let him see any emotion other than contentment trickle across my face. "Yes."

Our elbows touched when he moved even closer. This time I shut my eyes at the simple connection. The heat of his body soaked into mine, teasing me with what I couldn't have. But then Niyol did the unspeakable, stealing the breath from my lungs when he threaded his fingers through mine.

I stared down at our interlocked hands. *Why?* was the first thought that passed through my mind. The second? *Thank you.*

Wordlessly, he pulled me deeper into the ocean until the water engulfed our ankles completely. Once we were in place, he began to speak.

"Summer, I have something I need to tell you." He reached up and grabbed his hat with his free hand, turning it around.

"What is it?" This was it. This was his goodbye.

"It wasn't just me making a promise to myself to get to San Diego." He took a deep breath, slowly blowing it out. "I also made a promise to get you here too. *That's* why I didn't want Maya taking me the rest of the way."

I blinked. "But you said Maya had to work, and she couldn't take you because of that."

"I did." He cringed. "But I lied. Maya had work, but that's not why I didn't wanna go with her."

My shoulders tensed. "I don't understand."

He grabbed my other hand, pulling me around to face him. I stumbled a bit, my bare toes brushing against his beneath the water. He wrapped his uninjured arm around my waist, and a sensation of *home* rushed through me.

"I'm not staying in San Diego, Summer."

"What are you talking about?"

He lifted his bad arm to touch my waist. But then he winced, and I stepped closer, so he didn't have to stretch as far. Confused or not, I didn't like the idea of him hurting.

"The night I was shot," he continued. "I decided that I wanted to go back to Illinois. Try to make things right with the club."

My lips made a tiny O, but I couldn't figure out exactly how his words made me feel. Relieved wasn't the right thought, mainly because his old world seemed so incredibly dangerous. But I also couldn't deny how my heart skipped a few beats at the thought of him coming home, being close to me all the time. It was a thought I'd entertained far more often than not over the last week.

"I was getting ready to come back and tell you, but that didn't work out."

"Obviously." I snorted.

Using his good arm, he let go of my hand and pinched my chin with his thumb and forefinger. "You gonna let me finish?"

I folded my arms, not trusting myself to keep distance between us. "I'm listening."

"Like you pointed out," he grumbled, dropping his hand away. "I couldn't come back to the hotel. But in the hospital, when I woke up, I realized something else."

"What's that?" I asked, remembering the exact moment when the nurse had come in and told me he was going to be okay. It was ten minutes after I'd met Maya.

I'd been crying when she found me there. And the second I looked at her, there was a connection between us, one I could only describe as a mutual affection for a man that was only meant for one of us.

"I didn't want to go back home till I finished this trip with you."

I spread my arms out, feeling my throat swell, refusing to think beyond just his words. He didn't mean anything by it. He was just being Niyol.

"Well, we're here now. Can we go?"

"You are so damn stubborn, you know that?"

There wasn't any malice in his words. And the smirk on his face proved just how crazy relaxed he was. I, on the other hand, felt like I was walking on a tightrope, no restraints attached.

"No. Getting you here was only half my plan."

"Plan?" My lips twisted. I wanted to be angry. Angry because he'd wasted my time and money on the remaining part of this trip because he was too chicken to fly on a plane. Too prideful to take a bus or train either.

"Yeah. This moment, telling you the truth, was the second half of my reason for wanting you to finish this with me."

"Then tell me the rest," I barked angrily. "Because if this is some spiel about *it's been fun messing around with you, but I need space*, then fine. Take your space, Niyol. Take it all."

"Stop it." He reached up and squeezed my elbow. "Please. You need to hear me out. Please." His voice held a tinge of desperation to it that I couldn't ignore. Which was exactly why I decided to hear him out. Desperate Niyol was about as appealing as sexy Niyol because he was actually real in that moment. Vulnerable, too.

I nodded, because speaking would hurt my already clogged throat.

"That night in your truck at the campground? When you were telling me about your mom and that bracelet? I was listening, Princess."

My chest squeezed tight at the thought of him remembering something so small, even if it meant the world to me. "What about it?"

"You wanted to come here, for your mom." He reached over and grabbed my bracelet, fingering the tiny shell.

My eyes welled with tears at the simple touch, his simple thoughts, his simple reasons. "You wanted to finish this trip with me because *I* wanted to see the Pacific Ocean?"

"Yeah. I wanted to give you this…" He lifted his good hand and pointed out at the ocean behind me, a boyish smile on his face. Then he reached over and touched my bracelet again. "…for this. Your mom."

I blinked, the warmth of my tears falling down my cheeks.

His face paled a little, brows furrowed in confusion, maybe fear too. "Shit. Did you not want to? I thought…"

I shook my head, then touched my mouth, lips shaking beneath the tips of my fingers. Words were robbed from my throat, but the tears falling couldn't be stopped. Niyol didn't want to finish the trip for himself. For Maya neither. Nor did he want to finish for a chance at a new life. He wanted to finish so I could see the Pacific for the first time, so I could try and connect with a woman I'd never known but would always love.

My mom.

I stepped even closer, our thighs brushing. Then I swatted his chest like one of the middle-school girls at school when they wanted attention from a boy.

"You are so *stupid.*"

"Huh?" He jerked his head back, frowning.

"You could still be in danger! You never know about those *rogue* people. There could be more laying low and waiting to strike." And now I was starting to talk like him. Joy. "I didn't *need* to see the ocean, Niyol. It was a want. Do you know the difference?"

Though if that was the case, then why the hell was I blubbering?

He shrugged and smiled, like everything I'd just brought forth was the lamest reason as to not do this.

"Your differences between needs and wants are a hell of a lot different than mine."

My idiot heart stopped, restarting at a pace I couldn't control. The thunder of my pulse echoed along with the splash of the ocean in my ears. Inches apart, I stared up into his eyes, my stomach swirling at the look inside. He grinned even wider, likely realizing he'd done an amazing thing, no matter how risky it had been. So as much as I wanted to berate him, I couldn't find it in me to do anything but wrap my arms around him and hold him close.

"You could've been happy without doing this," I whispered, my cheek pressed to his chest. I was so thankful for this man in front of me. For his selflessness when I didn't think he had it in him at all.

"Hell no," he kept going. "All my happiness and promises and future? They're all connected to one thing now. And that's you."

I leaned back enough to prop my chin onto his chest. "Me?" My voice quivered.

His lips kicked up on one side. "Hell yeah."

I squeezed my eyes shut, none of this making sense. He was sealing me over like I was a cut that wouldn't cease bleeding, sucking me all in with his emotions. That had to be it. When I stepped back, he must've seen the question in my eyes, because he kept going, like he had this entire speech planned out in his head.

The paper in his hands from the car? I blinked the thought away. *No. It couldn't be.*

"I knew things were changing the day I met you at that diner. Then, at your grandparents' house, up in that bedroom when I nearly kissed you…" He shut his eyes, almost like he was reliving the experience. "It's like… Shit, I wanted nothing more than to make a life with you happen. I just wasn't sure how to go about doin' it."

"Niyol," I whispered, pressing my palms to his face. "Look at me." He opened his eyes, the dark pools nearly scorching. "Of course you were bound to feel something for me when we went through all of the things we did. This entire trip was fueled with adrenaline-packed emotions. It's not… healthy. You and me? We wouldn't make it in the real world. We're too different."

It hurt to say the truth, but the speech I'd told myself just hours before was the right one, even if I didn't mean it. Even if I wanted to believe in everything he was telling me.

"Stop. Right now." He dragged his thumb in a slow circle on my cheek. "I've *never* felt what I do for you with anyone else. Ever. So don't try to tell me it ain't right, when we both know it is."

"W-we don't even know each other." I blinked, running out of excuses.

"Sure we do. I know you better than you probably know yourself. We have a lotta games under our belt to prove it."

I rolled my eyes. "We played *two* games, Niyol. Two."

"And guess what, I won the first one, and you still owe me for it."

"What? No way. I—"

"Don't argue with me." His hot breath washed over my face as he lowered his forehead back to mine. "I won by forfeit when you gave up."

"What does that have to do with anything?"

"Simple." He grinned, so slow, so dang sure of himself. "You owe me a favor." He pulled back before I did, only to trace his finger down my neck, across my pulse point.

"I want *you*, Summer. All of you. Nobody else. And my favor is for you to let all your excuses go and give us a chance."

My heart leapt into my throat. "Don't play games with me. No more, Niyol. Please. I can't handle it."

"No games." He held his good hand out in front of him and pressed it against my heart. Then he leaned forward and kissed my temple, lingering there as he said, "You called Maya. You called Archer, too. When I was in the hospital, you could've taken off, left me. You could've abandoned me. But you didn't."

I looked at my wet toes, remembering how awkward that had been. It had been an instinctive reaction, calling the two of them, one I would never regret. Niyol had people who loved him, regardless of what he thought. And those people had come through, proof that he wasn't as alone as he assumed.

"I wouldn't leave you like that."

"I know." He pulled away, cupping my face with one hand.

In turn, I reached up and gripped the neck of his shirt, settling my wrist against his heartbeat. It thudded like a zillion racehorses were powering down inside, the fight to the end just seconds away.

"Can't you feel what you do to me? To my heart?" he whispered, lightly squeezing my wrist.

"Yeah, I feel it." It was the same thing he did to mine.

"*You* are the one I need now, Summer." He stroked a hand down the middle of my spine, his fingers taking their time. "You're the new life I need."

"But that club… You're going back."

"Yeah, I am. That gonna be a problem?"

I thought about my answer, what I wanted to say, and how I felt about possibly dating a man who did illegal things for a living, even if he said he was going to try and change that club and turn it into something good. The problem was, Niyol was only one person. There was no way he could take all the bad away at once.

Still, I didn't say no because I couldn't. I just wasn't a woman who could spout off emotions at the drop of a hat, was the thing. I stuttered when I was nervous, cried when I was mad. My emotions were all over the place, never feeling the way they should in a moment like this. Granted, I'd never actually *been* in a moment like this before, not even with Landon. And it was scary and right and everything I didn't know I wanted. But the question was, could I let him and his life into mine? Forgo all my fears and insecurities because of a five-day fling of chaos and high emotions?

"Talk to me," he pleaded.

When I didn't respond, he took a step back, tugged off his baseball cap, then ran his fingers through his hair, likely sensing my internal dilemma. "I get it. We're different. You're a-a teacher. I'm an ex-con. But this thing between us? It's more fucking right than anything I've ever known in my life. You can't deny it, Summer. Don't try to."

I couldn't. That was half of my problem. "I'm scared, Niyol."

Our eyes locked then, and the setting sun drifted through his long, dark locks. "If you're scared, then it's because you know it's real. Us. You and me…" He pointed a finger between my chest and his. "Six years I thought I only wanted one woman. Then six *days* with you and I feel like my entire life's been one fucked-up lie that led me to the only truth I've ever known."

"What truth is that?" I asked, throat burning.

"You're my truth." He leaned forward and kissed one of my cheeks, then moved on to the next before he said, "You're the only person that makes me *not* afraid to do what I need to do. Be who I need to be." He kissed my nose. "You're not some figment of my imagination, or a memory. You're my reality, Summer. And I can't run from reality, not when it's got everything I've always wanted."

My eyes blurred through tears. "What are you saying exactly?"

He grinned, lowering his mouth just inches from mine. "I'm saying that if you're good with this, with us, then I'm gonna take you home with me, fix my relationships at the club. Then I'm gonna fix myself to be a prince who's worthy of a princess."

I couldn't help but roll my eyes at his cheesy line, but at the same time, my heart flipped, proving to me that this thing we had might be exactly what I needed too. I could still work on myself as a woman; venture into my career, find my place in the world, but at the same time, being with Niyol would also mean having someone who cared about me like I did them, without being their second.

Really, though, what good had a straight-and-narrow path done for me in the long run anyway? Nothing. Absolutely nothing.

That's when I made the best and scariest decision of my life.

"Okay." I smiled. "Okay, we can try."

"Really?" His eyes popped wide, bright pools of happiness I didn't think his body could manufacture.

I giggled at the expression, nodding once. "Yes. Really." And that's when I kissed him.

CHAPTER THIRTY-ONE

Niyol

I was on the verge of exploding right there in my fucking jeans and all she'd done was kiss me. But then the tide rose a bit, surrounding our knees, and soon we were falling, me tipping to the right, her coming straight at me with a squeal.

Biggest. Cock-block. Ever.

We both started laughing as we laid in the wet sand. Why? Hell if I knew. Maybe when you're happy, even the shittiest of luck can be funny.

"Holy crap, the water is cold." Summer shivered at my side, fingers touching my stomach beneath my wet shirt.

I yanked her up against me. Using my good hand, I stroked strands of wet hair from her face, watching as her lips curved into a smile. "You okay?"

"Never been better." She smiled at me. Fucking smiled so bright it lit up my world. Shit, I was turning into a nut case for this woman, and I didn't give two shits how I looked or sounded either.

My arm ached like a bitch, not to mention the salt was screwing with my road rash. But I couldn't find it in me to care—not when Summer was there in my arms, agreeing to give me—*us*—a chance.

"Mmm." I moved in closer, gripping her hip. "I can think of a lotta ways to get us warm." I nuzzled her neck and smiled against her skin, the water still splashing over our thighs.

She shivered. "Oh yeah?"

I nodded, grinning like a fool.

As if a fire had begun building within me, my body started to come even more alive as I kissed her lips, her chin, her pulse. I wanted her naked. I wanted to be inside of her. I wanted to explore every single inch of her body.

"I want you, Summer," I whispered in her ear, pulling back, urging her to straddle my lap. She didn't hesitate to press our shivering bodies close. Breathing her in, I dropped my mouth to hers and pulled her bottom lip between my teeth.

Pain rocketed up my arm again, but I worked through it, loving when she slipped her chilled hands under my shirt and pressed them both against my bare stomach.

"Do you want *me*?" I mumbled over her mouth, needing her yes.

"So much." She brushed her hand through the back of my hair, studying me, my favorite hat likely floating away.

"We should go then," I grinned.

"Let's." She grinned back.

I walked us to the hearse, stopping only once to grab her shoes. At the front bumper, I kept my free arm wrapped around her waist, unable to get close enough.

"Today is my birthday, by the way." Not sure why I felt the need to tell her. I hadn't cared about my birthday for years.

Her eyes widened. "Crap. I didn't know. I'm so sorry."

I shrugged, sticking my hands into my pockets. "Not a big deal. Twenty-seven is just a number."

"Not a big deal? Are you serious? Of course it's a big deal." She muttered something under her breath. Eyes now narrowed, she pointed to the passenger side door. "Get into the car."

I reached for her hand, pulling her to me, kissing her neck again. "What's the matter?"

She huffed, not answering as she stomped away toward the door, eyes downturned as she hopped into the driver's seat.

"Summer." I jumped into the passenger side a few seconds later, fucking confused as hell. Was my age some sort of deal breaker for her? "What the hell's wrong?" I reached over and touched her thigh as she typed in something on her phone. Seconds later we were peeling out of the lot.

"It's just…" She puckered her lips.

"What? Just what?"

"We need to celebrate while it's still sort of light out. You have five more hours left." As if mocking her, the sun lowered even more in the sky.

I relaxed in my seat and laughed. This woman was nuts. And I was *nuts* about her.

"That so?" I ran my hand over her thigh, inching my fingers close to her center. She slammed on the gas pedal in return, making me laugh even harder.

Damn. I hadn't felt so good in my entire fucking life.

"It's a well-known fact that sex during the day is a hell of a lot more fun than sex at night." She slapped her hands against the steering wheel and we swerved once into the other lane to pass a truck.

"We got lots of *days* to practice. No rush."

She rolled her eyes. Again. But stayed silent.

Somewhere along the way she pulled into the parking lot of this tiny beachside motel. I didn't want to question it, but the *L* on the sign was backward, and the group of pink flamingo statues sitting by the front door seemed to be having an orgy.

Still. I didn't care *where* we had sex, long as I had a woman to do it with.

More specifically, *this* woman.

CHAPTER THIRTY-TWO

Summer

As far as hotels went, this place was the crappiest of the crap. Still, it'd do the job, give us both what we wanted. And then when we got back home, Niyol and I would christen every bed sheet—every *inch*—of my apartment. Including my shower.

"We don't have to do this, you know. We can wait until we go home," Niyol mumbled as he stepped up behind me in our room. Pressing his lips to my neck, he wrapped his good arm around my waist as I set his duffle onto the desk.

His erection shifted against my backside, and I couldn't help but moan. "Yeah, we really do."

Plan in motion, I lifted my arms up behind me and wrapped them around the back of his neck. Like *my* neck was a magnet, Niyol lowered his mouth to the spot below my ear, just barely letting his lips caress the sensitive skin.

I shivered, my breaths increasing as his good hand moved up over my ribs, settling just between my breasts.

I wanted this man. Needed *every* piece of him.

As I whimpered from his teasing, he finally cupped the base of my heavy breast, kneading it like it was a gift from God. Taking his time, he used his thumb to graze my nipple, the hardness almost painful as it peaked through my wet shirt and bra.

"I can't wait to be inside of you," he whispered against my ear.

"Now. Please." I turned, facing him, and rose up on my toes to take the lead. This kiss was slow, everything I wanted and more. Just not right now. For some reason, I felt as if time was still running out, that there was an urgency I couldn't explain.

Niyol opened his mouth first, inviting me in to explore. I took the opportunity and traced his tongue with long, fluid movements.

"Take my shirt off." His voice was sure, the heat in his eyes primal as I pulled away from him. I reached for the base of his tee and lifted the still-wet material up and over his head and down his bad arm, in a matter of seconds.

Toned abs greeted me, along with his marred, tatted skin. He was bruised and bandaged, reminding me how close he'd been to death. I shuddered at the thought, tracing the ink on his chest. His belly twitched as I moved my hands back up to explore his arms and neck. It made me grin knowing I had such influence over his reactions.

I craved to feel every line, every indent, every mark, but my mind screamed at me to hurry once more.

Reaching for the button on his jeans next, I glanced up at him from under my lashes for silent permission. He shut his eyes and blew out a breath as he nodded, giving me just that as I slipped them down over his thighs.

"Summer." He shuddered as the pads of my fingers trailed a gentle path over his bandaged and unbandaged hips and thighs. He was kind of a mess right now.

"Your turn." I raised my arms up over my head, biting down on my lip as he reopened his eyes.

As I'd commanded, he slipped my shirt off with his one good arm, the pads of his fingers taking their time to explore my ribs, the side of one breast. I gasped, my body instinctively grinding against his thigh. His throat bobbed up and down, and he wrapped his good arm around my waist to hug me closer.

For a second, I feared he was having second thoughts, until I felt the slip of his hand curl around the clasp of my bra.

One lone lamp lit the barren room, setting the soft tone of his touches on my skin. And when he pulled back, slipping my straps off my shoulders, I couldn't help but hiss. Cold air hit my skin when he backed away; my nipples grew even more rigid, desperate for his mouth or his hands on the peaks for warmth. But he did none of those things. Instead, he sat on the edge of the bed, his eyes never leaving my face as he beckoned me closer with his finger.

Knees shaking, I moved toward him, stopping when his hands reached for the edge of my shorts. He urged those down one-handed, leaving me only in my ocean-soaked panties. He leaned forward once he was done, kissing my hip bone, only to let his tongue trace a line lower and lower, until he hit the inside of my thigh.

"You're so gorgeous," he moaned.

I swallowed, my hands freezing in his hair. He blinked up at me in question, the thumb on his good hand tracing dizzying circles against my hips, dipping lower into the front of my panties. Seconds later, they were off, my doing, and he was on his knees, tongue buried inside of me.

"Niyol," I gasped, knees nearly buckling as I gripped his hair.

"Tastes so fucking good," he hissed, sliding his thumb against me too.

Bracing one hand on his good shoulder, I threw my head back, crying out as he teased me with his touch, his pierced tongue. "Please, I need more," I pleaded, knowing I couldn't hold off much longer if he kept at this torment.

Like a bolt of lightning sparked him to life, he stood, his boxers falling to the floor in the process. I pushed him back onto the bed and straddled his waist. The head of his erection pressed against my entrance, teasing the bundle of nerves he'd worked over so well with his lips and tongue.

But it was his voice that stopped me short. Not because it made me not want him. But because it made me want him even more than I already did.

"Condom."

I bit down on my lip, lowering my forehead to his. "Um, I don't have one."

One side of his mouth tipped up into that adorable smile as he whispered, "Guess it's a good thing I do."

I slipped off his body while he reached down to the floor to grab his wallet. The sound of ripped foil indicated he'd somehow gotten it open with only one hand—probably paired with teeth. Rolling over, it took him but a second to crawl on top of me and straddle my thighs.

"Are you sure?" His cock hovered just at my opening, his eyes serious, full of emotion as he looked down at me.

"Are you?" I asked, watching as he tried to hide a wince.

He met my eyes with a nod. "Very."

And then he lowered his mouth, kissed me, and entered me with a gentleness that should have been forbidden.

"Niyol," I moaned against his mouth, our lips not quite touching. I arched my back to let him in even deeper, helping him, in case he hurt too much to move.

Incoherent rumbles sounded in the air as he settled his face into my neck. "Fuck, Summer. It's not supposed to feel this good so soon."

I smiled, shutting my eyes as he held himself still inside of me. "Not true." When feelings were involved, sex was so much better.

"Not gonna last long."

I stroked my fingers over his back, kissing his neck, the familiar tingles of my orgasm already coming to life. "Me, either."

Like he feared the process, Niyol began to move with tentative pushes of his hips to mine. My body responded of course, urging him to go faster, but the growl in his throat insisted I lay still. He sat up, reached for my hands with his one good one, then pressed them above me on the mattress over my head.

"Keep them there. I won't last with you touching me like you are."

I cried out at the loss of control, my body craving the intensity. And when he pulled back, staring down at me with his heavy-lidded gaze, I understood then what it meant to speak with the body and nothing more.

His hips moved faster as he lowered himself onto his good elbow, spurring my own hips to do the same. I cried out once more, not caring that the headboard was crashing against the wall. Not caring that the sheets were coming off the bed, the mattress scratching at my naked back. I reveled in the sound of our bodies together, our skin sticky from sweat. Unbridled and out of control, I screamed his name as he angled his hips and pushed in deeper.

"Summer, God." He pressed our foreheads together, crying out my name louder than I did his. My fingers ached from gripping the edge of the mattress so hard, but nothing else mattered other than this moment of him and me, together.

The tingles hit, the warmth in my belly coming fast. Our gazes locked, and I couldn't help but wrap my legs around his waist. I had to do something, the pressure brought me to the edge, the intensity too much. The angle, his looks, the feel of his thickness buried so deep inside of me, pushed me into a mindless state of orgasmic bliss.

"Yes, Niyol," I moaned, meeting his thrusting hips beat for beat. I came hard with a force, harder than any orgasm I'd had in a long while. Seconds later he was behind me, groaning so loud I couldn't help but smile into his neck at the sweetness of the moment.

Gasping for breath, we remained locked together for minutes, his body never fully losing the erection as he stayed buried inside my clenching body.

"Are you okay?" I ran my fingers along his spine. His skin was slick with sweat and cold, but his breath was hot against my neck.

"Mm, hmm. Never fucking better."

I giggled then, lost in the euphoria of happiness and sex.

Lost in Niyol, our moment, and everything we suddenly were.

CHAPTER THIRTY-THREE

Summer

He was going to break one of my fingers. Or my entire hand at the rate he was going. When Niyol mentioned that airplanes were not his thing, he wasn't freaking kidding. For the entire flight, he'd clung to me. And by the greenish tinge of his cheeks, I wasn't about to tell him to stop.

He gritted his teeth as the plane descended into the airport back home. "You didn't tell me that landing in one of these things would be like that."

I smiled, laying my head on his shoulder. "Is your stomach in your knees?" A nod. "Don't worry. We're just circling the runway now."

A few minutes later, he lifted my chin with his finger, forcing my gaze to meet his. For a long while, he studied me, only to lean forward and whisper against my lips, "Thank you."

I touched his cheek, heart swooping. "For what?"

He swallowed hard, his Adam's apple bobbing. "Everything."

With a sigh, I shut my eyes and kissed him once, lingering with my version of a *You're welcome*. This was the beginning of something I was scary unsure of. A territory I'd never known I'd be in. Something unsaid, unscripted, and un-plotted out. But it was exactly where I wanted to be.

There was a jolt as the wheels skidded to a stop. Niyol's head jarred back against the seat and he cursed under his breath. This time I squeezed *his* hand. "It's all over now."

His head fell to the side with a shaky breath and another nod.

"Don't forget, I had both of our bags delivered to my dad's house by the insurance agency. My father was supposed to pick them up and keep them until we got home."

He scratched at his neck, an uncomfortable look passing through his gaze. "Home, huh? Not real sure where that is at the moment."

"I mean, I don't know what you have planned, or where you'll be living, but you're more than welcome to stay with me."

"Are you asking me to move in with you?" His dark brows rose in question, but the smirk on his lips had my tummy twisting with insecurity.

"I mean, if you want to. No pressure." Was it too soon? Probably. Was I crazy? Most likely. Did I want to stick my head in the dirt and hide away? Absolutely.

The engines rumbled beneath our bodies, while the captain spoke his thanks over the speakers. I paid zero attention to anything else, my focus now on Niyol, and his on me.

He nuzzled his nose against my cheek, inhaling my hair as he said, "Let's just take this one day at a time. Figure things out as they come. I'm gonna be wrapped up with club business for a day or two, I'm sure, so there's no need to make a decision about anything yet."

"Right. Yeah. Totally." My face went hot from embarrassment, my sudden need to rush into things making this entire conversation cringe-worthy. And then there was the matter of the *club business* he was referring to.

Still. I'd told him I wanted to give this a chance. And I did. But something just didn't feel right yet. And it was unsettling.

"Summer." He urged my chin back with his fingers. "Don't shut me out."

I frowned. "I'm not shutting you out. I just…" I took a deep breath. "I didn't mean to imply that you actually move *in* with me, in with me…" *Which I had.* "I just meant, you're more than welcome to hang out at my place anytime. If you want to, that is. Like, you know… do the normal, dating-sleep-over thing."

I gnawed on my lower lip, suddenly unsure of where we stood. Him and I, together, this *thing* we shared… It was so new, with so little time in between. Landon and I had dated for six months before we slept together. It took a month for the two of us to even kiss. To say things were moving fast was an understatement.

Yet somehow, I felt closer to Niyol than I ever did Landon. He was everything I never thought I'd want. What suddenly scared me the most though, was one very important question: *What if he changed his mind about us once he got back in with his club?*

He reached into the overhead compartment and grabbed our two small bags, handing me mine as he said, "I know what you meant, by the way. And I don't mean to be a dick, but I got some things I gotta take care of first. Flick's likely gonna give me shit for taking so long as it is. I just wanted to warn ya."

"Oh!" I feigned disinterest and scrunched up my nose, waving a hand out in front of my face. "Yeah, I mean, of course. Whatever it is you need to do." I just wished he'd tell me what his *club business* entailed.

When I got to my feet, he wrapped his arm around my waist and pulled me to his chest. "Don't overthink this." He tucked a lock of hair behind my ear. "This is all new to me. Gotta get my legs back. Figure shit out. Just know that you and me? We're end game, Princess."

I tried to smile, especially since he'd turned that dreaded nickname into an endearment. But everything weighed on me regardless. Still, I said what I could. "Okay."

Uncertainty hung in the air as we walked off the airplane and into the airport. Even with his hand in mine, I felt like every bit of progress we'd made over the last two days was about to be wasted, regardless of his reassuring words. I knew nothing of how a motorcycle club worked, and if he was going back to them, did that mean he'd be doing illegal things again? That whole drug-running endeavor... I couldn't be a part of that. Which meant there would always be a side of Niyol I'd be missing out on.

"Niyol!"

His eyes narrowed at the voice. I stared over his shoulder inside the bustling airport, only to find Lisa shooting her way through the crowd. Dressed in black jeans, a hot pink blouse, and lacy black scarf, she looked incredibly young for her age.

"I'm so happy to see you!" She wrapped her arms around his neck and squeezed, the sight doing warm things to my chest. Niyol claimed he had no one, but he was wrong. Lisa held him like a son. Like she hadn't seen him for months, not days. Most importantly, she looked at him as though her heart held nothing but love for the boy she'd taken under her wing pre- and post-prison.

With a deep laugh, Niyol picked her tiny frame up and twirled her around in a circle. I grinned, despite the weird jealousy creeping up inside. More than anything, I wished *my* dad was here. He knew I was flying in today, even knew about the tornado and my Rover's destruction. But supposedly he couldn't get off work to pick me up. We'd agreed to do dinner that night at least, but after everything Niyol and I had gone through, I was wishing, for once, that he'd put work aside for his only daughter.

"Good to see you, Lisa." Niyol set his stepmom down on the floor, a wide grin plastered on his face.

She patted his cheek once, then looked to me, her arms going wide. "And you..." Lisa put her lips to my ears and whispered, "Thank you for bringing him home to me. I'm so glad you're both all right."

Tears filled my eyes, and I nodded, squeezing her closer. Before I could speak, a brunette bombshell came running my way. "Summer!"

Lisa backed up, making room for Emily. I frowned, happy to see her, yeah, but confused as to why she wasn't on her cruise.

"I'm so happy you're back." She rocked us back and forth, never letting go. "Sam and I left Orlando just as soon as we heard what happened to Niyol. Got back in late last night."

"Hi to you too, Em," Niyol said behind her, winking at me before guiding his stepmom toward the exit, likely giving us space.

Emily rolled her eyes, ignoring him as she kept her gaze solely locked on me. "I'm so glad to see you." I buried my face into her neck. "But how did you know what happened?"

"One of Niyol's idiot club brothers called my mom. In turn, she called me. We cut our trip short, and voila, I'm here." She pulled back and smiled, but it didn't reach her eyes.

The stress of the week, my crazy emotions, were grabbing me in a chokehold. Adrenaline and Niyol's touches and kisses had kept me together, but now I felt like I was seconds away from crashing. Seeing Emily, hugging her, it was my last straw.

"Hey, hey. What's wrong?" She held my face between her hands and frowned. "I knew I should have been the one to go with him. I feel awful that you've been dragged through so much."

I looked to the floor and shook my head. No matter what had happened, I would never regret the time Niyol and I spent together. The *good* moments, even if they were few and far between, would always outweigh the bad.

Sensing his gaze on me I looked up, finding Niyol a ways ahead of us now, looking back at me with a sly grin.

My face grew hot in turn, and a smile beat back my tears.

"Oh, God."

I lost my grin at my best friend's voice, meeting Emily's eyes once more. "What?"

Shaking her head, she reached into her purse and handed me a tissue. "It all makes *perfect* sense now."

"What do you mean?" I asked, wiping my tears. Niyol's gaze was locked on Lisa's profile now as he laughed at something she said. "Emily, I asked what you meant."

She lowered her hands, along with her voice. "What happened between you two?" she hissed at me, her mood flipping so fast, it made my stomach twist.

"Nothing happened." At least, nothing that I was ready to get into.

Stupidly, I'd thought she'd be excited over Niyol and my new relationship. But, apparently, I'd played that out wrong in my head.

"You're the reason he's back," she said.

"Well, part of the reason, I suppose."

"No, no, *no*." A loud huff escaped from between her lips. "I didn't want him to leave," she said. "But him coming back here is even worse of an idea." She sighed, the sound tearing me to bits. "That club is toxic. Those terrible men will *ruin* him again. And now he's about to bring you on the ride to hell. I thought this would work. I thought..." She froze, raising both hands to cover her face.

Goosebumps danced across my arms. "Emily?"

"What?" she snapped, rubbing her face—avoiding my gaze when she dropped her hands away.

That was when it hit me. The truth. "Did you write Niyol a letter while he was in prison, pretending to be someone from his club?"

She stiffened. Biting her lip. It was the only yes I needed.

"I can't believe you would do that. He's been a wreck, thinking someone was against him. It's half the reason he left in the first place," I mumbled, angry that my best friend thought it was okay to try and mess with someone's life so much. This wasn't her. Not at all. And if Niyol or anyone from his club found out...

I shuddered at the thought, glancing around the terminal and half-expecting a group of bikers to take her down.

She grabbed my wrist and tugged me toward Lisa and Niyol by the door. Her voice dropped to an even lower, angrier, whisper as she continued. "I was doing him a favor. Can't you understand that? That stupid club *ruins* people. It nearly ruined my mom, which in turn, nearly ruined me."

In a way, I could understand her reasoning behind it. But to make such a drastic move, one that could put her in danger at the same time?

"They're trying to find out who did it," I whispered back, yanking her to a stop. "Do you know what they'll do to you if they find out it was you who sent that?"

Emily shrugged. "I'm not scared."

I shook my head, disbelief making me look at my best friend of six years so incredibly differently now. I might not have been a fan of Niyol's lifestyle, but I would never interfere like that. Maybe she had her reasoning beyond just protecting her stepbrother, but Niyol had his reasons to want to go back. And I respected that. She should have too.

"Don't tell me you've fallen for his BS about *club life*, and *brotherhood*," she sneered.

I couldn't respond, mostly because I had fallen for his BS. More than anything, I wanted to trust him because I was *falling* for him.

"Jesus, Summer." Her shoulders drooped, as though she carried the world on them.

I took her in fully, disbelief washing over me. Not only was I going to have to keep this a secret from Niyol, but I was also going to have to try and figure out a way to keep my best friend safe.

Me. A middle-school teacher. A cheer coach. *Good God.*

Before I could tell her what I was thinking, Niyol was there, pressing a hand against my lower back, and Emily was off, hands tight at her side.

"Ready?" he asked, his eyes narrowed after his stepsister.

I nodded, a knot forming in my throat. "As I'll ever be."

CHAPTER THIRTY-FOUR

Niyol

"Well, well, well… What the fuck do we have here?" Flick looked me over, a huge smirk on his face as he stood on the front steps of the Red Dragon clubhouse. His beard had grown longer than I'd remembered, as had his hair. But his eyes looked tired. Bags hung beneath them. I could only imagine the shit he'd been dealing with since I'd been in prison. But he didn't have to do it alone anymore. I just hoped he wasn't too pissed that I'd taken so long to come home.

Shifting back on my heels, my brothers flanking both sides of me, I tucked my hands into the pockets of my jeans and nodded. "Flick."

I hadn't even been in town an hour before I'd Uber'd my ass here. Greeted by Slade and Archer at the gates, they'd let me right in, leading me up to where I stood now. We were a force, the three of us.

Flick motioned Slade and Archer away with his chin. They looked to me for affirmation—a ballsy move to make against their Pres. Regardless, I nodded. Flick and I needed to head this off. Alone.

"I want my cut back," were the first words out of my mouth.

"And I'm guessing you think I should give it to you?"

My boots crunched through the gravel as I stepped closer, sending a chill down my spine. On the outside, I kept my cool, chin held high. But on the inside, my heart raced, proving my nerves were as fucked up as my current head-state.

"What do I gotta do, Flick? Tell me." I stood before him, willing to beg if I had to.

"You ran."

"I did." Paid for it too, though my brothers had nothing to do with the wound on my arm.

"What makes you think I wanna give you another shot?" His left eye twitched, but otherwise, his face stayed emotionless.

"I don't deserve it." I dropped my head. "But I want to earn my place again. Here, as an RD."

"And, what, you think running to my niece cross-country was how to do it?"

"No. It was stupid. But like I said, I'm ready now."

He chuckled, the sound scary as fuck. I looked up at him again, trying to remember the man who'd once taken me fishing. Who'd been more of a father to me than my old man ever was.

"I was willing to give you that chance, boy. Before you left. You didn't take it though."

"Did Slade or Arch tell you—"

"'Bout that letter?"

I nodded.

"Yeah. Not a good enough excuse though."

I swallowed, looking to my right. The gravel parking was littered with bikes and old cars, along with broken beer bottles and God only knows what else. It was proof that everyone was there tonight. Plus, the music was loud, the wide door open, welcoming, as people, brothers and groupies filtered in and out of the building.

My stomach twisted at the view and my thoughts drifted back to the kiss I'd shared with Summer outside her apartment. She'd offered to drive me home if I stayed there with her, but I knew if I did go inside, then I'd chicken out and not come here. Now, seeing the place in motion, I missed Summer already. Not sure what that meant, but knew it wasn't good.

Could I have both worlds, though? Or would I lose both instead?

"I'm pissed, Hawk." Flick's voice echoed in the night, the music in the air heavy. Angry like the beat of my heart. "Not being able to trust your brothers is a pretty shitty thing in our world."

"It wasn't about not trusting. It was about Emily and Lisa. I could've put them in danger by sticking around."

"And, what, you think leaving put them in any less danger?" He threw his hands up, then let them slap against his thighs. "We protect what's family. And those two are just as much our fucking family as you are."

I swallowed hard, regret heavy in my chest. He was right. My *new life* plan was also one of the reasons I'd left. But he'd never let me back in if I told him that.

"You assumed the worst. That's not how this shit works round here, Hawk. And frankly, I'm fucking pissed."

"You got every right to be."

"Wasn't lookin' for your permission, boy."

I nodded, dropping my head. The one big difference between Flick and Pops was Flick didn't use his fists as punishment, but his words, his shame, could hurt just like a knife to the gut.

"I know I fucked up." I shook my head. The darkness outside now matched my black boots—possibly my soul. "And I know I sure as hell don't deserve another shot either. But if you give me one, I promise I'll make it worth your while. I'm devoted for life."

Keeping my eyes on the ground, I couldn't find the guts to look at him. It was my lowest point in life, begging for reinstatement. Lower than the day I stepped into prison.

"What about my niece?"

I blinked, confused when I glanced up at him again. "Maya? What about her?"

"She doing good?" He folded his arms, gray eyebrows bunching together.

"Yeah. She's fine." *And not for me.*

"No. Not anymore she's not fucking fine," Flick growled. "By you leaving the way you did, going to her, you automatically brought her back into the world you were runnin' from."

Unease rushed through me. "What do you mean?"

"What it means, is, I'm gonna have to figure out a way to get her ass back here when she's settled and happy."

"The Vegas brothers. I thought they took care of things. I didn't think—"

"Hell the fuck no. They're good with us, but nobody wants to go against your old man, not even behind prison bars."

"Fuck," I whispered, pinching the bridge of my nose.

"Fuck's, right. Your old man's got connections all over the damn place. That small group who shot your ass were just a few fuckers the Vegas crew took care of. By leaving, ratting your old man out, you've caused one hell of an uprising round the country with some of our brother clubs."

I knew it. I god damn *knew it.* My narking had not only ruined my shot at getting back my cut, but it'd messed up whatever shaky balance the club did have with brother clubs around the country. "What can I do?"

He shrugged. "Not a damn thing."

I shut my eyes. So, that was it then. He didn't want me back after all. Nodding once, I turned on the toes of my boots, even more lost than before I left.

"Hawk," he yelled at my back. I froze but didn't bother looking at him. "I never did like Pops. That's the thing." I heard Flick stepped closer.

I turned around, facing him.

"So consider yourself lucky."

I stiffened, not expecting those words.

"We'll take a vote on reinstatement," he continued. "Call an emergency church meeting about what to do next. Tonight."

Slowly, I lifted my head and looked him in the eye, trying to make sense of what I was hearing. Take a vote... As in, take a vote to let me back in?

"*If* your brothers decide to let you come home, it's gonna take a hell of a lot of work on your part to make things right. All your time. Your effort. Your blood, sweat, and tears."

A vision of Summer flashed through my head right then. Me and her in her Rover, the backseat, the Colorado sky. The tornado, her wrapped in my arms, the beach, my confession, and finally burying myself inside of her. What we had was confusing as hell already. Me, telling her my devotion was going to be fully dedicated to the club instead of her for a while, would be me doing exactly what she didn't want. Putting her second to something else.

Still... If I wanted a life with her, I needed to fix this part of myself first. And second chances were hard to come by when it came to being a Red Dragon.

I just hoped Summer would understand that this choice was being made for *us*, not just me.

"I'm willing to do whatever it takes," I said.

He lifted one brow. "Are you? Because you leave again, things ain't gonna be good for you."

"Yes. I'm fucking positive, Flick."

Smirking, he lifted a hand, shoulders relaxing as he propped a hand along the back of my neck. "Well then. Let's start with a drink."

CHAPTER THIRTY-FIVE

Summer

Three weeks had passed since we'd returned home.

Three very *long* weeks of Niyol completely shutting me out and cutting off all contact.

I'd been a fool to think that things were going to be different between us; that he was nothing like Landon, or any guy I'd been with for that matter. He would put me first. For once, someone wanted me as their top priority.

How wrong was I?

To obliterate my madness, on the eve of day twenty of not speaking to him—AKA last night—I did something that nearly broke me: I deleted his phone number from my cell.

Screw Niyol.

It was time to disregard every promise *he'd* made, for good.

From here until the day I went back to work, I was determined to bury my nose in lesson planning and restyling my loft apartment. Nothing said *life-revamp* like new furniture. My brother Caleb's truck had just pulled up outside of my complex. He was bringing my new stuff—him and a couple of his buddies. Normally, I'd get giddy over the fact that there would be an abundance of sweaty, sexy hockey players in my place, but I wasn't much in the mood to be sidetracked by more men.

In a rare fatherly moment, Dad had decided he wanted to do something to celebrate the start of the new school year for me, which led to the furniture spree. I think it was his guilt talking, honestly. He hadn't bothered to swing by but once to see me since I'd returned home from my trip. It *was* disheartening, to say the least.

There again, that's the way it had been my entire life, so I shouldn't have been as upset as I was. Dad loved me to pieces, but he loved his job more. I'm not sure why I expected anything different. It's not like he knew—or would ever know—what I'd gone through with Niyol during our trip.

What I needed was a shoulder to lean on. An occasional hug. And I needed ears and simple company most of all. Was that too much to ask? I'd already been on the phone with my grandparents three times more than I had been during the past four years. Listening to Grams talk about her crazy cat, laughing at Grandpa's jokes… It was the perfect therapy. Until they brought up Niyol and our trip. That was usually around the time when I feigned exhaustion or a bad signal on my phone. Was it the most mature way to handle things? Absolutely not.

But I could only be so strong.

Though Emily had been keeping a healthy distance the past few weeks as well, claiming wedding-planning stuff as her excuse, she was supposed to be swinging by to help me with a little reorganization. After a long talk with her about the whole letter thing, she'd finally agreed that what she did was wrong. In turn, she'd also started to panic. I tried to reassure her that there was likely no way the Red Dragons would ever find out, even if I didn't believe it. She wasn't as easily convinced as I feigned to be, but what else could two twenty-four-year-olds do?

We had plans to order pizza and consume a little wine tonight. Most of all, we were going to play catch-up, talk bridesmaids' dresses, normal stuff, even if that was the last thing I wanted to think about.

"You look like hell." That was the greeting I received from Caleb as he barged into my apartment. He motioned to someone down the hall with a hand, and the echo of laughter and heavy footfall rumbled through the loft.

"Hi to you too." I motioned him and the four dudes inside, the rustle of plastic sounding around my new couch.

"Nice place," one of the guys said—Kyle, I think, his name was. He was good-looking, single, and according to Caleb, had a slight thing for me. My brother had been trying to set us up for months, claiming he was twice the man Landon ever was. What my brother didn't realize was that my heart had in no way ever ached over Landon the way it now did over Niyol.

Still, Kyle *was* worth a second glance. Dark hair, blue eyes… every girl's dream. Every girl's dream but mine, that is.

"Thanks." I smiled despite myself. "And thanks for helping."

"Sure. No problem. Happy to help." He winked at me—playful, flirty, sweet. I begged my heart to do that jumping thing it did when someone seemed interested me. But of course it stayed stagnant in my chest. I'm pretty sure Landon had paralyzed it, only for Niyol to rip it out permanently.

Regardless, I invited the guys to stay and hang out for a while, offering them beer and pizza for their services. They were nice. Surprisingly respectful too. But, sadly, they all bored me to tears.

Now there I was, mindlessly exchanging cell numbers with Kyle as he leaned against the doorframe, the last to leave, other than Caleb.

"A couple of us are hitting the downtown scene tonight. You want to join?"

I waited a breath, glancing at Caleb, who was texting and oblivious, likely chatting with his fiancé. Saying no was what I wanted to do. I wasn't interested in the least. But memories of the road, Niyol's dark eyes, the beach and the water and the plane… It pushed me to a place I didn't want to be.

"Sure." I smiled and tucked a loose strand of hair behind my ear. "I'd love to."

He smiled so wide his eyes seemed to sparkle, and a rush of sadness forced me to hold my breath at the view. God, Niyol… I'd kill him. He was ruining me far worse than Landon had.

I shut the door behind them and stared at the empty pizza boxes and beer bottles left behind, realizing something. This was my life now, the way I was meant to live it. Fall for a nice guy, who didn't call me princess. Who didn't tease me. Who didn't suck me into his dangerous lair for the sole purpose of living his life. I was a freaking middle-grade teacher for God's sake. Not some biker dude's… what had Niyol called them again? *Old lady?* Nooooo, thank you. Not me. No way, no how.

Still, why did it hurt to breathe so badly again?

♥

"We're going out tonight. I don't want to sit around and be bored." I looked at my best friend who sat on the other end of my new couch, a glass of Moscato in hand.

"Us? Out?" She scrunched up her nose.

"Yes. Like, we're going to a club."

"We haven't done the club scene in almost two years, Summer."

I kicked my feet out in front of me on the coffee table. "I realize that. But I'm *done* with sitting around and watching life pass me by, you know?"

A beat passed before she looked at me with sad, accusing eyes. "*He* did this to you."

I froze, not having a good response. She was right. But admitting it wouldn't make me feel any better.

"Don't deny it. Stupid Niyol and his *stupid* motorcycle crap… God, I still can't believe he got to you. I love him, I do, but he crossed an uncrossable line with me by messing with you."

I flinched at her harshness. This was the first time she'd voluntarily talked about him since we'd left the airport that day. It hurt. A lot. Not just because I missed him, but because she seemed to think I was an idiot for feeling the way I did—even though a person can't exactly always help how the heart responds. At the same time, I didn't want to be the reason for any bad blood between her and her stepbrother. He was her family, always would be, even if they weren't blood relatives.

"You're not allowed to hate him." I nudged her with my toe.

She sighed and looked toward the picture window that looked over the streets of Rockford. "I never should've agreed to letting you go on that trip. This wouldn't have happened if I had."

"It's fine. Seriously. I'm okay now."

"It's better this way for you, ya know." She looked at me, smiling sadly. "He would have been a super-shitty boyfriend."

"Yeah." Sadly, though, I'd never get the chance to truly find out now.

"I saw what it was like for my mother to be with his dad. The man would leave her to go deal with club business in the middle of the night, or during important life events. Then she'd sit in her room and just cry." She looked down at her hands and shook her head. "Mom always felt so trapped. Like, he was holding something over her to keep her with him. She was miserable with that man, but she refused to leave, saying she had to stay because she didn't want to abandon Niyol." She made a funny face, scoffing. "I never understood her loyalty to the guy and that stupid club, but I'm glad he's finally out of our hair for good."

"It doesn't matter either way," I said, lying through my teeth. "What Niyol and I had was a fling. Temporary. I'm over him and

Landon both. Which is exactly why I want to go out tonight. A couple of Caleb's hockey friends will be there."

"Oh yeah? A certain blue-eyed hottie who's been eyeing you for months?" Her eyes lit up, a bit of *my* Emily returning to the here and now.

I'd missed her—this. Us. Our friendship, most of all.

I smiled and glanced at the ground, hoping to look coy instead of broken. It was hard to declare interest in one man when I was pretty sure I'd never be over another. When would I ever learn?

"Yeah. Kyle's sweet. Maybe it's time I gave him a chance." Even though just earlier I'd declared yet another fruitless man-ban.

"Okay. Let's do this then." She scooted closer and patted my knee. "Operation Hottie Hockey is officially a-go."

♥

The club was packed. Body after body lined the walls and dance floor. I stood at the bar, nursing my rum and Coke, watching the crowd with disinterest, while Caleb stood to one side of me, talking about his stats at a game earlier in the year. So, either my clubbing days were over, or this funk I was in couldn't be healed by grinding dancers, shots of tequila, or hot hockey studs. God, life sucked.

Emily stood next to me on the other side, shoulders sagging. "This sucks."

I sipped on my drink and shrugged, leaning close to her ear. "We're ancient."

"We're supposed to be in our prime," she argued.

I looked at her, then her at me, before we both started laughing. The two of us were old souls, twenty-four going on forty. If we could've lived in a coffee shop drinking dark blends and creamers for the rest of our lives, we probably would have.

Still, this was my idea. And I needed the distraction.

So, we danced a little. I flirted with Kyle on occasion, never once feeling that spark. The majority of the time, Emily was texting Sam, all smiles and swoons and making me completely jealous. I wanted that, not this. Not the bar scene, the dance scene, nothing that felt like so much effort.

"Wanna dance?" Kyle asked after an hour and a half. He settled his hand between my shoulder blades, but, again, nothing happened. Not a spark. Not a shiver. Not a single. Damn. Thing.

I sighed, looking away. Did I want to dance when it meant I might inevitably be leading him on? No. If anything, I wanted to go home and curl up on my couch, eat Ben & Jerry's and cry over romantic tragedies. But that was no way to get over a heartbreak either. Not in the least. Which was why I did what I did.

"Sure." I smiled, leading Kyle back to the bar first. "But let's do a couple more shots. I need some liquid courage." He smiled, doing as I asked. And then when it was time to dance, we did. His body against mine, his hands staying below the breasts, and above the ass. Respectful. A gentleman. Perfect.

No matter how much alcohol I pushed down my throat, though, nothing could get me to feel anything but sadness and longing and a deep sense of regret that this was what my life had come to. Still, those wretched thoughts didn't stop me from inviting Kyle home with me.

Kyle held my hand in the cab, talked to me about hockey and his schedule, life on the road, and the NHL. We both loved kids. We both wanted to stay in the suburbs instead of moving to downtown Chicago. We enjoyed reading, though he preferred thrillers and I loved romances. On paper, Kyle and I were perfect for one another.

But paper disintegrated eventually, just like he and I would too.

"Thanks for inviting me back to your place." His hand stayed perfectly centered along my back; even with all the alcohol we'd indulged in he never stepped over the line. God, what I wouldn't give to just feel something for him. *Anything.*

"You're welcome."

The buzz in my head at least kept me numb to my surroundings as I walked down my hall to my apartment door. I unlocked it but didn't turn the knob. The problem with me drinking into the late hours of the night meant I wouldn't sleep. At least not soundly. Sure, I'd fall asleep right away, but an hour or two later I'd likely wake up with a headache and a churning stomach.

Maybe I just wouldn't sleep at all. I could stay awake and eat some ice cream… Ice cream cured all, didn't it?

Yes. Absolutely. My now sole purpose in life was drowning my sorrows with a tub of Vanilla Bean and bingeing on rom coms until I passed out cold.

There again, doing so with a man I was in no way interested in, standing just outside my door, wasn't possible.

Until it was.

"Listen, Summer…" Kyle touched my elbow, a sad smile on his lips when I spun around to face him. "I don't think I'm going to be coming in after all." He pulled his hand away and tucked both into his jean pockets. "You're a sweet woman. And I like you a lot, in fact. But… you're not with me."

I flinched, blinking up at him outside my door. "I'm sorry?"

"Sorry. Let me rephrase." He cleared his throat. "Whoever he is, the man who has your heart? He's a lucky guy."

My eyes welled with instant tears, and I stood on my tiptoes to wrap my arms around his neck. "And you're going to make some woman very happy someday."

He chuckled against me, his hand sliding along the back of my neck. "Talk soon?"

"Yeah. Soon." Though we both knew that wouldn't be the case.

♥

I slept fitfully that night, until the sun crept through the lone window in my quiet living room. Through the glass pane, I blinked my sleepy eyes, and watched the trees from the courtyard out back flit and flutter in the wind. I thought to myself: *This could be my life*. Alone most nights, waking with wretched hangovers. All I needed now was a cat.

Head throbbing, I leaned over to grab my cell. No new calls. No texts, just the lonely time of nine-twenty a.m. flashing back at me. I sighed and settled the phone on my chest, ready to sleep the day away. Until a knock sounded at my door.

Groaning, I slowly sat up, kicking my blanket onto the floor. Another knock sounded just seconds later, louder. Angrier.

"Coming, damn it."

I looked out the peephole, lip curled, finding the last person I ever expected.

CHAPTER THIRTY-SIX

Niyol

I shouldn't have been there. It was early, and she was probably still sleeping. But I couldn't be without her any longer than I already had.

A few brothers who were still undecided when it came to my coming back had put up a fight about my return at church. Said I needed to pay for my abandonment. In the end, the rest were good with my return, having picked their sides long before Pops got put away. But the new prospects replacing the rogues who'd left were not as trusting.

In the end, one church vote later, I was back in. Permanently.

It just wasn't with open arms.

Flick had been right when he said I'd be making up for my running away. What I never counted on, though, was sacrificing my life with Summer, completely, for three weeks. Now, though, I was finally in a place where I felt that I could have both. If she'd have me, that was.

I had to earn back my brothers' trust. Doing so meant cutting off ties with the outside world, no warning. Ties that included Lisa, Emily, and worst of all, Summer. It was brutal. It was fucked up. It was complete and utter hell. But in the end, it was worth it because when they gave me back my cut, along with a new bike, I was proud to wear it and ride it for the first time in my life. I was home, with my family. Now I just needed Summer at my side to complete it.

For the past three weeks, my life had been a living shithole. I wasn't punished physically, thank fuck, but mentally I was tested. Locked away from all the meetings in church, doing the grunt work as a prospect, living in the shittiest dorm, and not allowed to do anything club related. I was treated like the fucker I was. Worse than a prospect, really.

Archer and Slade had been right though. Things were already changing for the better now that Flick was Pres. Drug running with shit suppliers had been halted for the most part. Dealers had changed, kept on lockdown most of all. The club had gotten pickier as to who they dealt with in the end. Anyone who wanted otherwise was told to leave. Flick even took in my ideas about what I'd hoped to see done with the club, claiming he wanted that too, but would need my help making it happen. First though, we needed to make it right with the other clubs that were still with Pops.

Now Flick, along with Archer as temporary VP and Slade, the new Road Captain, were already trying to figure out how to go about doing so. Money was a big thing, financially buying out others' loyalties. It sucked that it had to be that way, and yeah, it *was* my fault. But in the end, it'd be worth it—though their final plans on getting the cash to make it happen wasn't something I was necessarily okay with.

They were tapping into Pops' drug money, the hundreds of thousands he had tucked away. If the guy ever got out of the pen, he'd lose his shit if he found out what the club had done with his cash. But at the same time, if the money *had* to be used, then it was at least gonna go toward something worthy: Peace.

Blowing out a breath, I knocked on what I hoped was Summer's door. Lisa had told me the building name, but I couldn't remember the apartment number exactly. And Emily? Well, she wasn't talking to me—still pissed that I wanted to bring Summer into my world.

I'd tried to explain to both her and Lisa why I'd done what I'd done—been away for three weeks. But Emily told me to fuck off and left the house, while Lisa told me she understood, probably because she was more used to the club's ways than Emily was. Still, knowing my stepsister was pissed at me sucked.

I stuck my hands into my jean pockets, kicking the toe of my boots against the floor. A minute passed, then two, until the door flung open with a whoosh.

And there she was.

"Niyol?"

I reached for her hand, drawn to her, needing her in my arms. "Hey, Princess."

Her eyes started watering and she put the hand I was grabbing for over her mouth. Messy hair, flushed cheeks, dressed in a pair of tight leggings and an off the shoulder tee, no bra… She looked worn out, but incredibly sexy. The picture I had stored inside my head hadn't done her beauty justice.

I swallowed so hard I could feel it in my nuts.

"Where have you been?" she asked, face paling as she rubbed both hands up and down her arms. "It's been three weeks!"

She moved to my right, not wasting any time with her questions. Not that I expected anything less. I was a dick, fucked up for thinking she'd still want me after abandoning her like I'd done. But I was here to apologize. It was a start.

"You told me you'd call, but you didn't. You told me you wanted to be with me, but you made no effort to do so," she continued.

I moved in closer, reaching up to hold her cheek in my hand. She stiffened but didn't push me away.

"I'm so fucking sorry. I just… It was club stuff is all."

She pushed my hands down when that was all I had to offer, anger burning in her baby blues.

"Is this what being in a relationship with you would have been like?"

Wincing at her *would-have-been*, I took a small step back. I couldn't lie to her, not when I didn't know the truth myself. I'd never been in a real relationship with a woman before. Had no clue how they worked. I wanted to claim her, though, in front of the club's eyes—tell them with my words once and for all. She *was* my old lady, whether she liked the term or not. That was the first step to a forever in my world.

I cleared my throat. "Not all the time. I had a lot of shit to take care of."

"And you couldn't have picked up the phone and called me?" Her voice pitched, lips stretching into a tight line. "Jesus, Niyol. You have no idea what you've put me through."

My throat burned as I spoke, regret hitting me hard that I didn't try and sneak away somehow. Get a message out through Slade or Archer. But if I had, and was caught, I would've been done for good.

"I couldn't. I'm back with the club and…" I squeezed my eyes shut. "They cut me off. From everyone. *Everything*. It was the only way they'd take me in again. I had to prove my loyalty to them. Today's my first day of freedom, and I came straight to you."

"You're a grown man, Niyol. You shouldn't let people dictate what you can and can't do."

"Club life is different, Sum. It's a brotherhood. A family. We don't fuck around and we don't walk away. Not like I did. The fact that they're giving me another shot is—"

"You don't need to explain. I get it, all right?" She sighed, losing some of her anger, hands up in the air at her sides. "But I just don't know if that's something I want to be a part of now."

I flinched. "Don't say that. Please." Terrified this was gonna be it, I ignored her need for space, stepped forward, and buried my face into her neck. "Summer, I need you. You're my life now."

If she didn't take me back, accept this, I'd lose my shit. My *life*.

She didn't hug me back. Instead, she sounded robotic. Annoyed, even. "I'm not a second anymore. I refuse to be."

My eyes began to water. Fuck, I never cried, hadn't in my entire life. But the thought of losing this woman wrecked me.

"You're the reason I came back to face this. You made me believe I could do anything."

She shook her head, hands still at her side. "Then maybe you shouldn't have come back at all."

"Don't say shit like—"

"I get it." She finally lifted a hand, pressing it over my heart. Leaning back, she looked up at me with an emptiness I'd do anything to fill.

Fuuuuck. She'd made up her mind before I even got here.

"You're trying to find your way, Niyol. And I'm fine with that. Hell, I'm trying to do the same thing myself now that I'm home. But I don't think we fit into each other's lives the way we're supposed to."

"No," I begged, pressing my forehead to hers. My heart twisted like a vise in my chest, *throbbing.* "Don't do this. Please. I need you."

She finally let me touch her face, and when I held it there between my palms, I willed her to see my soul, how it fucking ached when she wasn't near me most of all. I was bared to her and only her, she needed to know that—see that. Feel it too.

Her eyes grew wet, filling with the same ache that was breaking me down inside. Seeing her like that, feeling the things I did… I knew what it meant—no doubt in my mind.

I was falling in love with her.

But was it too late?

CHAPTER THIRTY-SEVEN

Summer

I didn't give Niyol a chance to speak much after that. But much to my chagrin, I invited him in anyway. Instead of getting right to it, I sent him to the couch like a toddler and told him I needed to shower.

Maybe I shouldn't have invited him inside at all. But the part of me that was falling for him, the one who knew who he really was, deep down, couldn't say no.

If he and I were going to be having some deep conversation, I needed to wake up. Plus, I smelled like cheap liquor and last night's perfume, two different scents that did nothing for my hangover.

Inside the shower, I turned the water to scalding hot. As I stood under the head, I willed the tension from my shoulders, trying to breathe and prepare myself for whatever bullshit excuses Niyol was about to throw my way. If I forgave him, accepted him, what kind of future would we have? I knew nothing about his world in the club. And I'm pretty sure I didn't want to if it meant he'd be disappearing for weeks at a time without my knowledge again.

From what I knew about his world, it was illegal and tainted. And if I were to involve myself in it, what would that mean for me? Would I have to go to all of his club parties, see him getting mauled by other women? Would I be awake all night, every night, worrying about whether he'd come home or die on the streets? That wasn't the life I wanted to be a part of.

There again, a life without Niyol felt like an impossible life to live. Which was why he was still here. *Stupid heart.*

In the middle of one of my mind-boggling scenarios, the creak of the bathroom door sounded. I sighed and shook my head, knowing it was him—the man had no patience.

Facing forward, I continued to let the water fall down my chest as I waited for him. He wasn't polite enough to stay outside and, in all actuality, his abrasive behavior turned me on. It was a shame all the raging-mad questions in my mind had not tamed my Niyol-fused libido.

The curtain was peeled back, rings scraping across the rod in the process. A hand touched my waist, warm, solid, man.

"Please. Listen to me." He pressed his fully clothed body against my backside.

I sighed, my shoulders falling. "Talk then."

"I've got nothing else but you and the club. I don't want to fucking choose, but if it comes down to it, you know where I'll go…"

My face grew hot, and humiliation struck me like a guitar pick to a string, a sour note that had chills of unease dancing down my spine. I was *such* an idiot.

"I don't expect you to pick me, if that's what you mean."

He moved in closer, his hips flush with mine from behind. With slow fingers, he lifted my chin, forcing me to look at him from over my shoulder. "Is that what you think?"

"I don't know how else to think."

Niyol tucked a lock of my hair behind my ear, then caressed my shoulder with his calloused fingertips. Wordless, he leaned around me, shutting off the water. I didn't move, other than the chattering of my teeth.

"Come on. Let's get you warm." Niyol pulled back the curtain and stepped out, water dripping from his jeans, onto my floor, soaking the tile. He grabbed a towel, forgoing his own clothing to tuck it around me. Then, without a thought, he picked me up, cradled me to his chest, and carried me to my room.

The worst part about it? I let him.

Both of us were drenched, soaking the carpeted floors. Along the way, down the hall, he grabbed another towel from a closet and wrapped it over me like a blanket. In my room, he lowered me onto the bed, taking care to wipe my body down with the extra towel. Again, I let him, watching with trembling breath, and remembering our nights together on the road.

His hair fell over his eyes like a curtain, wet from the shower. Every drop caressing his lips was a seduction of its own. Part of me knew I shouldn't have let him do it. I wasn't even sure if the two of us were meant to be together now—he'd basically told me the choice was already made. The club over me. Yet there I was, a sucker for someone, again, who'd basically just told me I would never be their number one.

He stripped out of his own wet clothes, staying in his damp boxers. Both of us shivered as we lay beneath the comforter, our bodies pressed close. Not thinking twice, I laid my head on his chest, a natural reaction to being close to him now. I draped my arm over his stomach and he kissed my forehead in turn.

It felt amazing to lay with him like this again, even though this very well could have been our last goodbye. Maybe that was why I wasn't pushing him away.

The comforting sound of his heart was like a lullaby in my ears, almost lulling me under. But I refused to fall asleep when there was still so much to be said.

"Are you happy, Ny?"

Fingers danced in my hair. "With you, like this? How could I not be?"

"Not with me." I sighed. "I meant, being back with your club."

"It's where I've always belonged, Summer. And now that Pops isn't there, I feel like I can breathe again. Live the way I've always wanted to within the club."

"That's good." I paused, genuinely happy for him. "I just... I'm so confused about what's going on right now. It's going to take me some time to wrap my head around everything. You being a part of my life *and* the club..."

"That's not a no." His words were a whisper, as though he was speaking them out loud for his own sanity.

I shook my head, feeling his smile against my forehead when he pressed his lips there again. "No. I guess it's not."

"I'm willing to wait, Summer. However long it takes you to decide."

I shut my eyes, letting go of the words with my heavy breaths. "You're willing to wait, but..." I swallowed hard. "What if I don't want you to?"

"What do you mean?"

"I don't know if I can live my life never knowing if you'll be home or not. I'm not sure if a non-traditional relationship is something I want."

It wasn't. I'm not sure why I was sugar-coating it. My entire life I've dreamt of the house with the huge land where my kids could run free. Just like my grandparents had. We could host holidays and Fourth of July bashes. Maybe buy a few goats and a horse even. I wanted to be the mom mine couldn't, and have a dad, right there by my side. I'd go to work as a teacher during the day and then, at night, come home and live the life I'd always dreamed of.

Committing to Niyol meant losing all of that.

"Who says we wouldn't have traditional?" he asked, lifting my chin so I could settle it on his chin and meet his eyes. "Just because I'm an RD doesn't mean I can't give you everything you want." His brows furrowed as if a thought had just slammed into him. Lips quirking up on one side, he said the last thing I ever expected. "Move in with me."

I jerked my head back a little. "Move in with you?"

He was kidding. He *had* to be kidding.

"Yeah, I mean, I'm living in the dorms at the compound right now, but we could rent something for a while. Halfway between the compound and your work. Once we save up enough money we can build a house on the compound land."

Build a house on a *motorcycle club compound?*

"I…" His eyes were wide and serious, searching my face. Nothing about this was a joke to him, but to me, it felt like I was living in some sort of alternative reality.

"I'm not talking today, or tomorrow, but soon," he continued. "We can be together. See where things go."

I frowned. "You want me to move in with you?"

"There a parrot in the room?" He smirked, stroking his fingers along my cheek. "Yeah, Summer. I want that. A lot."

I chewed on my bottom lip, not doubting his sincerity. Laying my head back on his chest, I glanced over at my small work desk that sat across the room. It was piled high with lesson plans and new cheer routines. My planned life. My career. Almost everything I wanted was right there in that stack of papers, organized and ready. I liked my apartment. The location was ideal for now. The simplicity of it all. My very own world where I could just come home and be me. Drink my coffee in the morning, grade papers at night. The only thing missing would be Niyol.

"Say yes." He stroked a hand between my shoulder blades, his voice practically cooing. "Come be a part of my world."

"But what about *my* world? The things I want."

He frowned. "You can have that too. Told you. I'll take you to work on my bike. Be there to pick you up at work every night."

"But I *like* my apartment. And I'm getting my new car next week, so I'll be able to drive myself around again. I want a farm, Niyol." I shook my head at the thought.

He chuckled. "A farm, huh?"

I winced, hating that he could joke about this. "Yes. I want that. Like my grandparents have. I want *that* life someday."

He paused for a little bit, his fingers stilling too. "Someday, yeah, but what about right now? You don't wanna move in with me?"

"Niyol… I told you I wasn't even sure if we should be together a few minutes ago, and now you're talking move-ins and changes. I just—"

"But it was okay if *I* moved in with you, though." His voice cracked angrily. "You asked me on the airplane, remember? To move in with you once we got back."

Technically, I *had* asked him. But that was before he had a place to go to. A home to stay at. A motorcycle club to be a part of. That was also before I realized what him being back with his club would mean when it came to us being together.

It was better to be blunt and state the truth, rather than hold back, which was why I said what I did next. "Your world scares me."

He pulled me closer. "You'll always be safe with me." When all I could do was shrug, he kissed the top of my head again. "At least think about it?"

More insecurities piled on top of me at his question, but I wouldn't let them overrule my head. I was not going to agree to something I wasn't sure of. And I sure as heck wouldn't let him put me on the spot either. We barely knew one another, so what was wrong with waiting before delving into each other's worlds so quickly? I should have never asked him to move in with me on the plane in the first place. It *was* too soon. Too much for both of us. These three weeks apart had only proven that. We needed to slow down. Date. Get to know one another more.

There again, was that what I even wanted? I was sure I was falling for Niyol, but did that mean I wanted to sacrifice my chance at happiness for his?

Maybe that's what love was truly about. Losing yourself to make others around you happy. I'd done it for so long that it was a natural reaction.

Stress had me yawning, exhaustion creeping in with a vengeance. And though my mind swarmed with confusing thoughts, I found myself falling asleep against him.

Life was complicated, life was stressful, life was full of too many choices and decisions.

But naps, on the other hand, were not. And I needed one.

CHAPTER THIRTY-EIGHT

Niyol

If I was truly a good man, then I should've never snuck out of Summer's bed after she'd fallen asleep in my arms. I should've explained why I had to go, that there'd been a call from the club. Someone had broken into the compound after I'd left. Cut through the barbed wire of the fence, snuck the fuck inside, and stole some of our guns and ammo right out of the War Wagon, the trailer we kept our weapons in. More rogues, we'd figured. But were they the same ones? And what the fuck did they want with a few bullets and a couple of Glocks?

We'd only seen one dude on video getting out of their car. Dressed in a black cut, no patches, and a ski mask. He was a twig-like thing who obviously could move around unseen. A tool for someone else? Likely. By the time Slade got a crew to the corner of the compound where he'd been, the guy had split.

To be fair, I did leave Summer a note saying that I'd call her tonight. I'd make it up to her, for the rest of my life if I had to, but this *would* be my life for a long while, if not forever. Run, run, run. Stop. Go. Stop. Go. Over and fucking over. And if she didn't like it, or wanna be with me because of it? I had no clue what I'd do, but I cared about her enough to accept it.

I wasn't kidding when I'd said she was one of the main reasons I found the balls to come back. Without her? I'd be a worthless man. But making her miserable by sticking it out with me wasn't who I wanted to be either.

It was later in the evening when Slade, Archer, and I got our first and only lead. Couple of guys driving an old Chevy down the interstate toward Iowa. They'd made it just to the edge of the Illinois/Iowa border, their car dying alongside the roadside. When we'd found their piece of shit ride, the guns were right there in the backseat, along with the ammo, door unlocked. We couldn't figure out what their angle was, but we were all relieved that no blood had to be spilled to get them back.

The three of us, along with a couple of other prospects, wound up stopping for the night at a run-down shack of a motel with a makeshift bar in the lobby set up on stilts. It wasn't any worse than the places Summer and I had stayed in, but it wasn't golden either.

I'd texted Summer about a half hour ago, apologizing again. Saying I'd pick her up tomorrow, do something date-ish, because I knew that was the kind of shit she needed. I had to try and keep our two worlds apart for a little while, until the time was right to mold them together. Especially if she was still unsure about everything.

Sitting there with Archer and Slade like I was in that bar, felt like old times. Drinking and celebrating the world we were about to be living in. An awesome fucking world where there'd be no more Pops to mess with our lives.

"Tell me about this woman of yours." Slade leaned back in his chair, curly hair hanging over both his eyes and a Bud bottle pressed to his lips. The guy was quiet and deadly most of the time, always on high alert. The trifecta that rounded out our crew.

"What do you wanna know?" I asked.

"What's she like?"

Like heaven bottled all its perfection and put it inside of this one person that was made for me.

"You saw her. She's damn perfect." I settled with that, not wanting to sound like a pussy-whipped fool.

"And she's gonna accept this?" He spread his arms out wide. "Our world. *Your* world?"

I shrugged, peeling the label on my beer, hating how I didn't have a real answer anymore. "Hope so."

She told me she feared my world, and I didn't blame her. Summer had grown up with a doctor daddy and two big brothers. A situation where she didn't have to want for, or deal with, a whole lot, I'm guessing. The lifestyle I lived was something that wasn't easy for an outsider to get used to.

"She's a feisty one." Archer grinned, taking another drink of his beer. "Thought she was gonna bust my balls trying to keep your ass hidden in that room in Colorado." He laughed, jabbing his thumb at me. Slade smirked at that, and I couldn't help but do the same. "I got mad respect for a lady who tries to protect her man."

I remembered listening in the hall that night, waiting for her to get back. I'd been pissed as hell that she'd taken off, but in a way, that also proved she could handle anything. It's the only real hope I had left when it came to the possibility of her accepting me and the club.

"She's a good girl." I clapped the bottom of my bottle on the table, not really in the mood to drink now. Instead, I wanted to call her, get home to her, get inside of her again, most of all.

"Good for you two. Thinking she'll make a fine old lady." Archer leaned back in his chair with a smug smile.

I grinned, rubbing my hand over my mouth. "I wouldn't label her as that just yet. She'd likely bust me in the balls."

"You sure she's what you want?" Slade leaned forward onto the table, his eyes narrowed. As my cousin, the two of us shared the same dark eyes and skin. Unlike me, though, he saw the world as a black hole, ready to suck you in at any moment. I could be like that sometimes, but never as bad as him.

"She seems like a lotta work," Slade added.

"She's not."

"But you were so fucking adamant about going cross-country and finding Maya." Unconvinced, Slade kept going, defense for the woman there in his stare.

"Maya's my past. Summer's my future now."

"Sounds ridiculous." Archer laughed, then put his hand on my shoulder. "But if that's what you want, I'm all for it. Long as you don't take off again." He turned serious. "The club needs you."

"I'm not running."

"Swear it," Slade demanded.

I put my elbows on the table. "On my life."

Both my buddies slowly leaned back at my declaration, respect flickering in their eyes. They knew I didn't make that vow lightly.

"Well, all right then." With a grin, Slade lifted his drink into the air. "A toast to the forever kind of pussy."

I shook my head but lifted my bottle anyway.

The tension eased in the air after that. We spoke about the club's future, the plans we all had. It was a damn good night, all in all.

Until my phone buzzed and Emily's name flashed across the screen.

THIRTY-NINE

Summer

The road was pitch black, while the rain beat against the windows like tiny drums, echoing throughout the cab of my rental car. The insurance company said my Rover was totaled, which I figured was the case, and now I was just waiting for the insurance check to buy something new.

Somewhere along the drive, amid my disappointment over being ditched by Niyol, I let my emotions take hold and guide me to Lisa's house. Sometime after I'd fallen asleep in Niyol's arms this morning, he'd left. And next to me on a pillow when I woke was a Dear Jane letter. What a stupid, stupid man he was saying one thing, then acting another way.

At the same time, I should have expected this to happen. After hearing what he'd gone through during his three weeks of isolation, only for him to run straight to me the second he was free, I wanted to give him the benefit of the doubt, even if I didn't understand it right now. Just as long as he let me in every now and then; communicated instead of ditching me while I was sleeping. Then maybe I could try to accept the ways of his club. It could take some time, but that's all I had anymore.

I pulled into Lisa's driveway ten minutes later, my inquisition prepared. Emily had told me little about her mother's life with Niyol's father, and from the sounds of it, things hadn't been great.

So, it was time I went straight to the source and found out exactly what I was about to get myself into when it came to the world of the Red Dragons.

Dressed in a pair of jeans and a long, black tank top, Lisa opened the door looking as though she was ready for the runway.

"Summer? What are you doing here?" Her green eyes widened as she took in my disheveled form.

"Would you believe me if I said I was in the neighborhood?"

She ushered me inside with a sad smile on her face. "Sadly no."

Soaked to the bone and wearing my hoodie and shorts, I walked inside, looking around, and asked, "Is he here?" It was a long shot, not to mention the perfect excuse.

"Niyol?" she asked.

I nodded.

"No, I'm sorry, sweetie, he's not."

She took my coat and ushered me into her kitchen. Uncaring that I was dripping water all over her beautiful floors, she grabbed a blanket off the back of her couch and placed it around my neck as I settled at her kitchen table.

"What's going on, Summer?"

Not wanting to beat around the bush, I let it all go. "He wants me to move in with him, but I'm not sure if I want to."

Lisa prepared a pot of coffee and set a cup in front of me on the table. She tapped her finger to her lips as she sat down beside me in a chair with her own. "So, this is deeper than I originally thought."

"What do you mean by that?" I frowned.

"*Meaning*, Niyol's in love with you."

"Um, no. We only just met." My face heated, but there was no denying the extra pitter-patter of my heart.

"Did Emily or Niyol ever tell you the story about how I met Charles?" She sat down across from me, hands folded on the table top.

"Niyol's father? I asked.

"Yes."

"He mentioned it."

She ran a hand up and down her throat. Something flashed across her face when she looked away, but it was over before I could analyze it.

"Niyol has never been the biggest fan of his father."

"For good reason." I hated how nonchalantly she put it. Charles Lattimore was a no-good piece of crap, something she didn't seem to fully comprehend.

"I'm sorry. I know you care about him. And I do, too. A great deal, actually." She reached for my hand and squeezed, her green eyes going soft. "It also kills me knowing what his father did to him. But Ny…" She sighed. "He's turned out so well. A good, strong man who is nothing like his father. From the second I laid eyes on him, I knew he was different."

I nodded, agreeing with that sentiment. Niyol might have been rough around the edges, but he was a good person. Loving, protective, *and* loyal. All the qualities a woman wanted in a man. Including me. Which was why this was so confusing. I thought I was falling for Niyol: *the guy I'd driven cross-country with.* But in the end, I didn't know Niyol: *member of the Red Dragons.*

"Charles was a bad person." She tapped her lips methodically. "But when I first met him, he wooed me and promised me stability. Something I'd never known growing up." She laughed under her breath, but the sound was that of heartache more than humor. "I had nobody in my life. No mother or father, just a brother who never cared much about what happened to me and another one who was fifteen years older."

I didn't know this. And part of me felt terrible for her about it. But from what little I knew of Charles Lattimore, I wouldn't put *woo* and his name in the same sentence. But to each his own, I suppose.

"Charles sweet-talked me. Promised to give me this *wonderful* life." She smiled nostalgically. I shifted in my seat, uncomfortable with the thought of her thinking anything positive about a man who'd hurt Niyol the way that man had.

"He was so good to Emily and me for a long while. Bought us this home. Funded my business." She smiled softly, eyes locked on nothing in particular. "Emily wasn't happy about relocating in the middle of her sophomore year of high school, but she survived. Then she went away to college two years later and met you, the answers to her prayers." She winked.

The two of us had lived in the same dorm and ran in the same circle of friends. We may not have had much in common, but we always managed to make each other laugh. That had been enough to solidify an amazing friendship that lasted four years of college and beyond. What neither of us ever expected was that our home towns had only been an hour apart our whole lives.

"Emily would do anything for you, even then," I said.

Lisa stared through the dark window of the kitchen. "And I'd do the same for her in a heartbeat."

A mother who loved her child: something I wouldn't ever know, but something I still appreciated all the same. Had my own mother survived my birth, then I could only hope she would have loved me like Lisa loved Emily.

"I didn't want to hurt Emily, but we were days away from losing our apartment. I'd just lost my job and we were living on a meager savings account. I'd taken her to Chicago for her birthday that weekend, was going to tell her we were set to move in with my brother the next day. I'd wanted her to have happiness once more before I broke her heart." Her lips turned down as she studied the table. "Then Charles came along, becoming the answer to our prayers." She shrugged. "It was easy to pretend he meant something when he promised to provide for Emily and me."

I sucked in a sharp breath, shock rendering me speechless. Emily was under the impression that her mother had fallen for Charles and moved to Rockford because she loved him. I'm betting she had no idea it wasn't true.

"Anyways." She waved one hand in front of her face, wiping at her newly wet eyes with the other. "I made a decision, and though it wasn't always easy, I still got my daughter the second chance she deserved, one where she could live comfortably."

"Have you ever told her the truth? That you didn't love him?"

She shook her head. "I won't either. But the reason I'm telling you this is because I know you'll understand."

"Understand what?" I asked.

"That sometimes a person feels like they have no other choice in life but to make one decision in order to find the right one."

Something clicked in my chest at her words and I sat up straighter. "Like Niyol choosing the club."

She sipped her own coffee, but didn't meet my eyes when she said, "Yes. Like Niyol. Though he'd argue for days that those boys in the club are his brothers."

It all made perfect sense now. He felt like he had no other option than to go back to the club. And now he was trying to rectify his past. Be someone his father could not be. I sighed, then took a long gulp of my drink as I pondered my decision.

In the end, the answer was plain as day. I'd go to him. Visit his club. Attempt to blend into his world *for* him. If we were truly meant to be together, then things would fall into place. I wouldn't move in with him yet, but that didn't mean I wouldn't rehash the idea later down the road. Facing your fears is half of life's battles.

"H-have you ever been there?"

"To where?" she asked.

"The Red Dragons' compound."

"Many times, actually. It's about a twenty-minute drive from here."

I licked my lips. "What's it like there?"

"Different. But not as bad as you'd think. The guys are all a bit rough, though. At least they were back in the day. Flick though..." She looked away, clearing her throat. "He's a good man."

I frowned, wondering what that was all about. Soon, I'd question it, but my mind was laser-focused, my plan already in motion.

"Do you, maybe, have the address to hand?" I held my breath, praying she'd understand. When a smile curved her lips full, I knew I'd asked the right question.

"Actually, I have more than that." She stood, grabbing my coffee and pouring the remains in a Styrofoam cup at the sink. When she turned to hand it back, she said, "How about a little drive, just you and me?"

♥

"How's Emily been since she got back from her trip?" I leaned back in my seat and stared out the window of Lisa's car. The rain hadn't let up at all. If anything, it seemed to be getting worse. Lightning flashed in the distance, exploding in the night sky. Ominous goosebumps pebbled my flesh and I rubbed my hands together after finishing the last of my coffee. My belly was warm and sated, but my nerves were skyrocketing.

"Things are great with her, but she's been worried about you." Lisa smiled sadly, turning down the radio.

Emily and I needed to spend a day together where we weren't drinking or moving me into my apartment. I missed her—us. The simplicity and ease of our friendship most of all. At the thought, I pulled my phone out from my purse and sent her a quick text: *Lunch soon?*

Sure, she replied within seconds.

And because I felt like she needed to know, even if she wouldn't accept it in the end, I said: *Your mom's taking me to see Niyol at their compound. I want to know his world. Please don't be angry.*

The little bubble popped on the screen, proof that she was typing. But then it stopped, not a single answering text coming through. Frowning to myself, I set it in the cup holder, not wanting to know why she'd ignored me. I had enough to deal with already. So, I set the thoughts aside, determined to figure things out later when my head was a little clearer.

"Emily was really upset about you and Niyol getting together. She's scared you'll get hurt, especially knowing what that lifestyle entails."

"I know." But it was my choice in the end, not hers. Someday I'd tell her that, but not now, not with a text.

"She's been keeping busy though," Lisa continued. "We're supposed to have lunch tomorrow. They've moved the wedding up to the end of October."

This was news to me… which also made me feel like crap. Why wasn't I told this last night?

"I didn't know."

"Don't worry." She leaned over and pressed her hand on top of mine. "She's a little scatterbrained right now. But she'll need you over the next few months. Maid-of-honor duties and all."

I frowned. "You're a wedding planner, Lisa. She's not going to need me."

"Of course, she will. You're her best friend."

I leaned my seat back and shut my eyes at her words, wishing for a freak emotional reprieve to all the unclamped energy inside of me. I was excited at the prospect of seeing Niyol in his element. Nervous to be in his world at the same time. Then, to top it off, Emily's distance was freaking me out.

We had another ten minutes or so left until we would arrive at the compound, according to Lisa, so I decided to rest. Maybe a little shut-eye would help uncloud my head. A few more minutes passed, and my lids started to grow heavy, sleep catching me in its claws. But just before I settled in deep, Lisa cried out, just as something slammed into our bumper.

"What was that?" I asked, jerking upright, hands braced against the center console and door.

Her eyes flashed to the rearview mirror. Bright lights glared through the rear windshield, blinding me when I turned around to look.

"I-I don't—" Before she could finish, another crunch sounded through the air, the same car shoving us forward even more. Lisa swerved to the left, crying out as she tried to avoid going in a ditch.

Another crash, the car slamming into our bumper once more. My face smashed against the window from the force. Lisa screamed, only for her forehead to hit the steering wheel.

And then we were swerving, swerving, swerving…

"Oh, God." Dizziness washed over me as I braced myself, hands on the door, the console.

And then the car flipped, metal screeching, cracking, breaking.

Once.

Twice.

Three times…

Until there was nothing.

CHAPTER FORTY

Niyol

"Where is she?" Three hours after my phone call from Emily I stormed through the front door of the compound. My pulse seethed, cut soaked down to my skin from the rain, every bit of pissed-off fury I had in me ready to burst through the surface of my skin.

Our brothers parted the room, half on one side, half on the other. We made our way through the crowd, headed toward Flick, who sat at a table toward the back of the bar. He stood upon seeing us, stubbing out his smoke before coming around to the front of the table.

Some of the brothers hovered over the tables, while some leaned against the bar, and others stood around the room with their thumbs up their asses, waiting for orders.

"Last room on the right," he said with a scowl, pointing toward the dorms.

Slade and Archer were at my back, following me as I took off down the hall. I was met with Emily's sobs the second I stepped inside the room. She was on the small bed next to the wall, her hazel eyes red.

"This is all your fault." My stepsister stood and raced at me, hands swinging. "Mom's car is totaled, neither of them were inside, and it's all because of you and this stupid club."

"Woah, there, pretty girl." Flick slipped in between us, his gray hair pulled back into a ponytail at his neck. "Don't go blowing out accusations like that against my boys."

"How do you even know Summer was with her?" I moved around Flick to stand at his side. "You got proof?"

Emily reached out, swinging at me again, but Archer grabbed her by the arms and pulled them behind her back.

"Calm the fuck down, Firecracker. This is bigger than you right now."

Her shoulders fell as he whispered something else in her ear. Then another louder sob burst out of her mouth before she fell against him and sobbed. I stood with my hands in my hair, restless, sick to my stomach. Emily had been to the club only a couple of times, but she knew a lot of the brothers. Pops, Flick, Archer, and Slade. But here, alone, dressed in street clothes without her mom, she looked a hell of a lot lost, and it was my fucking fault.

Once Arch seemed to get her under control, he stepped back, keeping a protective hand on her back as she started talking.

"Summer texted me that her and Mom were coming here, a-and I didn't want her facing this place alone, so I got in the car to come meet them." She put one hand over her mouth, knees weakening.

Archer pulled her closer, whispered something in her ear. She nodded once, taking a breath, then starting again.

"Th-that's when I saw the f-firetrucks, the police…" She jerked her head back and forth, gaze filled with fear as she looked at me, then Flick. "When I tried to get to their car, the officer said there was nobody inside." She stopped to take a breath. "I thought maybe they'd been sent to the hospital, but when I asked, they said there was nobody in the car by the time they'd arrived." She covered her eyes with a hand. "Something's happened to them."

"Fuck, fuck, fuck." I paced back and forth, hand running over my mouth. I'd heard some of this on the phone, but not all of it.

Was it more rogues? Someone working for Pops on the outside? Jesus Christ, I'd kill them all.

I looked to the ceiling, mind growing unhinged. Yet all I could think of was Summer's sleeping, peaceful, gorgeous face this morning before I'd left her.

God, if I hadn't left…

"What do we do, Boss Man?" Archer looked up to Flick, urging Emily to sit back on the bed.

Flick took his place at my side, opening his mouth, only for someone to say, "It was a distraction."

I blinked, glancing back at the doorway. My cousin stood there, quiet, assessing, deadly.

"What was?" Flick asked, folding his arms.

"The stolen weapons, the ammunition. The fucking *Chevy*. It was all a distraction, so we'd leave town today."

"Son of a bitch," Archer hissed. "Makes sense."

Desperate, I looked at the rest of my brothers, gaze zeroing back in on Flick, whose chin was to his chest in frustration, anger, maybe fear. That's when I figured out the truth—as plain as fucking day. My back growing stiff, my heart beating like mad against my chest.

Fuck, no. It couldn't be possible…

"Somebody tell me this is all some big fucking joke, right?" I looked to each of my brother's faces. I wasn't a praying man, but I sure as fuck wanted to be if it meant waking and finding out this was all some nightmare.

Still, nobody said shit to me. And the more I felt myself rage, the darker everyone's faces grew. They were all thinking the same shit I was.

Pops had gotten out.

I moved in front of Flick, who was motioning for a phone from one of our other brothers, Bull.

"Tell me Flick… Tell me Pops is still in fucking jail!" I closed the distance between us, watching his face for the answer I feared.

He didn't say nothing, just pulled his phone from his pocket, and dialed a number.

I dug my nails into my palm, needing to draw blood. Feel pain. Because just the thought of Pops getting to Summer had me wanting to die.

"...then get someone on it, damn it," Flick yelled at whoever was on the other end, his face beet red beneath his gray beard when he turned back around. "Find out if he's still in. If not, then figure out where the fuck he is!"

"Fuuuuuuck." I turned to my left and kicked a table onto its side. Glass shattered all over the floor, causing Emily to cry harder.

"Slade's gonna get a crew ready." Archer squeezed my shoulder, suddenly there. He was trying to be the calm I needed, but it didn't work.

Still, somehow, I managed a nod, breath heavy, heart racing.

One second passed, two seconds, then three. That's when things spurred into action.

I had to get them back.

I had to get *her* back.

"Follow me."

Slade nodded, knowing what needed to be done. That was why he was who he was. A calm, dark motherfucker who would stop at nothing to get what he wanted. He pointed at a few other brothers in the room, the expression on his face deadly.

Flick turned around and said to Archer, "You, stay with her." He motioned to Emily who stood by the wall now, eyes still wet, but her face now completely blank. Comatose even.

Shit. If she didn't hate me before, she sure as hell did now.

"You got it." Archer moved toward my stepsister like a man approaching a wounded animal.

Slade and I ran out the side door of the compound and headed toward the church.

"What do you need?" I asked Slade when we moved inside.

"Weapons, ammo, a lead."

"Workin' on it." Flick moved alongside us, never losing his stride. The man may have been pushing sixty-five, but he was still a badass, and a damn good leader too.

"Is he out?" I froze, hands in my hair as I looked to the man who'd been more of a father to me than Pops ever was.

It was a gut reaction, but we all knew my old man was a tricky son-of-a-bitch who could talk his way out of prison. Or get someone to do it for him. And if anyone hated me enough to steal Summer and my stepmom, it was that man.

"Don't know yet," Flick said, opening the door, his eyes filled with pity when he glanced at me.

I nodded, needing him to know I was keeping it together now. I'd had my moment, and it didn't do me any good—sure as hell didn't get Summer and Lisa back.

Inside the main room of the church, fifteen brothers were already gathered, packing, and ready to go. Flick switched another set of lights on, gathering all eyes and attention.

"Emily's gonna have to stay at the club," I said before he could speak. "It's too dangerous for her to be out there now. Somebody's gotta stay with her."

Flick opened his mouth, only for the doors to bust open.

"You can't keep me here!" I spun around, finding my stepsister's wide eyes glaring back at me from the front door. "I have *Sam.* I need to get back to him. I need to search for my mom. I—"

"Just until we can figure something out, Em." I gritted my teeth.

Holding his hands over his junk, Archer came stumbling into church behind her.

"Woman kicked me in the fucking nuts." Accent thick, he shook his head, face pale, sweaty blond hair falling over one of his eyes. I would've laughed, if I hadn't felt like killing someone.

"What about Sam? What if he's in danger?" Emily asked, ignoring everyone but me.

"I'll send a group out to keep an eye on him," Flick answered, rubbing a hand over his mouth.

I added in, "Tell him you need a vacation or something. You've got to stay here. It's not safe for you to leave the compound right now."

Her eyes narrowed at me. "I already *had* a vacation, remember? *With* Sam. My *fiancé.* Sam who I *live* with."

My body shook with anger and I pinched the bridge of my nose. I wanted to have patience, but how the hell could I knowing Summer and Lisa were missing? Possibly in danger?

"Fine. We'll set you up at home." Flick exhaled, coming to the rescue. "I'll send a crew out to watch your house."

"I don't need anyone to *watch* my house." She moved in front of Flick, poking his chest with a finger. A couple of brothers chuckled under their breath, but Flick looked ready to snap.

"The hell you don't, girl." He growled back at her, his eyes moving over her face. I gripped her upper arm, pulling her away.

"This is all your fault." She shoved me then, two hands on my chest. "This club, your stupid father…" she roared, then lowered her voice for only my ears. "You should've stayed away like you were warned."

I stiffened. "What'd you just say?"

"You heard me." Her upper lip curled. And that's when it all clicked into place. Emily was the one who'd written that letter to me before I left the Pen. *Emily* was the reason I'd nearly fucked up my whole world.

I lowered my chin to my chest, taking it all in, seething. "You need to get the fuck out."

A slap. Her hand. My cheek. "I hate you," she hissed.

My blood ran cold. *"Good."*

Giving her my back, pretending she hadn't just stabbed it, I looked to Flick and said, "We gonna do this or what?"

CHAPTER FORTY-ONE

Summer

Tremors racked my body, and the wood-paneled walls of the barely lit room did little to keep my imagination from running wild. Everything inside of me ached, the pain so excruciating in my head I'd rather die than experience it another second.

I'd been in and out of consciousness for God only knew how long, my body dried up of blood and tears. For the first time in days, hours, minutes, I was finally awake and somewhat aware, though I'm pretty sure I had a concussion.

Someone had tended the wound on my head while I was out. It no longer bled into my eyes but was covered instead with a dirty, white bandage, which hung over the side of my head haphazardly. I was dressed in the same clothes though, all layered with the stale stench of mildewed rain, blood, and my sweat.

On a bare mattress across the dark-lit room, Lisa lay on her back, asleep. Her arm was bent out at an odd angle off to the side, likely broken, while her neck and face were covered in tiny cuts and dried blood from broken glass. She'd refused treatment when it was offered—I vaguely remember her screaming, *Don't touch me*, before I'd lost consciousness.

After the car had flipped, we were pulled out and put into another one within minutes. Lisa was awake the entire time, while disorientation kept me from focusing on faces or locations. I'd woken partially to find we had stopped just outside the front of what looked to be an old, abandoned cabin somewhere in the woods, only for my eyes to shut again.

How was I not dead? That had been running through in my head since the moment I was pulled from the car.

The windows to the old cabin were boarded off, the doors locked from the outside. I couldn't tell if it was day or night, and part of me didn't want to know how long it had been. If I found out only hours had passed, I would likely cry again. If it had been days on the other hand, I was certain I'd give up altogether.

Amid my fear and confusion, I'd finally garnered enough energy to stand. But the second I was upright my legs gave way as dizziness nearly encompassed me whole. It was why I was on the floor by the door now, knees to my chest, head tipped back against the wall. I could barely stand without feeling as though I was going to pass out or vomit. Regardless of the nausea, my stomach growled, proof that it had been a while since I last ate. Proof too, that more than a few hours had passed.

I opened my mouth to try and wake Lisa again, but my throat burned so terribly it was as though razorblades were embedded inside. I pawed at my neck, like that would make it work better. I was dehydrated and desperately in need of water.

We needed to get out of there, somehow. Soon. Preferably before whoever brought us here came back.

Thoughts of my father's face flashed through my mind right then. I hadn't spoken to him since the night I'd gotten my new furniture. He'd be worried sick, frantic in a search to find me.

My hands shook as I braced them against the floor, warmth gathering in my eyes once more, sans the tears. With a giant breath that hurt to take in, I pushed myself up again and managed to croak out, "Lisa?"

Body throbbing, I limped closer to the bed, head spinning, knees and legs on fire. I'd do something to try and wake her, I just had to make it there first. Then I would try to find something to break through the windows, though I knew it was a long shot. Another step closer and I was there at her side, but voices sounding from outside the house had me freezing in place.

"They were both out cold. Checked on them myself a few minutes ago," a small, masculine voice said.

"I've got to get them as far from here as I can."

A lump lodged itself into my throat at the unfamiliar voices, choking me. The lock twisted on the door, and I jumped, turning just in time to see the shadows of two men step inside. Bright sunlight entered the room from behind them, and I lifted a hand to hold over my eyes. The door creaked shut with a click, and two sets of footfalls sounded across the plywood floor.

Breathing fast, I lowered my arm, blinking up at the faces now lit by one, lone lantern.

I gasped at what I saw, shock keeping hold of my screams.

One of the men looked so much like Niyol, I had to blink twice to make sure I wasn't hallucinating.

That couldn't be…

"You shouldn't be up moving around," the Niyol lookalike growled.

"Do not…" I gasped. "Come near me."

"Hey, now. That's no way to treat your future father-in-law." He chuckled lazily, the sound sending a shot of fear into my belly.

Charles Lattimore had gotten out of prison.

A hand grabbed mine from behind and squeezed. Lisa was awake. I didn't turn to acknowledge her. Instead, kept my gaze trained on this evil, awful man.

"Why are you…" I managed another breath. "Doing this?"

He put one hand on his hip, fingering the gun in his holster, his head cocked to the side as he studied me. A tattoo ran the length of his cheek, numbers I couldn't make out.

"Because my son deserves to pay for what he did to me." He shrugged casually, legs crossing at the ankle as he leaned against the door. "Death was too easy an out for him."

I shivered at the thought of what this man planned to do with me, but deep down, the thought of him hurting Niyol made me thankful I was here instead.

"Besides that, he's blood." Charles shrugged. "Can't kill blood. It's an unspoken rule in my world."

A whimper sounded from the bed, distracting me from continuing. Instinct and fear had me turning toward Lisa. She was struggling to sit up, her arm pulled to her chest. Ignoring Charles and his friend, I managed to sit on the bed beside her, careful not to jostle her with my movements.

"Let her go," she whispered to her former lover, glassy green eyes meeting mine. "She's too pure for this."

"No." I squeezed her good hand. "Stop it, Lisa. I'm not leaving you."

"This is all my fault." She began to sob, heart-wrenching bellows that echoed loudly throughout the barren room.

"True." Charles laughed at her. "But now that I've got you both here, *wifey*, what better way to drive Niyol insane than by taking what he thinks is his?" Niyol's father's eyes zeroed in on me and winked.

I continued to plead with him, hoping there was a shred of decency left inside of him somewhere. "Please. Don't do this."

He scoffed. "Hate to break it to you, girl, but there is no other way around this." His upper lip curled. "Guess you should've thought about that before you took a liking to my son's dick."

Movement behind him caught my eye, and I glanced up, seeing a younger guy's face flashing with both fear and distrust. I remembered what he'd said outside the door and tried to use that to our advantage.

"Please, help us."

"Do not talk to him," Charles snarled, grabbing for my chin, digging his nails in so deep I was sure he drew blood. My shoulders began to tremble, and soon my whole body followed their movement.

I shut my eyes, hope falling away. "Please don't do this."

"Go ahead." He grabbed me around the neck and squeezed. Hatred laced his dark eyes—eyes so blistering I feared they would explode. "Beg me not to kill you. That'll make it so much more fun." With a grunt, he shoved me back onto the bed, my body landing on top of Lisa's legs. He straddled my waist, never removing his hand.

I clawed at his wrists, eyes blurring from the lack of oxygen.

"I don't blame you for getting sucked into his world," he snarled, never losing his grip. "Us Lattimores are charming men who always get what we want. It's just a shame one of them isn't worth the pot he pisses in."

Lisa began to scream, her form jumping at Charles from the bed. The other guy was there to intercept, slamming her back and onto the floor. My eyes shut, my fight, my struggle, wavering the harder he squeezed.

Before another round of darkness could overtake me, Niyol's father shoved me back against the mattress, but thankfully let go of my neck. I gasped for air and pressed a hand to my throat as I rolled onto my side and coughed.

"Do as he says." Lisa crawled up next to me on the bed, her body close.

"Get them ready, boy," Charles growled low from the other side of the room. "We're wasting time."

"He wants to hurt Niyol," Lisa whispered into my ear. "And in order to keep him and Emily both safe, we have to go with him.

But I won't let him hurt you again." Her face had grown paler as I blinked open my eyes to face her, right before she said, "I should have never let things get this far. This is all my fault."

I blinked in confusion, my throat too sore for me to speak. That was the second time she'd mentioned that. What did she mean?

"Put these on." Something landed on the bed between us. Two new dresses and blindfolds. I had no idea how I'd put them on when the simple act of breathing hurt so badly. "You got five minutes." The kid's feet thudded across the room, followed by the slam of a door.

I gasped for more air, panic overtaking everything. Oh, God, what if this was it? Truly?

"Shhh, Summer, I won't let them hurt you again. I promise." Lisa helped me undress, her voice far too calm for this. But her words made no sense; ramblings of a crazy person. "I made so many stupid, idiotic choices when I was a teenager." She helped me get my arms through the dress, tossing my old clothes onto the floor. "If I hadn't, then we would have never been put in this position."

"What… do you mean?" I managed.

"I've known Charles Lattimore since I was sixteen years old." She stared down at her hands, which both trembled on her lap.

My face fell at her words, my body still nearly limp on the mattress beside her.

"I got pregnant then by Charles. Then I married him not long after that. I lived as a Red Dragon old lady for almost two years before I got pregnant again… with Emily. Once she was born, I took her, and left."

Slowly, I managed to sit up, a hand still pressed to my throat. I felt savaged, brutalized, the pain beyond the worst I'd ever experienced. Somehow, though, I managed to sort through the thoughts swirling like mad inside of my head; all the lies Lisa had told Emily, about not knowing Charles until later in life, about Emily being the result of a one-night stand…

Yet none of those things were true.

Lisa dropped her face into her hand, her bad arm still hanging limp. "I'm such a fool."

The pieces began to put themselves together in my mind. Emily was almost three years younger than Niyol. Two years after her first child was born, Lisa got pregnant *again*. Her first child *wasn't* Emily.

Oh, Jesus…

Tears streamed down Lisa's cheeks when she met my gaze and the second it all clicked into place, she spoke words I was in no way ready to hear.

"Charles is Emily's father, Summer. And Niyol…" She sucked in a breath. "Niyol is my son."

CHAPTER FORTY-TWO

Niyol

It took us less than an hour to figure out the truth. Several phone calls to some guys on the inside of the prison that Flick knew, people he'd done dirty work for, gave us the answer we'd been dreading.

Pops had gotten out.

Escaped.

Then, thanks to a few guards he'd paid off, his revenge plan against me was put into motion.

I don't know how it happened, the logistics of his escape. Didn't really care all that much either. The only thing I wanted to know was where Summer and Lisa were—and whether or not they were safe.

We'd been sitting in church for an hour, me pacing the floors, the rest of my brothers too damn calm for my own good. I looked to Flick, my entire body raging with fire.

"I'm done sitting around, motherfuckers. We need to be out there, looking for 'em."

"Tryin', Hawk." Flick didn't look like he was trying. If anything, he looked bored, least to everyone else. But I saw the twitch by his eye, felt the shake of the floor as he bounced his knee. He was ready to feel the blood of my old man on his hands, maybe even more than me.

Not sure what had happened within the last two years to break the two of them apart. Sure as hell couldn't be because of me. But there was something there, something bad. Something I'd find out about in the coming weeks, if I was still alive.

Before I could punch another hole in the wall, Flick's phone rang.

I was at his side before I could blink, reaching for it, until a hand grabbed the back of my shirt and tugged me away.

"This is not your job," Archer growled into my ear.

Against him, I shook with rage. "Let me the fuck go."

He yanked me back, then shoved me against a wall, getting into my face. "Let the man do his fucking job, Hawk."

"That's my fucking woman out there, damn it," I seethed, shoving him back. He didn't budge, solid mass under my hands. Archer had always been a skinny guy, but the past two years, I'd noticed, had done something to him.

"Yeah, I get it. We all do. Why the fuck do you think we're here?"

I rubbed a hand down my face. "I can't..." My throat closed off, my eyes blurring. I would not fucking cry, damn it. I *didn't* fucking cry. Ever.

He dropped his forehead to mine, squeezing the front of my shirt, knuckles digging into my throat. A warning. A comfort.

"Get your shit together," Archer shook me. "You want her back, then be a fucking Dragon. Not a pussy-whipped boyfriend."

I nodded, swallowing hard. He was right. No way would I get through this thinking with my heart.

"We got a lead." Flick slapped the table and stood. "Young kid. Dee is what he said his name was."

"Who the hell's Dee?" someone asked.

Archer stepped away, meeting Flick at his side. He looked down at the paper in Flick's hand, swiped it up, then gave it to Slade, who'd been like a fly in the room, hovering. Quiet.

"Prison guard. Said he was with Pops," Flick barked. "Give me stats on the motherfucker. *Someone.* We need a real name. Credentials."

The brothers went in full-on research mode. Phones to their ears, until someone came back with news.

"Former Army," Slade was the first to reply, now sitting behind a computer at the table. Smart motherfucker he was, he'd hacked into the prison system. "Name's Andre Lopez, a former Marine from So Cal."

"Good." Flick nodded, then looked to another guy, a new prospect turned member while I'd been put away. I'd met him once. His patch name said Chop. "Location stats?"

"Looks to be a cabin outside Springfield, Illinois."

"Let's go then." I balled my hands into fists. "Now." Then stepped toward the door.

"Where the fuck you think you're going?" Flick growled at my back.

I froze. "To get them."

"No fucking way. Not with Pops there," Slade said, grabbing my arm.

I narrowed my eyes at him, then Flick. "You can't stop me."

"Think I can." Flick folded his arms. "You showing up there would be suicide, especially if this is a trap."

Teeth gritted, I snarled out, "I'm. Fucking. Going."

"Let him," Archer argued, coming up on my other side. If I could've, I would have hugged the guy. "Anyone one of us would do the same if we had an old lady."

"Fine." Flick stood and shook his head. "It's your fucking head."

I nodded. Slade growled. And Archer... he slapped me on the back and whispered, "You owe me big time, asshat."

♥

We got to the outskirts of St. Louis around six, the sun barely hanging onto the sky. "We're goin' in around seven. Bone and his boys are on their way." Flick scratched at his jaw, an unlit smoke hanging out of his mouth. He was straddling his bike to my left, eyes scanning the perimeter, his doo-rag on.

Bone was his old Marine buddy from a different club an hour or so away from St. Louis, I'd come to learn. We were riding heavy as it was, at least forty of my brothers had come along, but Flick wanted to be prepped in case there were any surprises. This sort of collab wasn't one I'd come to know within the club. Archer and Slade were right when they said shit was changing for the better. It was like Pops being put away had inspired a rise within it in the last few weeks.

For the first time in all my years as an RD, I felt a true brotherhood within the group.

We were waiting for Slade to come out of a McDonalds' bathroom now. Archer was to my right, reading something from an old magazine. He looked so fucking calm, almost bored. I knew better, though. The guy was just as anxious and primed for a fight as I was.

I blew out a cloud of smoke and tossed my cigarette onto the cement, crushing it with the toe of my boot.

"You ready for this?" Slade asked as he stepped through the doors and off the curb. The button of his jeans was open and his fly was down. A mother and her daughter raced around him to the front of their car, eyeing his tats like he'd curse them from one look alone.

"Fuck yeah," I growled.

"Do me a favor, would you?" Slade put his hand on my shoulder.

"What?"

"Keep a clear head while you're in there."

Keep a clear head? Yeah, fucking right. There'd be no clear head till I had Summer in my arms and Pops beaten bloody.

Our contact pulled into the lot forty minutes later. He was Flick's age, but bald. His eyes were evil-looking, red clouding the whites. When he pointed that gaze at me, I knew right away I wouldn't get any respect.

His bike rumbled, not once did he turn off his engine. He looked at Flick, then the rest of the brothers we'd rode up with before he spoke.

"This it?" he asked.

Flick nodded. "Simple. It's how we roll."

The guy shoved some glasses over his red-rimmed eyes and nodded. Then he was off, no warning as he moved toward the street.

"Bone, I take it?" I asked, eyeing the back of his cut. A devil with fanged teeth and pointy ears sat in the middle of it.

"Said he was an old buddy. Didn't say he was a good guy." Flick took off before me, forcing me to hit the road hard. We followed as a crew, not taking long to catch up. Driving through backroads, along a couple of abandoned streets, I searched for landmarks, things to remember in case shit went bad.

What felt like forever later, we pulled up to a small backroad just a few miles off some country road and slid off our bikes.

"We'll head the rest of the way in on foot," Slade announced once engines were off.

Quiet, so as not to warn anyone we were coming.

"Slade, Arch, Hawk." Flick nodded at each of us. "You all follow me. Bone and the rest of the boys are gonna watch our shit. We'll call in backup if need be." He motioned his chin toward his bald friend, along with the rest of our brothers. "We go in there, all of us, shit could get real crowded, real fast."

Nobody argued with Flick's logic, and if the snitch who'd called us was telling the truth, that it was just the four of them, we wouldn't be there for long.

Guns locked and loaded, we rushed down the path, a single-file line of deadly stealth. Trees covered our heads like canopies, and the stench of dead animal filled my nose. Sweat dripped down my temples, my cheeks, the back of my shirt, but none of that mattered. I was too lost in my memories to care.

This entire situation, the environment, it reminded me of the night Summer and I had camped. Something lodged inside my throat at the memory, but I cleared it away, not wanting to clog up my head.

Bottom line? I needed her back. And I needed it to happen *now.*

A good few minutes passed, then five, then ten. Impatient, I picked up speed, pushing away branches and swatting bugs out of my face. Nobody questioned me, just kept pace with a once-upon-a-time rat.

"Something don't feel right." Slade broke in first.

"We got this, boys, no worries." Flick reassured us, his gaze flitting left and right even with his confidence.

Just then, the sound of a door slammed ahead. I froze, hand on my gun as I looked up through the woods. A rusted, silver car with Wisconsin plates sat outside a broken-down house.

"How we gonna do this?" Archer asked.

A woman's voice cried out before anyone could answer. "*Please, don't make me go. Please…*"

My body grew rigid. "That's Summer," I growled. The door shot open then, and out popped—"*Fucking Pops.*"

No. No, no, no, no. Fuck.

With his arm latched around Summer's shoulders, and dressed in cop blues, he led her down the steps, grabbing her by the hair. I jerked forward, but Flick grabbed me by my shoulder, a finger to his lips. Summer stumbled and fell to her knees, crying out. My stomach grew hot with mad fury and I shoved him back and drew my Glock.

Years of pain.

Years in prison.

Years of hell that *he* stole away. Not again. *Never* again.

Refocusing on Summer, I watched as Pops grabbed her by the hair and tossed her into the backseat of his car.

"What the fuck are we waiting for?" I hissed.

Another voice slipped through the air. I jerked my head back to the house door, finding Lisa stumbling down the cabin's front steps. Behind her stood a younger dude. Our informant? Had to be.

"Now!" Flick yelled, taking off, his gun blazing. He shot the front tire, then the front bumper.

Someone went for the windshield next, but before they could get the back, I yelled, "Not the windows." They might hit Lisa or Summer if they did.

Flick hid behind a tree, Archer too. The rest of the brothers scattered, dispersing in the trees. Shots rang out from all over, a few from Pops' end, nearly hitting my head in the process. I fell to the ground, burying myself behind a downed tree. Archer dropped next to me, a *Holy shit* muttered under his breath.

"Drop your motherfucking weapons," Slade roared, his back to a tree near Flick.

Sweat dripped over my eye when I looked up again. They'd stopped shooting, but I couldn't see or hear them now either. This was too damn easy.

"Fuck, where are they?" I roared.

Death.

Murder.

Kill.

Three words I was ready to use. It didn't matter if the guy was my own flesh and blood. He had my life in his hands, and I'd do anything to keep it safe.

"Good to see you again, son." Pops laughed from somewhere up ahead. "Was wondering if you were gonna show."

I stiffened and glanced at Archer. He shook his head, a silent way of saying, *Don't take the bait.* A minute later Pops popped out from behind the car, dragging Summer along with him.

"Let her the fuck go. It's me you want." Taking things into my own hands, I tucked my gun into the back of my pants, instinct leading me closer to the cabin, hands up.

"The hell, man?" Slade hissed, attempting to stand. I jerked my head no—this was my job, not his.

"Awww, look at you." Pops chuckled. "Getting all worked up over some pussy."

Summer cried out as he put his gun to her temple. Tears streamed down her pale cheeks and everything inside of me fell apart at the view. Blood dripped across her temple. Down her cheek. Landing on her chin, where it was caked across her face. She swayed, both knees bent. Terror filled her blues when they met mine, and from where I stood, I could feel her quiet plea as much as I could see it.

I'd never fucking forget that look for as long as I lived.

"Get the fuck down, Hawk," Archer whispered, his hand on my calf, pulling on my pants. But that wouldn't hold me.

"You've ruined me," my father shook his head. "You realize that, right? So, we gotta do it the RD way now."

"How so?" I growled. Another step closer, then another, until I was ten feet ahead of my own flesh-and-blood old man. I'd never hated someone as much as I did him.

He shrugged. "An eye for an eye."

"I'm the one you want." I took a step closer, ignoring Flick and Archer. Slade was gone, maybe going to get help. Not that it mattered. My father wanted vengeance on me and me alone.

I could see the man's bloodshot eyes from where I stood. See the yellow on his teeth too. See the numbers perfectly tatted across his cheek. Prison numbers. They were new.

"Niyol, no, please," Summer whimpered, struggling against my father's hold. All that did was piss him off more, and he slammed her down on the ground.

"I'm gonna kill you." My words were calm. Deadly. Yet I shook all over. My hands, my legs, my shoulders. "I'm gonna shove my gun inside your mouth and pull the motherfucking trigger, you hear me?"

Pops laughed at that, head tipped back, eyes to the sky. "You got some good and worthy goals there, boy." He lost his smile. His lips going flat. Stoic. *Evil*. Murder. Death just seconds from his hands. "Goals that'll never. Fucking. Happen."

The gun clicked.

Like a bull seeing red, I charged him, head down. His weapon went off, pointed at me. Seconds later, a shot of pain slammed into my right shoulder. It was nothing compared to what I was about to do to him though.

I knocked the gun from his hands, grabbed it, and shoved the barrel against the center of his head, using my other hand to hold against his neck, I straddled his gut. Something wet spilled down my forearm, onto his chin, blood likely. I knew I'd been shot, but I was numb to everything but my hate for my old man.

Instead of being met with a plea for his life, he laughed. *Laughed*. His face red, gasping for air. "You ain't... got the guts... to kill me."

I opened my mouth, to tell him how fucking wrong he was, only for another voice to butt in first.

"He may not, but I sure as hell do."

Jerking my head up, I spied the beat-up, bloodied face of my stepmom hovering.

"Lisa. Step the fuck back. I got this." I blinked, suddenly dizzy... my world spinning.

"Let me go!" Summer's voice cut through me like a knife, painful, pleasuring... *mine*. My instinct to protect her had me loosening my hold on my father's neck. His eyes slid shut, but he wasn't dead. Still, taking the chance, letting him go completely? I couldn't risk it.

"It's fine, Summer. Stay back," I managed, eyeing Slade, who was holding her back.

My stepmother dropped to her knees in front of me. "Go to Summer." Lisa motioned her chin over my shoulder. "You're going to need her now."

I gave my head a fast jerk, slipping off my father's gut, landing on my knees beside him. My head spun, her words didn't make sense.

"I'm sorry, Niyol." She began to cry, tears dripping as she looked at Pops, then me, then Pops to me. I blinked, trying to make out her face, my eyes narrowing, shutting... "I'm so, so sorry," she repeated.

Before I could ask her what she was sorry for, I was on my back, flat, a gorgeous, familiar face hovering over me.

"Niyol." Summer shook as she laid on my chest. "You're okay. Things will be okay."

Little did either of us know that things never would be okay again.

CHAPTER FORTY-THREE

Summer

Two days had passed with no word about Niyol's condition, other than the occasional 'He's alive,' thrown at me by Archer. Out of the forty-plus club members who had been in Springfield for my and Lisa's rescue, all but three had come back to Rockford: Niyol, Flick, and Slade.

I wasn't allowed to stay with him, no matter how much I'd begged. Apparently, they only had so many places for people to get treated there, and since my injuries weren't nearly as bad as Niyol's and Lisa's, I was forced to leave after being treated briefly by some hairy-faced doctor, within the walls of a crappy building that served as a motorcycle compound, for my concussion and dehydration.

I didn't ask why I wasn't taken to the local hospital because, truth be told, I already knew why. These club people didn't mess around when it came to anything related to the police or hospitals.

Three hours after that, while Ny was still in surgery to get the bullet removed from his shoulder, I was whisked away in a strange car, driven back to the Red Dragons' compound without even knowing if Niyol had made it through surgery. Archer said the rush for me getting back was for my own safety, which I didn't understand. Niyol's father was in custody with the police again, as was his little minion—as far as I knew—and, well… who else was there that might want me dead? Or kidnapped, or whatever it was that Charles had planned on doing to me and Lisa.

Lisa, who was able to stay at the compound. With her *son*.

A son who, technically, didn't even know he had a mother at all.

Now there I was, alone with nobody but my scared, lonely heart… oh, and some bikers who I was oddly coming around to—including Archer. Big men, all different shapes and sizes, skin tones and languages, nationalities, it was a melting pot. The best kind. Intimidating or not, I could see why Niyol loved it here. He was exactly like them.

The second I was settled into a dorm at the compound, I called Emily to let her know I'd left St. Louis, but that her mom was still staying with Niyol. I asked her if she wouldn't mind coming to be with me until they were brought back to town. Her response, though, made sense, even if it hurt: *I love you, but I can't go to that club again.*

Part of me wanted to tell her that she'd be forever a part of the club, even if it was only by blood. But it wasn't my place to tell her the truth about who her father was.

That was her mother's job.

Knowing that Lisa had walked away from Niyol when he was only two wasn't something I could wrap my head around. Worse yet, she'd kept the truth from Emily. I'm sure she had her reasons, but until I knew what they were, I couldn't get behind them—or her. Nor could I fully support her being around Niyol either. When I'd told Flick the truth about what Lisa had admitted to me before being put inside that car, while Niyol was in surgery, he explained how he already knew. I didn't like that he'd hid it from Ny either, but he told me he had his reasons. And I, oddly, chose to accept his answer.

Guess the fact that I'd nearly died at the hands of an escaped convict was proof that there were worse men in the world than a bunch of bikers to be around.

I paced the length of the bar. It was the first time I'd shown my face in this area since I'd arrived. I'd slept a lot over the past two days, recovering from my injuries. I was lonely, though, missing Niyol so badly I'd do just about anything for companionship.

The main part of the compound—which, apparently, they called the *clubhouse*—wasn't as crowded as I figured it would be. There were no scantily clad women lounging around, no raucous parties with endless flowing drinks either. Instead, only a few members of the club lined the length of the room. Other than that, it was quiet. Painfully so.

"You gotta stop pacing, Feisty. It's givin' me a complex."

At the end of the bar, I glared at Archer. I hated the nickname he'd labeled me with more than I did Niyol's *Princess*.

He was sitting on a stool, long, muscular arms stretched across the old wood of the bar top. His dimpled smile was smug, and one piece of wavy, blond hair hung over his clean-shaven baby face.

"Giving *you* a complex?" I jerked my head back, laughing. "You're pretty much the epitome of badass, while I'm the lone girl who may, or may not, belong here. I am the complexed one."

"Aye, maybe that's why everyone's avoiding you." A breath whooshed from his mouth before he leaned back in his seat and winked at me. His Irish accent grew thicker with every drop of liquor he drank. And believe me, the guy drank a lot.

My face burned as I slouched down onto a stool beside him. Sure enough, when I looked around, various odd glances flickered my way. Some held disgust, some disinterest, while some gave me the heebie-jeebies, straight up.

Deciding it was better to get my questions out of the way, I leaned forward on top of the bar, mirroring Archer's position.

"I need answers, please."

"Nope."

I groaned, determined not to give up. "Is Niyol healing from his injury okay? Does he know about Lisa yet? And where is Charles?

Back in custody with the police?" I rubbed my hands over my upper arms, a small chill rocketing through me at the thought of that awful man.

I wasn't immune to everything I'd been through; someday I was sure I'd crack completely. And out of all the images, that one of Niyol, strangling the life out of Charles, having no mercy in his eyes whatsoever, should have scarred me the most. Yet after everything that had happened, it barely fazed me. I was numb, possibly in shock. The only thing I really wanted now was a sense of normalcy.

"You don't need to worry." Archer leaned across the bar once more and tried to pour himself a drink from the keg. Of course, he failed—the fact that he'd been drinking since he rolled out of bed that morning didn't help matters. "Things are best if you don't know what's going on. Trust me."

With a scowl—and a sure-fire plan in mind—I stood and walked around the bar, grabbed his mug, and poured from the keg. I slammed the glass in front of him and finally said, "Tell. Me. What. You. Know."

He grinned wider, two full dimples popping in his pale cheeks this time. He was incredibly good-looking, reminding me of Tarzan more than a biker. But he was so… so *lazy*. It drove me nuts, and I barely knew him.

"Nope." He winked.

I pulled at my hair, then reached under the bar. "No?"

He nodded, watching me, his smirk falling when I pulled out something I'd seen him cradling in his arms the night before when he'd swung by my dorm to check on me.

"Well. How about I do this then?" I popped open various bottles of liquor, one after the other, drawing a few more biker eyes as I began to dump drops of the alcohol into the sink. Archer chuckled at first, probably thinking I wasn't ballsy enough to keep this up. But after a full six-shots' worth was dumped out, his high and mighty laugh went dark.

"Not the whiskey, Feisty. I had that delivered from home. It's expensive as fuck."

I lifted my eyebrows. "This stuff?" I sniffed and pointed at the bottle. The label said *Redbreast*. I shrugged, then began to pour it down the drain even faster.

He was up and around the bar before I could get it emptied, his stool falling to the floor with a loud crash.

I pulled the half-emptied bottle to my chest, then limped quickly around the bar. Crap. What was I doing? Granted my brain was half-fried and this was the only way I could think of getting any real answers out of anyone, but I wasn't part of this group, hadn't been accepted by anyone but Niyol. And oddly enough, I kind of wanted to be.

The second I moved to hide behind a table full of ginormous men, most of whom looked like they could crush watermelons with one hand alone, all of them stood in front of me, arms crossed, chins high in defense.

For me.

I did a small shimmy, grinning in success. *Well, then.*

Archer leaned over onto his knees, gasping for breath. Or maybe he was trying to keep himself upright? He cursed, and I winced myself, my own body throbbing, even days after the accident. Pain or not, I wasn't ready to let this go until I got the answers I deserved.

"You going to tell me now?" I asked, hands on my hips, breathing staggered.

One of the club members in front of me looked over his shoulder and gave me a knowing nod. Something almost respectful. This guy was one of the quiet ones in the club, I'd come to know. Chop. I liked him already.

For the first time in a week, I felt the tightening in my chest ease. Maybe I wasn't so out of line after all.

"You should tell her what we know, Arch," Chop said. One of his arms was bigger than both my thighs combined.

"Put the baby down first," Archer slurred, his glassy eyes never leaving mine as he pointed toward the bottle in my hand. His face had fallen, the teasing gone completely. Evil Archer was here. I should've known that version would make an appearance sooner or later.

"Tell me. Please. I'm..." My bottom lip quivered as the adrenaline in me crashed. "So scared."

"Settle down, Feisty," he said on a sigh, cradling the bottle in his hands when I turned it over. "Hawk is fine."

My shoulders fell in relief and I followed him to a table.

"Something's happened with Lisa, though," he continued.

My knees grew weak, and I pressed my hands along the back of a chair for support. "Is she okay?"

He sat down, putting the bottle on his lap. "She's taken off. Left. Charles... She took off with him in the night. Nobody knows where they—"

"She *what?* How is that even possible?"

Archer put his hands up in the air, opening his mouth to respond, but the front door of the clubhouse blew open, a gust of summer wind slamming it against the wall and interrupting him.

"They're back," Chop said, his eyes narrowed, lips pushed down into a frown.

My face grew hot, eyes stinging with unshed tears as I turned to face Archer. Ignoring me, he stood and took off, heading outside.

I pushed away from the table and hobbled after him, my feeble body protesting the movement. Just alongside the cemented road outside the front door I stopped, watching as a group of motorcycles rolled in. Relief rocketed through me, yet the closer they rode to the front, I realized that none of the riders were Niyol. Though I was certain he wasn't in any shape to ride a bike after getting shot—again—the letdown of not seeing his face right away burned my chest.

"Where is he?" I scanned the road.

Archer stood by my side as he said, "In the car."

That's when I saw it. An old Buick coming through the gates. I could finally, for the first time in days, take a breath that counted.

I knew very little about any of the men here, but the solidarity they showed as the convoy of bikers and the car pulled in front of the clubhouse proved just how devoted they all were.

These men were so much more than I'd thought.

As they parked their bikes and jumped off, nobody moved to open the car's doors. Instead, Flick and Slade came directly toward Archer and me, a two-man force, with an army at the ready behind.

"How is he?" Archer asked the man with the long gray beard—Flick. I recognized him instantly.

He paused for a second, taking me in before he finally answered. "'Bout as good as anyone who's been shot twice in a month could be."

Ignoring them both, I pushed through the rest of the men standing by, shoving right and left with my shoulders. Chop was there, he seemed to notice me before anyone else. He nodded in acknowledgment, then stretched his arms wide, making room for me. I smiled and mouthed *Thank you* just in time for the rear door of the car to open.

Breath held, I stared and waited and waited…

In the backseat, two young guys got out next, both looking no older than sixteen, followed by…

"Summer."

Tears filled my eyes as I zeroed in on… "Niyol!"

I limped forward and slammed into Ny's chest as he stood. He was alive. He was here. He was safe. We both were.

He let out a hiss at my tight squeeze. I jumped back and dropped my hands, fear making my lower lip wobble.

"I'm so sorry. Did I hurt you?"

"I'm tough." He tried for a smile, reaching for my cheek. I leaned into him, feeling like I was finally home. Looking into his eyes though, I could see a type of pain that wasn't there before. A pain which stemmed beyond just the physical kind.

"Are you okay?" I tried for gentle, my voice shaking as I stepped closer once more. This time, I reached for his hand and brought it to my mouth, kissing his palm.

His eyes closed at my touch. "I'm good. Nothing to worry about."

"I missed you."

He blinked open his lids, mouth opening and closing. Something was on the tip of his tongue, but a man cleared his throat from behind, reminding us we had an audience. Niyol leaned forward, kissing my ear, only to whisper, "We'll talk tonight."

"Church. Now," Flick barked throughout the group of men. I swallowed and looked around, about as foreign to this world as, well... a cheer coach to a motorcycle club.

Niyol squeezed my fingers just once, bringing me back to attention. "I'll be in your room in an hour."

CHAPTER FORTY-FOUR

Niyol

"She's dead to us."

Flick was the first to speak as we settled around the table. His eyes were as black as the night, bone-chilling. I'd seen a lot of angry men in my life, but nothing like this before. He looked vengeful. Like this was a personal vendetta for him, and only him, when really, this was mostly about me.

He told the room the story. How Lisa had betrayed the club by working with Charles and helping him escape. He also told them about her being my real mom—something I still couldn't wrap my head around. A few eyes flashed my way. One or two with pity, couple more with disgust. But I ignored them all, too fucked up in the head for any words.

I leaned back in my chair, covering my face, wishing like hell we didn't need to have this vote at all. If only Lisa hadn't been so stupid, left like she had, we wouldn't have to make this damn decision. I'm not sure what the fuck was going through her mind, but I knew her well enough that there had to be a good reason for it. And my guess was, that it had everything to do with Emily.

When I was almost three years old, Lisa had left me behind with Pops, only so Emily—my sister—didn't have to be part of club life growing up. Over and over at my bedside, just hours after I'd had surgery, she'd told me how badly she wanted to take me with her, that she had tried hard to do so. But the first time she'd attempted to run, Pops had found her, beat her, raped her... Then he threatened to kill her if she ever tried leaving again. Terrified, Lisa had called one of her friends from school, an old boyfriend or some shit like that, and the next night, when Pops had gone out on a run, that friend had come to get her; waited outside the compound gates where she'd been forced to stay until Pops got home.

She'd gone to look for me after grabbing Emily, but I was missing. Apparently my fucked-up father had hidden me somewhere that night. Then Emily started crying in her arms, and she knew it was too late. That she'd never get out of there with the both of us. So, she left with my sister, leaving me behind.

Apparently when Pops found out that she'd split, he went ballistic. Found her friend, killed him, then put a hit out on Lisa. Somehow, she'd gotten lucky though, and escaped.

But shit went down, life messing with her. She ran out of money, lost her job, got evicted from her apartment, only for her brothers to turn their backs on her too. She thought that was Pops' doing but didn't know for sure.

Then bam, there was me and Pops that night along the road. Karma, Lisa had called it. Now that I look back on it though, I'm guessing Pops knew exactly where she was, probably had all along. That's also why he'd taken me with him. Not for a hooker to celebrate my patch in, but to rub it in Lisa's face that he'd turned me into the exact man he was. Or so he thought.

Pops took one look at Emily through the car window that night, and Lisa knew she was stuck for good this time. Only good part was the fact that Pops didn't want Emily. He just wanted the pussy Lisa could provide, anytime he wanted it.

So, she made a deal with Pops that night. If Lisa gave it over, he'd not tell us the truth and keep both her and Emily well provided for.

The rest is history, guess you could say.

Not sure why Lisa never bothered to tell me the truth. All those years she'd been back in Rockford but hadn't said shit. Maybe she was scared of what Pops might do to her and Emily if she did. Either way, I didn't question it. Not knowing all the answers was better right now anyway.

It was gonna take me a long time to forgive her, and I'd told her that.

But then she left, took Pops with her. Now no one knew where they were. Gone in the fucking night. Took out a few prospects in their wake. When they were found, Lisa would be treated like Pops, according to tonight's vote. Death being the punishment.

Regardless of who she was.

"All in favor of making Lisa an enemy say Aye," Flick continued, his upper lip curled as he stared around the room at the brothers.

Votes were tossed around, most with no hesitation until the end when it got to Archer—whose eyes had been trained on me the entire time.

"Archer," Flick barked. "Vote. *Now.*"

I watched him swallow, his throat moving up and down. If he did this, he'd not only be putting a death sentence on Lisa's head, he'd be ruining Emily's life.

"Aye." He looked to the table, shaking his head. His yes felt like an instant stab to my back.

He and I were best friends, but his yes was the first time he'd ever betrayed me.

In the end, the only nos were from me and Slade. Obvious reasons, no doubt. Lisa wasn't just my stepmom now, but my blood. And for that, she was Slade's aunt. His family too.

"Then it's agreed. Lisa is as good as dead."

I couldn't listen to anymore, so got up quietly from my seat and left the room.

Nobody followed. Not that I was surprised.

As I walked through the nearly empty clubhouse toward the dorms, I kept my head down, laser-focused on one thought: *Get to Summer.* But even as I stood outside her door, I couldn't go in right away. Instead, I settled my head against the wood, praying like hell that what awaited inside was a woman who wouldn't push me away.

I couldn't take anymore fucking heartache. Not tonight. Not ever. Pushing through the door, I sucked in a quick breath at what I saw. Dressed in only a white t-shirt and her panties, Summer's sleeping body. Laid out on her stomach, a blanket covering only her ass. The shirt she had on rode up high, showing her lily-white skin. I moved closer, until I stood beside her, knees touching the edge of the mattress, wishing I could stop time. Stay here with her, like this, forever.

Restless, Summer's face grew tormented as she whispered in her sleep, *No, no, no, stop, please.*

I reached down and ran my fingers over her cheek. She jerked at my touch, eyes blinking awake. The bruises on her face nearly killed me; made me want to punch a fucking wall.

"Niyol?" she whispered, slowly sitting up.

I nodded, not able to say shit for fear I'd break down. Seeing her there made me wanna do just that. Did she hate me because I'd gotten her involved in everything that was my fucked-up world? She'd been so unsure before this all went down, and now I had this horrible feeling in my gut that she wouldn't wanna be part of my life anymore at all. And because I felt the way I did, because I'd fallen fucking hard for her, I wouldn't ask her to stay. Not anymore. She deserved better than my world. Better than me.

"Hey, you." She reached up and touched my chin with her fingers, tracing my jawline. "I'm right here. Don't be afraid."

I swallowed hard, wondering how she knew... feeling more than I ever thought I could for a woman at the same time. Maya was fleeting, a big picture in my mind that I'd built up over the years. Summer, though, was *endless*. A forever I wanted so bad I could taste it.

"I tried to stay awake." She bit her bottom lip.

I traced her cheekbones, the side of her nose, every curve, every inch… remembering, in case this was it.

"Sorry. It took longer than we thought."

"It's okay. I knew you'd come this time."

My stomach hurled, had me damn near losing my lunch. *This time. This. Time.* She didn't think I'd find her at the cabin. She thought I'd given up.

"I'm sorry…" I breathed, dropping to my knees, placing my head against hers. I wrapped my arms around her calves, begging silently for her forgiveness. "So fucking sorry for everything."

She cradled my face between her hands, urging me to look at her. "Don't apologize," she said on a whisper. "Don't *ever* apologize. Just be with me. That's all I want."

I nodded, slowly standing, though it hurt to do so. She patted the bed beside her and I took a seat, no idea where to put my hands—knowing at the same time where I wanted them.

Summer took the initiative, though. Her fingers, so cold against my stomach, unbuttoned my jeans, and slipped them down to my ankles. Leaning over, she pressed a small kiss to the underside of my cock, causing a groan to rip through my throat. With her tongue, she played with the small bar beneath, tickling, touching, exploring. Before I could beg to be inside of her, she reached behind me and grabbed a condom from under her pillow, tearing it open, then slipping it on.

She'd wanted this to happen. She'd *planned* it.

Relief and need washed over me as she took off her panties and carefully straddled my lap. "Against the wall, Niyol," she urged with a small tap against my shoulders. I did as she asked, hissing the entire time in pain, but she didn't make me stop. Didn't ask me if I was hurting. Didn't even attempt to slide off of me. For that, I was thankful. Because I needed the pain to remind me that with it, pleasure would follow.

When I was finally in position, she ran her palms over my chest, my neck. Then, before I could breathe her name, she sank over the top of my cock with a long, whispered moan.

"Summer, baby…" My head fell to the side in sweet agony as she moved. My chest hurt, the position pulling at my shoulder against the wall, but her beautiful body rubbing against mine was the only remedy I needed for the pain.

She didn't stop moving, her hips going slow, as she rolled her pussy up and over my cock. Her heavy eyes watched my every move through half-closed lids, under the shadow of her hair. She needed this as much as I did. Pink, parted lips just barely grazed over mine, a silent admission that told me all I needed to know.

Summer wasn't going to let me go.

Her fingers never left my face or hair and she worked my body like she owned every piece of me. Which she did.

All of me.

Forever.

I touched her breasts, fingers spread wide, cock aching with pleasure as her pussy surrounded it whole. I was already so close.

The tip of her tongue trailed up and down my neck when she leaned over, alternating with her lips that kissed and sucked and played. Sweat collected at my temples, but I refused to wipe it away. I needed to feel this moment in all the fucking ways I could.

Wanting nothing more than to taste her again, I grabbed the sides of her head bringing her mouth back level with mine.

"Kiss me," I begged. And Jesus, did she ever.

Minutes later, I came with a growl, calling out her name and barely able to hold out as she followed me with a cry. I should've been embarrassed for blowing my load so soon, but the pain running through my body was damn near explosive. I was lucky I made it as long as I did.

"Did I hurt you?" she asked, pulling off me. I reached down, grabbed the condom, and shoved it back inside the wrapper.

I leaned forward just enough to kiss her forehead, barely able to catch my breath as I dropped the foil packet into the garbage by the bed.

"No. You gave me everything I needed."

With a small smile, she kissed my cheek, then stood and reached for the bottom of my shirt. Slowly, she brought it up and over my head, careful of my wound. She peered down at my bandage, her hands trailing over my arms, my shoulders, goosebumps forming under her touch. With ease, she tugged the white gauze back, and I heard her breath catch the second she saw the bullet hole.

"Oh, God, Niyol."

"I'm gonna be okay."

She stroked the area around it, gentle in her Summer way.

"Almost even with the other side now." I chuckled, but my thoughts were anything but humorous. More so wild with things I needed to say to her but couldn't figure out how to.

Instead, I let her touch me, selfishly enjoying her care. Then I dropped my chin, praying she'd talk first.

"Do you know where they went?" was the first thing she asked. "Charles and…"

I squeezed my eyes shut, knowing who she meant. Pain burrowed itself inside my chest this time. "No."

After undressing completely, I laid on the bed beside her, wishing I could tug her closer, but knowing my injury wouldn't let me. Instead, I rolled onto my good side to face her and rubbed bits of her hair between my fingertips, the back of my hand grazing the space above her heart.

"She's my mother, Summer. My fucking mother. And she's left me. Twice."

"I know." She paused. "She told me at the cabin. I don't know what to say other than I'm so, so sorry, Niyol."

"Don't be sorry. Not when I've dragged you into all this bullshit. You were scared already and then…" Fuck. I couldn't even say it out loud.

Summer grabbed my hand and held it between both of hers under her chin. "The future is never certain, no matter who you're with, what you do, or what's in store. And knowing you could have died, twice now…?" She slowly shook her head. "I couldn't lose you then, and I'm not gonna lose you now."

"Even if it's not gonna be ideal?"

Her nose scrunched up in that way I loved. "Ideal is a word I'm beginning to redefine."

I chuckled, but at the same time, I also knew this was only just beginning. And whether she realized it or not, Pops would get even deeper revenge on me now.

A shiver raced through me. Summer tugged the blanket up and over my shoulder, probably thinking I was cold.

"Will you tell me what happened after I left?"

I nodded, starting from the second after I'd woken up from surgery, finding Lisa hovering over my bed. I told her everything, rehashing it out loud again. Getting it off my chest helped a little, but not a lot. I was confused and worried, pissed and frustrated. The only good I had in that moment was the woman in my bed listening like nothing else mattered but me. Not real sure how I'd survived this long without Summer in my life. But now that I had her, I wouldn't know what to do without her.

"I had this vision of my mom in my head for so damn long. Then to find out that she's been here all this time… Shit, I don't know." I rubbed a hand over my face, not realizing how bad they were shaking until Summer put her fingers on top and held them.

Minutes passed. I thought maybe she'd gone to sleep. But then she surprised me…

"Have you ever been in love before?" She studied me, her bottom lip pulled between her teeth.

I swallowed, nervous. Nobody had ever asked me that before. Thing of it was, I hadn't been. Least not until her. Which was why I said, "Yeah."

"Maya?" She bit her bottom lip.

I shook my head. "No Princess. Not Maya."

Her eyes widened a little as I leaned over to kiss her just once on the lips.

Shivering against me, I felt her fingers graze my stomach. Slipping a leg over my thigh, Summer settled even closer, kissing my chest.

Summer knew exactly who I loved.

"Does it scare you?"

"Does what scare me?"

"The thought of someone like me loving you?"

She didn't hesitate. "Nothing about you has ever scared me. You've always put on this big, tough guy act, but deep down, I know there's a teddy bear inside."

"Jesus, you really know how to make a man feel like a man."

A giggle slipped out from between her lips. It was the first sound I'd heard her make at the diner where we'd met. A sound I'm damn sure was made only for me to hear.

"Look, Summer." I leaned back and pressed my forehead to hers, breathing her in. "Nothing about my life is ever gonna be normal. You won't get the white picket fence or the minivan. You'll get barbed wire and a bike. So, if you don't wanna be part of my world, I'm gonna give you an out. Right now."

I sucked in a breath when she didn't say yes right away.

"If I didn't want to be here, I would go."

Hope flickered in my chest. "But it's only going to get worse. Your entire life is gonna change by being with me."

And at this point, there was no telling what would happen. With the club, my father... Even if she didn't want me, there'd forever be a target on her head. Pops didn't take into account break-ups when it came to an RD old lady.

Like she knew what I was thinking, Summer slowly rolled me onto my back, crawled onto my lap, and laid her head on my good shoulder. She didn't press into me hard, but I felt her deep inside still. Always would.

"I'm not going anywhere. We're in this together now."

My body relaxed, her words soothing; music to my ears that I'd never take for granted. "Okay." I kissed the top of her head and stroked a hand over her spine.

We laid like that for a long while. I concentrated on her breath against my neck, the heat of it, the way her fingers made circles on my chest. Our bodies moved in sync as we inhaled, my eyes drifting closed with thoughts. Feelings. Needs.

Love.

I kissed her forehead once more, only for her to sit up. She stayed on my lap, legs straddled over my waist. Her fingers touched the blanket covering my legs, and I could easily see the wheels moving in her mind, see the tiny lines forming between her eyes as she frowned.

"You need to know something first. Before we make this official and all."

I grinned, regardless of everything in my life. I think I liked that word: official. "What's that?"

"I'm likely *not* cut out for this life you live."

My world stopped spinning. Fuck, fuck, *fuck*. I knew this was all too good to be true. But I also understood where she was coming from.

"I get it." I dropped my head to the left, looking out the window.

Summer grabbed my chin between her fingers and pulled my face back, eyes flashing with frustration. "Let me finish."

"Go on then." But it didn't hurt any less.

"Good. Now, when I said I wasn't cut out for this life, I meant it, but does that mean I'm not going to try to accept it? God, no. I just need you to know that it's going to take me some time to adjust. Especially after everything that's happened." She drew in a breath. "I won't *live* here with you yet, but that doesn't mean I won't maybe stay with you on the weekends, or on an occasional night during the weeks. We could be, like, a normal couple. Then once I get used to this... this *biker* life, we'll talk again."

"You wanna *date* me, Princess?"

A shy smiled covered her pretty lips. "Why wouldn't we date? You and I didn't exactly have a normal courtship to begin with."

I tipped my head back and laughed. "You just said *courtship* in the same sentence as *you and I*."

She pulled at the end of my hair, not hard. "And *you're* being a jerk."

I was. But the thing in my gut, spinning and jumping and leaping like frogs and butterflies all put together? Yeah, that was a happy-ass jerk. *Summer* wanted to date me. Figure this thing out between us. *Be* with *me*.

"You wanna be my girlfriend then? Go steady with me?" I winked, secretly fucking *loving* the idea.

She rolled her eyes. "Kind of thought we'd established that already." If it weren't half dark in the room, I'd almost bet her cheeks were pink.

"It's established, all right."

"Well," she huffed. "Good then. Glad that's... established."

I yanked the blanket off our bodies, hiking her up to where my cock brushed over the lips of her pussy. She let out a little hiss of pleasure, and I damn near exploded all over her again.

I knew this was it—the answer to my minimal prayers. Summer was the only family I'd ever need again. Just as long as I could be hers.

"You know you've been mine since the second I laid eyes on you in that blue waitress get-up."

"Really?" Her nose curled up. "I thought you hated me."

I shook my head and grinned, tucking some of her hair behind her ear. "Never hated you. Just got confused about the way you made me feel."

"Could've fooled me." Fingers traced around my stomach, shifting between my hip bones.

At her touch, I said the biggest truth I'd ever told. "How could I hate the one thing I love?"

Her eyes grew heavy, and a smile spread over her lips. "You really love me?"

"More than anything." I didn't hesitate. No reason to when I meant it. I did love Summer. And it might not have been that long, but I knew she was it for me. She was *the one.*

"Niyol Lattimore." She lowered her head to mine and kissed me once on the lips. "You and your sweet words slay me."

I grinned and grabbed her bare ass. "Plus, you made me hard as a fucking rock that night. Had to go back home and jerk one out, only to jerk another one out right afterward."

"Way to ruin a moment." She squeezed the side of my stomach, not too hard, but just enough to make my cock twitch.

"Come here." I kissed her lips once more, tangling my hands through her long hair. Tasting her slowly, I let her know, without words, that she was mine and I was hers and together, no matter what, *we* were lifers.

EPILOGUE

Summer

Three months later

Niyol promised me dinner and a movie after I got off work. It was supposed to be one of our rare date nights; the only source of normalcy we had all week. During my lunch period though, he'd called to say he was going to be late picking me up from work. Apparently, he had *club business to take care of* first. Because I'd grown used to the constant fluctuation in our schedules, I didn't question it. Guess that was the life of a Red Dragon old lady.

My need to keep a routine outside of school and coaching was seriously messing with me, yeah. But at the same time, Niyol was also helping me see the dark side, where we lived on whims and spontaneity. Nothing about our relationship was perfect, that's for sure. Case in point, my brothers *hated* him while my father *dealt* with him.

But when it comes to love, you don't necessarily have a choice in the matter. And I was certifiably, head-over-heels, in love with Niyol Lattimore.

With that thought, I walked down the stairs of Rockford Middle School with a stupid, goofy grin on my face.

"Hey, Mute." I waved to the club member who'd been following me around, acting like my bodyguard, for the last few weeks. Niyol insisted I had someone constantly close by when he wasn't there, explaining that this Mute guy, was the best man for the job. Mostly, he made himself scarce, except for instances like tonight, with me being the last one to leave the building. I purposely hadn't driven my new Rover because Ny was supposed to be picking me up.

Mute nodded at me, a pair of black glasses over his eyes—even with the thunder clouds brewing to the west. He was tall and muscular, tattoos for days on his neck and every other inch of his skin I had seen thus far. He was polite to me, but didn't speak much—hence the name Mute, I'm assuming. Niyol said he was a new prospect, him and his brother Talker, so he was trying to do right by everyone in the club, which apparently meant not being overly friendly with the ladies. Still, I was determined to know him in some way or another, even if all I ever got out of him were a few nods and an occasional smile.

Thinking I had a few minutes left to spare before Niyol arrived, I headed toward the curb to sit, intending to yank out a book, only for the roar of a Harley to rev from the parking lot the second I sat down. Like a silly school girl, I couldn't help but jump to my feet, then skip to meet up with him in the middle of the lot.

God he was sexy.

"You're early," I hollered over the roar of his engine.

He greeted me with that side smile I loved, handing me over my helmet. "Didn't want to keep my princess waiting."

I rolled my eyes as he reached for my hand and tugged me to his chest. Like always, I inhaled the scent of his aftershave and the leather from his cut. The one thing that was noticeably missing? The smell of menthol and smoke. He'd quit six weeks ago.

I called it a milestone and he called it an act of true love.

At the thought, I pulled back to kiss him, threading my fingers through his hair. It was the kind of kiss that said *I love you.* The kind of kiss that said *I missed you.* It was my favorite type.

Completely breathless, I dropped my forehead to his. "Got room on that thing for me?"

He patted the seat behind him. "The only woman who's ever going to be on this bike again is you."

Laughing under my breath, I slipped on behind him, waving at Mute who just pulled out of the lot. Like I'd grown used to, I tugged the helmet on over my head, only for Ny to turn and strap it beneath my chin.

"Ready?" he grinned back at me.

My belly swirled. Then I nodded and wrapped my arms around his waist. Seconds later, we took off down the street, weaving through the cars, until we hit the highway. I didn't ask where we were going, just shut my eyes and savored the moment. The thrill of riding behind my boyfriend, feeling him between my legs, while the rumble of his bike engine vibrated beneath me, was like an adrenaline rush I never wanted to end.

Which pretty much summed up our entire relationship at this point.

My boring version of normalcy and career-dom was balanced by his crazy. We were opposites in the best possible way. I may not have been his first, but I knew I was his forever. And for that, I was happier than I'd ever been in my life.

Forty minutes later, when my legs were weak, and my backside numb, Niyol pulled down a gravel road just inside the Red Dragon compound. I could see the high fences from where we stood.

"What are we doing here?" I asked, looking around.

"Come on." He parked just outside the padlocked entry, trees tucked around both sides. A shiver of unease ran through me, as nothing seemed safe anymore in life. Niyol said he would never let anything hurt me, but I knew even the strongest, toughest group of men couldn't necessarily keep me safe if Charles Lattimore had his way. Still, I chose not to think like that, living in the moments I had with Niyol while all was calm.

We stumbled down a gravel road once he unlocked the metal padlock, his hand clasped in mine.

"I've been thinking a lot about things between us lately," he said, his gaze switching between me and the road ahead. He looked nervous, a look he didn't sport that often.

Niyol and I thought about our relationship all the time, so his statement wasn't entirely new—though his behavior was. Usually it was me doing the talking about futures, while he sat and stared at me, occasionally playing with my hair, a mindless, warm gaze on his face. I'd never felt so devoted to in my life.

"Verdict is?" I studied the plants and vines growing up the length of the pathway, mesmerized by the ivy and flowers. They weren't roses exactly, but similar looking. Gorgeous all the same. It was a quiet path of perfection back here, reminding me a little of our Colorado camping adventure. I smiled, thinking about that night in the back of my Range Rover, our fingers on the window, his lips on mine.

"Verdict is, I miss you like crazy."

I squeezed his hand and smiled sadly at him. "I miss you too."

Our time together was rare. Once a week and the weekends… It could be worse, of course, though for Niyol and me, it wasn't enough. But between my job and coaching, and his running the new on-site motorcycle shop, we didn't have much of a choice.

Niyol's dark eyebrows pulled together over his even darker eyes in thought. He'd cut his hair shorter on the sides last month but kept it long in the front and middle. Kind of Mohawkish. Not to mention badass sexy.

"I need you to come live with me."

I skidded to a stop. "What?"

He rubbed the back of his head, peering through a layer of hair with a nervous stare. "I need you close, Summer. All the time. I know I said I would wait, but I can't. Not anymore. You're on my mind all day and all night. And it fucking drives me nuts that I can't come home with you." He shook his head. "Fucking sucks even more that Mute get to see you more than me."

The first thought that went through my mind, surprisingly, was Emily.

She'd go nuts if I moved in with Niyol—not that she controlled me. Or that it was any of her business. But after discovering the truth about who her father was, that her mom had supposedly 'taken off' with him, she'd gone completely off-kilter. Broke off her engagement with Sam, sold their home, and moved into the apartment next door to mine. She was always at my house. Always sleeping over. Always crying too. I felt terrible for her, knowing she'd lost so much. The thought of leaving her alone like that... It killed me.

"I'm not really sure what you want me to say." And I wasn't. Maybe because he and I were still so new to this relationship thing.

"Just, come on. Follow me."

My curiosity was still piqued, so I followed him like he asked, my hand automatically folding into his again. Our footsteps were the only sound we could hear as we moved down the road, other than the occasional bird and the gust of a fallen leaf. The further we walked, the less I could hear. Not even the highway traffic that ran due south could be discerned in the distance. Peace washed over me, regardless of the bomb he'd just dropped, and I leaned my head back, soaking in the late, evening air. It was chilly, but perfect, reminding me of my grandparents' Iowa farm.

"Here we are."

I blinked, focusing ahead, only to frown and look at Niyol. "What's this?"

Ahead of us was a wooden frame lining the ground, inside the frame were two lawn chairs and two cans of beers. It was about as romantic as Niyol got. Still, I grinned, loving his makeshift picnic. "You did this?"

Not bothering to wait for him, I stepped toward the middle. But it was the set of blueprints sitting on one of the chairs that caused the sudden shaking in my hands.

"Niyol?" My voice cracked when I turned around, holding it in my hands. "What's this?"

He remained on the other side of the frame, his hands in his pockets. Then shrugged one shoulder before closing the distance between us. "Blueprints for the house I'm gonna build you."

I swallowed hard, blinking in confusion.

"I was late tonight because I wanted to make sure the guys broke the ground. I wanted to surprise you." His face turned red, a rare blush covering his dark cheeks. He took a few steps closer, until he settled in front of me. Slowly, he trailed a finger down my cheek. "Do you know how much I love you?"

I nodded, stupefied, really.

"We're opposites, Summer, but that trip we took nearly four months ago, everything that's happened between us since, has made me want to be what you needed. And every damn day I try harder to do that, even if I'll never be traditional."

Tears filled the corners of my eyes and I tugged him close by the end of his t-shirt. It was gray today, a change from the normal black. "If I wanted traditional, I wouldn't be with you."

"But I wanna be traditional in some senses. For you."

"Oh?" I tipped my head back to look him in the eyes.

"This, right here?" He motioned toward the ground, the two-by-fours surrounding us. "I'm building it for you and me." He pointed a thumb back toward a smaller spot to the back left of the lot. "Got Emily her own mini place going a few yards away, that way she can be next to you too."

Tears filled my eyes from his thoughtfulness. He was so much more of a man than any other I'd met.

He kicked the dirt with his boot, suddenly shy. "We can live on this land together, be with each other. Maybe, someday when you're ready, we can, you know, think about doing *other* stuff that's traditional."

Marriage. Children. The words didn't need to be spoken for me to know what he meant. I could envision that with him. My chest warmed with the possibilities.

"You really want to move in together."

"Yeah, Princess. I want that a lot." He grinned, like he hadn't just dropped the bomb of the century on me.

But I couldn't say yes… could I? Driving to and from here and work would make for two hours on the road every day. That could get draining, not to mention it would waste a lot of gas.

But at the same time, I only had three months left in my apartment lease. And moving to the compound would actually bring me closer to my dad, even if he wouldn't likely be okay with my moving in with Niyol.

There were so many pros and cons. Yet at the same time, life wasn't made for order and perfection, I'd come to learn that. Chaos ruled the world, and everything that was me and Niyol thus far. So, the more I thought about it, the more I looked into the hopeful eyes of the man I never thought would be mine, the more I realized how right Niyol was. And to be honest, I was damn tired of living apart too.

I loved him, and he loved me and apart we sucked, but together? We were real.

"Okay." I blew out a breath, barely believing what I was agreeing to.

"Yeah?"

I nodded.

"Fuck, that makes me happy." He grabbed me around the waist and swung me in a circle, both of us laughing and hugging, close, but not close enough.

I must've been crazy. Truly, madly crazy. But one kiss on the lips later, and I discovered the truth about crazy. And order, perfection and doing the right thing…

It was totally overrated.

A LETTER FROM HEATHER

First and foremost, I want to say thank you so much for picking up *Her Wild Ride*. If you enjoyed it, please leave a review. This helps newbie authors like me, so, so much. Also, if you want to keep up-to-date with my past or future releases, feel free to sign up using the following links. Your email address will never be shared and you can unsubscribe at any time.

www.bookouture.com/heather-van-fleet

I hope you loved *Her Wild Ride* as much as I enjoyed writing it! This was one of the most challenging books I've written to date, but also the most fun too. Yes, I know this wasn't the typical MC romance a lot of you are used to reading, but I'm not exactly a typical kind of girl either. No matter, I've had Niyol and Summer's stories in my head for years, and am just so crazy happy that Bookouture was willing to let me share this wild pair's adventure with you all.

I love hearing from my readers – you can get in touch on my Facebook page, through Twitter, Goodreads or my website.

Thanks,
Heather

authorheathervanfleet

@HLVanFleet

www.heathervanfleet.com

ACKNOWLEDGEMENTS

I have a million and a half people to thank, but I'm going to keep this as short as possible.

Chris: You're a Rockstar husband. Thank you for understanding when I have to order pizza five nights a week because I *need* to complete my edits or reach a deadline. YOU are my happily ever after.

My girls: There are not enough words to describe how amazing you three are. I love you like nothing else in this world. Thanks for making me a mom. For believing in me most of all.

Jess: You're my rock. My bestie. Thank you for being one of the only people who really gets what life is really like for me. Thank you for being you, bottom line.

Michelle: Without you, HWR would never have seen the light of day! I'll forever be thankful for your notes and guidance.

Katrina and Jen: You ladies read this book when it was at its ugliest. God, do I love having CPs that understand it's okay to have cruddy first drafts. Love you both, so, so much.

To my Hot and Heavy Ladies: I promise to make up for my absence in the group with more Thom Evans pictures. You're the best ladies ever.

And finally, to the fans that have decided I'm worth sticking around for. *You* are the reason I am here, every day at my kitchen table, writing my words. Thank you for remembering me out of the fifty million other authors out there.

Made in the USA
Las Vegas, NV
24 December 2024

15263976R00194